PRAISE FOR SARAH READY

PRAISE FOR FRENCH HOLIDAY

"Ready (The Fall in Love Checklist) whisks readers to the South of France for a saucy enemies-to-lovers romance... This is a winner."

— *Publishers Weekly* starred review on *French Holiday*

"Ready has written a tale that deliciously taps into its French trappings...A charming dramedy featuring a promising sleuthing duo."

— *Kirkus Reviews on French Holiday*

PRAISE FOR JOSH AND GEMMA MAKE A BABY

"Romance author Ready gives Gemma rich and complex motivations for wanting a baby...An unusual and winning read about a little-discussed topic."

— *Kirkus Reviews on Josh and Gemma Make a Baby*

"A lively, entertaining, romantic comedy by an author and novelist with a genuine flair for originality, humor, and narrative driven storytelling..."

PRAISE FOR JOSH AND GEMMA THE SECOND TIME AROUND

"In this sequel—which stands well enough on its own—the happily-ever-after moment is merely the starting point...Ready effectively leads readers to wonder if she isn't going to upend every single one of the genre's expectations. It's a testament to her exceptional writing skill that even the most romantic-minded readers won't be sure which outcome they prefer. A charming and disarmingly tough story of the many ways that love can adapt to crises."

PRAISE FOR CHASING ROMEO

"A fun and sweet love story..."

ALSO BY SARAH READY

Stand Alone Romances:

The Fall in Love Checklist

Hero Ever After

Once Upon an Island

French Holiday

The Space Between

Josh and Gemma:

Josh and Gemma Make a Baby

Josh and Gemma the Second Time Around

Soul Mates in Romeo Romance Series:

Chasing Romeo

Love Not at First Sight

Romance by the Book

Love, Artifacts, and You

Married by Sunday

My Better Life

Scrooging Christmas

Stand Alone Novella:

Love Letters

Find these books and more by Sarah Ready at:

www.sarahready.com/romance-books

JACE AND ANDREA. ANDREA AND JACE. FROM THE MOMENT OF THEIR FATE-FILLED FIRST MEETING IN CENTRAL PARK THEY'VE KNOWN ONE TRUE THING—THEY'RE MEANT TO BE.

Life doesn't have many certainties but for Andrea and Jace forever is one of them.

Andrea Leighton-Hughes—shockingly wealthy Upper East Sider, a chess-piece in her family's games since before she was born—knows what it's like to hide behind a mask. Her world is one of lies, manipulation, and reputation. Jace is the first and only person to see who she truly is.

Jace Morgan is no stranger to tragedy and every day is a struggle to get by. A musical prodigy from the Bronx, Jace and his brothers will do whatever it takes to climb to the top of the music charts. Andrea is the first and only person who has helped him play from the heart.

No one understands their connection. No one understands their love.

As Jace and Andrea struggle to stay together and prove that love defeats all obstacles, life sets out to prove them wrong.

What happens when two people promise forever, but life tears them apart?

What happens in the time they aren't together—in the space between?

A love that lasts decades and a friendship that never dies. Sarah Ready's The Space Between is a novel full of passion, betrayal, longing, and redemption—where love and lyrics hold the key to everything.

The Space Between

SARAH READY

CROWN

W.W. CROWN BOOKS
An imprint of Swift & Lewis Publishing LLC
www.wwcrown.com

Library of Congress Control Number: 2022915660
ISBN: 978-1-954007-52-9 (eBook)
ISBN: 978-1-954007-53-6 (pbk)
ISBN: 978-1-954007-54-3 (large print)
ISBN: 978-1-954007-55-0 (hbk)
ISBN: 978-1-954007-56-7 (audiobook)

the space between

For the music and for love

PROLOGUE

JACE

I FLY ACROSS THE GRASS, SPRINTING THROUGH CENTRAL Park, desperate to stop the only woman I'll ever love from marrying another man.

I weave through the crisscrossing paths, past green benches that stand empty like mourners, over hills and jutting gray rocks.

There's the Alice in Wonderland statue where Andi fell when she was small.

A playground with kids shouting and sliding.

There. Gone.

My lungs burn as I round the path climbing toward Bethesda Terrace, the angel of the waters rises high, her hand outstretched, her wings flared.

Tourists crowd around her, the bronze angel of healing in her fountain, holding a lily in her hand.

There's a raucous wedding party taking photographs,

a bride in white, a groom in black, my heart thunders—but it's not Andi.

My feet pound across the red brick, past the arched stone, past the lake and the rowboats with couples bobbing in the sparkling green waters.

The sun is already high over the leafy green trees, the dirt and grass smell strong with the evaporated dew, the bright blue sky mocking.

It's the perfect day for a wedding.

He'll be at Wagner Cove in the morning, she said.

I charge down the path lined with tall shade trees and leap over the wire mesh fencing separating the grass from the path.

When I land, my leg screams in pain, the old injury flaring, and I grab my thigh, dig my fingers into the pain and keep running.

I jump over another fence. I don't have time to take the prescribed path.

I dodge a bicyclist and keep running as they shout after me. Then I'm on the small stone and dirt path tumbling down to the lake and the cove.

The woods are thick with green, the boulders rise out of the ground and trees dig their roots into the stone.

The path winds down, down, and my chest heaves as I drag in the summer air.

Sweat runs down my back, and every step down the stone path is like a hot poker stabbing bone.

But I see her.

I see her now.

I round the path. Down below, cascading down the forest toward the lake, there's a rustic wooden gazebo, hewn from roughly cut logs, perched like a fairy tale on the edge of the shimmering lake.

And standing underneath the sloped wooden roof, surrounded by a carpet of red rose petals, is Andi.

She's in white.

Of course she's in white.

She's getting married.

But the white nearly strikes me down. She looks like an angel, radiant and beautiful.

I almost can't reconcile the Andi lying in my arms last night with the Andi standing in the gazebo.

Her dress is the most brilliant white I've ever seen. It floats around her like a cloud and must have a thousand diamonds sewn into the fabric because it gleams like the noonday sun.

The top of the dress is tight, strapless, showing the thin line of her shoulders and the smoothness of her skin. The bottom, though, flows out, like a cloud blowing in the breeze, sparkling as the sun lights over her.

Her veil is pulled back, settling over her hair, a diamond and pearl tiara rests on her head. And on her neck, there's the thickest diamond and ruby choker I've ever seen.

She looks like a billion dollars.

She looks like a bride.

The sight punches me, robs me of breath, but I fly down the stone path, desperate to stop her.

She hasn't noticed me yet.

No one has.

Andi's holding his hands, staring up at him with a solemn, grave expression, her face pale and serious.

A gust of wind hits me then, bringing the voice of the officiant...do you take...to have and to hold...

Andi tilts her chin, that defiant, stubborn, take-on-the-world look I've dreamed about for years.

It means she's going to say *I do*. She's looking at him, holding his hands, and she's going to say yes.

I reach out my hand, as if I can stop it all with a gesture, and say raggedly, my lungs burning, "Andi, don't."

At that, Andi turns to me, but the only part of her that shows surprise is the flaring in her eyes. I can see it, the surprise, but also the overwhelming love.

I take another step forward, my leg burning, my chest aching. I reach out my hand, palm up.

She can take it, she can take my hand and we can walk away, leave all this behind together.

"Don't do this. Come with me."

I let my hand hang there and all she has to do is take it.

My heart thuds a heavy, desperate beat as she looks into my eyes, a bright, shining love there.

Around us, her family is shifting, her brother laughing, her dad murmuring angrily, the groom's family confused and stunned.

And him, he's still holding her hands, a somber expression on his face.

But I don't see them, I don't hear them, I only see Andi.

None of them matter.

None of them.

"Andi," I say, the taste of her riding on my lips, the memory of her kisses, the memory of her laugh, the memory of her touch.

When I say her name she gives me a brilliant smile, one like the sun coming out from behind the clouds on a rainy day.

It's a joyful smile, the one that first made me fall in

love with her all those years ago. The one she's only ever given to me.

The one that says, *I love you.*

And when she smiles that smile, I know exactly, without a doubt, what she's about to say.

PART I

1

Jace

My dad loved only three things in life—my mom, his sons, and Louis Armstrong.

His entire world revolved around us and Louis.

Every day at six-thirty when he walked into our windowless, railroad-narrow living room in the Bronx, he'd line us up—me, River, and Dean—and then we'd play.

Not play as in board games, or catch, or video games, but play as in *play music.*

Me on the Martin I'd been strumming since before I could talk. River on the busted-up, moldy church piano we nabbed from the curb on trash day. Dean on his second-hand bass. My mom beating the drums, crooning Ella to my dad's trumpeting Louis.

The building actually vibrated from our music. The plaster walls shook—my mom took down the pictures after the third frame fell and shattered—and the old wood floors rumbled.

But no one in our six-story former tenement building ever complained about the nightly concert reverberating through the paper-thin plaster walls.

First, because my dad was six foot five and as wide as a door. Second, because we were good. Better than good.

So a little thing like plaster dust raining from the ceiling when my mom had a drum solo, or cracks running down the walls from when we really turned it up, didn't bother anyone.

From the time I was conceived to thirteen years old, I was surrounded by music and love.

My dad came from Ghana. My mom from Switzerland. They met at a jazz club in Geneva when they were eighteen and fell in love over "What a Wonderful World." They married right away and left for America, the home of their idol.

Dean came along. Then River. Then me. And Dad did what all self-respecting cover artists do. He made a family band.

Sometimes you hear horror stories about parents who mold their kids into actors or musicians. There's punishing practice, verbal abuse, physical abuse, all for the ultimate goal of fame and fortune.

That wasn't my dad. He loved the music, he loved my mom, and he loved us.

And if he could have all that combined into one—our band—then that was his version of heaven.

After we finished playing we'd be sent to bed. Then my mom and dad would have their time.

Sometimes, when I was really little, I'd sneak out of the bedroom that I shared with River and Dean. I'd tiptoe down the hall and peer around the corner, just to watch them.

Every night it was the same.

My dad would pull out a shiny black vinyl record, hold it up to my mom with a smile, then drop it into the record player. The stylus would scratch over the spinning record. It would crackle, settle, then Louis would start to croon.

And my dad would take my mom in his arms. Him— larger than life, loud and brash. Her—tiny, calm in every storm, and quiet.

They would dance, folding into each other, until they became whole. That's what it was like. When they were apart they weren't complete. But as soon as they held each other, they were exactly as they were meant to be. One couldn't exist without the other.

Then, always, they would kiss.

Even when I was young, I knew that was my cue to go to bed.

I'd lie there, on our thin, lumpy mattress on the floor, squeezed between River and Dean, and rest safe in the fact that this was the only kind of love there was. That I'd always have my parents. That when I grew up I'd have this kind of love too.

The all-consuming, soul mate, need-you-so-much-I'm-not-whole-without-you kind of love.

No one was surprised, not even me, that when my dad died—horribly, senselessly, viciously—my mom was right there with him. It only made sense that they'd die within minutes of each other. One couldn't live without the other.

Not us kids, not even Louis was enough to keep either of them here. Not without the other.

I didn't blame them.

I understood.

My mom loved my dad enough to die for him. And my dad loved my mom enough to die for her.

When they were gone though, it left a vacuum. All that love, suddenly gone, was like a supernova. Their star exploded and left behind a black hole.

And that black hole sucked all the joy, all the laughter, all the color out of the world.

I saw for the first time, maybe, what the rest of the world had seen all along.

A gray, dirty, cockroach-and-rat-infested apartment building musty with the smell of grime and mold. A graffitied, vandalized, trash-strewn street soaked with dog urine and littered with used needles. A subway full of lonely, hard-faced, closed-off people, wary and shifty-eyed. A city, a world, where love like my parents had wasn't the rule but the exception.

All that love I had for my parents, it had nowhere to go, so it collapsed back in on itself and caved inside my chest.

Sometimes, when I played my guitar, tears would leak out, racing down my cheeks, falling like rain flooding the city streets, overflowing into the East River.

Dean pretended not to notice. He isn't good with feelings.

River understood. But he's like that. He understands everyone and everything.

But Dean didn't like it when I cried, so I stopped.

I stopped thinking about magic, and color, and laughter.

I stopped.

I never thought I'd feel that kind of love again. In the

four years since my parents died I never saw any evidence of it.

Not until I saw her. The girl in the red silk scarf.

While my guitar vibrated under my fingers, and I squinted into the bright setting sun, I took one look at her and knew—that girl, with her haughty brown eyes and condescending look, taking in and then discarding my brothers and me playing music in Central Park—that girl had my heart, and I was never getting it back.

2

JACE

WHEN I PEER INTO THE DARK, TWISTING SHADOWS OF THE Ramble, I have only two things on my mind—catching the 7:08 bus home, and the girl in the red scarf.

I thought I saw her, the bright crimson flag of her scarf bold against the gray stone of Belvedere Castle. Then she disappeared into the bowing green limbs of the thickly wooded Ramble.

The air is still here, humid and loamy wet, the mossy, wet wood smell tickles my nose.

I let my eyes adjust to the dim, gray light. Only a few specks of sunlight filter onto brown bark and green leaves.

My brothers—and even Dallas and Pauly—don't like to walk through the Ramble. Like many New Yorkers born and bred they believe trees belong spaced twenty feet apart sticking out of a sidewalk. They have an instinctual distrust of deep, wild, wooded places.

But I don't mind it.

Sometimes I come to the Ramble after playing a set in the park. I like to take the meandering paths deep into the shadows. The bright sky, the rumbling, yelling noise of the city, the metallic, street cart, subway smell, all that disappears beneath the tangled canopy of the forest.

The city is muted. And if you walk far enough, the city is lost.

To guys like Dean and Dallas, who thrive on the thickly clustered buildings and the unending noise, I imagine, that's unsettling.

But I like to come to Central Park and then escape into the Ramble. If you slip far enough into the brush, where the smell of moss and rain-soaked granite boulders becomes overwhelming, you can find a little hollowed out cave hidden behind thorn branches and thick vines.

Inside the opening, a small waterfall trickles like a tambourine. I often pull out my guitar and pluck out melodies. I like to imagine the acoustics in that little hollow echo like Red Rocks Amphitheatre.

Even so, Dean doesn't like me going into the Ramble after dark.

He thinks it's safer to walk through a gang fight unarmed than to walk into the Ramble after nightfall.

After our last song, I told them I was going to take the bus home. I nodded at the Ramble, and I could tell by the tightening around Dean's mouth that he wanted to say no. So I hefted my guitar, waved, and hurried toward the darkened tree line.

Now, I'm not so sure Dean wasn't right all along.

I knew the girl in the red scarf wouldn't be here. It's been more than thirty minutes since she passed beneath the hanging limbs. There isn't any chance I'll meet her. But stupidly, I still had a sort of hope.

I look over my shoulder, back at the lengthening shadows snuffing out the last flickers of light. There's a crawling sense of unease working its way over me.

Suddenly, the bitter tang of cigarette smoke in the humid air snakes around me—someone else is near.

There's a scraping sound, like a boot sliding over rock and sand. Chills slither up my spine.

It isn't that the Ramble doesn't have plenty of people walking through it—usually. It's that no one is here. No one is near.

But there's the smoke.

And the scraping.

My skin goes cold and sweat runs down my back. That's what happens when I'm scared, it always has.

Which is why, when a limb cracks like a gunshot, I hunch my shoulders, heft my guitar and walk *fast*.

"Gutter. Hey, gutter rat. Slow down!"

I let out a hard breath. It's relief but also anger.

How is it possible that in a city of millions, I manage to run into the same pricks day in and day out? Isn't it enough that we have to share the halls and classrooms of Darby School?

"Gutter! Slow down. You too good to say hi?"

I scowl and hunch my shoulders. Let me tell you, it doesn't feel great to have "gutter rat" shouted after you whenever you pass.

I pick up my pace, although I won't run. I've never run and I'm not going to start today.

My guitar thuds against my back as I move faster, the gravel crunches, like it's egging on a confrontation.

Behind me, Reid, Scott, and Breck round the bend. Their figures are dark, all except the pinpoint of orange light glowing from the end of their cigarettes.

What a bunch of pricks.

They're the Jetters. I don't call them that. Everyone else does.

They go to Darby, the private school in lower Manhattan, just like me.

But unlike me—there on a community outreach scholarship—they are there because their great-great-great-grandfathers founded the school.

Me and the Jetters, we're different.

The Jetters are in the newspaper for things like crashing their dads' Lamborghinis into Madison Square Garden, meeting the Prime Minister of Japan for tea, or winning gold at a fencing tournament then trashing the hotel suite where they stayed.

Meanwhile, the "Gutters," as they fondly call me and anyone else from my neighborhood, we're in the paper for things like vandalism, theft, and assault.

We don't have the Lamborghini to soften the blow of public property destruction.

I'm not saying I've never done anything that would make my parents ashamed. You do what you have to do.

Pauly likes to shoplift. Dallas has a fondness for throwing bricks through car windows. River likes to fight. Me, I try to keep out of trouble.

Anyway, I'm not saying the Jetters are better than us. They're not.

But I'm not saying we're better than them.

We're just different.

They have their problems and I have mine.

It'd be nice if they saw it that way too.

By the sounds of their shoes scraping over the gravel, they're close. The smoke of their cigarettes burns my eyes, and their breathing is loud.

"You too good to say hello?"

That's Reid.

He's golden-haired, square-jawed, with a wide smile, straight white teeth, and hard blue eyes. He's the leader of the Jetters. I saw an old movie once, with a young Paul Newman, and I did a double-take because for a second I thought he *was* Reid. He's a real doppelgänger.

He has the build of a quarterback, but like I said, he prefers fencing.

Sometimes I think the problem with Reid is that he's too ambitious. If he'd been born poor he would've had some way to expend all his energy. But since he was born on top of the world he has nothing to do but spend his dad's money. I think he hates it.

I'm only about two hundred feet from the tree line. I can make out the yellow glow of a streetlamp through the dark branches. My breath comes out in a relieved exhale.

But then one of them reaches out and grabs my arm.

Swings me around.

His fingers dig into my skin.

I jerk my arm.

But it's Breck and I can't pull loose. He's the size of a linebacker and from past experience I know that his hands are clamps and he hits like a semi-truck.

"Hi Gutter," Reid says, stepping close.

There's a wild light in his eyes. They reflect the orange of his cigarette, and they glow blue, black and orange like a hot, angry coal.

For the first time in four years, I'm worried they're going to do something we'll all regret.

I clamp my mouth shut and calculate my chances of pushing past Scott and Breck and making it to the edge of the Ramble. There'll be people in the park.

"Nothing to say?" Scott asks.

Reid flicks his cigarette to the ground and smiles.

The coppery flavor of fear fills my mouth. I lower my shoulder and hit Breck, twisting my arm to free myself. Instead of pulling free, Breck shoves me to the ground.

My guitar cracks at the impact. It's in a thin gig bag and the fabric rips with a loud tear. My back screams in protest as the wood splinters, the shards stabbing into my spine.

The breath goes out of me.

I fight.

Breck holds my arms.

Reid jumps on top of me, his knee in my chest, cutting off all air.

Scott hits me. Knocks my head to the side.

The gravel and dirt of the path flies up around us. The sand scratches my eyes. Blood pours down the back of my throat and my nose swells.

Sparks light in my eyes.

Then Reid leans close. His hot breath is on my face and through the rushing in my ears I hear him.

"You're too pretty to be from the gutter. We're going to fix that for you."

I reconsider my decision to remain silent.

"Go to hell." I spit the warm blood out of my mouth and try to jerk free.

Then the orange light of Breck's cigarette flashes along the edge of a knife.

You know, one of those stupid knives you peel an apple or pop a tire with. A nothing knife.

But it's long enough to cut up my face.

When the cold edge of the metal presses against my cheek I lose it.

I punch.

I kick.

I hit.

I bite.

I hear them shouting—hold him still—shut him up —do it—cut him—I can't breathe, my vision's swimming, the trees wave above me, salty coppery blood fills my mouth.

When Reid hits me I bite my tongue.

Pain bursts through my head. White sparks swim around me. Sharp, hot pain slices through me.

I fight like crazy.

And then there's someone above us all.

They're a dark, small figure, descending on us like a ferocious hurricane.

They beat Reid with a large black object.

Reid shouts when he's struck. He jumps off me, throwing himself to the side.

I yank in a desperate breath, choke on my blood, and breathe through the pain in my chest.

My rescuer turns on the other two.

Beats them with the black object, swinging it like a weapon.

The Jetters are yelling.

They're running.

My rescuer chases after them, kicking up dirt, and shouting.

I don't know what. I still can't hear through the rushing and ringing in my ears.

I lie there, breathing heavily, swallowing the salty copper taste of blood. I'm on the hard, rocky ground, and the sharp splinters of my guitar dig into my back.

Wetness leaks down the side of my face, and I'm certain it's blood because I've not cried in years.

The tightness in my chest is from Reid's knees, not from fear. The ache in my throat is from yelling, not from fear at seeing a knife.

They could've killed me with that stupid little knife. One slip. One mishap.

What. The. Hell.

I stare at the dark sky, the trees obscuring the starless gray heaven.

The hot breath of the humid air blows over my face and I slowly pull in air, willing my heart to slow. I dig my hands into the rocky soil and let the dry dirt crumble through my hands.

I concentrate on the feel of the grainy soil sifting through my fingers.

My knuckles ache. They're already swelling. Good. That means I got in a few hits.

Although, Dean will be upset because this means I won't be able to play until the swelling goes down.

I shift and then wince as the remains of my guitar scratch my back.

Above me, the tree branches look like skeletal hands reaching down to grab me, and even over the scent of my own blood, I can still taste cigarette smoke hanging in the air.

The rushing, ringing in my ears finally subsides, my

heartbeat slows to a normal rhythm, and the world slowly stops spinning.

I groan. It's time to sit up and head home.

But then, out of the darkness, I spy my rescuer, jogging over the rocky path.

They lean close and peer down at me. They're so close their nose nearly touches my own.

I lose my breath again.

The world tilts.

I'm punched right in the gut. But this time, it isn't a real hit, it's all in my head.

"Well, are you alright, or aren't you?" asks the most beautiful girl in the world.

3

JACE

HER RED SCARF HANGS DOWN, THE TASSELS BRUSH OVER MY cheek. I stare at her dumbly.

Up close, she isn't as perfect as I first thought.

Sure, her long thick hair is my favorite color—it's the color of the sweet, reddish-amber honey that I drizzled on the biscuits my mom used to make on Saturday mornings. And her eyes are deep set and dark. They're the rich shade of the butter-brown wood on my (now splintered) guitar.

But beyond that, there isn't anything special about her.

Her nose is straight and a bit too long. Her chin has a small dimple, which I've never seen on a girl before. Her cheekbones are high and her face is angular. Her eyebrows fly up in straight, questioning lines. Her top front teeth have a small gap.

I guess, though, it's hard to notice that she isn't what you'd consider *beautiful*, because there's something about her that's arresting. Something that makes it almost impossible to turn away.

I think it's the way she carries herself. Like she knows something. Some secret. And the expression on her face...

"Are you going to answer me?" she asks, her voice a rich husky alto, just like Ella singing "Dream a Little Dream of Me" with Louis.

It shocks me so much that I find I *can't* answer her.

"Oh no. Are you dying and I'm blocking the light?" She steps aside and gestures at the dull, cloudy sky, a bit of filtered light shining down on us. She frowns at me, "Well?"

I stare at the light playing over her, highlighting the honey color of her hair and the flecks of gold in her eyes.

"You're beautiful."

I blink.

That's not what I meant to say.

The girl tilts her head. "Nope. I'm Andi. Nice to meet you."

She smiles and holds out her hand for me to shake, like we're at a tea party at the Waldorf Astoria and she's in a silk dress and I'm in a three-piece suit. Instead of the reality, where I'm still on the ground covered in blood and bruises, and she's in a baggy cotton dress and a tattered red scarf.

I push myself up and swallow down the nausea as my head spins. The scent of cigarette has left, blown away on the humid breeze. It's replaced by a soft smell, like sun-warmed strawberries and cherry blossoms freshly fallen.

I sit in the dirt and take her hand.

Her fingers are warm and when she squeezes my hand, it feels, for all the world, like coming home.

When I was three, and my dad gave me my Martin, it felt like this too. Like I'd been born to hold it.

"I'm Jace."

She squeezes firmly and shakes my hand. Then leaning close, she frowns.

"Did you know you're bleeding?"

I nod and feel a little woozy when I do. But I push past it. "It'll be fine."

She quickly unwraps her scarf from her neck, her hands working in brisk, efficient movements. "Here."

And before I know what she's doing, she's kneeling close and pressing her silk scarf to the cut on my forehead. I stay still, breathing shallowly, as she holds the fabric to the cut, stemming the bleeding.

"My name's not really Andi," she says.

I shift on the ground, trying not to think about the broken guitar bits beneath me. Some of the wood even fell out of my gig bag and scattered around me.

"It's not?"

She shakes her head. "It's Andrea, but I always wanted people to call me Andi. No one will, of course. Since we've never met before and you don't know me, I thought it'd be nice for you to call me that."

"Andi," I say, and when I do she gives me a wide, happy smile that makes my stomach dip in response.

"You know, you shouldn't walk alone in the park at night. You could get mugged." She dabs at my forehead then my cheek, wiping more blood away.

"Really?" I ask, smirking at her.

"Sure. And then you'd have to be rescued by a girl.

Which could really hurt your ego. How old are you, by the way?"

"Seventeen," I say, trying not to laugh. "My ego is not hurt. It was three against one. Did you see those guys? Giant. Huge. This big." I hold out my arms wide.

"Hmmm." The corner of her mouth twitches. "I'm seventeen too. I saw you playing in the park. You're good."

I stare at her, stunned. "You liked us?"

She pulls away the scarf, wads it into a ball, and then shoves it in her purse. The "black object" that she'd been hitting the Jetters with.

"Sure. You're really good." Then she glances down at the broken lengths of my guitar. "I'm sorry about your guitar. They really had it out for you, didn't they?"

I shrug, but she's studying my expression.

"It meant a lot to you?"

I nod, looking away to gather myself. "It was my dad's."

"Can he get you another one?" she asks, running her finger over a piece of the splintered wooden body.

I shake my head no, but don't say anything.

She stands quickly then and brushes off her dress, whacking her hands briskly against the fabric. I stand too, hiding a wince at the pain in my ribs.

For a second we stare at each other.

The silence stretches.

Is this it? Are we going to say goodbye?

Andi peers into my eyes, then takes a deep breath.

"Do you want to get something to eat with me?" she asks, her question coming out in a rush.

"Why?" I ask, surprised.

"You don't have to," she says tightly, tilting her jaw and fisting her hands.

"No. It's not that, it's only...you don't know me." Doesn't she have any concept of self-preservation? I'm a kid from a rough neighborhood. I haven't always kept my nose clean. There's a reason the Jetters call me gutter rat.

I'm nothing special to look at. I mean, if you want someone good looking all you have to do is find River. He has thick glossy black hair, golden brown skin, dark eyes with long eyelashes that can make *any* female do *anything* he asks, a square jaw, and a mischievous smile that makes girls go wild.

He has a shoe box full of business cards from all the agents who have asked him if he'd ever consider modeling. He gets a laugh out of it every time.

River is two years older than me. He's filled out and is four inches taller. At seventeen, I still haven't had my growth spurt. A late bloomer, I guess.

I also have gray eyes, not brown like River and Dean, which sucks, because everyone I've ever met with gray eyes is a real prick. Mom said I got them from her dad, but I never met him, so I don't know if he was nice or not.

Other than the height and the eyes, people say I look a lot like River, but I don't see it.

Anyway.

"You don't know me," I repeat.

"Sure I know you," Andi says, scowling as I bend to gather up the broken pieces of my guitar. "Your name is Jace. You play the guitar in Central Park on Friday nights. You're seventeen. You live in..."

"The Bronx."

"The Bronx," she says, like she knew it all along. "You can't fight. At all."

"I take offense at that."

She smirks. "You like Louis Armstrong."

I raise my eyebrows, then stop halfway, because of the sting in my forehead. But how'd she know I like Louis?

"You and your band played a bunch of his songs."

"What else do you know?"

"You go to Darby," she says, pointing at my shirt.

We wear a uniform to school, khaki pants and a tailored navy shirt with the Darby crest embroidered on the chest. I usually change before we play but today I was running late.

"True."

She's observant.

"And..." She purses her lips and then her eyes light up triumphantly. "You're a bibliophile."

"How'd you know that?" I ask, surprised.

She points at the small poetry chapbook sticking out of my front pocket.

"Right. Okay. But...still."

"What?"

I frown at her. Even though I'm only five nine, she's about six inches shorter than me. She's dwarfed in the shadows of the reaching trees and their bowing branches. The night has gone heavy and quiet, the humidity of early May smothering the city and traffic noises from outside the Ramble.

"You don't actually know me. How do you know I won't hurt you?" I ask.

She weighs my expression, regarding me solemnly.

"Will you?"

I don't hesitate. "No."

Never.

I'd never hurt her.

"I didn't think so."

She bends down and picks up a piece of my guitar that I missed. She presses it into my hand.

Then she says, "Besides, maybe you should be worried about me hurting you."

"Will you?" I ask as I take the last broken piece of my dad's guitar.

She smiles at me, and the way she smiles is so infectious that I can't stop myself from smiling back.

"I don't know," she says, "I'll try not to. But I can't promise anything."

She says the last cheerfully, although it seems like a warning. As we walk toward the edge of the Ramble I think about heeding it, but what's life without risks?

4

JACE

I UNWRAP THE PAPER FROM MY BURGER, STEAM RISING FROM the bun and burning my fingers.

The grilled burger scent slathered with melted cheddar spirals around us. I take a bite and then lean back against the boulder, watching Andi from the corner of my eyes.

She's nibbling on a French fry, staring at the lamplight shining across the grass, ending just shy of us. It's full dark now.

I texted Dean to let him know I was getting dinner with a friend—otherwise he'll get upset. He's like that. If I come home straight away he gets upset because I don't stay out. If I stay out, he's upset because I don't come home.

But he just texted back: *Don't stay out late.*

It's because we have a gig tomorrow. Our first paying gig.

The thought makes me queasy, because how are we going to play if I don't have a guitar?

"I've been thinking," Andi says. She reaches into the paper to-go bag and digs around.

We went to the outdoor burger stand at the edge of the park and loaded up with fries, burgers, ketchup packets, and dill pickles. I paid, even though the crumpled twenty-dollar bill I pulled out of my pocket was supposed to be for next week's lunches.

It was worth it.

I'd rather eat this one meal with Andi then five meals alone. So I'll go hungry. So what.

"What about?"

"I think, you and I, we're going to be best friends." She grabs a handful of French fries and shoves them into her mouth, chewing with relish. She's watching me with a laughing glint in her eyes.

My mouth goes dry, so I reach out, grab my chocolate milkshake, and take a long swallow. I let the cold drops of condensation run over my fingers then drip to the grass.

We're secluded from the rest of the park by a giant boulder, one of the gray, tall, wide hulks that line the edge of the park, butting up to the stone wall.

I lean against the curve of the stone and sink into the soft grass. At the dusky edge of the park, the round softness of nature hits the uniform straight lines of tall well-lit buildings.

Andi's smiling at me, watching me consider where nature meets city.

I turn back to her and say, "I already have a best friend."

She lifts an eyebrow. "Oh yeah. Who?"

"My brother, River. He was the one playing the keyboard. What do you like to do?"

She considers me, pursing her lips.

"If I tell you, you can't laugh," she finally says.

I lean forward. Now I really have to know. "I won't."

She narrows her eyes, then nods. "Okay. I like to go to the park, or the museum, and just sit there, on a bench or in the grass, and watch people. I like to watch all the people walking by. Then, I make up stories about them. For instance, there's this really old guy who comes and sits beneath the Obelisk behind the Met every Tuesday at five. He sits in its shadow, crosses his legs, puts his hands on his knees, and closes his eyes. I made up this story that he's an alien, stranded on earth, from the Alpha Centauri star system, and he's trying to use the Obelisk as a locator device to send a distress signal to his home planet— where his wife and kids are waiting."

She peers at me, her long amber hair falling across her cheek. She pushes it back and says, "Well?"

"What else?" I ask, taking another bite of my burger.

"Hmm. There's a woman who brings her dog to the park every morning. It's this little white fluffy thing, looks a bit like a rat wearing a wool sweater. She's been trying to teach it to play fetch for almost a year now. I couldn't figure out why she was doing it—it's obvious that dog hates balls—but then I saw the big guy with the Great Dane. I made up this story that they were star-crossed lovers, doomed to be apart until her dog learned to play fetch."

"Do you make up stories for everyone you see?"

She nods. "Pretty much."

I grin. "What did you make up about me?"

She turns away so I can't see her expression, and takes a long minute to meticulously pick the lettuce off of her burger.

"That bad, huh?" I've finished my burger, so I crumple the paper and throw it into the to-go bag.

"No," she says. "Look. It's just a made-up story."

I shrug. "Alright."

She turns and frowns. "You don't want to know?"

I do. But... "Not if you don't want to tell me."

"Okay. Thanks."

I nod. Then take a long drink of my chocolate milkshake. It's too sweet, but the cold feels good against my busted lip.

"Tell me about your guitar," she says, leaning back against the boulder and letting her legs sprawl out.

I hold out the bag of fries to her and she takes one with a smile.

"My dad gave it to me when I was two. It was his from when he was a teenager. I learned to play on it. My parents always said I was playing music before I could talk. I don't think a day has gone by in fifteen years that I haven't played it."

The heavy weight of losing my guitar hits me and suddenly it's hard to breathe.

"I'm really sorry. Your parents won't get you another one?"

"My parents are dead," I say.

Her eyes meet mine and she sucks in a breath.

Suddenly I'm sorry I told her. Now, I'm not Jace, the bibliophile who plays the guitar, and gets mauled by pricks in the park, I'm Jace, the kid with dead parents. I'm not someone to like anymore. I'm someone to be pitied.

Next, she'll say I'm sorry. Then there'll be awkward

silences because she doesn't know what else to say. Then she'll leave. And I'll never see her again.

Here it comes.

Three.

Two.

One—

"How'd they die?"

You're not supposed to ask that. No one *ever* asks that.

I stare at her.

"You aren't supposed to ask that," I say.

"Why not?" she looks at me curiously, tilting her head.

"Because it's callous. Because people don't."

"Are you sure?"

Ha.

I shake my head, and suddenly, the pain of losing my guitar—the last connection I had with my dad—isn't so heavy.

She isn't looking at me differently, she isn't looking at me with pity, she's...still here.

"I'm sure," I say. "You know, you're kind of terrible."

She nods and sits forward, resting her chin on her fist. "Tell me more."

And funny enough, I want to. I want to tell her everything.

"I write songs. When I can't figure out what to say or how to say it. I write lyrics."

She studies me for a second, focusing on the cut over my eye, then on the bruise I think is spreading over my cheek. "If you had to write a lyric for this moment, what would it be?"

I look back at her, try to figure out all the emotions I'm having, all the things that are hard to put into words.

Finally, I say, "*We'll be friends. You'll tell me your secrets, I'll tell you mine.*"

My fingers tap against my thigh and I can feel the rhythm of the song coming to me. It's the moment I love, when a song comes to you and you decide whether or not it'll be written. It's the space between dream and reality. Will you. Won't you? There's never as much anticipation as in that moment.

"I like it," Andi says, smiling.

"What about you? What's your lyric?"

She purses her lips and wrinkles her nose as she thinks. "*Sitting in the park, on a summer night, half in and half out of the light.*" She frowns, "I'll work on it. I've never made up a lyric before."

"It wasn't terrible."

She laughs and I move closer, the short grass matting beneath me.

Outside the park, a car horn sounds, long and insistent. We sit in silence for a long moment. She chews on her straw, taking small sips of her strawberry milkshake. I press my hands into the grass, down to the night-cool dirt, digging a small hole with my pointer finger.

Then, I say, "They've been gone four years."

"Your parents?"

I nod. "Sometimes it feels like they were here yesterday, but other times it feels like they were never here at all. My Martin, my guitar, it was the one thing that let me feel like my dad was still with me. You know, he played my guitar, he played the same notes, the same songs. So when I played it, it felt like we were together. Like he was there next to me. I could pretend for a song that he wasn't gone. Now that it's broken, it feels..."

I pause and the weight is back, pressing down on me, as heavy as the large boulder we're sitting against. I swallow and admit, "It feels like he's really gone."

I stare out at the darkness of the park. The wide, mounded humps of the large boulders. The fuzzy line of trees with their leaves rattling in the breeze. The lamps light the park, but they don't light it enough. My dad, he's disappearing into that darkness, isn't he?

Irrational anger sparks because it feels like Reid wrecking my guitar was the same as Reid killing my dad. I almost hate him in this moment.

"Let me fix it," Andi says.

I shake my head. "You can't fix it. The neck's broken. The body's splintered."

"Anything can be fixed," she says. "Let me fix it. I promise. I can do it."

"Why?" I ask, which seems to be the question I ask her a lot.

"Because. I said we were friends, didn't I?"

"You're sure?"

"Of course I'm sure." She stares at me, daring me to contradict her.

And I realize that right now, she's offering me a choice. Friend or forgotten.

If I say yes, then we'll be friends.

If I say no, then we'll part ways and never see each other again.

I can't imagine never seeing her again.

"Yeah. We're friends."

She leans toward me, her body curving close, like a whole note, a long, happy exhale.

"That's what I thought. So, let me fix it. I promise. I can."

I don't believe her. But what do I have to lose? It's already beyond repair.

"Alright," I agree.

"Your dad isn't gone," she says at the same time.

"I mean, he is," I say.

Not even a guitar can change that.

She shakes her head. "I think, when we play music, we can reach anyone, anywhere. Music transcends the known world. If you love someone, all you have to do is play music, from your heart"—she touches her hand to her heart and says—"and they'll hear you, no matter where they are."

"What do you know about music?" I ask.

She smiles. "Not much actually."

I smile back, then say in a sudden rush, "My parents were shot. In an armed robbery at the bodega down the street from our apartment. They were shot for a six-pack of beer and forty-two dollars."

She studies me, her eyes steady. "Did they find who did it?"

"No." I frown. "My dad tried to stop the robbery. Instead of ducking behind a shelf, he tried to talk the guy down. He was like that. He thought, if you were good to people, they'd be good back. He always said to me, *Jace, people are good*. He thought that the best way to make people realize we were all the same was through music. Music doesn't have color, he'd say. Everyone, no matter their age, their background, they all can connect through music. He could make a whole crowd of people dance, and laugh, and smile—they wouldn't have anything in common, sometimes, they'd be inclined to hate each other, but as soon as he started to play, all that animosity would disappear. He could make a stone-cold man cry. He could make a hateful man smile. He could make two people fall in love. All from a song."

"You're that way too," Andi says. "You can do that too."

I wish.

I wish I were like my dad. I wish I were like Louis.

"Anyway, he was so used to making people smile that I don't think he believed he'd actually get shot. But he did. And my mom, she was there too. She jumped out from behind the shelf, right in front of him. Like, what? What did she think? That she was bulletproof? That her love would stop the bullets? I guess. She did. Some of them. But it was too late. My dad grabbed her. Spun her around. And that was the end."

When Dean told me how Mom jumped in front of Dad, how he grabbed her and spun her around, all I could picture was them dancing.

Wasn't this like a dance?

Dad holding Mom in his arms. Spinning her around the living room. Them curled into each other. Always together. Always one.

Holding each other.

This time though, I wasn't there, peering around the corner of the hallway, watching them dance to Louis.

No.

I was at home, waiting for them to come home with ice cream and chocolate syrup to celebrate Dean getting a full-ride scholarship to Tisch School of the Arts at NYU.

Dean was going to be a star. He was going places. Rising high.

Back then, Dean smiled a lot. Joked around. He had Dad's belief in the goodness of the world.

But at the funeral, when I broke down, and River let

me hang on to him, while he cried too, Dean sat, stone still, staring straight ahead.

He didn't cry. He never cries. And he never smiles.

Not anymore.

Sometimes I get upset at the world, for taking my parents, but also for taking Dean. It's not fair. Four years ago he was on his way to Tisch.

But then he took on the role of raising two kids and turned down his scholarship to work as a concrete hauler instead.

Six days a week, he goes into construction sites and hauls busted up concrete and construction waste. He comes home tired, wide shoulders bowed, dust coating him, a permanent, tired frown on his face. It only eases a bit when we play.

Because we do.

We still play.

Because what are we without music?

Would we even be a family?

"We have a gig tomorrow," I say, realizing that we're truly screwed. "I don't have a guitar."

"When is it? Where?"

"The Fireside Club in Williamsburg at nine," I say. "It's our first paying gig. Dean's going to kill me." And it's not like I can play well anyway. My knuckles are the size of grapes.

"I have a guitar you can borrow," Andi says quickly.

"Do you play?" I ask, surprised.

"No." She smiles. "Which is why you can keep it as long as you like. To use until yours is fixed."

"It's an acoustic-electric?" I ask, skeptical but hopeful.

She bites her bottom lip, rolling it through her teeth. "Yes."

"Alright. Okay."

She reaches over and grabs my hand and squeezes. Pain shoots up my hand. I think I do a good job of hiding my wince, but I guess not, because she pulls back.

"Sorry. I forgot. You're hurt." She studies my swollen eye and the cut on my forehead. "You know, you really should learn to defend yourself."

I scowl at her. "I know how to fight."

"Uh huh." She gives me a skeptical look. "You carry around poetry and play like an angel. I don't think you have a bad bone in your body."

Right.

"There were three of them," I say irritably. I'd prefer it if she thought I was tough.

But she just grins and holds up her purse. "That's why you carry one of these and fill it with rocks."

Then to my amazement she proceeds to pull five fist-sized rocks out of her bag, clanking them to the ground.

"You're something else," I say admiringly.

"I know."

She picks up her milkshake and plays with the straw, then takes a small sip. She got strawberry. She's sitting so close I can smell it on her lips.

A pigeon, one that hasn't found its roost for the night, pecks over the grass, hoping for a handout. I shoo it away.

Andi sets her cup down and bites her lip again. "So. I'll meet you...here? Tomorrow at three? To get you the guitar? I want to come to your show too."

I study her. She seems almost nervous that I'll say no.

Maybe she feels the same thing I do.

Like the universe is plucking a chord and it's our chord and ours alone. And we're tuned to it, and drawn together.

Some people, when you meet them, your notes clash, like a B flat with an A. It's a horrible, discordant noise, and you can't mesh, no matter how hard you try.

But sometimes, when you meet someone, it's like you're each other's keynote. The third. The fifth. An octave. You don't even have to try to be in tune. You're a harmony.

That's what my parents had.

I know now that it's rare.

I think, when you find it, you should hang on to it.

Keep playing that tune.

"I'll be here," I say.

She smiles, a wide, relieved smile, and I can see the gap between her front teeth.

"Good. Then I'll come to your show and see how you do."

There's a happy, ringing feeling inside me. I shake my head. "What kind of person pushes their way into someone's life like this?" I ask, although I'm not upset about it.

She leans close, her nose almost touching mine. I can feel the heat of her and see the spark in her eyes.

"The fun kind," she says, like I can count on it.

5

ANDI

SOME DAYS I FEEL LIKE I'VE BEEN LYING SINCE THE SECOND I was born.

But other days, I'm more honest with myself, and I realize I've been lying since *before* I was born.

Most of the world thinks that lying is a sin, but for me, lying is the only way to survive.

I leave the green shadows of Central Park and step onto the brightly lit sidewalk of Fifth Avenue. There are a few empty wooden benches stationed along the stone wall separating the park from the street. I briskly walk to one and drop my purse onto the painted green surface.

Bright yellow taxis and city buses blow past, leaving a constant swirl of exhaust and noise in their wake, but otherwise, the street is fairly quiet.

The Met and the Guggenheim are closed for the night. Cooper Hewitt too. All of the tourists are back at their hotels, or tucked in some restaurant enjoying dinner.

There's a man walking his golden retriever across the street, a couple meandering toward the park, and a doorman standing inside his building's vestibule, staring out at the darkness.

Otherwise, no one's near.

This section of the city is bustling during the day, but night turns it sleepy and quiet.

Taking one last, furtive look around, I pull the navy cotton dress up over my head and off.

The reason I bought the dress is because it's shapeless, baggy and can fit over my clothes.

With the navy dress off, Andi is gone, and Andrea is back.

Andi wears wrinkled cotton dresses, tromps around the park, sits in the grass, laughs when she gets jumped on by muddy puppies, and people watches while drinking cheap street cart coffee.

Andrea? She wears custom designer dresses, shoes and accessories, all perfectly coordinated by her personal stylist. She attends art openings, the opera, and charity events with her parents. She doesn't laugh or roll in the grass. She definitely doesn't meet boys in the park and demand that they become her friend.

Andi can be friendly like that.

But Andrea? She hasn't been friendly a day in her life.

I roll the cotton dress into a tight ball and shove it into my purse, refusing to feel upset about peeling it off.

Underneath, I'm dressed in what I was supposed to wear to the gallery opening in SoHo that I told my mom I was going to.

I kick off my boots and replace them with the Jimmy

Choo heels I had wrapped in their satin shoe bag, tucked at the bottom of my purse.

Then I put on lipstick, mascara, and roll my hair into a messy French twist.

Looking in my compact, my expression slides back to cold, aloof, distant.

I picture the glass bubble around me, the one that separates me from the rest of the world.

All I need to do is make it through tonight.

Tomorrow is another day.

～

"Good evening, Miss Leighton-Hughes." The doorman, Viktor, pulls open the brass-handled, sparkling glass door of the Tower.

The cold dry air hits me, sweeping away the sticky heat and bringing with it the lemon-ammonia scent of the freshly polished marble floor.

I stride into the lobby, my heels clacking and echoing in the cavernous space. The lobby is four stories tall and was designed to look like the Hall of Mirrors in the Palace of Versailles.

Crystal chandeliers adorning the ornately painted ceiling splash prismed rainbows on the white marble floor. The ceiling is lined with sparkling gilt and the paintings depict the wondrous and legendary early years of Robert Chatham Leighton-Hughes, real estate tycoon, tech giant, financial wizard—my father.

If, upon entering, you forget who owns the Tower, this forty-two-story building taking up a slice of prime Manhattan real estate, all you have to do is look up.

When I was old enough to understand, I realized that

my father had the paintings commissioned to disarm his opponents. When they walked into the Tower and saw his monument to self, surely the work of a bombastic, silly, egotistical man, they would underestimate him.

The greater his display, the greater their misunderstanding. I know for a fact that many don't see behind the pompous boasting to the shrewd calculations of his mind until it's too late.

My heels click on the marble as I head toward the elevator bank.

The marble walls are lined with gilded reliefs and statues. I glance at the mirrors as I pass, checking my appearance.

I'll do.

There are five wide arched mirrors that stand opposite the five arched windows overlooking the bustling city street. Like I said, an ode to the Hall of Mirrors at Versailles.

As I reach the elevator my phone rings. Not many people have my private number.

I answer.

"Who is this?" I say, biting out the words.

"My word. You are the coldest person I know."

There's the muffle of people in the background, a large crowd, and music. It's a party. Of course.

The elevator operator, Johann, wearing his tan uniform and white gloves, presses the up button.

I look down at my phone and glare at the phone number displayed.

"Is this a new number?" I ask my oldest brother, Robert Jr.

"I've had it for six months. My word, you're unfeeling."

"Yes. Yes. What do you want?"

"I was calling," he says, and I can tell he's gritting his teeth, "because you are *late*. He is your father too, if you recall. Don't embarrass the family by failing to—"

The elevator doors open, Johann holds them wide and I step inside the mahogany and mirror lined lift. The elevator doors ding as they slide closed and Johann selects the penthouse.

"—abide as a Leighton-Hughes, obligations dictate—"

"Goodbye, Rob."

"Don't you dare hang—"

I hang up.

My stomach rises and flips as the elevator speeds up to the fortieth floor. My family lives on the top four floors of the Tower. The roof is my favorite spot, there's a pool, a hot tub, a lounge deck with sun chairs, and a garden. But the best part of it is the fact that no one ever goes up there. Just me.

On the rest of the floors we have three-hundred-and-sixty-degree windows so that we can see the park or the city from whatever room we're in. The family bedrooms are on the top floor, along with two living rooms, a library, a kitchen (and a chef), and a dining room. The next floor down there is a movie theatre, a gym, my dad's home office.

The floor below that is our entertainment floor. It's mostly taken up by the catering kitchens, and the grand ballroom, which is as gaudy as the lobby and full of marble, frescoes, gilt, and nude marble statues.

There's also a grand piano from Carnegie Hall that a famous pianist played on, a classic Lamborghini, gold-plated and parked on a marble pedestal in the center of the ballroom, and on the far wall, a twenty-foot-tall painting of my dad in a tuxedo, smoking a pipe, with his Afghan hound, Fencer (RIP), lying at his feet.

The next floor down, we have more guest bedrooms, a kitchen, offices, etcetera, more of the same, decorated in the same gilt, burnished marble, and burgundy silk.

But I don't step out onto the family floor, or the roof, or even the guest floor.

When the elevator doors open, I'm greeted by the echoing noise of two hundred people singing "Happy Birthday" to my dad.

The ballroom sparkles. The bright light of the chandeliers reflect off the diamonds and precious gems plastered on the women and the gold watches sported by the men. It's blindingly bright.

There's a string orchestra, stationed beneath the Lamborghini, playing "Happy Birthday" in time with the guest's singing. The sound echoes off the marble walls and the round columns. It's overbearingly loud.

But when I step into the din, I tilt my chin high and pretend the noise and the shine aren't too much. Even though I'd much rather be in the fading evening light, listening to a boy playing guitar in the park.

Anyone near the elevator unconsciously moves back.

Part and parcel in being a Leighton-Hughes.

Everyone fears you.

A few respect you.

None like you.

Someone might wonder, if no one likes a Leighton-Hughes, then why are there more than two hundred people crammed into Robert Senior's ballroom, celebrating his sixtieth birthday?

Because he invited them.

And no one says no to my dad.

As the last chords of "Happy Birthday" fade, and the orchestra bridges into a classical piece, I move farther into the ballroom.

The air is warm and sticky from so many bodies pressed so close together, and the scent of expensive perfume is almost overwhelming.

But as I run my gaze over the guests, past flashing diamonds, colorful dresses, and forced laughter, I finally spy who I was searching for.

He's across the ballroom, insouciantly leaning against the grand piano, a glass of wine forgotten in his hand.

His long legs are stretched out, his shoulders relaxed, he has the carefree, nonchalant air that is often worn by boys who know they are good-looking, wealthy, and universally admired, and don't have any worry of that ever changing.

He's wearing a black tuxedo with a white vest, his blond hair is smoothed back from his forehead. He has a bored, supercilious expression on his face as he stares through, not at, the crowd of people.

I've known him my whole life.

We were christened on the same day. Our nannies rolled our strollers next to each other for art afternoons at the Met and took us to the same French language class for toddlers.

We attend the same polo matches on weekends. We stay at our vacation homes on the same Caribbean islands and in the same European cities.

I know him, and he knows me.

I stalk across the room, the crowd parting around me.

When I reach him, he smiles, as if he's been waiting for me to come to his side.

I don't smile back.

His teeth are straight and white. He grew when he hit fifteen, shooting up from five and a half feet to six foot one seemingly overnight.

Now he's seventeen. His shoulders are bulky, his muscles always taut, as if he's shifting his weight, ready to strike.

You'd think his golden hair, his sea blue-green eyes, his square jaw, and his smile would make my heart melt. But you'd be wrong.

His smile is too close to a shark baring its teeth. His eyes are too knowing and cynical.

No. This suave son, this scion of New York, he's as dangerous as I am.

I step close and say in a quiet steely voice, "Hello Reid."

6

————

ANDI

"ANDREA." REID BARES HIS TEETH. "FANCY SEEING YOU here."

I give him a hundred-yard stare and he laughs, delighted.

Now that I'm only a foot away from him, I study his face. It burns me to realize he doesn't have a scratch on him. Not even a slight bruise from when I walloped him with a purse full of rocks.

"Thank you for inviting me to your party," he drawls in his gravelly voice.

I still remember when Reid had a high, whiny voice. But of course, as unfair as the world is, when he hit junior high, he was blessed with a deep voice that sounds like honey rolling over gravel.

"I didn't invite you. And it's not my party."

When he smiles I stare down at my nails, studying my manicure and pretending boredom.

We both know that the reason he's here is because his family's real estate conglomerate is a direct competitor with my dad's. The motto *keep your friends close and your enemies closer* is alive and well in the Tower.

"You don't look any worse for wear," I muse.

Reid straightens to his full height and stares down at me. "So it was you." He chuckles and spins his wine glass, twirling the red liquid.

It reminds me of the blood on Jace's forehead and a burning red-hot coal of anger lights in my chest. I don't let it show, instead I casually turn and grab a smoked salmon mousse canapé from a passing waiter.

I nibble at it, the smoky flavor matching the burning in my chest, and watch Reid.

He eyes me, starting at my messy French twist and sliding down my burgundy satin mini dress, all the way to my four-inch gold heels.

The gold and burgundy is an homage to my dad *and* so that no one forgets I'm his daughter.

While Reid became muscled and herculean when he hit fifteen, I didn't change much.

I'm still thin, small chested, and with an unfortunate gap between my front teeth that no matter how much I hate, I refuse to have fixed. It doesn't matter what I look like though. No one sees beyond the fact that I'm Robert Senior's daughter. Not even Reid.

He sets his wine glass on the piano and less than a second after it's down a waiter whisks it away. Reid doesn't notice.

Instead, he scratches his jaw and says, "I wondered. But then I thought, no, that couldn't have been the illustrious Andrea Leighton-Hughes. She wouldn't possibly dress like a homeless vagrant, some deranged hobo, and wander the park, thrashing innocents with her bag of trash. I couldn't see it."

I bare my teeth at him, treating him to his own shark smile. "You'll stay away from him. From now on."

"The question is, why? Why would you dress in rags? Wander the park at night? Unless…"

He lifts his eyebrows.

"Unless nothing. I asked you to leave Jace alone and you will."

I'm not ignorant to the fact that Reid goes to Darby school too. That means he's likely been bullying Jace for years.

"Or what?" he muses, folding his hands behind his back and rocking on his heels.

Finally, I let myself give him a real smile. I let a bit of happiness fill my eyes, then I whisper, "Or I will break you."

He laughs. A gleeful, happy laugh. There's a wild light in his eyes. He knows I can. He even knows I might.

The Shillings may be powerful, but the Leighton-Hugheses are more so.

"You've always been my favorite person," Reid says. "Let's dance."

He holds out his hand, palm out.

The orchestra plays a waltz. There are even a few couples twirling around the parquet dance floor.

"Come on, Andrea. It's a party."

Reid knows that I can dance. We learned together after all. Dancing, etiquette, all part and parcel of the life. My parents have even roped him into being my escort at certain charity balls.

Yes. We've danced.

I look past Reid, see my mom watching me.

My chest tightens.

She's in a floor-length gold dress, satin draping over her curves. Her golden hair is piled on top of her head and her make-up is flawless. She's surrounded by people. Even so, her face is devoid of all expression, even as I give a hesitant smile.

Even though her gaze doesn't flicker, and her face is as flat as that of the marble statues lining the ballroom, I know exactly what she expects.

"Yes. I'll dance with you."

I put my hand in Reid's.

Reid doesn't know why I acquiesced. Maybe he thinks it's his charm. He spins me onto the dance floor and holds me with exactly eight inches separating our bodies.

This close, with the warm air swirling around us, and the orchestra echoing above us, I almost feel as if I'm in a bubble with Reid.

And I dislike him for it.

I can smell his cologne, a woodsy, leather scent. I can see a nick on his neck from shaving. I can feel the heat and smooth power coming off him.

He fences, I've seen him practicing, I've even been to one of his tournaments. He dances like he's fencing, and each step is a lunge or a thrust.

He steers us around another spinning couple and grins down at me.

"So. Andrea. You've fallen for a lesser mortal. Chosen one of the unwashed masses."

I go to give a biting response, but he dips me, and I automatically lean back over his arm, dropping my head and curving my spine.

He pulls me up and swirls us around again. "What does he mean to you?"

"Nothing," I lie.

He lifts an eyebrow and thrusts me forward, pacing the floor in harsh dance steps.

"I only met him today," I say.

"Then why does it matter what I do?"

He spins me out, then back to him, improvising. We've long since stopped dancing the standard waltz.

"Because," I say, "I don't like bullies."

Which is part of the truth, but not all of the truth.

The real reason why I don't want Reid hurting Jace?

There's only one.

The minute I saw Jace playing his guitar in the park, a secret smile on his face, the sun falling over him, I didn't need to make up a story about him.

The story was already there.

He was mine. And I was his.

I felt it, like someone had reached out, shaken me, and said, "That boy, that one right there? He's yours. And you are his."

Jace asked me, what kind of girl meets a perfect stranger and demands to be his friend. I'd said, a fun one. But what I really meant was a lonely one.

I'd felt alone my entire life, until the minute I first heard the notes of his song.

After that, I didn't feel lonely anymore.

Reid studies me, deciding whether or not he believes me.

Finally he shrugs. "I don't see why you care. He's a nobody. His friends have criminal records. His parents were involved in some druggie shootout. He has a disciplinary record at school. He comes from nothing. He'll go back to nothing."

Reid watches me, trying to see if any of this is sinking in.

"I'm not planning to be his friend," I say coldly.

Lie. Lie. Lie.

"I'm merely planning on making your life hell if you continue being a malicious degenerate. I don't like it."

"Hmm." Reid smiles and then the music fades, falling quiet like the petals of a rose, drooping with age, until they fall silently to the floor.

Reid lets me go, pulling his hand from my waist. Dropping my hand.

I step back and nod.

Reid gives a short, mocking bow, the tails of his tuxedo jacket flashing behind him.

He moves to go, but at the last minute, stops and turns back. "I forgot. I won't mention your foray as a vagrant. I wouldn't want to ruin your fun."

I walk away, wading into the sparkling, noisy crowd, hoping that was the last time I ever have to interact with Reid again.

7

ANDI

THE SCRAPING OF SILVER CUTLERY ON CHINA IS LOUD IN OUR family dining room.

Our chef outdid himself with my dad's post-birthday breakfast of caviar butter on fresh brioche, lobster spinach omelets, and for the sweet tooth, espresso waffles with mocha syrup.

I take a sip of my cappuccino, letting the steam waft up to me, and enjoy the taste of the Belgian cocoa powder sprinkled on top of the light foam. I peek at everyone from over the delicate rim of my ceramic cup.

My dad sits at the head of the long marble table. He's in a gray morning suit, with an orange handkerchief in his pocket and a bright orange tie to match.

Even though he's sixty, he looks forty. He has thick red hair streaked through with dishwater yellow, a slightly lined, very tanned face, and a wiry frame. He's short, five three without shoes on, and he has a wide, puffed out chest. When he walks his chest leads the way.

He reminds me of a banty rooster. I saw one once, in South America. There was a large population of wild chickens near the resort, and one evening I witnessed a cockfight.

There was this rooster half the size of all the others, it was red-faced, its red comb stuck straight in the air and it walked with its chest thrust forward.

I thought for sure that that tiny rooster was going to be pecked to death by the larger roosters. But no. That little rooster tore into the others. It was vicious. That banty rooster dominated, it was the king, and boy, did those other chickens know it.

Sometimes people laugh at my dad for being short, for his red hair, for boasting and swaggering around. Then they learn. He's clever, he's vicious, and he tears apart anyone that comes against him. Just like a banty rooster.

When he's loud—brash, bombastic, bragging—you can relax. When he's silent, that's when you need to be concerned.

Today, he's quiet, which is why I'm tense and twitchy. Although, I learned to hide that years ago.

Elliot, the second oldest, never learned to hide anything.

He's across the marble table, slightly obscured by the gold candelabra and the Titanic-sized cornucopia. He's tapping his foot on the ground, shifting in his chair, and darting his eyes between Rob Jr, sitting next to him, and my dad.

Elliot and Rob Jr are only a year apart, twenty-three

and twenty-two. For their entire lives they've wrestled like Esau and Jacob vying for our dad's favor.

Rob is a facsimile of my dad. Short, red-haired, hairy armed, hairy-backed (you can see it sprouting from his collar) and red-faced.

He walks with quick, cocky movements, demands instead of asks, and believes that he deserves to be my dad's right-hand man and successor.

As a kid he enjoyed tormenting our nanny, poking the eyes out of my dolls and filling the holes with black void-like rocks, and telling me that I was a bastard.

When I asked our nanny Grace, a gentle, smiling woman from the Philippines, what a bastard was, she told me it was a type of fruit.

It wasn't until I was six that I learned what one really was.

Elliot, though, he's not like Rob, or my dad.

He's tall and thin. So thin his suits hang on him like he's a clothes hanger. He has brown hair, already thinning, and he has a clever, fox-like mind. He's the fox among the roosters, and I'm not quite sure who will win. He's a genius, full-stop, and he knows it. He thinks by right of his brilliance, that he should be the most favored son.

He's my mother's favorite child and she has never withheld her preference.

When he was young, he was a mama's boy. Not much has changed.

At the opposite end of the long marble table, shining under the sparkling light of the rainbow chandelier, my mom sits with elegant poise.

She's in a gray Grecian gown, with pearls dripping over her like frosting on a wedding cake. In her teenage years, she was a famous heiress, often in the tabloids for her wild exploits. But once she married my dad, I guess she became what you see today, a woman similar to a marble statue.

Her pale skin is unlined and poreless, nothing can perturb her or make her frown (or smile), and she has never, ever, not once held me, hugged me, or said *I love you* in my entire life.

Sometimes I think it would've been easier having a statue for a mother, because then I wouldn't have expected anything.

But that's life.

Anyway, here we are, our little family, in the huge, trendily barren dining room, eating the post-birthday breakfast to celebrate my dad.

"Robby," Elliot says, darting a quick glance at him. He calls him Robby, because Rob Jr hates to be called that. "Lydia tells me that you lost two million last week. Didn't you think to read the predictions? Everyone knew that investment was bust. Or haven't you learned to read yet? Personally, I have serious concerns about your business acumen."

I take a bite of the espresso waffle and watch as Rob's face turns pomegranate red. He hates it when Elliot questions his intelligence.

"What's this?" my dad asks, sitting straight in his chair, scenting blood.

"Nothing. I've done well enough. I made it up this week." Rob darts a glance at my dad to see if he's convinced. My dad shrugs, so Rob turns on Elliot and lashes out. "What about you? Your fiancée has a running date with her plastic surgeon. Her nose, her chin, her breasts. I have it from Tim that she and the surgeon had lunch together at the Mandarin and then took a room. How can you manage your business if you can't manage your fiancée?"

Game. Set. Match.

That's how Rob plays. Vicious.

Elliot's face pales, but he doesn't deny it. Everyone knows his fiancée isn't faithful. But he'll have to cut off the engagement now that Rob has said it in front of my dad.

I set my fork down and dab my mouth with my cloth napkin.

"Enough," my dad says. "I don't need to hear your bickering at my table. Neither of you are the son I wanted."

I glance at my mom to see how she's taking this. Her face is as placid as ever.

"Perhaps I'll give everything to Andrea. She has more sense than the two of you combined."

This is a common threat, and although I know not to believe it, Rob Jr and Elliot don't.

"You wouldn't—" Elliot begins.

"She isn't even—" Rob Jr explodes.

"Enough." My dad hits his fist on the table and the china rattles. A bit of my cappuccino sloshes over onto the saucer. "I'll do as I like."

"Mother," Elliot turns to her, "You wouldn't let that happen, would you? It wouldn't be fair. It wouldn't be right. You wouldn't stand—"

She doesn't say anything. She merely glances at my dad, her eyes calm. She picks up her mimosa and takes a sip. Then, once she's set her glass down, she says in a low voice, "I believe, that your father shall do as he pleases. As he has always done."

The silence stretches.

It's not as if my dad is going to retire today and hand his seventeen-year-old daughter his company. It's all for show. I imagine we still have thirty more years of this game to play. What I wouldn't give to step out of it.

"Did you choose pre-law at Columbia?" my dad asks. He takes a bite of his omelet and chews loudly.

"Yes," I say, my voice flat.

I was accepted at Yale, Princeton, the rest, but my family has always stayed in the city, in the Tower. The thought of another four years here feels like the bars of a cell door closing.

It's hard to breathe if I think about it too much.

I stand, pushing my chair back. The metal feet scrape on the marble floor.

"Where are you going?" my dad asks, his face reddening.

"Shopping. Then a study group. I'll be home late."

They don't bother to ask more. I leave, Elliot and Rob renew their verbal jabs and counter-jabs, and my dad calls for more champagne.

I hurry out the door.

I have a few hours to find and buy an acoustic-electric guitar and then find an outfit that a regular high school girl would wear to a concert in Brooklyn.

8

ANDI

I'M EARLY.

Huge puffy white clouds move swiftly across the blue sky, casting shadows on the green grass of Central Park.

I'm hot from the afternoon sun and my skin is itchy from sitting in the pokey grass for the last thirty minutes.

I have so much nervous energy that I'd love to get up and walk around a bit, but I'm worried that if I'm even twenty feet from where I said we'd meet, then Jace won't see me and he'll turn around and go.

So instead of pacing, I sit, legs folded under me, plucking blades of grass and disassembling dandelions, their yellow petals staining my fingers. Dandelions smell bitter and grassy, and my hands are a bit sticky from the milk in their stems.

I frown and wipe my hands on my skirt. It only took an hour to find a short skirt, a faded midriff t-shirt, and a pair of Converse shoes to feel normal again. My hair's in a ponytail, I'm not wearing make-up, and I have about twenty plastic bangles on my wrists.

Next to me in the grass is a brand new acoustic-electric guitar. I told the salesman I needed a guitar for a professional. One that would sound good on stage and in the studio. One that would last a lifetime.

There were so many choices it was dizzying. Fenders, Martins, Taylors, I can't remember...there were walls and walls of guitars on display.

So finally, I asked the salesman to play a few chords on each one. Then, I closed my eyes.

The first guitar, the second, the fifth, none of them were right. Finally, on the eleventh try, the noise reverberated over me, whispered up my spine and settled in me.

"That one," I'd said.

It sounded just like Jace.

It was another Martin.

"Are you sure?" the salesman asked, eyeing me skeptically. "This one is expensive. A kid like you might want something—"

No. That was the one.

I bought it.

Then I bought everything he said I'd need to be able to play it in a show.

I also found a repair shop in lower Manhattan that swore they'd be able to fix Jace's guitar. All in all, it was a really successful day.

Which means, I shouldn't be so nervous. But my hands are sweaty, my stomach is turning over and over, and I can't stop looking toward the path leading off the sidewalk.

What if yesterday was an anomaly?

What if I don't feel the same connection today?

What if he was just being nice yesterday and he doesn't show?

What if me buying him a guitar is way, way too much? What if...

I shake my head and stop playing the what if game.

I learned years ago that what ifs are like a whirlpool and they'll suck you under and drown you if you let them.

Okay.

I wipe my hands on my skirt, take a deep breath, and square my shoulders.

It's fine. It'll all be fine.

"I wasn't sure you'd really be here."

I look up quickly at his voice.

Jace.

My heart skitters around my chest, chanting *he came, he came, he came.*

I grin up at him. "Funny. I wasn't sure you'd really come."

When his eyes crinkle and a smile spreads across his face, the last of my fears and all the *what ifs* fall away.

He likes me.

He more than likes me.

The sunlight spreads over us, like a warm blanket, and even though there are a hundred people within shouting distance, this little patch of grass feels secluded and private.

I pat the grass next to me, the blades scratching my palm. "Have a seat. I come bearing gifts."

His eyes flicker to the guitar case. "You really did bring one. Dean'll be happy. He wasn't convinced a total stranger I met in the park would actually come through. He nearly lost his mind when he saw my swollen hands."

Jace winces, probably remembering whatever Dean said.

He kneels down and settles into the grass next to me.

"I'm not a total stranger," I say, sticking my nose in the air. "I'm your best friend."

Jace covers a laugh, his eyes smiling, and says, "Exactly. That's what I told him."

"You didn't," I laugh.

He shakes his head. "I didn't."

There's a warm, lovely happiness settling over me. I've never actually had a friend before. That might sound strange. Bizarre even. I mean, what sort of person has never had a friend?

But there it is.

Because how can you have a friend when everyone knows who you are and what you are?

My mom taught me a valuable lesson when I was young. She told me, "Andrea. Girls like you don't have friends. Keep yourself apart. Don't care for anyone. Ever. Because when you're betrayed, the betrayal won't matter. You'll already have anticipated it and put in place the appropriate retaliation. Do you understand?"

I nodded. Told her I did. I was four when I received that tidbit.

I didn't really understand. But I came to.

But Jace doesn't know who I am. With him, I don't have to worry.

I don't need that cold hauteur honed to icy sharpness over the years. I don't need the imaginary impenetrable glass bubble I keep around myself. I don't need any of that.

"I still can't believe you showed," Jace says, staring at me with probably an identical expression to the one I'm wearing. It sort of says, *wow, I can't believe how lucky I am...you're here!*

"Let's get this straight," I tell him, leaning close and peering into his gray eyes. "I like you. I've already decided to be your friend. I don't have many"—*any*—"so be prepared for me to come to all your concerts and cheer even if you mess up—"

"Hey. I don't mess up—"

I wink. "Follow you to all the parks around the city to hear you play. Also, I'll eat burgers and milkshakes with you in the grass 'til we're stupid full and can barely stand up. I'll make up bad lyrics and you'll write better ones. I'll always remember your birthday—when is it, by the way—"

"June twenty-third—"

"Noted." I nod and fold my hands in my lap. Jace's eyes are lit with amusement as I continue. "Also, be prepared for some hellraising this summer. We'll both be out of school. This summer will be our playground. Do you have any idea all the things I've always wanted to do, that I've just been waiting for the right person to do them with?"

"Like what?"

I shift on the grass, excited by the mere idea of it all. "So many things. I want to eat a dozen hotdogs at Coney Island and then ride the rollercoaster until I'm sick."

He laughs, just like I hoped he would.

"I want to go to the Shakespeare plays in Central Park, the ones where you run around after the actors and pretend to charge in the battle scenes," I've seen them from afar. "I want to go bowling." I've never been.

"I want to spend the night in a museum. I want to go to M&M World and gorge myself on only the red M&Ms—"

"Red? Red is the worst. Green—"

"Is disgusting. It can only be red."

He smiles. "We'll see."

I ignore that.

"And I want to go to concerts and dance until I'm so exhausted I can't stand up anymore."

"What kind of concerts?"

"Yours, for a start," I say.

I scoot closer. My hand rests in the grass, and when I look down, I notice that my pinkie is right next to his. Just the edges of our pinkies are touching, a millimeter at most, but it has my stomach somersaulting over itself. There's a current running between us.

"What do you think?" I ask.

"I think this could be the best summer of our lives."

I hold back a smile.

He looks down at our hands too. Stares at the tiny point of connection.

I watch his face.

Study him.

He looks different in the light of day. His black hair is thick and long on the top and short on the sides. He has a masculine face, with thick eyebrows, a straight nose, and a solid jaw. His eyes are gray and his gaze is direct and honest.

I don't think you'll ever have to guess what he's thinking, his eyes show every emotion. It's like looking into the surface of a gray, rippling lake, and seeing his thoughts reflected back on the water's surface.

You might think, that with him being skinny and only

a few inches taller than me, he'd be easy to ignore. But that isn't the case at all.

He has that special something.

I bet that wherever he is, whatever he's doing, people's eyes are drawn to him.

He's magnetic.

He's in faded jeans and a black t-shirt, with a bruised eye, a busted lip, and an inch-long red cut on his forehead.

Everyone I know would say he looks like trouble. That he's headed the wrong way in life. Or at least, in the opposite direction of me. Actually, Reid did say it. *Jace comes from nothing. He'll go back to nothing.*

What do they know?

"Do you want to try the guitar?" I ask, and when I do, Jace's gaze comes up and meets mine.

Neither of us moves our hands away from the other's.

"Yeah. Are you sure though? It's really okay for me to borrow it?"

I nod. "It's yours. As long as you like."

I finally move my hand away, but only to tug the guitar case toward us. It's a black, hard shell case, which the salesman assured me meant the guitar would survive even if a van backed over it. I flip the brass hardware and lift the lid.

The smell of cedar and maple rushes out at us, mixed with the biting scent of lacquer and glue. It's smells just like a woodworking studio I once visited. It's so distinctive, this new guitar smell, that I breathe it in.

I throw the lid back and it thuds to the grass with a hollow noise.

Jace sucks in a loud breath.

The inside of the case is plush burgundy velvet, and deep enough to cradle the guitar inside.

"You..." Jace trails off. Stares at the guitar.

The wood on the front is light, a honey-colored maple. But the edges, which are still hidden, are a deep rich mahogany brown. I like the contrast. Different, but complementary.

There's inlaid pearl too. Gold.

It's a beautiful guitar.

But it sounds even better than it looks.

"You had this just laying around?" he asks, finally tearing his eyes away from the guitar.

The sunlight glints off the lacquered wood and the gold, winking at us.

His eyebrows come down and a wrinkle forms between them.

Doesn't he like it?

"Well..." I shrug. "Don't you like it? Isn't it...okay?"

He shakes his head, and gives me a wide-eyed stare.

I look into his eyes and read the emotion there.

I smile, even before he says, "Like it? It's unbelievable."

"You should try it. Make sure it plays okay."

He tugs the guitar out of the case, cradling it in his hands like it's a newborn baby. Then he runs his fingers over the glossy surface and the strings, eliciting hollow sounds and whooshing squeaks.

"Hello," he says to the guitar, his head bent. The shadowed sunlight dances over him, flashing light and dark.

"I don't think it can talk," I tell him.

He looks up, a smile on his face. "Sure it can." Then

he asks, "Whose guitar is this? Aren't they going to miss it? Are you sure I can use it?"

"It's nobody's. So nobody will miss it. Of course you can use it. I said so, didn't I?"

He runs his hands over the body. His fingers stroking the wood. His knuckles are still swollen, although the swelling's come down since yesterday. But there are cuts and purple bruises on them. I guess, even if he didn't hit Reid yesterday, he did manage to hit someone.

"You're not worried I'm going to take off with it? This guitar is worth a lot of money."

I roll my eyes. "Uh huh."

"It is!"

"Well. I'm holding your dad's guitar as hostage, so I doubt you'll do anything like that."

"Are you sure?" he asks again, and I wonder if I shouldn't have bought such a nice one.

But it sounded like him, so how could I not?

The money was nothing. But the look on his face, that means something.

"Give me a lyric. For right now," I say.

I lean close. He taps his finger against the body making a hollow drumming sound. "*Girl is crazy, but I like her that way.*"

I laugh.

"Play me a song," I demand.

I fall back on the grass, lying next to him. My shirt rides up, baring my stomach. The grass tickles my legs and my back. I can see him from the corner of my eyes, bowing over the guitar, tuning it, growing accustomed to it.

Then he begins, strumming gentle, rocking chords,

that thrum against me like a summer wind brushing over my bare skin. The honeyed sounds curl around me.

A slow, happy smile spreads over Jace's face, and then his whole body looks as if it's smiling. He rocks in time to the song, and I watch, swept away in his music.

I squint in the sunlight, wait for clouds to pass over the sun, and laze in the music, the tickle of the grass, and the smell of cedar and sunshine.

"Sing," I say, longing to hear him.

He looks over at me, his fingers still strumming. "I never sing in public."

"Why not?" I ask, lifting myself up on my elbow and curling toward him.

His eyes shift away, settle on the runners, the dog walkers, the tourists, the dozens and dozens of people moving past.

We're in Central Park, not a secluded forest. I guess he doesn't have a problem playing with his brothers in public, but singing must be a different story.

"I don't know. I just freeze up when I try. My throat goes tight. My vision gets all these black spots. I start to sweat. Dean hates it. I have the best voice of all of us. He wants me to sing, but I can't."

"You've tried?"

"Every show. Dean makes me try again every show. And when I choke, River steps in."

It seems cruel. If he doesn't want to sing, he shouldn't have to keep trying. Unless... "Do you want to sing?"

He strums another chord, moving into another melody. "Yeah. I do. My mom always said I had the face of a sinner and the voice of an angel." He grins at me.

"That's a terrible thing to say!"

"I was always getting into trouble for something." His

eyes crinkle and he looks like he's reliving a happy memory.

"What kind of trouble?"

He tilts his head. "I got into fights in the sandbox. I gobbled all my mom's cookies before they had a chance to cool. I found a can of construction orange spray paint when I was five and practiced my ABCs on the side of our building."

I stifle a surprised laugh.

He shakes his head. "Dallas took the blame for that one. He's a good guy. Even when he was nine."

I scoot across the grass until my knees are almost touching his and look into his eyes. Around us, Central Park is as busy as ever. Even in the half-shade of the large boulder, and shielded from the street by the stone wall, there are still families nearby, joggers, and people out with their dogs for a weekend stroll.

If Jace has a fear of singing in public, then this many people will make his throat tighten up, I'm sure.

"You can sing in front of your family though?"

He nods. "At home. It's fine. River, Dean, Dallas, Pauly, it's fine with them. But when I look out, and there are all these people watching me," he shrugs, "I feel like I'm trapped, handcuffed to a chair, and there are a thousand eyes staring at me. I can't see anything else but their faces, spinning around me, watching. It's..."

"Awful," I say.

"Yeah." His fingers slow and the melody he's playing starts to break apart.

"What if..." I stop, unsure.

He looks at me. "What?"

"What if I stand up, right there in front of the stage,

like five feet from you, and you just look at me. You can block everyone else out."

He stares at me. "I don't think that would work."

Oh.

"Of course it won't," I agree. I brush off a bug crawling over my calf and watch it take flight. Finally, I look back at him. "But what's the harm in trying? Just think, tonight could be the night. You'll wow the world with your masterful croonings."

He snorts. "You think so?"

"Absolutely. Your wonderful warbling. Your pleasant purring. Your vociferous vibrations."

"Wow. Okay."

"Okay?"

"Okay," he confirms. Then, looking down at the guitar, he says, "We could try it now."

His cheeks have spilled over to the faintest red. He's nervous, even though he's trying his best not to show it.

He plays the beginnings of a song. Clears his throat. Opens his mouth to sing. Nothing comes out. He tries again. Nothing.

My chest tightens at the look in his eyes. Like he knows he's failing. Like he's giving up.

So I reach up, put my fingers to the edge of my mouth, pull it wide, stick out my tongue and cross my eyes.

The wheezing cough he was making turns into a sputtered laugh. "What?" he laughs.

I cross my eyes harder and wag my tongue.

He laughs, and then he starts to sing.

And goodness, I can't help it, my hand falls away from my mouth, my eyes uncross and I gape at him.

His mom was right, he has the voice of an angel.

His voice pulls at something deep inside, it reaches

down into you and pulls out all the feelings you forgot you ever had. It vibrates deep down into your bones and settles there.

My goodness.

No wonder Dean keeps making him try to sing in public.

Jace could make a thousand people weep. Or fall in love.

When I realize he's singing his lyrics from last night, *We'll be friends. You'll tell me your secrets, I'll tell you mine,* I decide that there probably isn't anything that I won't do for him.

Even tell him my secrets.

Just not today.

9

JACE

THE FIRESIDE CLUB SMELLS LIKE STALE BEER, BLEACH, OLD fryer grease, and decades of cigarette smoke layered into the tiled ceilings and black walls.

The main room, or really, the only room, is about thirty feet by fifty feet. There's a small stage area, a black curtain behind the stage, an open area to dance, and behind that tall metal tables clustered near a long bar where every band that has played here sharpies their name on the wood counter.

I think the room was originally designed to look like a speaker, or maybe a boom box from the 90s.

The ceiling tiles are painted black, the walls are painted black, and the rubbery linoleum floor is black.

Dean said that when the lights go out there are blacklight designs painted on the walls. He claims that the dingy, dirty look disappears in the dark and the club becomes *something to look at.*

To me, it doesn't matter what it looks like, I've already decided that the only thing I'll be concentrating on tonight is Andi.

I'm going to sing.

I'm going to do this.

I've known since I was three, maybe before, what I was meant to be. A musician.

Even if my dad hadn't started our band, and even if he hadn't handed me his Martin, I still would've had this longing inside me to make music.

Dean has it too.

River, not as much, he mostly plays because he understands what it means to us. He doesn't do this for the love of music, he does it for family.

He once told me that the only thing he's ever been good at is music, so even if he doesn't love it like me, it's what he wants to do, because he likes being good at something. Anything. I'd argue with him, but it's pointless.

He'd just point out that he's a dropout and that's that.

River never cared about school like me and Dean. He can understand anybody, and any situation, but he could never understand school.

After Mom and Dad died he failed tenth grade. Then he failed it again. And he kept on failing it until he was old enough to drop out. It's not that he isn't smart, it's just that River and school never got along. It's like that clash between the B flat and the A.

We're behind the curtain, ready for the gig to start.

Dean and Dallas already set everything up. We're tuned. We did our sound test. It's all ready.

I'm tapping my fingers against my leg, trying to get out the jitters. When we play in the park or at Union Square or Grand Central, we just set up and start playing. Here, people are waiting on us. I can hear their expectation. It's this crackling, edgy sort of noise.

I glance over at Andi.

She's leaning against the wall, partially hidden in the shadows, staying outside the circle of the band. When she sees me looking she smiles, stands straight and gives me a double thumbs up.

I smile at her.

Now the jitters I was feeling have settled in my stomach. But I think that's because Andi's wearing a top that rides up over her belly button and shows the curve of her waist.

I wonder what it'd be like to dance with her.

I try really, really hard not to stare at her bare skin.

I can imagine my mom smacking me on the back of the head if she caught me looking.

I wince at the thought and send up an apology.

"Who's the girl?" Dallas asks, shooting a dark look at Andi.

Dallas is a big guy. Refrigerator big. He's our drummer and he grew up on the top floor of our building. He and Dean are the same age and have always been friends. Dallas's dad has been in prison since before he was born and his mom was always gone. From what I could tell as a kid, she was gone early morning to late at night.

If Dallas wanted breakfast, he came to our place. If he wanted dinner, he came to our place. If he wanted a mom to hug him, or a dad to reprimand him, he came to our place.

Mom always called him her fourth son. Let's just say he took their deaths as hard as we did, and when Dean asked him to take Mom's place at the drums, he didn't hesitate.

Dallas glares at Andi and cracks his knuckles. Most people are intimidated when a six-foot-five guy plastered in prison tattoos cracks his knuckles and glares at them menacingly.

But Andi just lifts her chin and says, "The girl is Andi."

"I don't like her," Dallas says, turning away.

I'm not surprised, Dallas doesn't like anyone outside of Pauly and our family. Mom once said that Dallas has *trust issues.*

I always thought that was a nice way of saying he doesn't like people.

It never really bothered me before though. Us five, we're loyal to each other, and we always will be. We'd do anything for each other.

When River was nine, and Dallas was thirteen, Dallas came home and found River getting beaten by this junkie who'd been sleeping on our apartment stoop. The junkie had snapped and was viciously kicking River, who was curled in this little ball. Dallas went after the junkie. He went after him hard. I didn't see it, but I saw Dallas after. It wasn't pretty. The police came. It was ruled self-defense.

Later that night, Dallas set our landlord's Cadillac on fire. He dumped gasoline all over that Caddy and then threw a burning match on it. Apparently, the landlord was the one supplying the junkie with his fix and allowing him to use our stoop as his bedroom. Dallas didn't like that.

So he went to juvie.

When he came back, his *trust issues* were even bigger.

But he says he'd do it again. Anything for his family.

But even if it is Dallas, I'm not going to let him bully Andi. "She's with me."

Everyone turns to look at me. And it's funny, because even though only Dean and River are related, they all have identical expressions of surprise.

River is the first to recover.

"Nice to meet you, Andi." A wide grin splits his face. "I'm River. The nice brother."

She grins back at him. "I find that hard to believe. I'm pretty certain Jace is the nice one."

She's right, while River is empathic and understanding, he also loves to fight. He claims that fighting is the best way to blow off extra energy. Not with knives, or brass knuckles or anything, just with fists.

Anyway, if there's a fight, you can guarantee that River was the first one to throw a punch.

I'm watching Dean, he's frowning between me and Andi.

"You have a girlfriend?" he asks, narrowing his eyes on me.

I almost laugh.

I'm weeks away from graduating high school, I'll be eighteen in June and Dean's getting upset because he thinks I have a girl?

Yeah. I got the *have unprotected sex and you could end up in prison like our old neighbor Kenny, for failure to pay child support. Have sex, make baby, go to prison* talk. I get it.

We have bigger things in mind than getting tied up in baby wars.

But this is bigger than that too.

At least, I think it is.

"She's my friend," I say. "She's the friend who loaned me the guitar. You know, the reason we can play tonight?"

Dean raises his eyebrows.

"I still don't like her," Dallas says. "I don't trust her."

I shrug.

"Everybody, this is Andi. She's my friend. I vouch for her. I invited her."

I don't tell them that Andi might be the reason I sing for the first time in public. If it happens, then I'll tell them.

"Andi, this is River"—I point to my brother—"he plays the keyboard. Don't let his charm fool you, he likes to get into trouble."

"Hey," River protests and Andi laughs.

I gesture at Dean.

"This is Dean, my oldest brother. He plays bass. He..."

He used to laugh.

He used to be happy.

The only thing he cares about anymore is music.

"He manages the band."

"Hello," Dean says.

He's wearing black pants, a tight black t-shirt, and you can see how carved he is from years of hauling thousands of pounds of concrete. His hair is shaved short, his brown eyes are flat, and his jaw is hard. I never realized before how intimidating he could look on first impression.

But Andi just nods. "Nice to meet you."

Either she has balls of steel facing Dallas and Dean and not quaking or she's a little bit nuts.

Or, I guess, she comes from her own kind of rough home. I've seen enough to realize that a rough childhood can prepare you for just about anything.

Or it'll make you like Pauly.

I nod at him next. "This is Pauly, he plays the trumpet, the cornet, the trombone, anything brass really. Saxophone too, sorry I forgot."

I think Andi only now realizes that Pauly is here.

He's like that though. Pauly grew up in the apartment below ours. His dad went after him a lot. Pauly said, though, he preferred those days when his dad was after him to the weeks where he got ignored. He said those were the worst because he felt like a ghost in his own home. He said he'd rather the loud, rough days to the silent stretches of non-existence.

Either way, when you finally notice Pauly—because he tries really hard not to be noticed—he reminds you of a bone-thin, big-eyed dog, who's been kicked around so much that it ducks its head and shies away even when you're offering it a slab of steak.

Yeah. Pauly's worry-eyed, skinny, scared of shadows, loud noises, and whatever other monsters are in his mind. Not that he's a coward. If we ever get in a fight he gives as good as he gets. But he's jumpy. And it got exponentially worse after my parents died. It broke something in him.

So, we all look after him and don't let anyone bother him, even though he's nineteen. He's too much like that kicked puppy to do anything else.

Dallas watches Andi closely to make sure she doesn't do anything to hurt Pauly. Not that she would, but Dallas is especially protective of Pauly.

"It's very nice to meet you," Andi says politely, and then she gives Pauly a big, comforting smile.

"You too," Pauly says, then he gets an embarrassed look on his face and stares at his feet.

He's not at all like any other brass player I've ever met. He's not loud or rash, the loudest he ever is is when he's playing a horn.

He played in the school band, and I guess when Dean heard him practicing in the courtyard one day he told Pauly he was going to play in our band. Pauly didn't argue.

"And this," I say, nodding at Dallas, "is Dallas. He plays drums as steady as a metronome. He's solid."

"Hi," Andi says.

"Okay. We did the introductions. Now leave," Dallas says, staring pointedly at Andi.

I'm about to say something when Pauly shakes his head. "Aww Dallas, leave her alone."

We all turn to him in surprise. He never stands up to *anyone*.

Pauly shrugs, embarrassed. "She's nice."

Andi turns her face to the side so only I can see it, then she winks at me.

"It's okay. I'm going to find a spot right up front."

Then as she leaves, she sticks her tongue out, crosses her eyes, and gives me a thumbs up.

God.

I think I love this girl.

10

BEFORE WE PLAY, DEAN ALWAYS TELLS US OUR SET LIST, THE order of everything we're going to play. It changes every time.

Since we've been playing together for years—my brothers and I for nearly twenty—we can play hundreds, maybe thousands of cover songs. R&B, jazz, classic rock, pop, alt indie. We once tried to keep count of the songs we knew as a joke, River lost track after three weeks counting and six hundred songs.

But our original songs, the ones written by us—The Morgan Brothers—those are the ones we're playing tonight.

When playing, you rehearse a song until you know it. Sometimes that takes one time, sometimes it takes much longer. It doesn't matter how long it takes, you play until you can play it *right*.

My dad taught us that. You can play music for the sheer love of it, but you owe it to the people listening to play it well.

The first time I played in public, my dad booked us a gig on a small stage at a county fair up north. I was ten and terrified that I'd mess up and disappoint my family.

My dad kneeled down, put comforting hands on my shoulders and told me, *"Jace, at first when you play, you're going to want to get every note right, every rhythm right. You're going to want to play the perfect note and the perfect song. Better every time. Right?"*

I nodded. I knew what he meant. Each time I played I *strived* to hit every single note.

Then my dad said, "*Eventually though, there's going to come a time when you stop caring about playing the perfect note, or the perfect song, and you'll only care about creating the perfect experience. Creating the perfect emotion. It will stop being a note and start being an experience. Okay? That's when you'll stop being so scared. Don't worry. It'll come.*"

I didn't understand what he meant. At ten I was still convinced I could play a perfect show if I managed to hit all the notes. It was only later, long after Dad was gone, that I realized what he meant.

I don't want to strive for a technically accurate, musically perfect song. Any computer-generated beat can do that. I want to make music that creates *emotion*.

That's why Dean changes up the set. He knows, just like we all do, that the songs you play shift along with what's happening in the world. What's in the news? What's on people's minds? What's the mood of the world? These things matter. A musician isn't separate from this, we're a part of it.

When you play—if you're doing it right—there's a

feedback loop between you and the audience. The energy you can create together is incredible.

So Dean has our set list.

We're all ready.

It's nine. From the noise out front, the Fireside Club is at capacity.

My throat is tight, it feels like I swallowed a lemon, and the sour fruit is still stuck there, draining battery acid into my esophagus. It's not a comfortable feeling.

"Alright, Jace?" River slaps my back.

I nod, but don't say anything.

"Nervous about your girl?"

I shake my head. "Nah."

If anything, Andi is going to make it so that I'll be able to sing tonight.

"Don't get distracted. Play a good show," Dean says, tight-lipped.

River grins at me, "Jace always plays a good show. Come on, you know that."

Dean shrugs. He doesn't give compliments. "If you mess up, she can't come again."

"I won't mess up," I say.

Pauly and River exchange a look, one that tells me they just placed a bet on it. I'm guessing River bet against me, and Pauly for, but who knows.

Dallas pushes past us and says, "She shouldn't come again period."

"Okay, sunshine," River calls.

Dallas gives him the finger as he leaves the curtained area and walks toward the stage.

It's time.

I bounce a bit on my feet and drum my fingers against my leg.

Every band has something they do to start a show. To build anticipation and let everyone know the show is going to be *good*. My dad came up with the idea for our start.

My mom—now Dallas—sat at the drums and then started to play the bass drum. Boom. Boom. Boom. Boom.

The steady thud would demand attention.

Every time, conversations stop, heads turn, people stop and stare.

In the park, people stop walking and drift close.

Now, the entire club quiets.

Boom.

Boom.

Boom.

We stride onto the stage. I pick up my guitar, make sure everyone's ready, and then we start to play.

Right away, I know it's going to be a good night.

Everyone is *on*.

There's energy in the club.

Dean was right too. The lights are dim, the black walls are glowing with cityscape murals in fluorescent bright paint, and the place looks transformed.

Even the smell of stale beer and cigarettes is overpowered by the strong perfumes and colognes of the people standing near the stage.

And by the smiles on people's faces, by the swaying of bodies, I know that this is the night.

I scan the people, looking for one person in particular, and find her, right at the front.

She said she'd be five feet away. She's more like three.

If she wanted to, she could reach out and touch me.

She waves at me and does the most awkward dance move I've ever seen.

I guess I know what dancing with her would be like. She's a terrible dancer.

I grin, watching her, my fingers playing the chord progression through muscle memory. Once you play a song enough, your fingers roll through the notes without you having to think about playing them. They just happen. It's a good thing too, because I'm too focused on Andi to think about the song.

I shake out of it. Concentrate on giving people a good time.

Dean told us the reason we were hired was because the owner heard us in the park. He wanted us in to boost his flagging food and alcohol sales. That's what bands do. If they're good, they bring in crowds. If they make people happy, then the people buy more food and more drink. If a band does a great job then they make the club owner money. If they do a bad job, then they aren't invited back. It's economics.

If we do a good job tonight, then we'll make more than the pay for just this job. Because we'll get more gigs.

It's good. Better than good.

The music flows through me. The drums shake the old stage, and I can feel the vibration rumbling from my feet all the way up to my hands.

River is dancing, beating on his pad controller. The lights flash purple and green, he reaches over and improvs a line on the keyboard. He does that sometimes. When he feels the energy of the crowd he can't help himself. He's impulsive like that.

Dean and I keep the structure of the song, and Dallas keeps us steady at one-twenty, which Dad always said was the perfect beat.

Pauly's at the back of the stage, nearly out of the reach of the lights, playing the trumpet.

Dean cues us and we flow into the next song.

It's mine.

I mean, it's the song that Dean always has me try to sing.

It's for a tenor, and although River sounds okay when he sings it (taking over when I inevitably choke), it really was meant to be sung by me.

I wrote it when I was fifteen, on my parents' anniversary. I was feeling low and I wanted a song about them. About their love.

Dad always told me, musicians have to be honest with themselves.

Up on the stage you can't lie.

It's impossible.

You have to be *honest*.

With the audience and, most importantly, with yourself.

You can't hide.

When you play a song, you have to play the emotion in that song. Honestly.

If you don't feel love, everyone will know it, and so will you.

So when you sing a love song, you picture in your mind that person you love, and you sing it to them. Dad said that every time he sang a love song he pictured my mom.

When I wrote this song, I pictured them dancing.

But now, thinking of the lyrics, *lay your head on my heart and feel the rhythm of my love,* I don't picture my parents dancing. Instead, I look at Andi.

The room is quiet, I can feel the hush flow over the

club as people lean forward, wanting to hear more of the soft strumming. The song plays, I always thought, like my guitar is weeping.

If I'd been honest with myself, I would've realized it was because I didn't believe I'd ever see love like my parents had again.

Andi stands on her tiptoes, presses her hands into the stage, and winks up at me.

I smile at her.

I can tell River's getting ready to sing.

I take a deep breath.

My throat is tight and aching. My eyes burn, the stage lights shine bright. A drop of sweat trails down my forehead and down my neck.

My heart thuds hard once, twice against my ribs.

It's now or never.

Don't choke.

I open my mouth, try.

Nothing.

The guys repeat the chord progression, as usual, giving me one more chance.

Andi frowns, gives me a determined, do-this-or-else look, and then puffs out her cheeks, crosses her eyes, and makes herself look so ridiculous that the stuck air bursts out of my chest.

I love her.

I do.

And that's an honest emotion.

After that, the words come easily.

I sing.

And then I sing the next song.

And the next.

And the next.

And I don't think about the fact that a seventeen-year-old can't know love like this.

That first loves don't last.

That I've only known Andi for a day and a half.

That I don't know her last name, or where she lives, or anything about her past.

I don't think about any of that.

I just make music.

And sing like I've never sung before.

11

JACE

THE SHOW'S OVER.

After two and a half hours of playing and a short intermission it's after midnight. The club is empty and the lights are back on, bringing into bright relief the spilled beer, the fries dropped and squished on the floor, and the layers of dirt and grime.

But unlike earlier, I can still feel the energy of the place and the buzz of electricity riding over my skin. Even empty, the club is humming.

During the intermission, Andi grabbed my hand and tugged me behind the folds of the black stage curtain. Then she grinned at me, grabbed my arms and shook me, laughing.

"You did it. You did it!" she said, her cheeks flushing. "And you were *amazing.*"

"You think so?"

"What do you mean, do I think so? I *know* so."

When I stepped back out on the stage, Dean didn't say anything, he just slapped me on the back as he walked past to get a cola from the bar.

Dallas said, "Not bad."

Pauly came up to me and with his eyes on the floor said, "Your dad would be proud."

And River—since he knows me better than anyone—just smiled and shook his head.

It made me remember a conversation we had years ago, when he asked why I couldn't sing in public.

I told him I was too afraid. Then he said that fear and courage felt the same. Same queasy stomach, same shaking hands, same adrenaline pumping through you.

He figured someday I'd meet someone that would make me flip from fear to courage.

I guess he was right.

Now that the show's over, we're heading backstage. We'll pack up, load up Dallas's old white van with all of our gear, and then we'll head home.

Dean has a specific method for tearing everything down and packing up. The instruments have to be put away just so, cleaned and cared for, the cords have to be wound just right, everything has to be loaded into the van in the proper order. He's efficient, anal, and strong, which means we're usually packed up in no time.

Tonight though, he's settling with the club owner, so it's up to the rest of us.

Andi's waiting by the stage, sipping a red and pink sparkling drink through a rainbow straw, staring at me with big butter-brown eyes.

"What's that?" I ask gruffly, nodding at the drink as I put her guitar away in its hardback case.

"A strawberry Shirley Temple," she says, popping the P in Temple, "Would you like one? I can procure another, if you like."

I shake my head. There's no way I'd be caught dead drinking that. The guys would never let me forget it.

Also, Andi's funny, because sometimes when she talks she comes off sounding very proper, like an old lady at a tea party.

River walks past, carrying his keyboard case and stand. When he sees Andi he pauses and gives her his smoldering, hey-baby look. "Hey Andi."

"Hey River."

She gives him a strawberry sweet smile and flutters her eyelashes.

I cough into my hand.

River laughs. He's used to girls falling all over him, but apparently Andi isn't interested. It's pretty clear. River's looking at her like she's a new species just discovered and not yet named. An anomaly.

Finally, he stops laughing. "I guess you like Jace, huh?"

She tilts up her chin and gets that haughty look in her eyes. "I guess I do."

I can't help but grin at him.

River looks Andi over. "You sure you don't like me? I'm better looking. I'm older. More experienced."

"Really?" Andi says, her cheeks dimpling. "I didn't know! Then I'm in. You and me. I've been looking for a man who'll give me eight kids and doesn't mind sleeping with my pet goat, Rascal."

"Uh..." River frowns.

"Don't worry, that time he nibbled his last owner's wiener off? It was because he fed him hot dogs. Rascal's been rehabilitated. He'll never make that mistake again. Should we do it? Should we get married? How's tomorrow?"

River stares at Andi, his expression a mix of horror and fascination.

I shove him. "Get out of here."

He stumbles across the stage, his keyboard and stand in his hands. When he gives one last look back at Andi, she waves and calls, "Hurry back, sweetums!"

"You're lucky he didn't take you up on it," I tell her jokingly.

Andi sets her drink down and then jumps up onto the stage. She walks close to me, until we're standing only inches apart.

She leans forward and I can smell the strawberry Shirley Temple on her. I think, from now on, whenever I smell strawberry I'm going to think of her.

"Hmm," she says and her eyes crinkle at the corners.

When she smiles the dimple on her chin gets deeper and the gap between her front teeth is so cute that I have the overwhelming urge to take one final step closer and kiss her.

Behind me, Pauly grabs his cornet and trombone cases and hurries out the side door. When he shoves it open I can hear Dallas yelling at River, telling him to be careful of his drums.

The metal door bangs shut and Andi and I are left alone on the stage.

It's just the two of us, standing at the edge of the elevated black stage.

I mean there are two waitresses clearing plates and a young guy pushing a broom across the floor, but they aren't looking at us, they're chatting about heading to some new bar down the street when they're finished cleaning up.

Nobody's paying us any attention.

I swallow the tightness in my throat and look into Andi's eyes.

"You guess you like me?" I ask.

She lifts a shoulder. "I guess I do."

And then, she puts her hands on my shoulders, her bracelets clack together, and her warm hands send a shock through me. Then she stands on her tiptoes and leans close until her mouth is only a fraction of an inch from mine.

She's going to kiss me.

I can feel the heat of her mouth, taste the sweetness of strawberries. My lips buzz like a guitar string just plucked. If we kiss, they'll stop aching. I hold still, keep my hands at my sides, wait to see what she does.

Slowly, she pulls back, and when she does my stomach rolls and I let out a shaky exhale.

Her cheeks flush, "Sorry. I got...carried away."

I nod. "It's okay."

When the door bangs open, I look back and watch Dallas and River stroll inside.

River takes us in, the flush on Andi's cheeks and my (probably) awkward expression.

Andi takes a step back and rubs her hands on her skirt, smoothing it out.

Dallas ignores her, but River sends a grin our way.

"You're coming to all our gigs from now on, right?" River asks.

"Or don't come to any," Dallas says. "We don't need a Yoko Ono."

Some—okay, many—people think that Yoko Ono was the reason the Beatles broke up. She wasn't, but Dallas is against girlfriends mixing with the band as strongly as Dean is against music mixing with drugs.

Dallas bends down, grabs his bass drum and hauls it back outside.

"Don't mind him," River says, staring after Dallas. "Come to all our gigs. Alright?"

Andi looks at me and I nod. "You should."

A change comes over her, a softness lights in her eyes, and I realize before now she'd been holding a bit of herself back.

"What are you doing tomorrow? Or—" She looks at the clock on the wall, it's nearly one. "Today? For lunch?"

"Why?" I ask.

She gives me an innocent look. "Because I thought we could eat a dozen hot dogs and then ride the rollercoaster at Coney Island."

"Only if you promise to come and watch us busk before that, from noon to two. Same spot, in the park."

We spend every weekend, and many nights, playing. Dean handles the permits and the locations. Dallas handles the transport. We split the cash we make, after expenses—fifty dollars here, a hundred there—and it helps us scrape by, adding to Dean's salary as a hauler and River's part-time pay from detailing cars.

Tomorrow, I'll use any money made busking on hotdogs.

"I'll be there," Andi promises.

I offer her a ride home, but instead she grabs a taxi. I

watch the brake lights of the taxi merge into traffic and stand on the sidewalk until she's out of sight.

"You're a goner," River says, walking past with the last of the equipment.

There's no need to agree, River knows me about as well as I know myself.

I'm done.

I'm a goner.

12

ANDI

THE OLD WOODEN ROLLERCOASTER, THE CYCLONE, RISES over Luna Park on the shore of Coney Island.

It looms above the boardwalk, like a bony old woman, stooped over her walker. It's been here one hundred years, and it shows.

The wood is aged from sea winds, blowing sand and humid air and the tracks have warning after warning stamped on white signs. The flags blowing in the stiff breeze at the top of the first hill seem awfully high up.

"Actually, I'm not so sure about this," I tell Jace as we scoot into the front car.

I press my hand to my stomach and slide along the warm seat until my thigh hits the edge of the car. Jace slides in next to me. The car is tight, so his leg is pressed to mine and his arm, warm from the afternoon sun, rubs against my side.

He dips his chin and peers at me.

"Don't tell me you're scared?" he says, the salty wind blowing across his cheeks, painting them red.

His eyes are bright and laughing. They've been that way ever since I ate four hot dogs to his three, and demanded chili and cheese on top too.

"After the Ramble, and then meeting Dallas, I was certain you weren't scared of anything."

His smile is like the sun. Looking at him feels like earlier, when we took off our shoes and walked through the warm sand, letting it sift through our toes. I sipped my root beer float, the fizz tickling my nose, and the vanilla ice cream melting on my tongue, while we watched the gulls fly over the blue-gray waves and I let my hand hang right next to his.

"You're right," I say, smiling as he nudges his shoulder against mine. "I'm not scared."

"Good."

Our hands are on the metal bar. There are plenty of warnings telling us to keep them on the bar—and nowhere else.

"Is this your first time?" he asks.

"Yeah. And maybe...I'm a little afraid of heights."

He gives me a quick look, his gray eyes widening. "Then...why?"

I lift a shoulder in a half-shrug. "I always do things I'm scared of. It helps me feel alive."

I realize as soon as I say it that Jace might think something's wrong with me for admitting that, but he doesn't say anything. Instead, he moves his hand puts it over mine, lacing our fingers together. I stare at our hands.

I grip the metal bar and he holds me. My heart

flutters and flips, like the rollercoaster has already started.

He's warm and the callouses on his fingers from playing the guitar rub against my skin. His knuckles are still slightly swollen and bruised. Still, he doesn't say anything. He just holds his hand gently over mine.

"Thank you," I say.

"Anytime."

Then the Cyclone starts and the clack clack clack of the rollercoaster bumping over the tracks rattles through the car. The people in line wave at us as we pass.

I tilt my chin up and as we climb, my stomach rises and rises, not so much from the rollercoaster, or the high-up view of the beach and the foamy sea-gray water, but from Jace rubbing his thumb over the back of my hand.

I can't...I can't think of anything else.

We pass the flags, hit the highest point, and then, we're dropping, and my stomach drops too.

I close my eyes, the sea-salt wind steals my breath, my hair flies out behind us, and the car shakes and rattles so much that I'm pushed up and against Jace.

We're up. Then down. Then up and around.

The rollercoaster car clatters and shakes. Behind us people shout and scream with each drop. The whole time Jace keeps his hand on mine. And me, I loop my ankle around his leg and press against him, and hang on.

When the rollercoaster finally slows, Jace doesn't let go of my hand.

It makes the queasy, dizzy feeling worth it.

I stumble out of the car onto the platform and then we head back out toward the boardwalk.

"I think...oh I feel sick," I say. "Horribly sick."

Jace squeezes my hand. "We could lay on the beach.

Next to that guy."

I squint at the sun shining off the glassy surface of the water. Jace is pointing at an old man in a hot pink speedo, sitting in a beach chair. He's leathery orange and has one of those homemade tin-foil reflective tanners. But what makes him really appealing is his portable radio. It's playing jazz.

"Yes. Double yes."

So we do.

We lay on the sand, Jace on his back. Me on my side, curled into him, my head on his chest.

The sand rubs over my bare legs and feet, and the breeze tugs at my hair.

The gulls call out above us, and the waves crash against the beach, mixing with the jazz melody crackling out of the old man's portable radio.

Jace's chest is solid and warm and I can feel his heart beating. I'm warm and I feel more alive than I've ever felt in my entire life.

Maybe I don't need to do things I'm afraid of to feel alive, or maybe falling for someone this fast is the scariest thing you can do.

I spread my hand over his chest and listen to his heart.

"This reminds me of your song," I say. "*Lay your head on my heart...*"

I stop, because the next line is about love.

We're quiet then, watching the waves, listening to the jazz.

The world has stopped tilting, my dizziness has faded, and now the only movement is the soft inhale and exhale of Jace's rising and falling chest.

"Are you staying in the city after you graduate?" he

asks, his chest rumbling against my cheek.

Graduation is only a few weeks away, final exams are at the end of May.

"Yes. I'll be here." And suddenly, the prospect of four more years at the Tower doesn't make me feel so cold or so alone.

"Are you...are you going away?" I ask, worried that Jace is leaving the city for school and I won't see him after this summer.

"No," he says. He takes a deep breath and I rise and fall with him. "Does it ever...do you ever feel like the city is a trap?"

"What do you mean?" I think about the Tower, about who I am when I'm there, trapped in a part written for me before I was born.

"It's like, you're born here, and you have your borough, your place, your role in life, and there's nothing you can do to get out. Dean tried. Dallas tried, that's why he bought his van. He took off one summer, but he got sucked back when he heard how bad off Pauly was after my parents...never mind. I'm not making any sense."

I push off his chest and look down at him, at the shadows on his face, the still-purple bruises around his eye. He makes a whole lot of sense to me.

I bet at Darby School they don't ever let Jace forget where he's from. Nobody lets me forget it either. We may be opposites, but we're the same too.

"You make perfect sense," I say. "You're scared if you don't leave now, you'll never leave."

He sits up and leans back on his elbows. "Yeah. That's it. I'm scared that I'll always live in the Bronx, down the street from where my parents died, scraping by, hoping that someday I'll manage to have people know my name."

"You want to be famous?" I ask, smiling at him and the way the wind tugs at his t-shirt.

He nods. "I want to play for the world. I'd like to make the whole world happy. My dad said that music is the one thing that can bring people together, and I agree. All I want is to make the world smile."

He shakes his head, then looks at my lips and then away.

"If I never leave here, if I don't try, I think I'll have let the world down," he says.

I wrap my hands around my knees and dig my toes into the sand, burrowing down until I find the wet, cool grains. He's watching me. I put my chin on my knees.

"You have a good heart," I tell him finally.

He flashes me a surprised smile and then asks, "What about you? Do you want to be famous?"

I shake my head. "No. If I was never in the news, or in a magazine, or on a blog, I'd be ecstatically happy."

He smiles at me. "You never know. You might like it."

I shake my head.

Then I cover my mouth as I yawn. It's unexpected, but I'm tired from the late night, the sun and fresh air, and the overindulgence in hot dogs.

"Do you want to head home?"

"I don't think I can walk to the subway," I say, yawning again.

He grins. "Then I'll carry you."

He gives me a piggyback ride down the boardwalk, past the rides, and all the way to the subway. I wrap my legs around his stomach, press my cheek to his shoulder, and close my eyes.

On the subway, I rest my head against his shoulder and pretend to sleep.

13

ANDI

SUNDAY NIGHT AND MONDAY DRAG BY. IT FEELS LIKE EVERY second scrapes over my skin, ticking oh so slowly past.

School is mainly review periods; the final week of classes is full of cramming and last-minute exam prep.

I've been at the same all-girls private school since I was five. It's a strict, rigorous academy concerned with molding "the leaders of tomorrow." Which is a polite way of saying *we charge nearly six figures a year, and if you can't afford that, don't bother applying.*

The school is housed in an ornate limestone three-story mansion from the 1800s that was built as a family home by an ostentatious banker.

When I first saw the lion heads carved on the stone exterior, the high gold gilt ceilings, and the hunter green and gold wallpaper, I thought the banker and my dad were related. Turns out they aren't.

Back in elementary school I had dreams of friends and visions of fun.

In first grade my friend Jeanine asked me about who we'd had over for dinner the night before. I was naïve. I told her. That playground tidbit ruined a secret business deal worth millions. Jeanine's dad had put her up to it.

In second grade, Mayura, my deskmate, gave me a doll as a token of friendship. I loved that doll. It had raven black hair, a pink rosebud mouth and green glass eyes. I took it with me everywhere.

I didn't realize it had an audio recorder inside that was battery-powered and WiFi-enabled. Why would I?

My dad's competitors beat him to market on the new tech he'd been planning to unveil. Then they did it again. And again. He didn't realize where the leak was coming from until they brought a bug detector into our home.

By the time third grade rolled around, I didn't have friends. Both my mom and the kids at school made sure I'd learned what I needed to know.

As long as I'm Andrea Leighton-Hughes, I'll be used or I'll be feared. But I'll never be liked and I'll never be loved.

School was just something to get through. Just like charity events, political fundraisers, product launches, and other family obligations.

I'd escape by dreaming about the times I could go to the park and just people-watch or walk through the trees, wearing an old cotton dress that my mom would never approve of. It was enough to take off the edge, but now... even a day away from Jace and I feel like I'm crawling out of my skin.

I want to run to him. See him. Talk with him.

It's four o'clock and he's playing at five. I promised I'd be there.

I walk through the living room. The light shines through the wall of windows, highlighting the low white couches and white marble floor. My heels click on the marble, even though I try to walk quietly.

My mom's the only one home.

She's on the couch reading a magazine, sitting in a stream of sunlight so that it portrays her in the best light possible.

My mom has never gotten Botox, instead she has a preternatural awareness of how to manipulate lighting, angles, and her surroundings for the most pleasing effect. She's in an ivory silk sheath with a chunky gold necklace, hammered gold bangles, and gold heels.

Mom has a personal stylist and a private salon downstairs. She visits it every morning for a blow-out and professionally applied make-up. Sometimes she visits twice a day, for the morning look and then the evening look.

I go too. Because...

There are two unspoken and unbreakable rules in my family.

One: you will be loyal to the family above all else.

Two: you will look and act like a Leighton-Hughes at all times.

That basically means you serve the family, not yourself. It also means that you are a physical representative of the Leighton-Hugheses. If you look sloppy, or tattered, or mismatched then it reflects poorly on the family.

Only my dad can be underestimated because of appearance, the rest of us have to be immaculate.

The first time I bought a cheap cotton dress at a bargain store, my heart was in my throat and my palms were sticky with sweat. When I got back home, I thought for sure my mom would be able to smell the plastic, chemical scent coming off the store bag tucked in the bottom of my purse. But she didn't.

I went to the park and walked around in that dress like a regular person.

And then I did it again.

And again.

All those times I never spoke to anyone. I just watched people.

Until Jace.

It was hard enough waiting for my moments of freedom, it's been almost impossible waiting for time with Jace.

I clutch my purse and pray that the lump from my cotton dress and converse shoes aren't too obvious.

I'm nearly past my mom when she looks up, her eyes flicking to me over the edge of her magazine.

I stop. Turn toward her. I don't smile, even though the urge is always there.

I've always very badly wanted her love. Maybe, it's because she doesn't give it and you always want what you can't have. But I think it's probably because she's my mom, and every kid wants their mom to love them.

I have this picture of us I keep out of sight in my nightstand drawer. It's one my brother Elliot took of Mom. I just happened to be standing next to her. I don't think she was even aware I was there. But it's a picture of the two of us, side-by-side, and really, it's the only one I have.

"I'm going for a mani-pedi," I say in an even voice. "I

noticed a chip in my nail."

She sets her magazine on the couch and then crosses her hands in her lap. She moves in slow, deliberate motions, always taking her time.

Sometimes I think the articles about my mom from decades ago—the ones that describe her as a wild child —can't possibly be true. She's the most contained person I've ever known.

Passionate love? Wild nights? Raucous living? I can't see it. It feels like she's always been as she is—and for as far back as I can remember, she has been.

"The Swenson Gala is in two weeks," she says, her voice carefully modulated, "I've directed Marika to procure a dress. Do give her the time to have it tailored."

Marika is my stylist. If there isn't time for a custom dress, she buys the dress slightly large so that she can have it tailored to fit my shape perfectly.

"I will."

She studies me for a moment and then picks up her magazine and flips through the pages.

I let out a silent breath, wait for a moment, then walk toward the brass doors of the elevator, shining like a beacon.

"Andrea."

I stop at my mom's voice. Turn.

"Yes?"

"Don't be late," she says without looking up from her magazine.

She means to the gala. She's reminding me that I was late to my dad's party.

Don't let it happen again is unspoken.

"I won't."

And with that, the elevator doors open and I'm free.

14

ANDI

THE BOWLING ALLEY IS IN MIDTOWN.

It's laser disco night. Pink, green, and blue lights jet across the alley, and a huge disco ball spins, lighting the room with rainbow sequins. Disco pop music blares from the surround sound. It's so loud, I feel like I'm vibrating.

There are twelve lanes and each one has its own private booth and table. Jace and I are in lane twelve. So far the score is forty-two (me) to one hundred and sixty (Jace).

The funny part is, neither of us has bowled before. Jace just has beginner's luck and I have beginner's trouble.

I'm at the table, having a quick drink while Jace takes his turn.

My glass is frosty and my fingers are cold; it's full of icy pink virgin strawberry daiquiri.

We have a full spread of food on our table. Since Jace bought our tickets, I told him I'd buy the food.

We have nachos—the kind with the nuclear orange gloop and jalapeños on top. Pepperoni pizza—where the pepperoni curls at the edges and grease pools in the middle. And chicken wings—the ones that are so hot they burn your tongue when you bite into them.

Jace surprised me after he finished playing in the park. He'd booked us a lane, all because I'd mentioned the other day that I wanted to go bowling.

River wanted to come too, but Jace told him to get lost.

I take a sip of my drink, enjoying the strawberry bits.

Jace is at the lane, holding his black bowling ball at the ready.

"You can do it!" I shout.

He looks back over his shoulder and flashes me a grin. The lights from the disco ball dance over him, and the music pulses.

I watch as he takes three quick steps then lets the ball roll.

He doesn't bother to see what happens. Instead he strides back to the table. Behind him, all the pins crack loudly as they fall.

"Strike," I say. Then I frown. "Strike, right?"

He smiles and looks back at the pins, collected and lowering back over the lane. Up on the monitor, his score increases.

"Strike," he agrees.

He scoots into the booth next to me. The smell in the bowling alley—Lysol and floor wax and fried food—is replaced by Jace. I decided yesterday he smells like the ocean, and the park, and the sun.

It's nice after years of only knowing people who smell like expensive cologne.

"If you don't want to be a musician, you might have a career in bowling," I tell him.

I wriggle my cramped toes, ignoring the pinch from the borrowed shoes.

"I might." He grins at me, then says, "I just realized, I don't know your last name."

I swallow and set down my drink. Even though I'm going to tell him who I am eventually...I really am...it still scares me.

"Hughes," I finally say.

"Andi Hughes," he says.

"Jace Morgan."

The music changes, the boom and crack of the falling pins fills the alley, and the disco lights strobe between us.

The red vinyl of the booth is warm and sticky, and my thighs stick as I scoot closer, so he can hear me over the music.

"Do you think we're moving too fast?" I ask him.

He knows exactly what I mean.

"My parents fell in love in one night," he says, and I have to lean even closer because he says it so quietly.

I clench my hands.

"But we're only seventeen," I say, giving the argument I know anyone else would give.

"I know," he says. "But if it's any consolation, we'll keep on getting older."

I laugh.

I look around the bowling alley, at the couples, work groups, friends. Everyone is having a good time. No one is paying us any mind.

I've wanted to kiss Jace since the second I saw him.

He has the prettiest lips of anyone I've ever seen. They're light pink, and his bottom lip is wide and firm. They look soft and hard at the same time.

And the way he smiles? I want to kiss him. I want to kiss his smile.

"Tell me your lyric," I say on impulse, "for right now."

He thinks for a second, then says, "*Seventeen, I fell hard. Twenty-five, still crazy for you. Thirty, I'm still here. Whatever, whenever you need.*"

"You're crazy for me?" I ask.

"What's your lyric?" he responds.

"I really want to kiss you," I say.

He looks at my lips then back up to me, surprise painting his expression. "That's your lyric?"

"No. Yes." I shake my head. "No. That's what I want."

His swallows, his Adam's apple bobbing, and says, "I'm scared to tell you how much I like you."

"I'm scared too," I say, "but since doing things I'm scared of helps me feel alive, I'll tell you first. I really, really, really, really…"

He leans forward.

"Really like strawberry shakes."

He stares at me. Then, "Are you kidding?"

I nod. "Yeah. I actually love strawberry shakes."

He shakes his head.

Then I lean into him and say, "I think…I think I'm crazy about you too."

The biggest smile spreads across his face.

Then he wraps his hands around my arms, presses his fingers into my warm skin. I tilt my face up, and he bends down. He presses his mouth to mine. And we kiss.

The flashing lights, the throbbing disco, the clattering pins, all of it was a prelude to this.

I've never been kissed before.

I had no idea that a kiss was like a song.

That it could make you fly.

While I soar, I pray *please, don't let us crash, don't let us crash, don't let us crash.*

15

JACE

LONG WALKS IN THE CITY. A HUNDRED RED M&Ms FROM M&M world in Times Square. Romeo and Juliet in the park. Lingering in museums until closing. Playing and singing every day, with Andi there, always.

It took one look to fall for her. It's taken two weeks to never want to be without her.

We're on the couch in my living room. Andi's lying down, her head resting on my thigh, her calculus textbook held above her head. She has her last exam tomorrow. I'm already finished with finals. Graduation is next week.

While Andi studies, I'm working out lyrics for a new song, writing ideas in a palm-sized notebook.

Since Andi's been here and I'm singing, we're switching up our set and working out songs that suit my vocal range.

Everyone in our band has written songs or come up with rhythms or lines that become a piece. Wherever the seed of an idea comes from, we go with it.

Sometimes we can pull together a song in an hour, sometimes it takes weeks. I'd say Dean and I have always been the most prolific, and now that Andi's here and I'm singing, I'm more prolific than ever.

River is all for me dating Andi. Dallas is vocally against it. Pauly says I deserve to be happy. Dean is cautious—he doesn't like Andi, but he doesn't dislike her either.

River, Pauly and Dallas are at the dining table in the corner, playing poker.

River's winning, as usual, because he deals from the bottom of the deck and counts cards. Both Dallas and Pauly know he's a cheat, but they don't care because when River cheats he inevitably feels guilty and buys everyone burgers and onion rings from the place around the corner.

Dean's leaning against the piano, working out a rhythm on his bass. It has a steady beat in A minor, and then it shifts into the bridge, and moves into A major picking up speed.

It's a nice feeling, the weight of Andi's head in my lap, her feet up on the couch's armrest.

Dean plucking out a new song, filling the narrow living room with music.

The joking and jabs coming from the card game.

"The next time you cheat," Dallas says, "you're buying me dinner."

"Or what?" River says.

"Or I'll beat you 'til you're blue," Dallas says.

That wasn't the best response. River loves to fight,

even when he loses. He likes the exhilaration of rushing headfirst into a bar fight or a street fight. He's so cover-model good-looking no one ever suspects he'll charge into a bar fight, fists flying. It got so bad when he was sixteen that Dean had to tell him if he kept it up he wouldn't be allowed to play in the band anymore.

That cooled things down a bit.

Luckily, Dallas doesn't mind going round with River every now and then. If I had to guess, I'd say that getting in fights is River's way of dealing with what happened to Mom and Dad.

At the table, Dallas stands and his chair screeches against the parquet. River lunges at him, driving a fist into his stomach.

Dean doesn't even blink, he just keeps playing.

Pauly sighs, sets down his cards, and leans back in his chair.

I look down at Andi to see how she's taking River and Dallas exchanging punches to the stomach.

Andi moves her textbook to the side and peeks up at me, then she smiles and gives me a wink.

I shake my head and shrug.

After a few seconds, Dallas has River in a choke hold.

"Dinner?" he says.

River elbows him in the kidney and Dallas grunts and lets him go.

They're both grinning like maniacs. River's eyes spark with happiness.

"Thanks, Dallas."

"You're welcome. I want barbecue on my burger."

River looks over at me and Andi, "You guys want anything?"

I'm about to ask for a strawberry shake for Andi when Dean stops playing.

"Hold up," he says. "I need to talk about something."

He puts down his bass and wanders toward the couch. He gestures at the guys.

"Come on over. This is important."

Andi sits up, smooths out her cotton shirt dress, and scoots closer to me.

"Should I go?" she asks.

I shake my head. "It's fine." Then I look at Dean. "Right?"

He shrugs. "Band business."

I pull Andi closer. "It's fine. Stay."

She nods. River squeezes onto the couch next to her, giving her a grin. He's still happy from the bit of fight he had with Dallas.

Pauly pulls the piano stool over and perches on the edge, his eyes wide and nervous. Not that he's scared about what Dean will say or anything like that, his eyes are always wide and nervous.

Dallas doesn't sit. He leans against the wall and folds his arms.

I take Andi's hand and hold it in my lap.

We've been holding hands since Coney Island. We've been kissing since the bowling alley. We've been officially together since M&M World, or probably, since the Ramble.

Andi first came to our apartment last week. We had a practice session and she asked to come along. When we stepped off the bus and she saw the long row of tired gray buildings, graffitied walls, trash in the bushes, and windows caged with iron bars, I worried.

But she didn't act any different than she does when

we're walking around the reservoir in Central Park or down Madison Avenue.

The rusted metal front door, the flickering florescent light in the entry, the water-stained ceiling tiles, the cracked and peeling paint, the curling, stained floor tiles, the cockroach skittering behind the recycling bin—she didn't seem to notice any of it.

She just held my hand, smiled, and said, "I can't believe I get to see where you grew up."

So I showed her my and River's initials carved into the metal of the elevator. I showed her the narrow, windowless living room, with River's piano, and all our instruments taking up half the space, and the old patched couch and table taking up the other half. I showed her the galley kitchen with two cupboards, a tiny fridge, and an efficiency stove where my mom made cheese fondue, Älplermagronen (a kind of Swiss macaroni) and for my dad, his favorite fried Ghanaian drop donuts. I begged to have the donuts for breakfast every Sunday, and usually, she said yes.

I show Andi the room River, Dean and I shared when we were kids. Now, Dean sleeps in Mom and Dad's old room, River sleeps on the couch, and I sleep alone in my room. It's just a mattress on the floor, a shelf full of books, a pile of my clothes, and a wall with pictures of Mom and Dad, and us playing as a family. Andi looked at the pictures for a long time.

I was worried what she'd think, but then she said, "Your parents look like the best people in the world. They must've loved you a lot."

Ever since then, she's been over plenty, and I don't worry about what she'll think about the cracks in the walls, or the cockroaches and rats in the halls, or the sirens that run constantly.

I'm guessing she must live someplace like this too. Especially since she never asks me over to her place, never talks about her family, and never talks about her life.

That's alright. Pauly never talks about his home life either. Nobody blames him.

Dean clears his throat and looks around the room. He has a serious expression, a slight frown. He worked a full day today, then played in the park, then came back here with all of us. He's tired. He's only twenty-two but he looks as tired as an old man.

"You graduate next week," he says to me.

I nod.

"My kid brother, a graduate," River says.

I grin at him.

"You'll be eighteen in a few weeks," Dean says.

"What's your point?" Dallas asks. "Are you planning on getting him a pony and throwing a party?"

Dean scowls, then folds his hands together and cracks his knuckles. "If he wants a pony, he can have a pony."

River laughs. "I want a pony."

Andi leans over and whispers, "I have your present already. Can I give it to you tomorrow?"

I squeeze her hand, "Yeah."

"What do you mean?" Pauly asks Dean, his eyebrows low. He leans forward on the chair, his black hair falling over his eyes. "Why?"

Dean's face is stoic, his mouth turned down, but suddenly I can see excitement flickering in his eyes.

"I got a call from a booking agent."

"What?" River asks, sitting straighter.

"He heard us at the Fireside. Then he came and watched us in the park yesterday. He wants to book us on a tour. Across the US, months on the road, making our way across the country. He'll take a cut, the rest is ours to split after expenses."

"You trust him?" Dallas asks, folding his tattooed arms over his chest. When Dallas wants to look intimidating he can look really intimidating. Right now, he looks like a tattooed refrigerator that could crush anybody with a look.

Dean nods. "I called around. Talked to bands he's worked with. He's solid."

"A tour," River breathes. His eyes are wide and there's this electric energy coming off him.

Pauly isn't saying anything, which is pretty normal. He'll wait to see what we all decide then go along with it.

"When?" I ask. "When would we leave?"

Dean looks between Andi and me, a frown tugging at his mouth. "The day after your graduation."

"But..."

That's less than a week away.

Dean shoves his hand through his hair and sighs. "Look. I've thought about this a long time."

River's shaking his leg, full of energy. "Damn straight you have."

Dean gives him a hard look. "We stayed here because Mom and Dad would've wanted Jace to finish school."

I swallow. There's a tight fist closing around my chest.

"But we all know, if we stay, we're going to keep doing the same thing, day in and day out. Breaking our backs at work. Playing for pennies on the subway platform. Coming back here every night." He winces and I suddenly realize what I never did before. Dean hates it here. He's been waiting for me to graduate so he can escape. "If we stay, we're going to die here, and we'll end up hating the music and hating this place before we do."

"You want to get out of here?" Dallas asks. And I guess, if anyone would understand, it's him. He bought his van to get out of here. He lived in the back of it for weeks before he got pulled back home.

"I want to leave this city behind, and not come back until they all know our name." He clenches his hands, and all I can see is longing and determination on his face.

"That could take years," I say. "Or it might never happen. Then what?"

"Then we keep playing," he says. "We do whatever it takes."

"You're talking about leaving our apartment? Leaving the city for maybe years?" I ask.

There's a hammering, like a hollow drum playing in my chest, and it's echoing inside me as I look around at our home.

I know I told Andi that I sometimes felt like the city was a trap, but...

We'd actually leave here?

We were born here. We were kids here. We learned to play music here. We were a family here. Mom and Dad danced here.

Andi squeezes my hand and leans closer, and I realize I won't just be leaving the only home I've ever known, I'd be leaving her.

She's going to college here. She wouldn't leave to travel the country in a rusty old van with me and four other guys.

Hell.

Hell.

River looks over at me, and I see understanding in his eyes. Even through his own excitement he can still see exactly how I'm feeling.

He says that I've always felt more than him or Dean, that I have big feelings. A softer heart. I think, when he said it, he always felt a bit bad for me. Like it was a detriment. Which I guess, it might be.

"I think we should do it," says Pauly. And even though his voice is quiet, it's loud in the silence. "Whether or not we knew it, we've all been waiting. If this guy says he can book us a tour, then I say we do it."

We all look at Pauly in surprise. He's never been the one to lead before.

He shrugs and ducks his head. "Your dad always wanted you to make it big. You'll regret it if you don't try."

"We'll more than regret it," Dean says.

He's right.

I know he's right.

I can picture Dean five years from now, the fatigue and weariness finally overwhelming him until he's bitter and too tired to care.

I can see River, a string of girlfriends, maybe a kid or two, cynical and getting into more and more fights.

Pauly, without us, well, he'd spend his time at home, getting beaten down by his dad until he wouldn't look like a scared puppy anymore, but more like a shell of human.

And Dallas, he always jokes that without our good influence, he'd be serving twenty to life.

And me?

I was going to take a year to work part-time, saving up for school. But then what? Get a job working in a company owned by someone like...Reid? Would I still have time to make music? Would I want to? Or would I be like Dean, slowly growing too tired and bitter to care?

"You should do it," Andi says.

I look over at her in surprise and she gives me a smile and a small shrug.

"You told me you want to play music for the whole world. This is your chance," she says.

Dean gives her a considering look. Then he says, "Let's vote. Raise your hand if you want to tour."

Pauly raises his hand right away.

Dallas gives him a nod, then he raises his hand.

Dean had his hand up as soon as he stopped speaking.

River studies me, concern in his eyes. "Okay, Jace?"

He knows.

He knows how hard it's going to be to leave home. If we leave this apartment, end our lease, we'll never live here again. I won't get to make donuts on the stove my mom cooked on. I won't get to hear how my dad's records reverberate off the plaster walls. I won't get to stand in the center of the living room and pretend my parents are still here, still dancing. All that will be gone.

"Okay," I say. "Yes."

I raise my hand. When I do River smiles and raises his too.

"That's five votes," Dean says.

Then for the first time in years he smiles. It's a smile held in for thousands of days, one full of disillusionment and hope, desire and dreams. He almost, almost looks like the kid that thought he was going to Tisch. His smile stretches across his face, burning away lines of fatigue and burden. I'm struck by the fact that somehow in the past few years, without my noticing, my brother started to look a lot like my dad.

I guess I never noticed because my dad was always smiling, and Dean never was.

But he is now.

"We're going on the road," he says.

I look over at Andi. She's clutching my hand and I wonder, is she holding on to me so hard because she knows that vote was the prelude to goodbye?

16

JACE

WE MEET THE NEXT DAY IN CENTRAL PARK, AFTER ANDI'S finished her calculus exam.

We're sitting in the grass at the edge of the lake on the north end of the park. The tall buildings on 125th Street rise up behind us, and the placid blue lake with turtles sunning themselves on the flat rocks spreads out before us. On the warm breeze there's exhaust, fried food, and pondweed.

A man nearby with a fishing pole casts his line, his spool whirs quietly beneath the taxi horns and bus engines rumbling on the street.

Andi has her legs tucked beneath her. Her dress is spread over her legs, and her honey-amber hair is in a high ponytail.

She's excited.

She's biting her lip and her eyes are dancing.

She has my present in her lap.

"Before you say anything," Andi says, pointing at the present wrapped in blue paper with a yellow bow, "this isn't your only present. I just wanted to give it to you as soon as it was ready."

The present is big and shaped exactly like a guitar case.

It's my Martin.

My dad's guitar.

My throat burns.

"Well, open it," Andi says. "I can't wait anymore."

Slowly I tear a small piece of wrapping paper from the corner of the case. Andi leans forward at the tearing noise. I can see the black hard case. So. She got me a new case.

I tear another section, slowly ripping the paper.

We don't do presents. I haven't gotten a real present since my thirteenth birthday. Sometimes River will toss an unwrapped shirt or pair of shoes at me, saying *happy birthday*, but I haven't unwrapped a birthday present in years.

"You're killing me," Andi says, looking like she wants to tear open the present herself.

I grin at her and she shakes her head.

"Are you always this slow?"

"I like savoring the expectation," I say.

She gives me an arch look, so I rip aside the paper. It flutters in the breeze as I tear it back. Then I click open the hard case and there... My throat hurts it's burning so bad. She fixed it.

She promised she could and she did.

Slowly, very carefully I lift my guitar out of the case.

The wood is smooth, I can barely see the repair lines, where it was glued, where it was pieced back together.

I hold it in my lap, stare down at it. It's too much.

I think I just might start bawling like a baby.

"You don't like it?" Andi asks. "They said they were the best in the city. I'm sorry. I thought—"

"No," I say. "It's..." I clear my throat, look up at her.

When she sees my expression, the anxious look on her face falls away and soft understanding replaces it.

"You like it." She smiles hesitantly. It's not a question.

I nod.

I play a note, then another, testing the sound and the feel. There's a tonal difference, less reverberation, less of the deep rich sound that once came from the decades old wood, but it's still undoubtedly my guitar.

Broken. Mended. Mine.

"You did it," I say. Then, "How?"

Andi shrugs, then shifts, suddenly looking uncomfortable. "I sought out an expert, then badgered them until they agreed to fix it."

I grin, running my hands over the expertly joined wood. "Thank you."

"I promised, didn't I?" she asks, her dimple deepening with her smile.

"You did."

She leans forward. "I have a lyric."

"Oh yeah?" I strum my guitar, reacquainting myself with the feel. There's a happy pulse shooting through me, brighter than the sun sparkling off the bright blue lake.

Andi grins. "It goes like this...happy birthday to you, happy birthday to you—" She's singing at the top of her lungs.

And okay, yes, she is a *terrible* singer.

I laugh.

Her eyes sparkle and she throws her arms wide. "Happy Birthday deeeeaaar—"

"Can it!" the man fishing shouts.

"Deeeeeeaaaar," she sings and somehow she manages to go even more out of tune.

I set my guitar aside and tackle her, gently rolling her to the grass beneath me.

She grins up at me, gripping my arms.

"Jace," she finishes.

I laugh at the satisfied look on her face and at the long grass tangling with her amber-gold hair and tickling her cheeks.

Her cheeks are pink and her brown eyes are bright.

"This is the best not-birthday I've ever had," I tell her.

"I want to come on tour with you," she says.

I stare down at her. I don't think I heard her right. "What?"

"I'll defer college for a year. I want to come with you. Don't look at me like that. I'm perfectly sane. It's just, you need me, right? You can't sing without me. And you said you're crazy about me, and I can help out, I'll be eighteen soon too, and I can—"

I can't listen anymore. She's worried. She's worried I don't want her to come.

I lean down and kiss her.

She keeps her eyes open for a second.

We stare at each other. My mouth on hers.

Then she grips my arms, wrapping her arms around me.

"You want to come because I'm crazy about you?" I ask against her mouth.

She presses a quick kiss to my lip, then says, "No. I want to come because *I'm* crazy about *you*."

At that, we stop talking and start really kissing.

"Get a room," the fisherman shouts.

We don't.

But unfortunately we don't stay long.

Andi has to leave after five minutes. She says she has a family obligation. But the way she says it makes me think she isn't looking forward to it.

Maybe getting out of the city and going on tour with us will be good for her too.

As I walk to the subway, Dean texts to say he's landed a gig through an old school friend. We're set to replace the jazz band that was booked at some charity gala in Midtown. They all have food poisoning, and the pianist recommended us in their place.

Dean's happy because the pay will go toward getting us on the road. I'm happy because I was dreading a night without Andi. Now it'll feel like no time until I see her again.

17

ANDI

THE BALLROOM GLITTERS FROM THE LIGHT OF CRYSTAL chandeliers bouncing off diamonds, sapphires, and rubies.

When I step through the doors, Elliot and Rob Jr on either side of me, I angle my chin up so that I'm not blinded by my own gem-studded gown.

It's black tie.

Ten thousand a plate or fifty thousand a table.

My dad usually pays for three tables to this sort of event and invites his top executives and their spouses. I've been attending these types of events since I was twelve and my dad decided I was old enough to start swimming with the sharks.

He's been grooming Rob, Elliot and I since we were born to be as cunning, as driven, and as successful as him. Both Rob and Elliot caught on quickly. I was a bit of a late bloomer.

My brothers are in crisp black tuxedos. I'm in a gold ballgown, flanked by my brothers. We pause at the entry, so that everyone seated in the ballroom can take a good, long look.

I notice quite a few raised eyebrows and whispers behind silk gloved hands.

The ballroom is gorgeous. Whoever designed the space was a master of understated lavishness.

A dozen crystal chandeliers hang from the vaulted ceiling, thousands of crystals tinkling between them like sparkling diamond raindrops. The room is thirty feet tall, with Venetian plaster walls and Corinthian marble columns shot through with pinks and golds. The floor is a masterpiece. The marble tiles alternate between ivory and gold, circling to the middle of the room, where a mosaic of the pink cherry blossoms and the white flowering dogwood of Central Park surround the dance floor. Tucked behind the dance floor, in the corner of the room, is a stage for the MC and later, when the dancing begins, the musicians.

There are fifty round tables, clad in ivory satin, set with fragile china and silver. The floral centerpieces are works of art, holding rare orchids and scented lilies.

Most of the guests have arrived. They're sitting at their tables, drinking wine and cocktails, or milling about the room.

Our arrival is very, very conspicuous.

The lull in conversation is noticeable.

"Why are you always making us late?" Rob Jr says through his teeth.

He drove us here in his new Aston Martin—an MBA graduation gift from Dad.

Mom and Dad are already seated at our table. Cocktails first, with hors d'oeuvres.

I bare my teeth in a smile and tilt my head at the room and all the people staring. "I'm never late. Everyone else is early," I murmur.

Elliot scoffs. He waited for me to finish preparing because he wanted to read the latest *Harvard Business Review*.

Rob Jr waited because he wanted to drive his new car to the gala.

Honestly, we're not late. The first hour is for mixing. For example, subtle reminders, casual business threats, and political jockeying. The main event, which includes dinner and an auction, doesn't actually start for another fifteen minutes. Then there's dancing. It's going to be a long night.

"I think we've let them look enough," Elliot says dryly, lifting an eyebrow at the room. He's sardonically aware that we will always be the center of attention wherever we go.

I'm surprised at the rush of affection I feel for him.

Rob Jr has always believed the attention is his due. Elliot just wants to bury his nose in a book and win Dad's approval.

We glide forward, letting the people stare.

The lights glint off my dress. My mom and Marika outdid themselves. I'm graduating next week, turning eighteen soon after, so I think my mom considers this dress my transition to full-blown Leighton-Hughes.

It's a classic ballgown shape, with a tight, strapless bodice and a wide skirt that flares out in elegant layers like a waterfall. It's gold. Not just the color gold, but actually gold. The bust and the skirt are shot through with strands and strands—yards worth—of 24 karat gold thread embroidered as flowers and leaves. It shines in the light, a burnished teasing color. And in the center of each of the embroidered flowers, there are rose red rubies, winking in the light. It's burgundy and gold, my family colors.

At my neck is my high school graduation gift, a gold necklace with three teardrop rubies surrounded by diamonds.

I look like Midas's daughter. I think, that was the point.

After I rushed home from giving Jace his gift, I hurried down to the salon, got an updo and evening make-up and then rushed to get dressed. I've never moved so fast.

The transition from fresh-faced, scruffily dressed, happy Andi, to cold-faced, pristine, Andrea has never been so stark.

When we arrive at my table, my expressionless mask slips for one tiny moment.

My mom didn't dress me up for my eighteenth birthday.

She dressed me up because of him.

18

ANDI

REID SHILLING.

He and his parents make up the final three at our eight-person table. He casually turns when I approach, a mocking glint in his blue-green eyes. Why is it that he's always sarcastic, always taunting and disdainful?

He's the only person who has ever been able to break my cool indifference. Because he's—I give him a haughty look—awful.

There's a flurry of hello, how are you, very well, cheek busses, and handshakes. Reid pulls the chair out next to him, and gives me a shark grin.

I sit.

The conversation starts again. Tuxedo-clad waitstaff take our drink orders and deliver artfully arranged bites of salmon mousse crostini, fig and brie wrapped in prosciutto, caviar and crème fraiche tartlets.

My mom watches Reid and me, then turns back toward my dad who has his boastful brash personality on full display. Which means he's angling to take Reid's father for a ride.

Reid studies me, my dress, the rubies, the gold dust the make-up artist brushed over my bare shoulders, the flush still in my cheeks from lying in the sun and kissing Jace.

He leans close and says low in my ear, "You look like a million dollars."

I look at him from under my eyelashes. Study his tux, the ruby cufflinks, perhaps a wink to my family. Maybe his father is actually courting my dad?

I pick up my glass of sparkling water filled with strawberries and peaches, and hold it in front of my lips, shielding them from prying eyes.

Then I smile and say quietly, "And you look like an ass."

I take a drink of my water as Reid grins at me with mocking delight.

I pretend to concentrate on selecting an hors d'oeuvres, the brie and prosciutto smell good, but I don't like fig. The caviar, yuck. What I could really go for is a burger from...

"I haven't bothered your friend. Not since you asked me," Reid says, keeping his voice low.

He's watching me, probably waiting for me to deny that Jace is my friend.

Or he's waiting for me to thank him.

I pick up a crostini and take a nibble. Reid sighs and tugs on the sleeves of his suit jacket, making his ruby cufflinks glint in the light.

As I take small bites of the salmon, I watch my mom

and dad.

Elliot and Rob Jr have already caught on. I should have right away. We're either angling for a business deal or starting some new hostility. Or my dad could be fishing for information.

Reid's father owns one of the largest real estate and development conglomerates in the tri-state area. I know he's working on a project that so far has sunk two hundred million into the development, but I heard he's had nothing but trouble since the project began. Equipment failure, worker issues, permit trouble.

Maybe my dad wants to take it off his hands.

As a friend, of course.

The charity auction passes quickly. The five-course dinner too.

I manage to ignore Reid and instead think about how in a week I'll be on the road.

I press my hand to my stomach when I think about telling my parents. The queasy feeling lets me know it isn't going to be an easy conversation.

"Too much to eat?" Reid asks.

It's the first thing he's said since the auction began.

He looks at me with polite concern. I'm not fooled.

I fold my hands on the table and say, "I'm fine."

"Good." He gives me a devious smile, his burnished hair glinting and his eyes laughing as he stands and holds out his hand. "Then you can do me the honor of a dance."

I stare at him.

Not *another* one.

"Go on then. Show us how it's done," my dad booms.

He's a small man with the voice of a giant.

He's red cheeked and red necked. His collar is too

tight and he's full of energy from an evening of chess-like business maneuverings against Mr. Shilling.

Even though my dad's voice is jovial, I know this isn't a request.

My mom dips her chin in command.

I stand and put my hand in Reid's. His eyes laugh at me.

At the table his parents watch us. His father has always given me pause. He has green eyes with a yellowish tint that remind me of a snake, and a bullet-shaped head. I think his father looks like what Reid is like on the inside. His mom, on the other hand, is very pale, and has washed-out blonde hair, washed-out blue eyes, and a large dark brown mole on her cheek.

Both of his parents watch us with silent expectation.

In fact everyone at the table is, except Elliot who is sneakily reading a copy of the *Wall Street Journal* hidden in his lap.

Across the room an old jazz song begins to play. It reminds me of the jazz on the radio at the Coney Island Beach.

Reid walks me to the dance floor his hand in mine.

"Why do you always have to maneuver me into dancing with you?" I ask, keeping a light smile on my face for everyone watching.

Reid holds my fingers gently in his. He gives me an ironic smile. "Because everyone expects it."

"Do you always do what everyone expects?"

"I try to," he says, a glint in his eyes. "Don't you?"

That's a dangerous question and one I'm not willing to answer.

"I thought you did," he muses, pulling me onto the

dance floor and spinning me into his arms. "But then...I saw you in the park, championing our friend."

"He's not your friend," I hiss.

Reid pulls me tight, rocking me closer in time with the slow languid jazz. We're dancing in slow motion, rather than the typical swing you'd dance with faster, more upbeat jazz. I wouldn't be able to dance swing—or even a waltz—in this dress anyway.

This music calls for an intimate dance. So that's what we're doing. I'm standing close, in Reid's embrace, moving our hips in time to the music.

We're the only ones on the dance floor. The rest of the couples haven't migrated this way yet. Some people watch, our parents do. My brothers too.

I still remember when Reid and I first had dance lessons together as awkward eleven-year-olds.

I didn't trust him then either.

"Whatever you think you're up to," I say, leaning close to his ear, "you can stop."

"My parents expect us to get married someday," Reid says.

I stop dancing. Not sure I heard him right.

Reid stops too. He stares down at me, inches taller even when I'm in heels.

Married. To Reid.

A laugh bubbles up in my chest but I smother it.

I stand on my tiptoes, lean close.

He leans down.

I can feel the heat of him, smell the expensive leather-scented cologne. Our faces are framed in the sparkling light of the chandeliers, when I promise, "I will never, ever, ever do what they expect. I will never love you. And I will never, ever marry you."

He stares down at me, his eyes filled with delight and mirth. "I don't know how you do it. You always manage to make me laugh."

"You aren't laughing."

"I'm laughing on the inside."

He leans closer, so close our lips almost touch, and then he spins me around, starting our dance again.

And that's when I finally look up, spin close to the stage, and see who's playing this old, languid jazz song.

My heart trips over itself, and my skin goes cold. I stumble over my heels, but Reid catches me and pulls me close so I can regain my balance.

"Clumsy?" he asks with a smile, but when he sees my face he frowns.

He's never been slow though. He glances at the stage, and understanding dawns.

His mouth tightens and he spins me again. When he does, my dress fans out, catches the light and sparkles like the noonday sun.

When I reach the end of the spin I look up, right into Jace's eyes.

A wrong note tears through the ballroom, a stuttered, clanging, discordant note. The guitar stops, but the rest of the band plays on.

He hadn't seen me before. Or I suppose he saw me, but he didn't match the girl covered in gold and diamonds with the same girl who wore cotton dresses and lounged barefoot on his couch.

I stop at the end of my spin, hold his gaze. My lips are numb, my skin clammy, not because he sees me, knows I've been misleading him, but because of the look on his face.

He's devastated.

Reid pulls me back, spins me to him again.

Jace starts to play again, seamlessly moving back into the rhythm of the song.

I look back to him, try to catch his eye, but he stares over me, past me, refuses to look at me dancing with Reid while he plays a slow song.

My heart races and I feel like I might lose my dinner all over the dance floor.

"I want to go," I tell Reid. "I want to go."

He nods, escorts me off the dance floor and then smoothly makes excuses at the table. He doesn't ask any questions. When he puts me into his family's Maybach and requests the driver take me home, all without a sarcastic comment or a taunting quip, I think Reid might not be quite as horrible as I always thought.

Then I remember him punching Jace in the Ramble. And I remember Jace's face when he saw me dancing with Reid just now. And I decide, yes, Reid is exactly as bad as I always thought.

I ride home, scared I just ruined the best thing that's ever happened to me.

19

ANDI

WHEN I GO TO MEET JACE ON MONDAY AFTERNOON, I don't expect him to be happy to see me.

I spent the night pacing my room and tossing and turning in my bed. I wanted to run up to his apartment and wait outside his door, but even though I was desperate to see him I knew that wasn't a good idea.

The gala didn't end until midnight. After packing up, he might not get home until two or later.

Because of my early exit from the gala, I knew my mom would come and look in my room to make sure I was home. Also, I wasn't oblivious to the fact that Jace lived in a rough neighborhood, and hanging outside his building in the middle of the night wasn't exactly smart.

So I texted him: *Can I still see you tomorrow?*

He wrote back the time and place: *Three o'clock. Belvedere Castle.*

I don't bother to change my clothes. I wear exactly what I put on this morning, an outfit that I wore last month on our spring trip to St Barts. It's a shimmery summer dress from a boutique in SoHo. The ones that serve you macarons and champagne or cappuccinos as you try on clothes. I'm in heels, because in my family, we always wear heels. And jewelry. My hair is in an intricate braid and my make-up is heavier than usual because the bags under my eyes are deep and my skin is pallid.

I thought about wearing a cotton dress and my Converse, but in the end I decided to show up like this. Maybe I'm punishing myself. Or maybe I feel this meeting will be easier if I look like Andrea Leighton-Hughes.

I stand in front of Belvedere Castle. The gray stone structure rises up behind me. It's a miniature fairy-tale castle, with a turret and arched glass windows overlooking the pond below and the greenery of the park. Tourists swarm in and out of it, taking the winding stairs to enjoy the view at the top, or leaning over the stone wall to view the tall trees or the buildings, far off, lining the edge of the park.

The breeze pulls a few strands loose from my braid and blows them across my face. The leaves on the trees flip and toss in the wind. It smells like rain, even though the sky is blue and the only clouds are heavy, fat white ones low in the sky and far, far away.

I shift on the hard gray stone and try to ease the pinching of my shoes. It's ten after three, and I'm not sure Jace is going to come.

Or maybe he saw me standing here and decided not to stay.

The arched stone entrance of Belvedere Castle is

dark, but the curved stone wall is inviting. I walk over and lean on it, setting my elbows down and resting my chin in my hand.

Down below, the pond is placid blue-green. It's surrounded by tall wispy grass, untamed foliage, and rocks dotted with sleepy turtles. I take a deep breath of the fresh, breezy, rain-scented air, and let out a long sigh.

Then, Jace is there.

He leans against the stone wall next to me, resting his arms on the ledge and looking out over the park.

My shoulders stiffen and I wait for him to say something. Like, *I don't want to see you again*. Or, *you are a liar*. But he just watches a little boy, running in the field past the pond, pulling a red kite behind him.

I stand with him, my breath short and painful.

His forearm rests next to mine. Only an inch away. His hands are folded together.

He stands there casually in old jeans and a t-shirt.

My eyes burn and I blink. "I'm sorry," I say.

He turns then and finally looks at me. His expression is closed off, he has sleepless bags under his eyes as well. He's watching me with steady, gray eyes. That's where all the rain is, I suppose. The gray in his eyes looks like thunderclouds.

"Who *are* you?" he asks, and I see how much it takes for him to ask even that three word question.

"Andi," I say, but it doesn't sound true, even to my own ears.

He shakes his head. "I don't think so."

The back of my eyes burn and I swallow back the denial.

He's right. I'm not Andi, I'm not even Andrea, I don't know who I really am.

"Look," he says suddenly. "I don't know what this was. What you were doing. I guess, you and Reid..." He swears then, and pushes off the wall, backing away from me.

I step toward him and shake my head. "No. I didn't—"

"Look at you," he says, his face full of confusion. "Last night, you looked like...who are you?"

I clench my hand tight, pray that this hasn't ruined everything. "Andrea Leighton-Hughes."

He shakes his head. He doesn't recognize my name.

"Robert Leighton-Hughes is my dad."

It takes a second, but I see the moment that he understands. You'd have to be living under a rock for the past twenty years to never have heard of my father. And Jace went to Darby School, where the newly renovated gymnasium was named after him.

I wait for the change. It's always the same. I'll become someone to be feared. Or someone to be used. Or, more likely, Jace will walk away.

It's easy to be crazy about a girl with normal troubles like where to go to college or how to find a summer job. It's not so easy being crazy about a girl like me.

"I have one question," he says.

I nod, my heart beating wildly in my chest.

He looks me over, the jewelry, the heels, the dress flitting in the wind.

"Did you and Reid have a good laugh? Was it hard to pretend you cared? Is your life so shallow that you have to play with people's feelings? What? Reid gets to punch my face. And you...you do one better, you get to punch my heart? What's wrong with you people? What happened to you that you think you can just play with people? What?" He laughs, and it's so unlike him, because the sound is painful and bitter. "Sorry," he says, "That was more than one question."

"Jace." I step forward.

He shakes his head, holds up his hand for me to stop, and then turns and walks away.

20

ANDI

OF COURSE JACE GOES TO THE RAMBLE.

His stride is long and his steps are fast. And for about thirty seconds I stand there, frozen, and watch him disappear. The dark trees and the shadows swallow him and I'm left there alone. A girl standing in front of a fairy-tale castle. But Belvedere Castle, as pretty as it is, isn't real.

And neither am I.

The only thing that's ever felt real is the past weeks with Jace.

I can't let it end like this.

He's leaving the city, and if Dean is right, they won't be coming back for a long time.

Decision made, I rush after Jace, my heels clicking on the stone.

The sun is bright. It's that soft yellow glow that bathes

the world in early summer and wakes up all the plants and the people. It's so sunny that when I hurry into the Ramble, I blink at the dark shade and the sudden cool, damp wood air.

I don't see Jace, but I hurry down the winding path.

My heels wobble on the uneven gravel and dirt and I trip over a tree root.

My knees jar against the coarse rocky dirt and my hands skid on the ground, dragging off skin. The sting sends a jolt through me and I shake it off. Stand.

Then I reach down, yank off my heels and shove them in my purse. I could really use my Converse right about now, but barefoot it is.

I run down the path, jagged rocks spearing my feet. I duck past a mom and dad with their two kids and stop at a split in the path. Which way?

Deeper, I think. Deeper into the Ramble.

I run that way, limping a bit, my knees red and raw.

Then I see him.

His shoulders are hunched, his head is down and his hands are in his pockets. He's staring at the ground as he walks under the shadows of the dark, green leaves.

If I had a lyric, it'd be just one word, *brokenhearted*.

I keep running, and he must hear my feet on the path, because he pauses, then turns.

Before he can shield his expression, I see it. He's surprised and so, so glad to see me. But then he shakes his head and frowns.

"Stop," he says. "I don't need you to apologize."

He turns to go, but I've reached him now and I grab his hand. It burns the raw skin on my palm, but I hang on tight.

He turns back. "Andi." He shakes his head, "Andrea. Whoever you are. I'm not—"

"Please," I say. "Let me explain. Just let me explain one thing, and then you can decide whether or not you want to see me again."

He considers me. Then he must feel the dirt still on my hand because he frowns and looks down at our hands, then at my knees, streaked in dirt.

"What happened?"

I shrug. "I was in a hurry to get to you."

That makes him smile. It's small, but it's there. "Alright. I'm listening."

I look around. It's Monday afternoon, you can hear kids and families walking, you can see the red and blue jackets of a couple on the path nearby.

"Do you know someplace private?" I ask.

He considers my expression, then nods.

Then he's pulling me along the path, into the deepest, quietest part of the woods, where only the birds and the wind in the trees makes a sound. He steps off the path and pulls me into the brush.

"Can you walk?"

The ground is grassy, with leaves, weeds, and fallen limbs covered in moss. It's cool and soft beneath my stinging feet.

When I nod he pulls me deeper into the woods, down a slope dotted with small boulders. Ahead is the trickling of water and the smell of wet stone. At the bottom of the little slope, hidden by thick foliage and intertwined branches, there's a small hollow. A rocky cave only a few feet wide and a few feet deep. The rock is deep slate gray and glistening from a small waterfall collecting in a tiny pool.

At the back of the space is a small dry area to sit. Jace gestures to it.

"No one comes here," he says. "You can talk all you want."

His voice is indifferent, but I'm encouraged because he's still holding my hand. We walk into the little stone nook, and the coolness and stone scent surround us. It's a small space, so much so that when we sit at the back, our legs are touching and our arms are pressed together.

Jace leans his back against the wall and watches me silently.

I pull my legs up and wrap my arms around my knees.

"I didn't set out to lie to you," I start.

He lifts an eyebrow.

"I didn't. A year ago, I started coming out to the park, trying to escape from life for a few hours at a time. Just being...normal."

He shakes his head. "Yeah. It must be real hard being wealthy. Poor little rich girl."

"Don't," I say, my heart twisting. "Don't be like that. You aren't like that."

His jaw hardens as he watches me, then he nods. "You're right. I'm sorry."

My fingers shake but I hold them tight against my legs. Jace notices, but he doesn't move to put his hands over mine.

"I've never told this to anyone," I say, my voice so quiet that even the trickling water over stone is louder than my words.

I look over at Jace, and I realize that his eyes aren't like thunderclouds, they're the exact color of the stone around us. And I decide, if this rocky hollow is a safe space to share secrets, then Jace, whose eyes are the same color, is a safe person to share secrets with.

Because I've never told this to anyone before, I'm having a hard time finding the words.

"Life in my family, it isn't easy. When I see you and your brothers, you're all so easy with each other. It's obvious, even though life hasn't done you any favors, you all still love each other."

Jace nods, but doesn't say anything.

"My dad, it's not that he won't love me, I think it's that he can't. Me and my brothers, we're not people to him, we're extensions of his ambition." I struggle to put it into words. "We're not his kids, we're...like a business entity. We have a purpose, a mission, if we act right, we'll earn dividends. If we don't, he'll sell us for a profit in a merger." I peer at Jace from the corner of my eye. He's looking at me like he can't fathom what I'm saying.

"I've never been a person," I tell him. "I've always been a chess piece in a game started long before I was born."

He lets out a breath, a sharp puff of air, and then shakes his head, like he can't believe what I'm saying.

"You didn't look like a chess piece when you were wearing a dress made of gold and dancing with Reid. I'm sorry, Andi, it looked like you liked being with him. You looked right at home."

He looks guilty saying it, but I guess it had to be said.

"I'm never more a chess piece than when I'm with him. Our families would like nothing better than to see us together. But he's never been my friend. I won't let them win by going down that path."

Finally, Jace reaches over, puts his arm around my shoulder and pulls me close against him. My thighs slide over the cold stone, and I shiver against his warmth.

The coldness of the stone reminds me of what I've spent years trying to forget.

"So that's it?" Jace asks. "That's what you wanted to tell me?"

"No." I scoot closer to him and then drop my head against his chest. He sighs, but then he puts his arms around me and holds me close.

I can feel the rhythm of his heart beating strong against me. His chest is hard and his arms are warm.

"My dad is Robert Leighton-Hughes," I begin, "but my mom..." I pause, stare out at the leaves flickering in the wind. "My mom was never affectionate with me. She gave Rob Jr and Elliot hugs, kisses. But not me. I had our nanny, Grace. She was the one who kissed my bruises and wiped away my tears. For years, I thought there was something wrong with me. I tried everything. I'd bring my mom flowers from the park. She'd throw them out. I'd buy her gifts with my allowance. She'd set them aside. I figured she didn't like gifts, so I tried to make her happy. I'd be very, very good. I'd dress in pretty dresses, and never cry, and never shout, and never fight with my brothers. I almost burst from how good I'd be. How still I'd sit, for hours and hours, just hoping she'd notice me. Then one day, when I was six, she did."

I let out a long sigh and close my eyes. Jace is holding perfectly still, his hand barely grazing my shoulder as his fingers fall over my skin.

I want to turn to him, bury my face in his chest and breathe in his ocean, woodsy scent, but I don't.

"My mom told me she was taking me to the playground for a special treat. I'd never been so happy in my entire life. My mom finally, finally had realized that she loved me. I thought that I'd somehow done it. Made my mom love me. We took the subway, something I'd never done before, all the way to the Bronx, far, far north, to a big playground there. I wore a pink dress with lace and ruffles, my hair in two braids. I skipped down the sidewalk as I held her hand. Once we were there, she pushed me on the swings for what seemed like hours. My heart was soaring so high. Then I went down the slides. I climbed, I ran, I played. I still remember how it felt. It was like I was in heaven. My mom was smiling at me the whole time. She'd never smiled at me before. I was blinded with happiness. Then she asked if I wanted an ice cream treat. I did. This was the most special day of my life. She sat me on a wooden bench at the back of the playground and told me not to leave. To stay right there. That she'd be right back."

Jace's hand trails over my shoulder in a gentle, soothing circle. In the woods, there's the lone call of a jay. That harsh, lonely caw.

"Right," I say. "I sat there. The hard wood of the bench digging into my legs. And all that practice I'd had being quiet and being still, it served me well. The sky went dark. The traffic beyond the fence slowed. A mom asked me, *'Where's your parent?'* And I said, full of confidence, *'She'll be right back.'* Soon, no one was left at the playground but me. The sky was black. I was hungry. I was thirsty. I was scared. Finally, I couldn't help it. I started to cry. But I couldn't leave the bench, because she'd told me not to. She told me she'd be back." I shake my head. "There were shadows, and then, you know, there are rats that hide in the bushes at the playgrounds. They come out at night. I heard them squeaking and skittering over the ground. The wind was cold. I started shaking and crying. '*Mom,*' I said, '*Mom please.*' Then I was so scared that I crawled underneath the bench, wrapped my arms around my legs and rocked myself back and forth, back and forth."

I stop, remembering the cold of the stone against my legs. The wet saltiness of the tears running into my mouth.

"What happened?" Jace asks, his voice low.

"A woman walking by heard me crying, she came into the playground and pulled me out from under the bench. I didn't want to go. I screamed when she tried to take me out. Then, my mom was there. She took me, walked me back to the subway, took me home. She didn't say anything about what happened and neither did I. No one knew what happened, not my dad not my brothers. My mom and I have never mentioned it."

"Why?" Jace asks. "Why would she do that?"

"I'm my father's daughter," I say. "But I didn't realize until my brother Rob Jr told me that I'm not my mom's daughter. Dad had an affair with my brothers' nanny. A woman named Marie. She didn't want me. My dad did. He and my mom had been having problems. He used my birth as a slap in her face. He knew that he could do whatever he wanted and she wouldn't leave him. She'd put up with anything to stay a Leighton-Hughes. Even raise a baby that she didn't want and wasn't hers. All I am is a chess piece in a game. My brothers see me as an interloper and my mom sees me as a parasite there to shame her and take her sons' inheritance. For seventeen years I've been used as a weapon. The only way I've been able to survive is by pretending to be someone I'm not. I imagine myself encased in glass, where no one can reach me and no one can hurt me. The only time I ever let myself out of that glass was when I met you."

I close my eyes and drop my head, breathing in the feel of him. "Please. I'm begging you, don't...please don't let me down. Please let me stay your friend."

His arms tighten around me. And then he pulls me into his lap and his warmth wraps around me.

"I'm sorry," he says, his breath a whisper against my cheek.

I turn up to him. "Why? You never did anything but make me happy."

"If you like," Jace says, "you can stay with us. You can come with us. With me. And just so you know, you don't have to do anything to make me love you, I'm already gone."

My breath cuts off and I stare up at him.

"You love me," I say.

He reaches his hand up, brushes it across my cheek.

"I do."

Something opens up inside me, something that's been locked for years and years. And I don't think I'll ever be able to lock it away again.

"Is it okay if I love you too?"

He smiles, his lips curving, and then he pulls me close and kisses me.

21

JACE

WHEN I TOLD ANDI I WAS COMING WITH HER TO TELL HER parents she was going on tour with me, I don't know what I expected, but I definitely didn't expect this.

At the downtown New York Public Library, the one with the lions out front, there's a huge mural on the rotunda ceiling with a massive Moses, holding the ten commandments. In Andi's lobby, there's an even bigger mural of *her dad*, holding solid gold bars.

It's one of the craziest things I've ever seen, and I've been on the subway at two in the morning.

The lobby was a flashy, gold and marble palace, perfumed with lemon cleaner and I'm sure, scrubbed by hand with hundred dollar bills.

As soon as we stepped into the cold marble hall, I felt transported to an entirely different world.

Even Andi looked different. The doorman held the

door, we stepped through, and all of sudden Andi was gone and in her place was...someone else.

She was like that girl in the gold ballgown, the cold, straight-backed, haughty girl I didn't recognize, even when she was dancing right in front of me. As soon as we stepped into the Tower, she became another person.

I shivered, cold from the dry lobby air, when I realized she reminded me of the Jetters.

She didn't acknowledge the doorman. Didn't look at the elevator operator as he ferried us up to the top floors. She was cold. Separate. Maybe unfeeling.

My stomach dipped with the speeding elevator and I looked at our reflections burnished in the bronze elevator wall.

We both graduated yesterday. We're set to leave this weekend. I'm nearly packed, I've said my goodbyes. Andi said she's ready too.

But is she?

I knew theoretically that she lived a much different life than me, even very different from the kids I went to Darby with. It's like, if the distance between me and my classmates is the distance between Earth and Mars, then the distance between Andi and them is like the distance between Earth and the sun. She's light-years above them all. And I'm only just realizing it.

When the elevator doors slid open and we stepped into her home and I saw the entire skyline of Manhattan bowing before the Tower, I knew that Andi fit here. Even if she didn't think she did.

The way she moved, the tilt of her chin, the look in her eyes.

She fit.

But then, she looked at me, and the glacial façade melted away and she gave me a beaming smile, one full of hope and love, and then she gripped my hand and squeezed.

"Thank you," she'd said.

Which it turns out are the only words I needed to stand against the shock, disbelief, and anger rolling off her dad and the icy dislike radiating off her mom.

"No," her dad says again, his hand slicing through the air.

He's red-faced, red-haired, and shorter than I thought he'd be based on his reputation. But he's barrel chested and full of sparking energy that reminds me of an amp turned up high.

While Andi told her parents that she was going with me on tour, indefinitely, and that she was deferring college, her dad watched me like a boa constrictor watches a mouse as it squeezes it to death.

Her mom, on the other hand, hasn't looked at me since she perused my old school uniform khakis and the collared shirt I bought for this meeting. I was weighed and found lacking.

It doesn't matter. I'm not here for their approval. I'm here for Andi.

"I graduated yesterday," Andi says, her voice steady. I wonder if her dad can see the way her hands are shaking. "I turned eighteen last week."

I resist the urge to look at her. She didn't tell me about her birthday.

"I'm an adult. I know this may seem ill-advised but I've thought it through and this is what I want. I'm going with Jace."

Her dad stares at her and I get the impression it's

taking quite a lot of effort for him not to pace the room. "Are you pregnant?"

Andi flinches. "What? No. Of course not."

Her dad weighs me again and I stare back. The light from the wall of windows shines over him and burnishes him with gold. He and his wife, sitting on the pristine white couch, look like a painting of Henry the Eighth and one of his unfortunate wives.

"I don't see any other explanation," her dad says. "The only reason you would throw away your life on... this"—he cuts his hand toward me, with a twist of his mouth—"is if you opened your legs so wide your brain fell out."

Andi's face leaches of color and goes pale.

"Robert," Andi's mom hisses.

I step forward, the battery-acid taste of anger searing my throat.

"Do *not* speak to her that way. She deserves respect."

Andi's dad finally stands, his chest out and his legs wide. His neck flushes red. I've seen enough brawls to know that he is considering taking me down. I think, though, unlike Dallas who uses bricks to smash windows, or River who uses fists, that *he* uses his power and his money to cut down people.

"You think you'll respect her?" her dad asks.

I look over at Andi and nod. "I already do."

"Where did you go to school?" he asks, bullet fast.

"Darby."

"Who are your parents?" he asks just as quickly.

"My parents are dead."

"And where do you live?"

I lift my chin. "The Bronx."

"Riverdale?"

That's a nice part of the Bronx, full of families and green parks.

"No. South Bronx."

Which is the worst part of the Bronx, full of homicides and concrete.

His lip curls.

"Dad—"

"Be quiet."

Andi clenches her jaw and lifts her chin. She takes a step closer to me.

Her dad notes this and takes a breath that reminds me of a bull heaving in a lungful of air as it scratches its hoof in the dirt and prepares to charge.

Her mom though has remained as still as a statue during the entire conversation. She watches Andi and me with unnerving stillness.

"Andrea," her dad says, stepping forward. "You may think you want this. I know, we all get tired of the glamor and want to play in the gutter. But that doesn't mean you *stay* there."

Andi shakes her head in denial, but her dad continues and I can see what I didn't before. Past the barrel chest, short stature, and brash personality, is a persuasive, guileful mind. He's determined to change her mind.

"This boy cannot make you happy. The chasm between you is too wide. You're not just from different boroughs. You're from different worlds. After a few weeks, maybe a month, the glitter will start to wear off and you'll realize the gold was only tin covered in cheap paint. The only future you'll have with him is the same present he's living now. No money. A run-down apartment. Cheap food. This ends only one way. With him angry and shamed that he can't give you the life you deserve. And you, tired and bitter, because the dream turned out to be a nightmare. You'll see that quickly, when you're hungry, tired, run-down, and just looking at him fills you with regret. I give it a month. Andrea, do not give up your future for a month."

Andi lifts her hand, sets it on her dad's arm. "Please understand that this is what I want. I'm leaving with Jace. I hope you'll support me in that decision, but it's fine if you don't."

"You are making a mistake," he says.

"I don't think so."

Her dad considers the set of her chin, her calm, steady gaze.

Then he turns to me, his chest thrust out, his eyes narrowed.

"If my daughter gets sick or hurt, how will you pay the hospital bill?"

"That's for me to worry about," Andi says.

I bite the inside of my cheek. This isn't something I thought about. I shake my head, "We'll manage."

He turns to Andi, "If you leave, you won't be on my insurance."

"I'm healthy," she says.

"If my daughter is hungry, how will you afford food? Healthy food? Food that she's used to? Salmon, veal, sea bass, coq au vin?"

"I don't need that kind of food. I'm fine with simple things. And I have money."

"Not if you leave you don't," he says. "No credit cards. No allowance. No trust fund. Nothing. You're cut off. You'll have to earn your own way in the world. And see how well he's done?" He points at me, at my clothes and the shirt I bought on discount.

"I earn enough," I say. "She won't starve."

Except, I won't be able to afford much beyond white bread, peanut butter and jelly, and cold cuts for a while. Our tour pay isn't that much, and I expect her dad knows that.

"And if my daughter needs a winter coat to keep her warm? Or a safe place to sleep at night? Or a new car? Or—"

"I can take care of myself," Andi says, cutting her dad off.

He shakes his head. "You have no idea what it takes to take care of yourself. When you"—he points at me, his finger shaking—"realize that you have stolen my daughter's future. When you see you've ruined her chances of earning a degree, of having a successful life, when you see that she's thin, and tired, and weary, then I hope you *respect* her enough to say goodbye. But if what I expect is correct, then you're an opportunist, and you think that my daughter is your ticket to wealth. I have news for you. I would rather my daughter stay in the gutter with you than give a grasping greedy child like you a cent of support."

I nod. That's it, I suppose. I get it now. Andi's dad only sees what I look like—a dirt-poor kid from South Bronx hoping to climb the social ladder by using his daughter.

He has a point too. I can't give Andi a home like this. I can't give her nine-course meals. I can't dress her in gold or fly her to Paris for her birthday. If she gets sick we'll be hard pressed to pay the bills. If she gets tired, I won't have a bed with silk sheets, I'll just have my shoulder. If she needs new clothes, I won't be able to take her shopping on Madison Avenue, it'll be the thrift store. I can't even help her pay for college. But she hasn't asked for any of that.

Like she said, she can take care of herself.

The only thing I can offer is my love.

And that's all she wants.

I reach over and grab Andi's hand. Hold it tight. "Sir, I love your daughter."

Andi looks over at me, her brown eyes wide. I smile at her, one that tells her to trust me.

"I love her and I respect her, which means I respect her decision. If she wants to come with me, she can come with me. If she wants to stay then she can stay. The only thing I can do is support her choice."

Andi squeezes my hand.

"Andrea," her dad warns, "think about this before you leave. No money, no phone, no driver, no home, no insurance, no college, no jewelry, no trips abroad. It's all gone. Your future is cut off. You know I don't accept dissension. I don't accept rebellion. If you leave you don't come back."

The room goes silent.

It feels as if everyone is holding their breath.

Andi lets go of my hand. My heart trips over itself and lodges in my throat as she steps forward.

Her heels echo on the white marble floors and the cloying scent of her mom's perfume makes it hard to breathe.

She stands between her parents, her shoulders back, her head high.

Then she pushes aside the fall of her honey-amber hair and slowly unclasps the diamond and gold necklace from around her neck.

Her mom watches her with rapt attention.

Her dad shakes his head.

The snick of the jewels hitting the marble coffee table is loud.

Then Andi takes off a ring with a sapphire the size of an almond and sets it next to the necklace. She pulls off a gold and diamond watch. The gold bracelet on her other wrist. The diamond studs in her ears. She pulls her wallet out of her purse and sets an Amex black card, the kind with no spending limit, and her debit card on the table. Then she pulls out a thick fold of cash and fans it out.

I've never seen anything like it. Her parents are rapt, watching Andi dump thousands and thousands of dollars' worth of jewelry and cash onto the table.

At last, she sets down her cell phone.

That's it then.

She steps forward, leans down and kisses her mom on the cheek.

"Goodbye," she says.

Her mom watches her, and I can't read the expression in her eyes.

Then Andi walks to her dad. He stares at her with a sort of stunned disbelief. She leans in and kisses him quickly. "Goodbye, Dad."

Then her head high, she grabs my hand and walks away from her future.

22

Andi

My dad gave us a month, and if I were anyone but me, and if Jace were anyone but Jace, he would've been right.

But from the minute we walked out of the Tower and Jace took my hand, I knew we were going to be okay.

Surprisingly, my brother Elliot found me minutes before we left New York. He shoved a suitcase in my hands, full of clothes, shoes, boxes of protein bars, two thousand dollars in cash, and unexpectedly, the picture of me and my mom. It was so unlike him, especially when he said, "Be happy, Andrea." I was too stunned to say thank you or really anything at all.

Elliot was the only one to say goodbye.

With some of the money Elliot gave me, Jace and I bought an old beater car to drive between gigs.

That way, Dallas drives the van with all the

instruments and the gear, and Pauly rides his sleek red Yamaha motorcycle.

He's as fast as a rocket on it, and beyond when he plays the horns, it's the only time that he's loud. His engine revs and he likes to dart between the van and our car.

I asked him where he got it and he told me he bought it a year ago with the money he'd made shoplifting. I didn't know if he was serious or not until Jace told me that Pauly's so slick he could walk out of a store with a microwave and no one would stop him.

One day I saw Pauly palming a snow globe at a gas station in Pennsylvania. After that, I told him, you can pick things up, but then you have to put them back down.

I still see him every once in a while, strolling a rest stop convenience store, his hands faster than a flying bird, but when he catches me looking he just smiles and shows me his empty hands. He promises he hasn't stolen anything in years, and he looked so deeply, achingly sorry about it that I believe him.

River and Dean take turns either riding with Dallas or riding in the back of our old beater.

The days I like best are the ones where it's just Jace and me together in the car. We roll down the windows, put on the radio and sing at the top of our lungs, as we drive miles and miles of wide open highway.

Or sometimes Jace will drive, and I'll rest my head in his lap, or lean against his shoulder and just drift off as the flickering light of the sun shines through the windows and the green smells of the fields we pass mixes with the old vinyl seats and the hot plastic of the dashboard.

We talk then. We talk for hours.

Sometimes about the past, but mostly about the future. And every story we tell about the future, we're in it together.

He likes to drive with one hand and hold my hand with his other. Or he'll run his hand down my arm, or touch my cheek, or run his fingers through my hair.

The only time we aren't touching is when he's on stage, and then, even if we aren't touching, he's still looking into my eyes and singing to me.

When River rides with us, there's more joking and a lot of laughing. River doesn't mind that I am who I am. Dean, though, he's been colder to me since he learned I was a Leighton-Hughes. Pauly doesn't care. And Dallas, he trusts me even less. I doubt Dallas will ever like me.

It doesn't matter though. In the three months we've been on the road I've become part of the family that makes up The Morgan Brothers.

I didn't want to be a tag-along or a freeloader, so I make myself useful. I help set up shows, I help tear down, I help plan the driving routes, and I've found that I have an uncanny knack for negotiating cheaper rates at the hotels we stay in.

Even more, after the first month on the road, when everyone was tired of gas-station sandwiches and cheap microwave meals, I bought a cookstove and a pan and started making simple pre-show dinners for everyone.

I found a cookbook for meals that cost five dollars or less and tried them all: sloppy joes, spaghetti, quesadillas, mac and cheese, beans and rice, more. Sometimes, if Jace is hungry after a show, I'll cook his favorite, grilled cheese with ham. It'll be three a.m. and he'll hold me, and sway to the sizzling of the butter on the stove, and sing me a song of my own.

Three months. Seven states. Sixty-three shows.

We're on the outskirts of Cleveland now. The show is in a bar with a cleared space for the band at the front. The bar is packed, there are people filling all the tables, and all the stools at the bar are full, with people standing behind them.

Sometimes gigs fill up like this, and sometimes they're playing to an empty room. It doesn't matter how many people come, though, they play the best show they can every time.

Even though Dean wouldn't like to hear it, he reminds me of my dad. He's driven and obsessed with professionalism. I hear him frequently saying to the others, *"This is our job, we play the best we can because we are professionals. It doesn't matter if there are five people or fifty thousand, we do our best."*

Jace is driven too, but he's driven because he loves to play and I think his soul is made of music. Either way, the combination of all five of them works some musical alchemy to create the best music I've ever heard. And by the response of the people that hear them play, I'd say I'm not the only one who feels this way.

The bar we're in is built like a warehouse; it's tall and wide with wooden beams spanning the ceiling and shiny concrete floors. The sound bounces around, especially Pauly's trumpet, which seems to zing between the ceiling and the floor. There's room for dancing, and a whole lot of people are. The whole place smells like stale popcorn, peanuts, and cheap beer.

I'm near the stage, sitting at a small bar table, a cold cup of ice water in my hands. The speakers are so close, I feel their vibration over my skin.

I asked Jace yesterday, "Do you still need to look at me when you sing?"

He said he tries every show to sing without me, but he can't.

"It's okay, I'm not going anywhere," I told him.

So now, Dean is playing a steady beat in time with River's chords, Dallas is hitting the drums, and Pauly waits for his cue to bring in the trumpet. Over that, Jace strums his guitar—the one I gave him—and sings.

I lean forward, my thighs sticking to the hard wooden chair.

Jace's eyes are on me.

It's a new song.

And I start to smile when I hear the lyrics.

"I got a car, and a stretch of road, and I got you. Can't go back, can only go on. But I'll drive a million miles, if the road ends at you."

The cold of the ice water sinks into my hands, but the rest of me is warm. My cheeks flush as I watch him and I see the memory in his eyes, of us in our old car, his hand playing with the hair at the nape of my neck, and me asking, *give me a lyric.* And he said, *I got a car, and a stretch of road, and I got you. And that's all I need.*

Then, I had him pull over. We waved Dallas, River and Dean on. Pauly sped past. Then, we idled on the shoulder of a country highway. I climbed into his lap, and we kissed and kissed until my lips were tingling and I was dizzy, and Jace was looking at me like he wanted to take me into the back seat and lay me down.

I feel heat spread over my cheeks and Jace gives me a small smiles as he sings.

He's taller now. He grew in the last three months. He's the same height as River now, six two or three. His shoulders are widening and with my cooking, and the miles he runs every morning after he wakes up, and him using the hotel gyms, he's gotten bulkier too.

I'd say that because of Jace's looks, he's a favorite with the crowds. His wide, gray, stormy eyes, his long dark eyelashes, his thick dark hair and square jaw, his secret smile—all of it combines to make him look like an unrepentant sinner.

I'm the only person who knows that the singer in the jeans and black t-shirt isn't a sinner but the kindest, most honest, most decent person I've ever known.

Meanwhile, River, who looks a lot like Jace but more angelic because of his chubby cheeks and the laughter in his eyes, is the one who has a bit of the devil in him.

And while River flirts with anything that moves, Jace only looks at me.

Which is good, because I'm only looking at him.

I take a long drink of my ice water, letting the cold run down my throat and cool me off. Then I hold the cup to my forehead, rolling it over my flushed skin.

The song comes to a close and Jace grins at me.

For three months, we've kissed, we've cuddled at night, but we've never, ever gone further than kissing.

I think...I think tonight might be the night.

23

JACE

THE TINY HOTEL ROOM IS DOMINATED BY THE queen-size bed.

Most of the hotel rooms we stay in are small. We hit the budget hotels and are lucky to get a bar of soap, much less a microwave or coffee maker.

It was worse before Andi started negotiating rates and booking our hotels. Before she took over, we stayed in roadside motels with stained, dirty sheets, mold on the walls, and dripping faucets. Dean looked for the cheapest rate and that's where we stayed.

I didn't mind that so much for myself. I'm always so tired after a gig that I usually fall straight into bed at two or three a.m. and then sleep until we have to hit the road for the next show. We get to the next gig, check into our hotel, then go set up for the show, play, take everything down, go back to the hotel for sleep, and then head out the next day to drive to our next gig. The only time we spend in the hotel is for sleep and sometimes for a few hours of rest if we make it in early.

The wild parties, the drunken nights, the orgies that popular culture shows in movies and on TV, I don't know who's doing that, but we all know our job is to play, rehearse, get rest, and then play again. There isn't room for anything but drive, set up, play, take down, sleep, repeat. Which is why I didn't mind that the hotels were basically a bed in a moldy box. Except, I minded for Andi. I didn't want her sleeping in hotels full of bugs, drugs, and stained mattresses.

She fixed it though.

Thanks to her negotiations, we save money and the budget hotels she finds feel like castles.

The light from the nightstand lamp colors the room dim yellow. The smell of butter and melted cheese fills the room. I stand behind Andi with my arms wrapped around her waist, soaking in the way she fits me.

She's at the portable stove making me a grilled cheese. The only counter is the vanity, so I watch her in the mirror, smiling as she bites her lip, concentrating on getting the perfect golden crust.

"Did you like the new song?" I ask.

We rehearsed it whenever she was out buying groceries or taking a nap. I wanted it to be a surprise.

She meets my eyes in the mirror. "I loved it. Was it for me?"

"Everything I write is for you."

She breaks our gaze in the mirror, turns and looks up at me. "Even that one about dancing in the dark?"

I grin, "Especially that one."

She stands on her tiptoes and brushes her lips across my mouth.

Her mouth is warm and she runs her tongue along my bottom lip. I never knew you could kiss someone for hours. For days. For months. I never knew that kissing could consume you.

I hold her close, feeling the heat of her pressing against me.

"Are you happy?" I ask.

That's the one fear that keeps holding me back from full-on happiness. Sometimes it keeps me up at night. Andi gave up everything, her entire life for this, and I'm scared that she's not happy. That a few days, or a month into this, she realized she made a mistake, but she can't bring herself to tell me.

I press my mouth to the edge of hers, bending down so we meet. "Are you?"

The look she gives me reminds me of her expression when I played her a song for her belated birthday. I parked on a country road, we sat with our backs to the car, our feet in the grassy ditch, and I played her a happy birthday song.

She smiles at me, her eyes glowing.

"Happier than I've ever been," she says.

"You don't miss New York? Your life?" My chest tightens as I wait for her answer.

"No." She tips her head back and her hair falls back over her shoulders. "If I wasn't here I'd miss you. You're the only thing I want."

"Someday you might want a home, a real stove, a bed of your own—"

She gives me an impatient look and puts a finger to my mouth. I cut off.

"I don't want to be anywhere you aren't."

I press a grateful kiss to her temple.

Then she sniffs and a wrinkle appears between her eyebrows. I smell it too. It's bitter, smoky, burnt.

"Oh. Dang it!" She turns and grabs the grilled cheese with her bare hand and throws it onto the paper plate. The bread is black and smoke curls off it. The cheese is brown and bubbling.

I flip off the burner.

Andi sticks her fingers in her mouth and says around them, "Burned myself."

I shake my head and pull her fingers from her mouth. The pointer and the middle finger are red on the tips. I take her to the sink, run the cold water and then hold her hand under the stream of water.

"I burned your sandwich," she says mournfully.

"I'll still eat it," I tell her.

She gives me a wistful smile.

Then, she says, "I have everything I need, in case that's what you were asking."

I stare at her, feeling the cold water from the bathroom faucet run over our hands.

The fluorescent bathroom light is bright, casting a glow over her amber hair and illuminating the gold in her brown eyes. She looks a bit like an angel.

"I know I'm supposed to want more," she says, "but I don't. I just want you. I think our life is pretty great. We might not be able to afford a tower, but our car and a hotel room is all I need. We might not eat caviar, but I like grilled cheese. You might think I want diamonds, but I don't. You're all I need."

I stare down at her, overwhelmed by how much I love her. She's my other half.

"You want to stay."

"I'm not going anywhere," she says.

I hold her tight.

"What's your lyric," she says, watching me in the mirror. "Your lyric for right now?"

I pull her hand out of the water and turn off the faucet. Then I keep ahold of her hand as we walk out to the bedroom.

The bed is wide, the bedspread brown, with red and green flowers. The sheets under it are pristine white. The carpet is low pile green, and the wallpaper is beige. There's a popcorn ceiling and olive green polyester curtains. The radio clock on the nightstand says two fifteen a.m. in red block numbers.

The lamp is dim but gives enough light for me to see the love in Andi's eyes.

My chest is tight, my heart pounds like a bass drum, my body feels electrified. I want her so much.

Three months we've been holding each other. Kissing. I've been learning all about her and she's been memorizing me.

I've been waiting, giving her time. I didn't want her to feel like she had to stay if she didn't want to. I know I'm not able to give her the life she had, but I can give her love, and I was raised knowing that love is much more important than money. I think she knows that too.

She looks at the bed, at the lamplight spreading over the floral comforter and the mound of the white pillows spritzed with her lavender spray. She smiles back up at me, a knowing look in her eyes.

I hold her hand, give her my lyric, *"Let me love you."*

She squeezes my hand. "All night long?"

I shake my head. "We only have five hours until we have to leave for Indianapolis."

At that, she tugs off her t-shirt, baring her smooth skin and her pink bra. Her breasts are pushed high.

"Then we better make use of the time we have," she says with a small smile. Then she unbuttons her shorts and kicks them onto her suitcase.

I let out a harsh breath and stare at Andi standing in front of me in pink lace underwear and a pink bra, and nothing else.

She flushes, from her cheeks all the way down to her chest. I stare at the pink lace covering her flushing breasts, completely speechless.

"What?" she says, frowning at me. "I'm not what you expected?"

"You are...are..." I'm speechless. "You're beautiful."

She grins at me then. "No. I'm Andi."

I remember then, it's the first thing I ever said to her and that's what she said back. It was as true then as it is now.

"You are," I say.

"Well, you can write a song about how beautiful you think I am later. For now, we should..." She dips her head toward the bed.

I take the hint.

I lift her up in my arms, she lets out a gasp and then laughs as I drop her onto the mattress.

I climb over her, press her into the soft bed.

"This works better naked," she says, tugging at my shirt.

"Shh," I say, "I'm warming up."

She snorts. "Don't tell me you're going to play me like a guitar. Warm up. Tune the instruments."

I imagine running my hands over her, stroking every part of her, listening to the noises she makes. It would be like music.

"Wouldn't you like that?" I ask, pressing my mouth to her neck and sucking on the feather-light beat of her pulse.

I'm ready. I've never been so ready.

She tugs my shirt over my head and throws it to the floor. She presses her hands to my chest and I feel like I'm going to levitate. There's so much energy arching between us you could plug a cord into us and light up a city.

"Do you feel that?" Andi asks, parting her knees and letting me settle on top of her.

I take her mouth. "I feel it every day," I tell her.

I press against her, feel her through the fabric of my jeans.

She closes her eyes and tilts up against me. I nearly lose my mind. I shake my head.

"I have to go slow or it's only going to last fifteen seconds."

I'm a virgin. So is Andi. This could go very, very badly. Or very quickly. Unless I do what I've been dreaming of doing every night that I held her in my arms and drifted off to sleep.

"I don't care. Next time will last longer," Andi says.

"I care," I say.

Then I sit up and do what I've dreamed of.

I kiss her. Slow and needy until I can feel the ache in both of us. I bite her lips, send my tongue over her, taste the strawberry flavor of her. I run my hands down her neck, over her collarbone, along her ribs, over the peaks of her breasts.

She moans into my mouth, the perfect note. I unstrap her bra and push it off the bed. Then I press my bare chest to hers. She wraps her hands around my back and holds me close.

"Feel the rhythm of my love," she says.

And I do, I can feel her heartbeat, pressing against my own.

"Andi," I whisper into her mouth.

Then I move down, spread my fingers over her spine, around her hips, I drag my hands down her thighs. I listen as her breath catches, as she makes a noise of pleasure as I trail back up her inner thighs.

Then I take her lace underwear and pull it down her legs, over her thighs, down her calves. I drop them to the floor. And then I go back to Andi. I draw my hands up her calves, trail my mouth over her legs. I listen, and each time she makes a noise of pleasure, or draws in a breath, I press another kiss, rub the same spot again, until I'm back up, right at her core.

She's naked underneath me.

Her skin is flushed. Her eyes are luminous and full of music.

If I listen closely, I'm sure I'd be able to hear it too.

I lean down to kiss her again, her thighs, her abdomen, her hip bone, then, I take her in my mouth. I've always wanted to kiss her here, to feel her raise her hips to me.

"Jace—"

She doesn't say anything more. Not the whole while I'm sucking on her, tasting her, and running my fingers over her.

Until finally, she bows beneath me, arches her back,

and cries out with the prettiest broken song I've ever heard.

She grips my shoulders, tugs at my hair, breathes my name as she kicks her feet out. Then I think she can't wait anymore, because she reaches down and unbuttons my jeans.

"Now," she says. "Now."

I kick my jeans off, reach down to the suitcase by the bed and pull out a condom. Rip it open and put it on.

She smiles at me. "Thank you."

I nod.

Then when I'm lying over her, our bodies running over each other, connected everywhere, and my tip is just there, at her entrance, we stop.

We both hold still.

Her arms are around my back.

I'm on my forearms, my hands buried in her soft hair.

I can feel every bit of her, every heartbeat.

The sweat, the heat, the love.

She smiles up at me, the happiest smile I've ever seen.

I lean down. Press my lips to hers. Taste her love.

Then I press inside her.

She stiffens, and I nearly explode. I go slowly, inch by careful inch.

She's hot, and tight, and nothing, nothing could have prepared me for how she feels.

Finally, I'm deep inside her.

My heart pounds. I'm dizzy. All I want to do is move.

But I have to make sure. "Okay?"

She nods. Reaches up and takes my hand. "I love you."

In that moment, my heart cracks open and I can hear

it, I can hear the music. It's us. The two of us. We're making our own song.

"I love you," I tell her.

I move.

I move to the rhythm of *I love you* and *I need you* and *I want you* and *please* and *I love you too*.

And then, everything crescendos, and I lose the world, I lose myself, I lose everything in Andi. She can have it. She can have all of me.

I bury myself in her and give her my heart.

When I pull her into my side and come back to earth, the first thought I have is, I'm going to marry her, and there's nothing in the world that can stop me.

24

ANDI

THE GIG IS IN A BOWLING ALLEY.

Dean didn't realize when the booking agent told him their next gig was at a place called The Strike and the Spare that it was a bowling alley and not a club.

But the stage can be seen from all twenty-four lanes, the lights are flashing with pink and blue laser lights, there's a smoke machine on stage, and the band sounds amazing.

The crack of the pins hitting the wooden lane meshes with the music. The pace of the bowling is fast and furious, matching the upbeat, swinging song. And between throwing their balls, people are *dancing*.

The place is packed. It's loud, it's flashy, and pitchers of foamy beer and neon yellow margaritas are flowing.

When we walked in the big warehouse space, with its high ceilings and rows and rows of shiny lanes, I felt a curl of happiness. It smelled just like the alley in Midtown—Lysol, floor wax, used shoes, old cigarette smoke, dirty carpet, and fryer grease.

I breathe it in and grin at Jace. He's up on stage. Sweat drips down his face, everyone is *moving* tonight. I think Dean took the bowling alley as a challenge, because they are playing every pop, electro-pop, and brassy swing song in their repertoire. The floor vibrates with the boom of the drums and the beat of the bass.

Jace winks at me and I fan myself. The bowling alley doesn't have air conditioning, just huge fans that blow a humid breeze across the space.

I rented a lane, the one closest to the stage, and every time I get up to throw my pink nine pound ball, it hits the gutter, and Jace holds back a laugh.

They've been up there for two hours. The show's almost over.

I'm surviving on a strawberry smoothie and a plate of fried brownies that taste like chicken and old grease. I think they probably haven't changed their fryer oil since nineteen seventy-eight.

But, beyond the nasty brownies, this place really puts on a good time for its bowlers.

I'm impressed.

Nobody else had a smoke machine, and nobody else had big bald guys dancing with their bowling balls.

When we pulled into the gravel parking lot of the alley—it's on the outskirts of Charlotte—Dean took one look, got that hard edged it's-a-challenge look he can get sometimes, and told everyone they were going to go old-school brass and make these bowlers dance.

I nearly laughed out loud at the glint in Dean's eyes, at River trying to work out whether the bowler girls would be cute, the disbelief on Dallas's face, the shy slump in Pauly's shoulders, and the pure *delight* on Jace's face.

Jace and I haven't been bowling since we went in Midtown, and this place is bringing back good memories.

The last time we went bowling we had our first kiss. I think Jace remembers that too, because he keeps giving me that secret smile from up on the stage.

I push my bangs back from my forehead, wiping the sweat lining my brow. A waitress weaves behind me and delivers double pitchers of beer to the lane next to mine. The three bald guys, brothers I think, and the women with them give a raucous cheer.

The show is almost over. They're on their last song, the one they always play, "The Goodbye Song," it's called, and they always shout out goodbye to the city they're in. People always cheer, no matter where we are.

It's been almost six months on the road now. We've made our way all through the Northeast, some of the Midwest, and now we're down South. You'd think, after nearly a hundred shows, I'd be tired of hearing them play. I'm not though.

Jace asked me why that was.

I said, "Do you get tired of playing?"

He said, "No."

And I said, "Well I guess it's the same thing. You won't ever get tired of playing, and I won't ever get tired of hearing you play.

I especially like to see him on stage. Jace becomes bigger somehow, he has a magnetism that draws people in, and when he sings, everyone in the room feels exactly what he does. It's like he plugs them all in and the room becomes electrified with his voice.

I love seeing the smiles on people's faces. The way they dance. The way they hug each other or hold hands. Sometimes they cry, but they're still smiling.

Every time I see him play, I fall in love all over again.

He said when he sings a love song, he's thinking of me. I'm thinking of him too.

They play the last chords. "Thank you, Strike and Spare!"

I laugh as Jace puts his hand in the air and all the bowlers cheer.

He jogs down to me and I grab his hand and pull him close.

"Hey you."

He tugs me to him, sets his hands on my hips and grins down at me.

When I met him seven months ago, I didn't realize he was going to get taller. I've started wearing heels again, otherwise I can't reach him for a kiss without him picking me up or me pushing him down onto a chair so I can straddle his lap.

Sweat drips down his forehead and he smells like the cedar and maple of his guitar and that fresh, clean breeze I associate with him.

"Fancy meeting you here," I say, giving him a wicked grin. "Want to bowl?"

"I don't know. Are you any good?" There's a laughing spark in his eyes.

"I'm terrible."

"What a coincidence. I love terrible bowlers."

"You're in luck then." I stand on my tiptoes and press a kiss to his mouth.

Back on the stage, Dallas and Dean are clearing up. River and Pauly have already started hauling gear out.

"Should we help?" I ask.

Jace studies them. We know our job. "Yeah. But then… we'll bowl."

So we help clear up the gear and pack the van, and then we play three games with River and Pauly, who I'm glad to say are just as bad as I am.

Dean and Dallas drink in the lounge. River picks at my basket of brownies, which he dubs "chicken-fried brownies."

Soon though, it's time to go.

It's late and we have to drive two hundred miles in the morning for the next gig tomorrow night.

I hold Jace's hand as we walk past the lanes, then to the lobby where there are rows of claw machines full of stuffed animals, flashing arcade games, quarter gumball machines, and a tall quarter machine chock-full of those little plastic tubes filled with plastic jewelry.

The door swings open, pushing in a cool breeze. It's early November, and even down South the temperature drops. Outside it smells like wet pavement after the rain. Dean, Dallas, River and Pauly all stride out, clapping each other on the back.

I'm about to head out into the dark after them, but then I see the spark of the fluorescent lights hitting a blue-gray plastic gem in the quarter machine.

I stop and smile up at Jace. "You know, that's my kind of ring. That shade of blue is my favorite color."

I point at the plastic stone surrounded by flecks of plastic diamond. It's the exact color of the water at Coney Island and the shade of Jace's eyes when he's kissing me.

He's staring at the quarter machine, a funny expression on his face. Like he's been working on a problem for a long time and the solution just came to him.

"What? Are you alright?" I ask.

He grips my arms, turns me to face him, and gives me an urgent look, one I've not seen on him before. "Stay right here."

I frown, not sure if I should be worried. "Okay."

He jogs off. I try not to think about what happened the last time someone I loved told me to "stay right here." I look over my shoulder, Jace is at the shoe counter, handing the worker a twenty-dollar bill.

When he jogs back he has two rolls of quarters and he's fighting a smile.

I shake my head. "What?"

"You like that one?" He points at the plastic gemstone ring, halfway up the machine.

I nod.

He drops to his knees and puts the first quarter in the slot.

Five minutes later there's a pile of forty plastic containers on the floor next to him, the machine is half-empty, and he's out of quarters.

I can't see the blue gem ring anymore, which means it's nearly out of the machine.

I've worked it out now. Jace is going to kneel on his knees, pushing quarters into the machine until he gets me the ring I want, and then...

I hold my hands in front of me, my fingers clasped together, my heart leaping around in my chest.

"I'll be right back. Stay here," he says.

I'm not going anywhere.

He jogs back, another roll of quarters in his hand.

He grins at me, like he hasn't ever been so happy in his whole life.

Then he drops down to his knees again and starts pushing quarters. With each crank of the handle, the creaking clacking, and the roll of the plastic container, my breath catches in my throat and I lean forward. And every time the ring is wrong, Jace grins, and chucks it into the pile. The containers clatter around. But he turns back to the machine and drops another quarter in.

I take a small step closer.

And another.

Until I'm right next to him, willing the machine to give us the blue-gray plastic diamond ring.

I run my hand over Jace's arm, he grabs my hand, and then sets another quarter into the machine.

I squeeze his fingers as the quarter drops. The plastic clatters. Jace opens the metal tray, and there it is. The ring.

Jace looks up at me. And the hope I see in his eyes is the same hope that he had the first time we made love. The one asking me to love him as much as he loves me.

He's on his knees. But if he's on his knees, then so am I.

I drop down onto the old carpet and lean close, the plastic ring between us.

"Andi," he says with a smile.

"Jace?"

"Will you be my wife?"

My throat tightens, my eyes burn, and my heart is so big that I think that my chest can't hold it inside anymore. "Only if you'll be my husband."

He smiles then, cracks open the plastic container and pulls out the ring.

We grin at each other as he slides it onto my ring finger. The plastic is cold, and the ring pinches my skin. The ends don't connect, he stretches it a bit, and slides it all the way down.

I hold my hand up and smile at the plastic blue-gray stone sparkling in the fluorescent light.

"We're getting married," I say. When I look back at him, he's blurry, and I realize it's because there are tears in my eyes.

"We're getting married," he agrees.

I told him I didn't need diamonds, that he was all I needed. I've never loved a ring as much as I've loved this one.

"We're only eighteen," I tell him.

He nods. "We're luckier than most. That means we have seventy more years to love each other."

"Exactly."

He stands then, picks me up, and carries me out of the bowling alley, back to the hotel and bed.

25

JACE

RIVER, DEAN, DALLAS, PAULY AND I ARE CROWDED INTO Dean's hotel room. We're playing a game of poker around a box of pepperoni pizza. River is cheating, as usual, and no one cares, as usual.

We got to town early, and instead of resting in our separate rooms, Dean wanted to play cards.

Andi saw a big box store from the highway on our drive in. She said she was going to look for Christmas presents. It's nearly December and she has plans for a big Christmas dinner with gifts for everyone.

"Jace, she's a crutch," Dean says, staring at me over his cards.

My shoulders tighten. Now I see why Dean wanted us all to get together for cards and pizza—guys only.

I look to the side, clenching my jaw. There's a generic landscape painting on the beige wall, stationed over the

MDF desk and the blue upholstered chair. I stare at the pastel swirls of the painting and take in a deep breath. The pepperoni and cheese pizza tints the air with garlic.

There are two full-sized beds in Dean's room, and we pulled the nightstand between them for a card table. Pauly sits next to me on the bed, Dean and River sit on the bed across from us. Dallas pulled up the lounge chair between the beds.

At Dean's statement, everyone goes quiet.

River sighs and throws down his cards. Apparently, the game's over.

When Dean saw Andi's ring the day after I proposed, well, let's just say he didn't offer any congratulations. In the month since, he hasn't thawed.

He hasn't said it outright, but I don't think he wants us to get married at Christmas.

River, he's happy for me, he knows exactly how much Andi means to me. Pauly approves. Dallas, he's Dallas, so he told me I was making a mistake because girls like Andi are bad for guys like me.

"She isn't a crutch," I say, dropping my cards to the nightstand.

Dean gives me a hard look. He hasn't smiled since that day we voted to come on this tour, but he is more alive. He doesn't look so old anymore, or so tired, he has his vitality back. But he hasn't gotten his smile back. Last week, River told him to lighten up and smile. Dean said, "I'll smile when we hit number one."

River laughed and punched him in the shoulder.

Right now, I'm reminded that even though Dean is happier than he was hauling junk in New York, he still isn't the carefree brother he used to be.

His eyes narrow. He looks so much like my dad, dark

brown eyes, thick eyebrows, his wide forehead and strong nose, that sometimes, I think it's hard to remember that Dean is nothing like Dad. He especially doesn't *understand* like Dad did.

"Jace, listen. She's a crutch. You can't sing unless she's there. You can't sing a word unless she's right up front. What are you going to do if she has to take a piss in the middle of a show? Follow her to the bathroom?"

He's speaking to me in that measured yet impatient tone that older adults use when speaking to kids that *just don't get it*.

"It's fine. She isn't going anywhere. It works."

Pauly sighs and his shoulders hunch. Anytime voices are raised or tensions run high Pauly sort of caves in on himself. I hate it because it reminds me of what he looked like when we were really little and he came to our place, shaking and trying not to cry.

Dallas watches Pauly, protective of him.

"Ease up," he says in his deep voice.

Dean shakes his head. "I'm only trying to say that things may seem rosy now, but what happens when she leaves. You can't keep using her as your crutch. You have to be able to go on without her. It's not right what you're doing."

"I agree." River nods and I give him a stunned look. Him too?

He shrugs and winces, "Sorry, Jace. I agree with Dean. He's right."

I shake my head. "She's not leaving. So there's no worry."

We're getting married in a month. Clearly she's not leaving.

And thinking about her not being at a show? It's so implausible that I can't even picture it.

"Fine," Dean says. "Andi's not leaving. You'll never have a fight. You'll never break up or get divorced. But what if she gets sick? What if she can't come to a show? What then? You're risking the future of the band by using her as a crutch."

I want to deny it, I want to argue, but when he puts it that way...I can't. I don't think of Andi as a crutch, but she is the reason I can sing at our gigs. She's my anchor. In the stormy sea of all those faces, she keeps me steady. So I can sing.

"She is a crutch," Dallas says, putting his elbows on the table, the black tattoos snaking over his arms on full display. "The only way to learn to walk without a crutch is to—"

"If you say break it, I will break you," River says.

Dallas lifts an eyebrow.

River hasn't had a fight in a few months and I think he's trying to rile Dallas up. He has that wild light in his eyes.

"Get stronger without it," Dallas finishes dryly, shaking his head at River. "You need to learn respect tiny man."

Pauly covers his laugh with a cough. Dallas smirks, glad he pulled a laugh out of Pauly.

I look between River and Dallas.

Dallas may be as tall as a doorway and his muscular chest is as wide as a refrigerator, but River is six three and wiry strong.

"It's not happening," I tell them all, standing. "Andi's not leaving. It's not a problem. I don't need to get stronger without her. Whatever that even means."

I wipe my hands off on my pants and look them all over. The pile of cards, the box full of pizza crust, the empty drink cans.

"We have a show in six hours. I don't know about you all, but I'm going to get some rest."

I turn to go, but Dean says, "Jace. Don't get married at Christmas. Wait a bit. Just to be sure that it's the right thing to do."

I study Dean. He's still looking at me like I'm a kid, like I don't know what I'm doing. I get that he's five years older, I get that he raised me after Mom and Dad died, but he's forgetting that I'm not thirteen anymore. I'm not that kid that cried at Mom and Dad's funeral and then slept at the foot of his bed because I was scared.

I shake my head. None of them are looking at me, they're all looking at the floor or the card table. It's only me and Dean right now.

I say out loud, what I've known for a long time.

"You're just worried about the band. It's all you care about. You're worried that if I get too involved with Andi then I won't give the band all I have."

Dean doesn't argue, he just says, "Will you wait? I don't want you to get hurt. I want you to make sure it's the right thing to do."

I let out a breath and shake my head. "I don't care if it's wrong or right. I'm hers. I've been waiting for her my whole life."

River finally looks up from the floor. I know he sees it, that this is the kind of love we grew up with. But instead of being happy for me, he looks sad, like he's seeing something in the future that he doesn't want to witness.

Maybe he's remembering what loving someone this much did to Mom and Dad.

"I'll see you later."

I walk out, worrying about what I'd do if Dean's fears ever came true.

26

JACE

ANDI'S CROUCHED ON THE GRAY CARPET OF OUR HOTEL room, slipping a green and red striped present into the front zipped pouch of my suitcase. She turns when the door snicks shut.

"It's a notebook for your songs. Don't open it until Christmas," she says, shaking her finger at me.

Like I'd do that and spoil her surprise. Not a chance.

I smile, walk forward and pull her up and against me. All that worry about her not always being around fades as easily as the evening light fades to night.

Our hotel room is clean, tidy, and smells like furniture cleaner and bleach. Andi already has the dress she's going to wear to the show laid out on the bed.

"I won't unwrap it. I'd rather unwrap you," I say, bending down and kissing her.

It's then I notice the taste of tears on her lips.

I pull back and frown, taking in the wet spikes of her eyelashes and the puffiness of her eyes. "What is it?"

She shakes her head and looks down, tucking her chin.

"Andi? What?"

When she looks back up she doesn't look sad, she looks angry. "I called my mom, to tell her I was getting married. I thought..."

My stomach drops. I know what she thought. I've heard Andi talk about her family enough to know that even if she doesn't admit it, she loves them and she wants their love back.

I pull her to me, tuck her head against my chest. "I'm sorry."

I lost my parents. And Andi, she lost hers too. Just in a different way.

"She said to never come back. She told me to never come back. That if I get married I shouldn't ever come back. My dad already cut me off. I'm..."

I close my eyes, bite back the anger I have for her parents. She's shaking, it's subtle, but she's trying so hard not to cry that she's shaking.

The light on the ceiling lets out a low buzz and the whooshing of cars speeding past on the highway nearby filters in through the thin walls. That's the only noise, because she's holding in her tears.

I wrap my arms tightly around her, press a kiss to her head.

And it makes me ill to say it, but it needs to be said. "If you want to, if you need to, you can go back. I know how much you love them. It isn't too late for—"

She shoves away from me, her face pale, her dimple deep beneath her quivering lips. She clenches her hands into fists and her eyes flash. Her chest rises in quick, sharp breaths. I've never seen her so angry.

"I made my choice."

I look down at my hands. I think about what Dean said. About how we should wait, to make sure we were doing the right thing.

I look back up. "I know what I want. Right or wrong, I want you. But you have so much more to lose."

The overhead light tilts over her, casting her eyes in shadow. "Funny. I always thought I had so much more to gain."

"I meant your inheritance. Your life. Dean said you should be sure—"

She wipes at her eyes then and I see that she was crying just now, she was just so quiet about it that I couldn't tell.

"Do you think that I want that life, that I want money more than I want you?"

I swallow down the burning lump in my throat. It feels like I'm choking, like I'm standing in front of an audience of thousands and I can't sing a note.

"Jace?"

There's a banging on the door and we both jump.

"We leave in five," Dean calls through the door.

"Alright," I shout back.

I look back to Andi, but she's already grabbed her dress and is heading for the bathroom.

"Andi." I reach out toward her, but stop when she shakes her head.

"No. I don't..." She trails off.

I stare at her face, her light brown eyes, her chin dimple, the spray of freckles over her nose. I know her face and her expressions better than I know my own. And right now, she looks lost. And I see that she didn't need me to offer her a way out, she needed me to tell her she was already home.

"We'll talk later," she says. "We have to go."

The door to the bathroom closes with a quiet thump.

I rub my hand down my face and let out a sigh. Why would I try to convince her to go when all I want her to do is stay?

27

JACE

THE SHOUTS REVERBERATE THROUGH ME, LIKE A DEEP rumbling bass. I strum my guitar and let the energy of the audience rumble over me. I'm buzzing with it, like I'm plugged into the feeling and I have to keep playing.

The club is packed. The style of the place reminds me of an old-school jazz club. Something Louis might have played in.

It has can lights beaming down on the stage but the rest of the club is dim. The walls are red brick, the floor is parquet, and there's room to dance up front, with dozens of round tables in the back covered in wine-red floor-length tablecloths. Behind us, at the back of the stage, is a floor-to-ceiling deep red curtain.

Every table is full. The bar is full. And in front of the stage, there's barely space to stand. There are at least two hundred people rocking, dancing, and singing.

The lights out front are dim, but the stage is bright, and sweat rolls down my neck.

My fingers fly and as I sing the lyric, *"Marry me, girl,"* someone at the back of the room shrieks, "I'll marry you! I want your babies!"

Andi lifts an eyebrow.

She's up front, right where she's been all tour.

I smile at her, keeping my eyes on her.

My fingers run over the notes, each one rolling into the next and then the next.

Not that I want to admit it, but what Dean said got to me. I've tried half a dozen times this show to look away and keep singing. But I can't.

Every time I try, my fingers shake, a vise closes around my throat, my mouth goes numb, and...I look back to Andi before the song can fall apart.

I try it again, *"Marry me"*—look away—*"girl"*—look back.

It's not working. My voice slipped there, it was raspy and pained sounding.

There's a wrinkle on Andi's forehead and she's watching me like something's wrong.

I give her a reassuring smile. Nothing's wrong.

Actually, we've never played with so much energy. It reminds me of how we played when Mom and Dad were with us.

Dean had us open with our version of "What a Wonderful World," which has a lot of Dad in it and a lot of grinding rhythm that always gets people moving. I think he did it first, because Mom and Dad would've loved this place, and second, to remind me of why we're all here.

When Dean said we were starting our set with "What

a Wonderful World," he gave me a meaningful look.

Like, *Dad's watching you, don't let him down.*

I get it.

The five of us, we're a family.

We've been together since before we all could talk. No matter our faults—Dean's single-mindedness, River's jumping into fights and any willing bed, Pauly's fear of just about everything, Dallas's mistrust of everyone except us—we don't care, we're brothers, and we'll do anything for each other.

You don't let down your family.

Except, Andi's my family too.

We'll figure it out.

I'll figure out how to sing even when she can't be around, and she'll figure out what to do about her family. It'll work out.

I give her a smile. It'll work out.

When Andi smiles back, I slide into the music, let the emotions and music capture me, and ride it through the whole show.

When we're finished, back behind the curtain, with the cheers of the crowd still echoing over the brick walls, Dean grins at us.

His teeth are white against his flushed skin and his eyes are shining.

"You're smiling?" River asks. He looks at the rest of us to make sure we're seeing what he's seeing. "We're not number one on the charts. We're not even on the charts."

Andi slips behind the curtain and I reach for her and pull her close. She's warm and she fits under my arm just right.

She gives me a questioning look, *are we okay?*

I nod. *We're okay.*

She leans into me and I rest against her. Playing a show can be physically demanding, but also once you're done, the adrenaline wears off, the energy dissipates, and the fatigue can hit pretty hard. I'm not there yet, I'm still buzzing, but I'm enjoying casually holding her in my arms.

Dean makes sure we're all paying attention.

He smiles at each one of us, his eyes blazing. "You're going to like what I have say."

"You look like one scary mother when you smile," Pauly mutters.

Dallas nods. "He does."

"I talked to a guy at the bar before we played," Dean says, ignoring them.

He reaches into his pocket and pulls out a slim white business card, flourishing it like a magician would a white dove. He's enjoying the suspense.

I squint at it but can't make out the small black type.

"I don't trust guys with business cards," Dallas says, his wide shoulders bunching as he scowls.

Andi coughs, covering a laugh, and turns her face into my side.

Dean waves the business card and it makes a whoom-whoom noise as it flaps in the air. I watch it, transfixed.

"Then I talked to him again during our break."

"That's a lot of talking," River says.

Dean's smile grows even larger, so big I can see his molars at the back of his mouth. It's a bit unnerving how much he's smiling.

"He's a producer," Dean says.

The word *producer* sends a jolt through all of us.

Producer.

A *producer*.

I stiffen, my heart triple beats and I get chills. A producer was listening to us tonight.

Andi looks up at me, her eyes wide.

Inside I'm waiting for what Dean will say. I'm keeping a tether on myself. I want to jump up and down, shout, spin Andi around and kiss her, slap my brothers on the back. But, if Dean says the producer was here but wasn't sure about us...then all the excitement will pop, fizzle out, and I'll shrug and move on. Keep going.

But none of us except Dean know what he said.

There's an expectant electricity flowing through backstage.

Out front, all the people still talk, laugh, yell. They're all energized from the show.

We're energized from the word *producer*.

I lean forward. "Well?"

This was Dad's dream. He always talked about us getting discovered, getting found by a producer. Then we'd get a record deal. We'd get on the radio. We'd get a big tour. We'd make it. We'd reach the world.

But after Dad was gone, it became my dream.

Dean dreamed of musical genius. River dreamed of helping his family. Pauly dreamed of escaping his life. Dallas dreamed of protecting us, helping us stay out of the trouble he found himself in. Me, I dream of lighting the world on fire—filling it with my song.

"Dean, tell us," River says. He's bouncing on his toes, holding his hand in a fist. I think he's aching to punch Dean if he doesn't tell us what's what in two seconds.

Pauly's eyes are wide and he's shifting on his feet, alternating between looking as if he's praying with fervent hope that a producer likes us and experiencing debilitating fear because a producer likes us.

Dallas is stone still; he looks like he's holding his breath. The only thing that moves are the tattoos on his neck as he swallows.

Then Dean gives a sharp, triumphant nod.

River sags. "Hell yes," he breathes. Then he shouts, "He loved us!"

"What did you expect?" Dean says. "Of course he loved us."

I let out a painful exhale, and I realize my lungs are burning because I wasn't breathing.

"A producer wants to sign us?" I ask.

Pauly's looking between us all, his eyes wide.

"Not just any producer." Dean hands me the business card. I hold it out so that everyone can see.

"Holy..." River says. He looks at us all, a crazy smile on his face. "We are getting trashed tonight."

Dean shakes his head. "We have a show tomorrow night. You know the rules."

"The hell with the rules. I'm celebrating."

"Yes," Dallas says.

Pauly shakes his head, like he's trying to wake up. "Guys. We're gonna...we're gonna be famous."

At that, Dean starts to laugh.

I hug Andi to me. Hold her close.

I'm flying. I'm flying and we're on top of the world.

Dean wipes at his eyes. "Fine. Tonight. Tonight we celebrate."

We're on top of the world and nothing can bring us down.

28

ANDI

IT'S THREE-THIRTY IN THE MORNING. THE PARTY STARTED AT
the club and then moved to the hotel.

There are lots of girls here, even the one who shouted
she wanted Jace's baby.

River is eating it up. He's many, many shots in and
slurring his speech. Dallas drank his weight in beer, but
he's still the same silent scowling giant. Dean loosened
up enough to have a few drinks and he's even laughing.

We're in River and Dean's adjoining rooms, playing
music on the stereo, playing cards, talking, drinking,
dancing.

It's the kind of night I think my dad feared I'd be
having *every night* on the road.

Me and Jace, we've been drinking cola and toasting
everyone and everything. Some of the women have been

making eyes at Jace. It's not the first time, he's popular at all his shows. But it is the first time the guys have had girls back to their rooms.

The room is hot, loud, filled with the smell of liquor, sweat, and cheap cologne. My eyes sting and my head spins from the heat and from fatigue catching up with me.

I'm sitting between Jace's legs on the bed. He bends close and wraps his arms around me. "You okay?"

"I'm alright," I rest against his chest and watch River dance with a woman in a short gold skirt.

Jace reaches around me and takes a sip of his cola, the ice rattling in the plastic cup.

We still haven't talked. I'm still...why did he tell me I could go home? And...why did he keep looking away from me at the show?

When he first looked away, I thought he was distracted. But then he did it again, and again, and I realized, he was doing it on purpose. He told me that when he sings, he holds me in his heart. But when he sang the lyrics *marry me* he looked away.

I had a terrifying thought that he didn't want to marry me anymore. That him telling me to go home and him not singing to me anymore were connected.

But then I pulled myself together and realized Jace wasn't like that. He *loves* me. Whatever this was about, it wasn't about not loving me anymore.

Another wave of fatigue rolls over me. But the party isn't over yet, and I don't want to dampen the celebration. They have a producer interested. This is huge.

Maybe some more caffeine will help.

"I'm going to go get another soda and some ice," I say,

leaning back and talking loudly enough for Jace to hear me over the music.

The stereo is turned to its highest setting and I'm surprised the front desk hasn't called up to tell us to stop the noise.

"Do you want me to come?" he asks, letting me free from his arms.

He's sweet to ask, but I can tell he wants to stay. Pauly's in the corner, shyly chatting with a girl, and River is shouting at Jace to come meet his new friends.

"It's okay." I shake my head. "I'll be right back."

He squeezes my hand. "Okay."

The hallway is cool, and after the door shuts behind me, it's surprisingly quiet. I breathe in the cold air and walk down the carpeted hall toward the vending machines.

The hall is long, it's about two hundred feet of beige walls, blue carpet with beige medallions, and beige doors spaced evenly. The ceiling lights are bright, even this late at night, and as I round the corner, the music from the party fades to a quiet rumble.

There's a sign on the wall, pointing to the vending machines and the ice machine. It's another twenty feet down the hall, past the utility closet, the stairwell, and the housekeeping storage room. Basically, it's as far from the rest of the rooms as you can get without putting it on another floor.

I push open the door and step into the small linoleum-floored room. The machines let out a low hum. There's spilled orange soda dried on the floor and my shoes stick as I step in front of the machines.

The room light is harsh fluorescent and the vending machine lights blink, flashing the display in green lettering. I look over the options, trying to figure out which one has the most caffeine.

Or there's a machine with snacks too. If I have enough quarters I could grab a candy bar and load up on sugar and caffeine.

Thinking about quarters has me smiling, remembering Jace putting quarter after quarter into the machine to get my ring.

I look at the flash of the plastic gem on my hand and smile at myself in the reflection of the vending machine.

I'm eager to get back to Jace. I'll tell him I'm sorry for getting angry, that I know he was trying to make sure I was okay. I'll ask him if he's okay, ask what was wrong on stage.

I hit a soda button at random and then start feeding quarters into the blinking slot.

Behind me the door swings open. I look over my shoulder.

It's three men. They're big. Not as big as Dallas, but bigger than River and Jace.

I turn back to the machine quickly, eyeing them in its reflection. The vending room is too small for the four of us. We're crowded together, and I swear I can feel the hot breath of the one closest to me on the back of my neck.

The hair on my neck stands on end.

They smell like beer, cheap liquor, and cigarettes.

They haven't said anything, there isn't any reason for me to think I'm in trouble, but my heart is squeezing in my chest and I taste the tang of bile rising in my throat.

The first thought I have is *Jace, where's Jace? I wish Jace were here.*

But he's not. He's back in Dean's room at the party.

"I saw you with the band," the one closest finally speaks.

His round head is shaved. They all have shaved heads, but this one has a thick brown goatee.

His mouth is so close to my ear that I jump. I can almost feel the moistness of his mouth.

Were these guys at the party? I don't remember seeing them.

I don't think they would've been. The hostility rolling off them is filling the small space so quickly that I'm finding it hard to breathe.

My hand shakes as I put the last quarter into the machine.

"You a groupie?" another one asks. He has thick black tattoos circling his neck that are so vivid I can see them in the reflection of the machine.

The can of soda clatters down the chute and hits the bottom of the machine with a thud.

"Hey," the man with the goatee says. "He said, are you a groupie?"

"No," I say, putting steel into my voice. I try to channel my old ice-cold demeanor, the one that let me walk through a crowd of hundreds without any fear.

All I have to do is reach down, grab my soda, and then push past them.

That's all.

My heart pounds painfully.

"I saw you tonguing the singer at the show. Up there, flaunting your bits at the stage. I know what groupies do. They suck off the band."

My hand has closed around the cold can of pop, the condensation runs over my fingers.

I pause. Grip the metal as tight as I can.

I'm bent over.

Wearing the same short black dress I wore to the gig.

I can feel the hard gaze of all three men slithering over me.

Every breath I take is sharp as a knife, painful and piercing.

Jace.

I should've asked him to come.

Slowly I straighten, turn to the men. The one with the goatee is so close his chest rubs against me. His eyes are cold with amusement, like a predator that enjoys catching prey just to play with them.

"Excuse me," I say, pushing the words past the fear gripping my throat.

I try to duck past him, get by without touching him, but the space is so cramped that my arm rubs against him.

He grunts and then grabs my arm.

His hand is wet with hot sweat, and when he digs his fingers into my arm I try not to flinch.

"Get your hands off me," I say coldly, yanking my arm.

He jerks me back against him.

"I'll give you a hundred dollars," he says.

He grabs my thigh.

My breath is short and hot in my lungs and my thoughts have narrowed to one plea—*get out, get away, find a way out.*

The other two men are blocking the door. If I had any hope of decency or embarrassment, it's extinguished at the look on their faces as their friend yanks at my dress.

The goateed man slides his sweaty hand up my thigh.

I lose it.

"Get off!" I scream, then I swing the can of soda like a

mallet and smash the metal edge as hard as I can into the man's nose.

There's a crunch. A loud, snapping crunch. And then the bright red bloom of blood.

The man shouts. It's a guttural pained yell.

He drops me. Raises his hands to his gushing nose. I spin to the door. Go to fight past the other two men.

My heart stutters. At the door, watching through the window, is Dallas.

His face is cold.

Expressionless.

The man with the goatee shoves me from behind, knocks me to my knees. As my knees slam to the concrete floor, and red coats my vision from the pain, Dallas turns and walks away.

Tears spill down my cheeks.

The goateed man grabs my hair, pulls my neck back. "I said I'd pay you."

Above me one of them laughs. I can't see anymore, my vision is clouded with burning tears. My knees scream with pain. My head swims. Dallas left. He saw me in trouble and he walked away. *He left.*

The goateed man jerks my head.

This close to the ground the smell of spoiled orange soda is putrid and rotten. I don't think I'll ever be able to eat oranges again.

If I have an again.

No.

I can't think like that.

I'm a Leighton-Hughes.

My dad, even though he's half the size of these men, would have all of them on their knees in seconds. What am I doing?

Why aren't I fighting?

I grip the can. Then I spin around and slam it into the man's kneecap.

There's a nasty pop.

A shout of pain.

He jerks back. Falls against the ice machine. I lunge at the door.

The two men at the door, too drunk or too surprised to do anything, stumble back as I shove at them, scrambling for the exit.

I fling the door open.

Clutch the pop can in my hands as I stumble upright.

Blink.

Dallas is there, in the hall, leaning against the wall.

I can't move. Even though my mind is shouting *run*, I can't move.

"You...you..."

The betrayal is too deep for words.

He was just *standing* there.

While three men roughed me up he just stood there and did *nothing*.

Behind me the door slams open, the three men shove out into the hall.

Run, my mind shouts.

"Get out of here," Dallas spits words at me.

Finally, my muscles unlock. I can move again.

I don't wait to see what happens.

I sprint down the hall, my battered knees shooting knives of pain up my legs with each step. I fly down the long hall, my heart pounding, feeling the gorge rising up my throat. I think I'm going to be sick.

The music from the party grows blessedly louder and louder, until I'm at the door to Dean's room. It's unlocked.

I push inside, wiping at my eyes, trying to block out the loud music and the laughter. They hit me like jagged knives and all I want to do is curl in a ball and let Jace hold me and tell me everything's alright.

He's not there though. He's not on the bed where I left him.

His empty glass is there though, the ice melting.

I check the adjoining room. He's not there either. There are plenty of people, still dancing, drinking, laughing.

The celebration hurts now. My ears hurt. My eyes hurt. My head pounds.

Pauly's in the corner, still nursing a beer and shyly chatting with a woman in red.

"Pauly. Where's Jace?"

He looks up at me and frowns when he sees my face. I sniff and shake my head. I can't talk about this here. Not right now. And not with Pauly.

"Where's Jace?"

Pauly looks around the room, anxiety pinching his face. It's almost like he doesn't want to tell me.

"Where is Jace?" I say, feeling desperate.

"Is he the tall, good-looking one?" the woman asks.

"Yes," I say sharply.

"He went with—"

"He went out. Just for a second. You should wait here," Pauly says, his eyes darting nervously around the room.

I shake my head. I can't wait a second. I grab my purse from under the bed and hurry out into the hall.

Our room is only a few doors down. I fit the key in the lock, open the door.

The lights are out, the curtains are closed, and the

light from the hall doesn't reach the depths of the room. But a slit in the curtains lets in a beam of light from the streetlamps.

That's enough to see by.

The woman, the one who wants to have Jace's baby is up against the wall.

Her mouth is open, her eyes are half-closed.

But when she notices me, frozen in the doorway, she smiles.

She smiles at me.

She's naked.

But Jace is naked too.

He's holding her up against the wall, his back to me, having wild, hard, sweaty, against-the-wall sex.

He's...

Jace is...

Bile rises, I'm going...I'm going to be sick.

I can't stay.

I can't stay here.

He told me I should go.

He couldn't look at me while he played.

He looked at *her*.

I have to go.

I can't...

The woman cries out. Loudly.

I can't look at them.

Next to me, in the closet by the door, Jace's coat hangs. I reach into his pocket and pull out the keys to our beater car. The smell of him, the wood and fresh air scent folds around me. I hold back the sob rising in my throat.

I grip the keys and slowly back out of the room.

I close the door without a sound.

When I turn, my purse in one hand, the car keys in the other, Dean is there.

He frowns at me, looks from my bruised knees, up to my stricken expression.

"What happened?" his voice is hard.

I shake my head, my throat burns. I look at the closed door, try not to picture what's happening behind it.

"How long? How long has this been going on?"

From inside the room, the very loud, finishing cries of a spectacular orgasm ring out.

Dean looks between the door and then to me.

I see the moment his eyes light with understanding. I see the second he realizes that I know.

Then I watch as he decides whether or not to lie to me.

"Tell me," I say, even though I really, really don't want to know.

"Months," he finally says.

His eyes fill with regret as soon as he says it.

My legs go weak and it's the biggest struggle of my life to stay upright.

"I'm sorry," he says, and by the pain and sorrow in his eyes, I know he means it.

I shake my head. He isn't the one who should be apologizing.

Months.

Jace has been having sex with other women for *months*.

The times when he said he was out rehearsing, hanging out with his brothers, staying out with Dean to work on a new song, was he actually...not?

"He's been having sex with other women for months?" I ask.

Dean looks down at the floor, refusing to meet my eyes.

The urge to leave scalds me, burning with insistence. I've been battered, bruised, betrayed. The pain is so deep and sharp, like needle-teeth gnawing at my soul, that I know, I'm going to break apart and not be able to pick myself back up again. Unless I go. I have to go right now.

The taste of ashes fills my mouth. Does grief taste like ashes? Or is that what it tastes like when someone's love for you dies?

I step forward. Dean meets my eyes.

I want to run into the hotel room, claw at Jace, scream at him, crumple into a ball at his feet and beg. I want to fall apart and have him catch all my pieces and help me stitch myself back together again.

But I don't. Instead I ask Dean for a favor.

"Please. Tell Jace I said..." goodbye? No. Not goodbye. I don't know how I was so wrong. So wrong about everything. I can't love another person that doesn't love me back. I can't do that to myself again. I can't sit on a park bench in the dark, waiting for him for the rest of my life. I can't. "Never mind. Just tell him...congratulations. I'm happy for him, and I think he doesn't need me anymore."

I consider taking off my ring, giving it to Dean to give back to Jace, but I can't. I need something to remind me of how it felt to be loved, at least for a little while.

"Where are you going?" Dean asks as I walk down the hall.

I'm keeping myself upright by sheer iron will.

I don't turn around as I say, "Home. Back to my life. Sorry, I'm taking the car. I hope you understand."

"Sure," he calls after me. "Andi, I'm sorry."

Then I'm out in the parking lot, out in the deep three o'clock night. The darkest, most horrible time of night.

I get into the car, I turn over the engine, and I drive north.

Back toward New York City.

I don't turn on the radio.

29

JACE

WHEN I WALK DOWN THE LONG HALL LOOKING FOR ANDI, I
don't find her. Instead I find Dallas slamming his fist into
the bloody face of flailing bald man.

Dallas's muscles bulge, his shoulders bunch, and he
crouches before snapping his fist and hitting the man
again. The bald man's head snaps to the side.

Dallas is in a rage.

He reminds me of a bull when he gets like this. He
told me once that he sees red when he gets angry. It coats
his vision and then he can't think anymore, he just has
to hit.

The first time it happened was when he saved River.
The next time, he was locked up. He fought a lot there.
He says he fought then he went into solitary confinement,
then when he got out he fought again. It was a cycle for

years. But I haven't seen him this worked up in a long, long time.

"Dallas," I say, standing far enough back so that if he turns around swinging, I won't get knocked flat.

The man's eyes flash to me. He's angry. His goatee is covered in blood and half his face is already purple.

There are two other guys, just as bald and just as big on the floor. They're moving fine, watching Dallas, so I know they're staying down so they don't attract his attention.

Like I said, he's just like a bull.

Dallas snaps his head toward me.

He's breathing hard, his muscles are flexed, and his black tattoos are stark against his skin. They flare menacingly over his sweaty muscles.

"What's going on?" I ask.

He shakes himself off, sweat flinging. His eyes, a little crazy, filled with adrenaline and heat, grab onto me. He rolls his shoulders, then jerks his head to the side, popping his neck.

The bald guy thrusts his hand against the wall to stay upright and spits onto the carpet.

I hold up my hands. "We should go."

The last thing we need is Dallas getting in trouble with the police. Dean is going to lose it. We get a producer interested and the next minute our drummer is in court? No thank you.

"Come on," I say, nodding back down the hall.

Dallas nods at me. He has a bruise forming under his right eye. I can't tell if his knuckles are busted up or if all that blood is from the other guys.

When Dallas starts to walk away, the bald guy behind

him jerks upright and lifts his fists like he's going to punch Dallas in the back of the neck.

I lunge forward and sucker punch him.

He goes boneless, like a puppet whose strings are cut, and collapses to the ground.

I shake out my fist, my hand stinging.

"Are we good?" I ask the three guys on the ground. "Are we good now?"

One of the guys has thick black tattoos around his neck. When I ask, he spits on the ground.

"They went after Andi," Dallas says, his voice tight and enraged.

My heart stops.

Cold dread hits me.

Fear and anger claw at me.

"What?"

"I had to keep my cool. I had to count to ten. Or else I would've killed them."

He would've. I know he would've. Dallas isn't like the rest of us. He doesn't have brakes.

Hell. Right now I don't have brakes. My chest burns, my blood is singeing my veins. I clench my fists. Dallas might not kill them. But I will.

"What happened?"

Dallas puts his hand on my arm. I shove him off.

"What happened?"

The man with the goatee climbs to his knees, starts to stand. "She's trash. She wanted it. She got on her knees and begged for—"

I kick him. He flies back.

I go after him. Whatever Dallas did wasn't enough. I'm going to—

Dallas grabs me, holds me back.

I fight him, struggle to get at them, but Dallas shakes me, and says, "It's taken care of. Go get Andi."

I stop.

Andi.

The fight goes out of me. Now the only fight I have is the one to get to her. Make sure she's okay.

"Where is she?"

Dallas jerks his head back toward the rooms.

He lets me go and I sprint down the hall, back to the rooms. Dean's there, leaning against the wall, his head buried in his hands.

"Where's Andi?"

I realize how harsh and guttural my voice is when Dean's head snaps up.

He looks drawn out and pale, but when he sees me he straightens. "What happened to your hand?"

I clench my fist. "Never mind."

I shove past him, go to open my room door.

But before I can, it opens, and there's River, pulling a woman out behind him. He's got that satisfied, just-had-some-loving look on his face. I don't have time for it.

"What. Are. You. Doing."

River frowns at me, then pushes the woman off with a smoldering look and a smirk.

He turns and holds out my keycard. "Hey. My room's occupied with the party. I didn't think you'd mind."

I shake my head. I have no words. "Stay out of my room. Don't do that again."

He has no shame.

"I have a fiancée," I say.

Dean pushes off the wall. "No. You don't."

He looks at me with determination, but also pity. Was she hurt? Did she...did those men...

"Where is she?" I ask.

I shove past River, flip on the lights and stalk into the hotel room.

Her suitcase is still here, set next to mine at the foot of the bed. The cookstove is still set up on the vanity countertop, a loaf of bread next to it. Her pajamas are set out on the bed. I can still smell her strawberry shampoo.

Dean stands in the entry watching me with the same exact expression he had when he told me about Mom and Dad.

There's pity, and steely determination, and sorrow.

I shake my head.

Shove past him into the hall, down to the party. River stares between us, confused.

"Something up?" he asks.

"She left," Dean calls after me.

I keep walking down the hall.

"She said to tell you that you were right. She wants to go back to her life in New York. To her family."

The words stab me in the back, hard punches to the spine, and I bend forward, pained.

I don't believe him.

I don't believe it.

She wouldn't leave without seeing me.

Even if...even if she was scared or hurt by those men. She wouldn't.

I barge into the party, push through the crowd, search for her. She's not here.

Pauly's there though, in the corner, nursing a beer.

"Have you seen Andi?" I ask him.

He stares at me, eyes wide, his lips pinching until they turn white.

"She was trying to find you," he whispers. He flinches

when he sees my expression, like I'm making him nervous. "She was upset. I told her to wait here. But she didn't."

"She left," Dean says. He's there again. "I told you. She said to tell you congratulations, that you didn't need her anymore, and she was going home. She took the car."

I swing to face him. "She what?"

"She took the car. She's gone. I told you. I told you she was a crutch. I told you—"

"Give me your keys," I say to Pauly.

I hold out my hand. His eyes dart between me and Dean.

River stands there, frowning at us all. "Andi left? Why would she do that?"

I shake my head. "She wouldn't. Something's wrong. Give me your keys."

Pauly hesitates, looking at Dean for approval.

"He's not in charge," I say. "Pauly. Just give me your keys."

Finally, he shoves his hand into his pocket and holds out his motorcycle keys. They glint in the light.

"Thank you."

I grab them, then say to Dean, "Dallas is down the hall, beating on three guys. You might want to take care of that. I'll be back with Andi. Then we should go."

Dean gives me a hard look and shakes his head.

But River is already heading toward the door. "Dallas got in a fight without me? Why would he do that? He knows—"

Then River's out the door.

"Go get her," Pauly says. "I like her."

Dean just sighs.

I run out the door, down the hall, and into the parking lot.

Our car is gone. Andi's gone.

Pauly's motorcycle gleams blood red under the streetlight.

I hop on, crank the ignition and rev the motor. It roars to life, a deep, guttural sound that tears through me.

Pauly used to let me race his bike down Second Avenue, speeding through the lights and weaving through cars. I was the only one he let ride it. Probably because he thought I was the most responsible and least likely to get in trouble.

Whatever the reason, I'm glad I know how to ride.

I throttle forward, gravel kicking up behind the wheels. The roar of the bike echoes over the deserted lot.

If Andi's going home, then she's heading north, toward the highway.

I can catch her though.

Stop her.

Hold her and ask her if she's okay.

She can't leave. It's not fathomable. I can't imagine a world where we aren't together.

It can't happen.

The motorcycle flies after her and I urge it on, faster, faster.

The wind claws at me, like it's trying to strip my skin from my bones, tugging at me and howling in my ears.

I clutch the handlebars and lean forward, fitting myself to the curve of the bike.

Faster.

Faster.

The bike growls beneath me as we dive over the hills

drenched in fog. The hills rise out of the mist like the back of a giant alien creature shrouded in darkness.

I throttle over the undulating hills. My stomach dipping, my heart speeding, my hands clenching the handlebars.

Please.

Let me find her.

Let me make sure she's okay.

Behind me, two headlights peak over the hill, the bright lights shining in my mirrors. I squint at the fog-swamped road, momentarily blinded by the light. The pick-up truck roars closer, riding my tail.

I pick up speed.

Check my mirrors.

When I look back up, a deer stands in the road.

It's huge. Giant antlers. Thick shoulders. Wide back.

And it's not moving.

It stares at me with flashing, shining eyes.

I don't have time to stop.

I don't have time to swerve around it.

I don't have—

The front tire of the bike slams into the deer.

There's a crack, a jerk, the bike skids, jolts to the side, I'm thrown, I flip over the handlebars, hit the antlers, then—

The pick-up truck.

They can't stop.

There's shrieking.

Glass breaking.

Metal twisting.

Deer.

Motorcycle.

The raging screaming noise is a terrible thunderous discord.

The smell of burning tires. Hot metal. Blood.

I'm in the air, thrust up over the deer, and then, I'm falling back down.

It takes only a breath, but lasts an eternity.

My arms and legs splay out, like a dancer twisting in the air, my spine bending.

As I fall, I see the pickup truck.

It's blue. The grill is large, metal.

The paint is dirty, scratched and covered in dried mud.

The window is splotched with dried bugs and dirt.

Two men sit inside.

They open their mouths to shout.

Time speeds up again.

I crash into the front end of the truck.

My right leg hits the grill.

Pain.

Life-ending pain.

An excruciating snap ricochets through me, agony devours me.

I scream.

Then I'm flying again, my leg twisting, my spine arching, and I slam into the pavement.

I was wrong, it wasn't the wind that wanted to tear the skin from my bones, it was the gravel.

Finally, I stop.

The discordant metal twisting music stops.

The sound stops.

The moving stops.

The only thing that doesn't stop is the pain.

My leg. It's...I reach down...I can't finish the thought.

The fog closes around me. I can't breathe. I can't hear. I can't see.

Then, there's a man. The driver.

He shoves his face close.

Through the mist I make out a beard, a hat, hard, cold eyes.

"Is he dead?" the second man asks.

His voice is far away, down a deep, yawning tunnel.

"Not yet," the driver says.

I try to lift my head.

Can't.

I try to speak.

Andi.

Andi.

I need.

Andi.

"Put him in the truck bed," the second man says, his voice far away. "Pick him up. Put him in the bed. I'll take care of it."

Take care of it?

Are they going to dump me somewhere? Is this a hit and run, but the run part includes dragging me into the woods and tossing me in a ditch?

The driver grunts.

Leans down and grips me under the arms.

Lifts me.

The pain.

The blazing, hot, killing agony.

I scream.

Dark, skeleton-fingered fog consumes me.

I dive, headfirst, into a drilling, killing screaming void.

And then, in a starburst of white, the pain, the world, and even Andi, are gone.

30

ANDI

I DON'T REMEMBER DRIVING THROUGH THE SOUTHERN states.

They pass in a numb, blue-green wave full of semi-trucks, wide highways, and sun glare. There was a gas station, maybe two, and eventually the still green south blurred into blue mountains jutting like painful scabs from the earth covered in bare, empty-handed trees. The trees had tossed all their leaves down and left themselves naked to the cold winter wind.

At some point, I found my fingers numb and my nose stinging, so I flipped on the heater.

Beyond that, hours and hours pass without me knowing how I got from Jace all the way to...here.

Because when I finally emerge from the numb hypnotic gray line of the highway north, I find myself in New Jersey.

I drove for miles and miles. And now, almost a whole country separates us.

The sky is lead gray, pressing down forlornly on the barren industrial towns that line the border of New York. As far as I can see, squat gray factories, abandoned mills, and graffitied warehouses line the highway.

Parking lots with tall barbed wire fences guard abandoned lots creeping with grass and winter-red poison ivy. The shift from the green, still-warm south, to the frost-covered, dead-brown north jars me out of the haze of grief that had wrapped me tight in its hard embrace.

Far in the distance, I can just make out the jutting skyscrapers of New York. They spear out of the flat land, a monument to man, reaching high for what he wants but can't have.

No matter how much you build something, or someone, up you'll never reach heaven.

I know that now.

The buildings stand in defiance to the heavy gray sky, straining up against it. And there, brightest of them all, is the Tower—home.

My chest wrenches, my heart clenching, and my hands shake on the steering wheel.

The traffic is thick. Plenty of people are heading toward the city, setting their dreams on that vision ahead.

And I don't...I don't want to go back.

The old beater car grumbles along the road, the wheel shaking as I push sixty-five miles an hour. In the air coming from the heater the old perfume of the city, metal, exhaust and treeless sky fills the car.

I don't...

Maybe I made a mistake.

Maybe Jace...

I blink.

Maybe it wasn't Jace.

He and River are the same height. The same build.

So many people say they could be twins.

I never saw it because I knew Jace before he grew to the same height as River. Plus, Jace is Jace. They move differently, they act differently, they smile differently. But from behind, in the dark, when I was crying and scared and shocked from what had just happened...maybe...

Maybe it wasn't Jace.

Maybe...Dean lied.

I shake my head.

Why would he lie?

But why would Jace cheat?

He wouldn't.

I cling to that hope, like a tree clinging to its last leaf in winter.

The air is cold, the frost is biting, the snow is coming, but I'm still clinging to that one leafy hope.

I let out a shuddering breath. I have to call him. I have to ask.

I turn on my blinker, signal, merge onto an exit lane and pull into the first parking lot I see, a fast food place pumping out scents of fries and burgers.

It's dinner time after all.

I reach into my purse and pull out my phone.

It's the cheap pre-pay phone Jace and I bought at a gas station after I gave my old one back to my parents.

I step out of the car and shiver at the biting cold wind. It's only weeks until Christmas, of course it's cold in Jersey.

But the cold does its job. It thrusts me into wakefulness.

My hands shake as I hit Jace's number.

I hold the phone to my ear.

My heart gallops and each time the ring sounds I feel as if I might throw up.

It rings.

And rings.

And rings.

He doesn't pick up.

I sag against the metal of the car and close my eyes as his voicemail picks up.

"Jace here. If I don't answer, it's because I'm making music. Leave a message."

My throat is raw and aching at the sound of his voice. I didn't know that I could miss it so much after only a few hours.

Except, that makes me realize, if Jace hadn't done anything, he would've called. He would've texted. He wouldn't have just ghosted me.

"Jace, it's me," I begin, my voice scratchy and hollow. "I guess you know I left. But..." I clench my hand, bury my nails in the palm of my hand. "Jace, tell me that wasn't you. Tell me..."

I hang up.

Let out a shuddering breath.

The smell of French fries and burgers is making my stomach churn.

I dial his number again. It's not late enough for him to be playing their next gig yet. He should answer.

It rings.

And rings.

And rings.

His voicemail picks up again.

"Jace," I say. "Call me back. I need to know. I shouldn't have left without talking to you." I shake my head. "I...I need you to tell me. If it wasn't you, if..." I blink, watching the line of cars inch past toward the urban industrial sprawl. "I love you," I whisper, my voice breaking. "If it wasn't you, please let me know."

I hang up and let my head sink down, dropping my chin to my chest. I close my hand around my phone and will it to ring.

I realize now that I'd turn around. Any word from him and I'd turn around. Even if he admitted it was him but said he was sorry, I'd go back. That thought fills me with shame, because it shows how much I want to believe in his love, but there it is. Even if it hurts, I still want to be with him.

I kick at the ground, scattering pebbles over the pavement.

The parking lot is full of cars, the fast food restaurant busy with the evening rush. I'm just another person among dozens, stopping for a break from the day's long monotony.

I shake my head.

I should go.

He's not calling back.

My cheeks burn from the cold wind, the tip of my nose is numb, and I'm shivering from the gray weather. It doesn't matter.

My chest feels bruised and aching, like a heavy boulder is crushing me slowly. I rub at the ache, cold icing over it.

Before I go, I'll try one more thing.

The display of the phone glows blue in the dusky light. I tap in a short message.

Hey, I tried to call.

I wait, my breath held, my chest heavy.

Then, a message appears.

Yeah. I saw.

I stare at my phone display. The words don't make any sense. The letters blend together and spin on the screen. My eyes burn.

I wait for a minute but he doesn't send anything else.

So I take a painful breath and type: *I wanted to be sure it was really you I saw. Dean said you've been cheating for months but that isn't true, right?*

I hit send before I can think about how desperate I sound.

My dad would throw a fit. I'm basically inviting him to lie to me.

It takes three minutes of standing in the cold, exhaust and fried food-perfumed air, before Jace writes back.

It was me.

I stare at my phone. My hands ache from how tightly I'm clutching it.

And my heart, it breaks, like a vase hitting the floor and shattering into a thousand pieces.

The damage is irreparable.

I turn, run to the curb of the parking lot, and vomit into the grass.

There wasn't much in my stomach, but anything left comes up between sobs and gagging and heaving pain.

I clutch my stomach until even the dry heaving has passed. Then I wipe my eyes, prickling with tears, and stand back up.

There's another message on my phone.

I never loved you, Andi. I felt sorry for you. You should stay in New York. I don't want you.

I can't stop myself. I type: *No. You said you would always love me.*

He writes back. *Your definition of always was different than mine.*

I squat down to the asphalt, and wrap my hands around my bruised knees. I lean back against the nearly bald car tire and cry.

The tears leak out of my eyes, running like a river, down my cheeks, onto my dress, onto the cold, gray pavement.

It hurts. My heart hurts.

I never knew that you could feel your heart break. But when I press on my chest, it aches, it hurts more than anything has ever hurt before.

I stare at the message.

I never loved you, Andi.

I never loved you, Andi.

The tears keep running, running, like a part of me is trying to find its way back to him.

But then, they stop.

The sky is dark now.

In the distance, New York is lit up, glowing like a bright beacon in the dark.

"I'm not Andi," I say, broken and alone.

I'm not Andi anymore.

Andi was a naïve girl who still believed in love.

She's gone.

She's dead.

When I stand up, I pull from deep inside me, someone I didn't think I'd ever have to be again. I dust her off, put the cold mask back on, push back my shoulders, lift my chin, and look toward the city.

I'm going home.

Before I drive toward the lights in the distance, I send a final text.

You're right. I belong in New York. I want money. I want power. I don't want you. I never loved you.

And then, because no matter what I say, I still love him and I know I always will, I send: *Write me a lyric someday. Be happy, Jace.*

It's done.

Over.

Then before I pull out of the parking lot, I put the phone under the car tire, and run it over, smashing my past into tiny fragmented bits.

It's done now.

By the time I step into the cold white marble lobby of the Tower, my eyes are dry, my heart is numb, and I don't think I'll ever smile again.

The elevator doors open to my family's living room.

Dad's there.

Mom too.

Rob Jr and Elliot.

I step forward, my head high, my spine straight.

Mom gasps, her hand going to her mouth, her ice-blue eyes startled and...disappointed. After all, she didn't want me to come back. She stands, her long gold dress falling around her in a waterfall of silk fabric.

It looks like I interrupted cocktails. They're all dressed in formal wear, probably back from a late-night charity event.

Rob Jr sighs, sloshing around the olive in his martini. "Oh joy. The prodigal daughter returns."

Elliot tugs on the sleeves of his tux and scowls at me from beneath thick black eyebrows.

My dad stands, red-faced and hard-jawed, and walks across the marble floor. I'm straight-backed and full of crumpled pride as I wait for his judgment.

His sharp searching eyes take in my bruised knees, my dirt-stained legs, my gritty dress, and my cold, unyielding expression.

At last he bares his teeth and says, "Welcome home, Andrea."

31

JACE

I WAKE UP TO PAIN.

It coats me in oily slickness, seeping into my pores and my bones. Even through the numbness I can feel the pain.

Pain over numbness.

I smell the tint of chemicals, bitter medicine, and Dean's cologne. I can smell Dean.

He's here then.

Maybe he's dead too.

There's rhythmic beeping, the television with the volume on low, I can barely make out the jingle of an advertisement for a mattress factory.

Then I hear Dean, growling, "I'll sleep when he wakes up."

"You've been awake for forty hours." That's River. He's

using the voice he gets when he's trying to reason with Dean.

It never works though.

I let out a sigh. I'm tired. Everything hurts.

I squint my eyes open and blink at the harsh fluorescent light.

Not dead then.

The white-walled cramped room is too sterile for death.

There are monitors, wires, tubes, an uncomfortable plastic-sided bed.

I'm in a hospital.

But... "You should sleep," I tell Dean.

He looks awful. Haggard and drawn.

My voice is scratchy and painful.

River and Dean turn as one.

They stare at me.

Then River's face crumples, his shoulders shake and he lets a loud, raw sob.

"Jace. Damnit. You're okay? You're okay."

He grabs my arm and shakes me, repeating "You're okay, you're okay."

"Stop shaking me. It hurts," I say.

I'm watching Dean. His face drains of color and he's looking at me like he didn't think I was going to make it.

And I finally see what I never recognized before. When Mom and Dad died, Dean never cried. Never. And he's not crying now. River's bawling like a baby, but Dean is just staring at me. He's staring like he's never cared about anyone as much as he cares about me, and he was so, so scared that I was gone.

He's been terrified all these years that he was going to lose one of us too.

Me. River. He's our big brother and he took on keeping us safe.

"I'm here," I tell him. "I'm okay."

He swallows and nods. "Good." His voice is thick with the tears he'll never shed. "Good."

Then I hear a cough and a sniff and turn to find Dallas and Pauly standing on the other side of my bed.

Dallas grins at me. "All your good looks are gone now, my man."

I don't know what he's talking about, but I don't really care. I'm alive. The men in the truck didn't toss me in a ditch, they must've brought me to the hospital.

Now I can find Andi.

She never cared what I looked like, she was too busy looking at my heart to bother with my appearance.

Pauly's shaking, his shoulders are turned down, and his mouth is pinched into a thin line.

"Awww, don't worry, Pauly. I'll get you a new bike," I say.

At that, River cuffs me.

I wince. "That hurt."

"I'll get the doctor," River says.

I lift my hand. "Wait. Where's Andi?" I ask. "How long have I been out? What happened? Did she come back? Did—"

I cut off at the look on River's face.

Then I see Dean.

His jaw is tight, his eyes hard.

"What?"

Dean pulls my phone out of his pocket. "You were in surgery for sixteen hours. You've been in a medically induced coma for twenty-four. Your right leg was shattered. You had internal bleeding. The driver behind you brought you to the nearest hospital. You're lucky to be alive."

"What happened to Andi?" I ask, staring at my phone.

"You have stitches down your temple, on your lip. Abrasions on most of your body. They say you need more surgeries for your leg. They thought they might have to amputate, but... You'll have six months to a year of physical therapy before you'll walk—"

"Where. Is. Andi."

Dean and River share a look. Dread curls in my stomach and slithers through me, filling me with foreboding. Dean hands me my phone.

I open it.

My hands shake. They're covered in bruises, my fingers swollen. I can barely turn on the display.

There aren't any missed calls.

No voicemails.

It's been forty hours.

Forty.

Why hasn't she called?

But then, I see a text message.

Actually, two.

The message before them is from days ago, from when she was out shopping.

And after that...

I stare at my phone, my hand shaking.

The guys wait, their silence oppressive.

Their pity suffocating.

Andi: *You're right. I belong in New York. I want money. I want power. I don't want you. I never loved you.*

And after that: *Write me a lyric someday. Be happy, Jace.*

There's nothing else. Just that.

I shake my head, refuse to believe it. I hit dial on her

number. It goes to voicemail right away. I call again. And again. She doesn't answer.

My hands are too swollen, too shaky to send a text.

"I'm sorry," Dean says.

"I didn't see this coming," River says. "I really thought she loved you."

"It's my fault," Dallas says, his voice rough with grief.

Pauly pats his arm, offering comfort to the giant who usually looks out for him.

"It's better this way," Dean says quietly.

I look at him, the room swims around him, and the pain claws at me, dragging up my bones.

"She would've left eventually. Now you can heal. Concentrate on the music. The producer called, we have ourselves a record deal."

I stare at him blankly, the dread snaking in tendrils, wrapping around my bones and my lungs, squeezing out my breath. She's gone. She's not coming back.

"Get better," River says, gripping my arm gently. "Think you can sing without her?"

No.

Never.

But then I look at the faces of my brothers, at Pauly and Dallas, not brothers by blood, but brothers all the same.

You don't let your family down.

Ever.

She's gone.

"Yes," I tell them. "I'll do it. I'll do whatever it takes."

I'll get better. I'll play again. I'll stand on a stage in front of thousands and when I look out on the crowd, she won't be there, and it won't matter.

And if I have to picture her ghost there, my memory

of her, to force myself to sing, well, no one has to know that but me.

Dean reaches down and squeezes my shoulder. "Whatever it takes."

I nod. Then I wince.

"Are you in pain?" River asks.

My leg is a ball of fire. My ribs scream every time I breathe. My face is raw and aching.

"Yes," I say.

Although the pain that hurts the most isn't from the accident.

She left.

She left.

I have a lifetime left and she won't be in it.

A million nights stretch in front of me, yawning with empty, aching loneliness.

She left.

Write me a lyric, she said.

I never loved you.

A tear stings the raw skin on my face, scraping my flesh with salty abrasion. The stitches and staples bite at me when I move. There are a thousand layers of pain, thin slices piled on top of each other.

Another tear falls.

"I'll get the doctor," River says.

He runs out of the room, shouting for help.

They pump painkillers into my IV, sending a cold, metallic numbness shivering through my veins.

"You'll get better," Dean says, and I can't tell whether he's begging me or promising me. "You'll get better. It will be okay."

I don't know that it will.

I don't think so.

But before I drift off, I make a promise of my own.

"Whatever it takes. We'll play for the world. Whatever it takes."

Andi may never see me again, but come heaven or hell, I'll sing so hard and so long that every time she turns on the radio, she'll hear my voice.

And maybe, when she does, she'll wish she never left.

PART II

EIGHT YEARS LATER

32

ANDREA

I HOLD THE THIN STEM OF MY CRYSTAL CHAMPAGNE GLASS and consider the drop of condensation slipping down the sloping side.

There's a heart-shaped strawberry resting at the bottom surrounded by the fizz of the pink champagne. The tart-fruit smell perfumes the summer-humid air.

It's July in New York. It's that time when those who can afford to escape to the cool breezes of the Hamptons to watch polo matches, frolic on the beach, and spend time together being rich.

At least, that's how I see it.

The great cottage mansions that spread along the water's edge, with graceful lawns leading up from the shore, are built as a retreat for those wealthy enough to join in the flight from the sweltering city.

But this particular July, unlike all the others, we're still here.

The setting sun spreads its golden rays across the East River and over the spires of Manhattan. The light shines over the burnished metal of the Tower so that it looks as if the entire structure is a stream of melting gold falling from the heavens.

I can see the reflection of the molten gold tower in the opaque black windows of the bank across the avenue.

It happens at every sunset and is the exact effect my dad wanted when he commissioned the Tower.

Make it glisten like gold, he'd said.

Across the street, the black-windowed building reflects our light. It's the headquarters of the bank that denied my dad a loan when he first ventured into business forty years ago. Now, they have to crane their necks to look up at his golden dominance every day.

I lean my elbows on the bronze railing, and peer hundreds of meters down to the city street below.

The wide silk sleeves of my dress blow in the breeze and my dress balloons up, catching the wind and flickering and snapping against my legs. I brush at my long hair tangling over my face and let out a long sigh.

I'm on top of the world.

I have everything anyone could ever want.

I hold my half-empty glass carelessly and squint against the bright setting sun.

"More champagne?" A waiter, a tall gray-haired man in a black suit, holds a bottle out to me.

I tilt my head to him. "Yes."

I dip my glass and he fills it with fizzing liquid. Then I take a long, fortifying drink, letting the champagne bite at my throat.

The rooftop of the Tower is draped in gold silk and faux marble columns. The sun glints off the gold veins in the marble, and the breeze twists the silk drapes, fanning them like flagged parachutes.

The wide rooftop pool sparkles with turquoise brightness and I'm tempted to kick off my heels and dip my pinched toes into the cool water. But that would mean leaving the relative solitude of the far reaches of the roof and wading through dozens of partygoers.

We're hosting a fundraiser for one of my mom's pet charities—a summer art camp for gifted youth.

Yes, she could just write a check and be done with it, but my mom likes to host at least four fundraising events a year. In fact, she's quite famous for her charity parties, and invitations are coveted.

We delayed our summer trip to the Hamptons for this party.

There are one hundred and twenty-five people here, the crème de la crème, all dressed as their favorite piece of art.

That is what the invitation stated. Dress code: Come as your favorite artwork.

And since this was my mom's most anticipated event of the year, I let her commission my dress, even though she hasn't done so in years.

I shouldn't be surprised that she dressed me to impress.

I'm the queen in *The Accolade* by Edmund Leighton. She told me she chose the painting because I have the same color hair as the queen, and of course, because the artist shares our last name.

The dress is ivory silk, medieval in style, with puffed sleeves, a tight bust, and a skirt that trails over the floor like a white cloud. The silk is soft and runs over my skin like a cool river.

It's held in place by a replica girdle—a wide twenty-four karat gold belt of connected squares inlaid with winking rubies. The sleeves are held with gold arm cuffs and a matching gold and ruby necklace rests against my throat. Gold thread, hand-embroidered in the silk, patterns the skirt's train.

When I first put the dress on, I didn't have any words. I didn't recognize myself.

I looked soft, romantic, like a young woman that still believed in fairy tales. The soft white lines of the dress were enough to detract from my hard brown eyes and the straight slash of my mouth and instead brought out the dimple in my chin and the freckles on my nose. Making me look *innocent*.

I hated the dress on principle.

But I wore it anyway.

I put on the heavy gold crown, ringed with pearls, and placed it over my brushed out red-gold hair.

When Rob Jr saw me, with the replica sword in my hand, he smirked.

Rob's thirty-one now, and he's aged from a shorter, redder version of my dad, to a man with a smile that borders on cruel and a stance that says, *I know I am better than you and you do too.*

Elliot, on the other hand, has remained the same—still squinting at books, still my mom's favorite, still fighting to be my dad's favorite too.

When he saw me he said sardonically, "They'll love that, won't they?"

He meant everyone at the party.

When I came back to New York, all those years ago,

my mom told me something I'll never forget. Her eyes were grave and intent when she said, "The next time you decide to fall in love, use your head not your heart. The heart is a liar."

I agreed.

My heart has never done anything except make me fall in love with the wrong people.

So I scoured every soft feeling, every bit of sunshine, joy, or semblance of love, and I locked it tight, deep down inside.

Rob Jr once said that I was the coldest person he'd ever known. At the time he was wrong, but now, he's right.

I've not cared about anyone or anything in eight years.

Sometimes men will try to chat me up, they want to be the one to win Robert Leighton-Hughes's daughter. They'll try to flirt, or amuse, catching me at a gala or a charity event.

And when that happens I turn and walk away.

Words aren't needed.

I don't need love.

I don't need friends.

I just need...

My mind blanks.

I don't need anything.

Across the rooftop, guests wander through the displays, dropping checks into golden vases.

My mom hired models to pose behind life-size golden frames. They are the real-life replicas of the most-loved paintings of all time. The models have to stand still for four hours, the length of the party.

There are women dressed in costume replicating the

Mona Lisa, the *Girl With a Pearl Earring*, *Portrait of Madame X*, and *The Birth of Venus*.

I envy the woman standing as *The Birth of Venus*, she's practically nude, and probably a lot cooler than the rest of us.

There are models posing as couples too: *American Gothic*, *The Kiss*, more.

Laughter drifts over the rooftop, splashing into the music. My mom took a modern turn, and instead of hiring a string quartet, she brought on a DJ.

I squint through the sun glare at my mom and dad, dressed as Andy Warhol's Marilyn Monroe, and Andy Warhol himself.

I tip my head back and drain my glass of champagne, then set it on the stone ledge.

"That bad?"

I turn to see which man has bothered to venture away from the gaiety of the party to attempt a conversation with someone who is known to *never* converse. Or smile. Or laugh.

He's a knight. An actual knight.

His hair is burnished gold, longer now, so that it feathers around his ears and brushes over the back of his neck.

His face is broader than it once was, his stubble darker, and his mouth has a sardonic, self-aware twist.

His shoulders are broad, his skin deeply tanned and his blue-green eyes full of a turbulent longing for some lost joy. It has to be a ruse—this man hasn't longed for anything in his entire life.

He's had twenty-six years of privilege and wealth. The favored son.

All the same, he looks like a fallen angel beseeching a

forsaken heaven. A deep red surcoat covers finely meshed chain mail, and a gold belt encrusted with pearls cinches around his waist.

I take him in.

Recognize that he's the other half of my painting.

He's the knight kneeling before the queen, pledging subservience and loyalty in *The Accolade*.

He's the Lancelot to my Guinevere.

My other half.

Across the rooftop I spy my mom watching us, her face carefully neutral.

Fall in love with your mind not your heart.

Right.

I haven't seen him in nearly nine years. His appearance has changed, but I doubt his character has.

But instead of walking away, something urges me to stay. It's like a pinprick needling at me, poking me and prodding me to engage.

After all, he's the only person I've seen in the past eight years who knew Jace too.

And apparently, I haven't totally eradicated every bit of yearning in my heart because I dip my chin and say, "Hello Reid."

33

ANDREA

REID SMILES AT ME.

His eyes lose that turbulent yearning and instead fill with sardonic mirth. The gold reflection of the Tower glints off of his armor and lights his hair so that he looks as if he's been illuminated by heaven itself.

"Hello Andrea," he says, and his voice has a gravelly edge that wasn't there when I last spoke to him.

In fact, a lot has changed. Nine years is a long time.

He's a little taller, a little wider, and if I cared about this sort of thing, a lot more beautiful. But with Reid, his beautiful golden exterior hides a black heart.

But at my expression his smile widens, it's lopsided and lifts more on the right. It's a smile that says, *I've just done something wildly fun, and any minute now, I'm going to do something wildly fun again.* It's a smile that would make anyone want to join him.

So instead of walking across the rooftop to the sushi chef constructing edible pieces of art to order, or grabbing an artisanal cocktail at the bar, I stay and stare coolly at my unwanted knight.

"I see my mother contacted you."

The breeze rustles Reid's hair, sending the modern scent of mint shampoo my way. I lean back, putting more distance between us.

Reid's smile turns careful and guarded. "Actually no."

I wait for him to elaborate. I'm not in any hurry. The party will last for hours more and I'm here to be seen.

That's the deal.

If I want to stay a Leighton-Hughes then I act like a Leighton-Hughes.

Always.

And I do. I put on this role so tightly, that even when I'm alone I don't smile, I don't laugh, I don't dream.

"I asked her what painting you were dressing for," he finally says, his gravelly voice scraping across me.

"Why?"

He draws in a long breath and considers me, as if he's weighing what answer to give.

"I heard about you. While I was in Paris."

That's right. I'd forgotten. After Yale, Reid left to head up his family's holdings in Paris. I never saw him after he went to Yale, and then he left the country, not even coming home for holidays. Apparently, he worked like a dog trying to prove himself worthy of the Shilling name.

Last Christmas my dad mentioned him in passing, saying how impressed he was with the heir to his competitor's business. It was a jab at my brothers that didn't go unnoticed.

"Men spoke of a beautiful woman in New York,

heiress to a fortune, who was so ice cold, so condescending and unfeeling, that not even the promise of millions of dollars could entice a man to want her."

Ah.

That's not anything I haven't heard before, I just didn't realize they were repeating the tale all the way across the Atlantic.

I slide ice into my gaze and say to Reid, "I'd wondered if you were still the same arrogant prick you used to be. It appears you are."

The right side of his mouth lifts in a smile. "And I'd wondered if you were still the same haughty princess from the Tower. I suppose I have my answer."

We stare at each other, and the image of the knight kneeling before the queen flashes in my mind, and I almost smile at the irony.

"I thought knights were chivalrous."

Reid smiles at me, then leans forward and whispers, "I'm not actually a knight."

There it is again, that smile that is part invitation, part promise of fun. I ignore it.

"I'm surprised you went to the trouble of calling my mother, seeking me out, all to see if I was still the same girl you knew all those years ago. I could've saved you the trouble. I'm not."

"That's a shame. I liked that girl."

Across the rooftop, a raucous laugh rings out, and I see at Rob Jr's urging, the Venus has taken her clam shell and climbed into the pool.

Reid doesn't turn to look, instead he studies me with searching eyes, a sheen of sweat coating his forehead. I imagine he's uncomfortably hot in all that chainmail.

But whose fault is that?

He's the one who wanted to meet me again.

"What do you want, Reid?" I ask, suddenly tired of the charade.

Then, across the rooftop, the DJ plays a new song. The sound weaves through the crowd, carrying on the wind, floating to me.

Apparently, my mom didn't tell the DJ that The Morgan Brothers are anathema to the Leighton-Hugheses.

The lyrics are crystal clear, Jace's velvet smooth tenor rolls over me, "*Marry me,*" he sings, "*Marry me.*"

He always intrudes when I least expect it.

In a coffee shop over the sound system, in an advertisement on TV, on a stranger's ringtone, during a movie. Every time I hear him, I'm frozen all over again, teetering between the pain of staying or the sorrow of letting go.

Somehow, even after eight years, his words still manage to sink into me, tug at the heart I buried long ago, and try to make me feel.

He gave me a thousand dreams and shattered every one.

"I see," Reid says, his voice soft. "I wondered."

I blink and try to pretend that the velvet warm tones of Jace's voice aren't affecting me at all. Haven't I been pretending this exact thing for years? My family is fooled. The whole world is fooled.

They say love fades. It doesn't. Pain does. But love doesn't.

That's why if you don't want to feel it you have to bury it impossibly deep inside. So that even a song written for you can't make you feel again.

I don't bother telling Reid that I don't know what he

means. He's too perceptive for that. He's smart and he watches people, he always has.

"You disappeared after graduation," he murmurs, and he's so quiet I have to lean closer to hear him. "Your family said it was an extended holiday. But then...I knew how you felt about him."

I take in a sharp breath, not wanting Reid to say his name.

He doesn't.

Thank goodness.

"A year ago, I met Elliot for drinks when he came to Paris on a business trip. He doesn't handle his liquor well. He told me this crazy story about you running off to marry some rockstar when you were eighteen. He claimed it's the only mistake you've ever made. I didn't quite believe him. But now..."

He shakes his head and I turn away because I don't want to see any pity in his eyes.

"What happened to you, Andrea?" His voice is soft, and stupidly concerned.

"Nothing," I say. "Nothing happened."

I know he sees the lie as clearly as if it were painted in front of us.

"What do you want, Reid?" I ask again.

He pushes his hair back off his head, mussed by the wind, and levels his gaze on me. "I want to see you smile. You used to be fire, not ice."

"No," I say automatically.

He nods, like he expected this.

The sun is down now, the rays of molten gold have vanished and left the trembling gray of dusk. Jace's song is fading, ending with a promise of always. Always to give his love.

"Then I'd like to take you to lunch tomorrow."

"No," I say. "I'm not interested."

"And if I say please?"

"I'm still not interested."

He rubs his hand over his stubble-covered chin and studies me for a long moment. He reminds me of one of the men that sits at the chess tables in the park, studying the board, weighing their next move.

"What if I promised you that all I want is one lunch with you? Just one. And if you're not interested in more, then I'll not bother you again. Ever."

"Why?"

"Because I need you," he says, and when I give him a disbelieving stare he says, "I need your help."

Jace's song finishes, the notes fading with the light. The sleeping, feeling thing that had perked up and opened its eyes at his voice curls up and falls back asleep.

Reid studies me as if he knows exactly what I'm feeling and he empathizes.

He's always been good at maneuvering people to do what he wants though.

"Please," he says, his voice rough.

I stare at him. I didn't think he'd actually say it. I doubt he's ever said *please* in his entire life.

"I don't know," I tell him. "I have to think about it."

His shoulders fall, and I'm not certain whether it's with disappointment or relief. "Don't think too long," he says. "I don't have a lot of time."

With that he gives me a tight smile and then walks away, leaving me to stand in solitude at the top of my Tower.

34

ANDREA

THE LONG BREAKFAST TABLE IS FILLED WITH STEAMY SWEET brioche, chocolate babka spiraling with paper-thin pastry and thick melting chocolate, and crepes rolled tight with strawberries and icing sugar.

I wrap my hands around my mug of scalding black coffee and let the heat sink into my fingers.

You used to be fire, not ice.

As if to emphasize his words, my hands are cold, even when they're wrapped around the warmth of a mug of steaming coffee.

I take a sip of the bitter black drink and gaze across the table at my family.

We're in the wide, window-surrounded dining room of the Tower. The ceiling soars high, the floor-to-ceiling windows show a hazy washed-out blue morning, and the chandelier sprays light over the white-tablecloth breakfast.

It's Saturday, a workday.

And even though we are all grown, living in our own apartments—Rob Jr in Tribeca, Elliot in the Upper East Side, me in a starkly bare modern space in Midtown—we gather every morning for family breakfast.

My dad is in his late sixties now, and his red hair, which was once his prominent distinction, has lost its fiery sheen and faded to a translucent dirty orange. His barrel chest still stretches out, but he's lost the muscle in his arms and legs, they're thinner, bony, like chopsticks holding up a wide piece of orange salmon. That doesn't mean he's gone soft though. If anything, he's harder, wilier, and more bent on winning than ever.

He loves the game of business and money is the scorecard.

"Updates on the Carraway project," he says in that rapid-fire, gruff way he has.

I set down my mug while Rob Jr and Elliot turn to me. My mom doesn't bother to look my way. She's nursing her matcha and spirulina smoothie, recovering from yesterday's party.

But me, I'm wide awake and have been since five in the morning. I expect my brothers and my dad were up even earlier.

"There is an issue with the title work," I say, speaking in the direct, monotone manner my dad prefers when reporting on business matters. "An eight-foot strip of land between the parcels was detached from the original title in 1957. It was never properly assigned to the neighboring parcel. The title is a mess. There is no adequate documentation. The city is refusing permits because ownership cannot be verified via title. I'm—"

"Did you call the assessor?" my dad interrupts.

"Yes. I'm working on it. I have legal, the surveyor, the assessor—"

"Good. Fix it."

"I will."

He nods. And the conversation is done.

Rob Jr and Elliot had been watching with interest, but when they realized there wasn't any chance of me losing the deal or messing up, they went back to their babka and brioche.

This is what I do.

I went to Columbia after I returned to the city, graduated with honors, then went on to manage development projects.

My dad started me on small projects, and then when he saw that I worked eighteen-hour days with a single-mindedness and cunning dispassion that matched his own, he gradually moved me onto larger and larger projects.

Four years after I began, I'm producing multi-million-dollar deals and bringing in more income than Elliot and Rob Jr combined.

It's not exactly a fair comparison though since Rob Jr is CFO of Dad's hotel brand and Elliot is VP at the tech firm. They don't bring in income, per se. But still, the knowledge burns them, and Rob Jr especially is waiting for me to stumble. Again.

Suddenly, my mom looks up from her smoothie and gives me a startled look, as if she's only now realizing that there are other people in the room.

She blinks and then takes in my appearance.

I don't want to admit it, but I took my time dressing today. I put on a red dress, it's shorter, tighter, and I wore it because, of course, I wanted to prove to myself that I'm not completely dead inside, that there is still fire burning in me.

By the stunned, intent look on my mom's face, I guess I haven't looked this *alive* in a long time.

I even went by the salon downstairs. They put my thick hair in an elaborate twist. It's shining and soft-looking and I *almost* took it out as soon as I saw it. Then the make-up artist put on fire-engine-red lipstick to match my dress, and I decided to leave it all.

I did look alive. I looked like fire.

It doesn't matter if I still feel like ashes on the inside. It's how I look that matters.

Because I decided in the early hours of this morning, as I tossed and turned in bed, that I am meeting Reid.

I am.

"You spoke with Reid yesterday," my mom murmurs.

She always speaks softly, and most people say she does it on purpose, so that you have to lean close and listen intently to *only* her. They don't mind though, my mom is so beautiful that most people want to lean closer.

Rob Jr stops tearing at his babka and shoots me a surprised look. "Reid Shilling?"

Even my dad sits back at that and waits for my answer.

"I did."

I don't say anything more, instead I reach for a strawberry crepe.

"What did he want?" my dad asks, leaning forward, like instead of coffee he smells scheming.

I put the crepe in my mouth, letting the tart sweetness

of the strawberry linger on my tongue before swallowing. Then I pat my mouth with my cloth napkin.

"He wants to take me to lunch."

Elliot drops his coffee cup to his saucer, making a loud clattering sound. "He's after you. If he marries you, he'll expect—"

He stops then.

I watch as everyone travels down the same mental road. Reid's father is Dad's competitor in real estate and development. Reid is already shooting past his father in terms of reputation in the European market. If Reid somehow manages to seduce me and marry me, then he'll want to take over Dad's real estate ventures after dad retires.

Suddenly, my brothers don't just have an upstart sister to worry about, they have a potential brother-in-law to fear.

My dad rubs his silver-stubbled chin, his eyes darting around the table. He's always enjoyed a good fight for dominance.

I push my plate away, leaving the rest of my crepe. I'm not hungry anymore.

Then I ask, "What makes you think, Elliot, that I'm not the one after him?"

Elliot slumps his shoulders and stares mournfully at his coffee.

Rob Jr shakes his head and I can practically hear what he's thinking, *my word, she's so cold.*

My mom gives me a considering look as I stand and push back from the table.

It's time to head to my office. Then lunch.

"Have fun," my dad calls after me.

Which means, of course, that I have his blessing to marry or to screw over Reid Shilling. Whichever is more fun.

35

ANDREA

REID ARRIVES EARLY. HE'S AT MY OFFICE AT ELEVEN, JUST
as I'm finishing up a call with legal.

He stands in the doorway, leaning casually against the
doorframe, his arms crossed and a small, patient smile on
his face.

"Call me when you know," I say, hanging up the
phone.

I take a moment to study Reid.

He has a long-limbed gracefulness, an appearance of
self-awareness that most people would find attractive,
and a strong, masculine face that makes him look wiser
and older than his twenty-six years.

I imagine Reid uses his appearance to his advantage
in both business and his personal life. He's never been
one to let any advantage go to waste.

As I stand, pressing my hands to my desk, his

eyebrows rise at my red dress and I feel a flare of satisfaction.

See? I'm not dead inside. I'm not ice. Thank you very much.

He recovers quickly and pushes off the doorframe, walking forward with an assured stride.

"I hope I'm not too early."

Then he holds out something that had been hidden behind his back. It's a bouquet of bright yellow daffodils wrapped in red paper. The sunny yellow petals are so cheery, so happy, that I don't know what to say.

I don't know what I expected today, but it wasn't this.

Reid holding out daffodils, his longish hair messy, his smile lopsided. He's in a soft, worn t-shirt and faded jeans —it hits me hard, the sight of him.

I've received countless vases of red roses, rare orchids, extravagant bouquets wrapped in gold-shot ribbons. All of those left me cold and unmoved. But a fistful of unassuming daffodils has my throat tightening and my heart thumping.

I think Reid expects me to refuse the bouquet, at least the way he's watching me tells me he does.

"I wanted you to have something to remind you of me," he says, when I reach forward and take them.

The paper crinkles in my hands and a light sweet pollen scent puffs up to me.

"Daffodils?"

"They're in the genus narcissus," he says with a mocking look.

"Are you telling me you're self-absorbed? Because I already knew that."

The small smile lines around his eyes crinkle. "No.

I'm telling you, I'm impossibly handsome, and I won't mind if you stare at me all day long."

He's not wrong about the impossibly handsome bit, but I'm not in any danger of staring at him all day long. There's only one man that I've ever wanted to stare at all day long—I used to as well, on long car rides, or lying in bed and looking into his eyes—but Reid isn't him.

And even if my heart thumped when he held out the daffodils, well, it doesn't mean anything. When I met Jace, the universe said, *he's the one*. When I met Reid, I was a baby and I think I cried.

"Thank you."

Reid nods, and I get the feeling he's disappointed that I didn't smile or laugh.

He's so out of place in my industrial-modern office, which is strange because he used to fit in everywhere. But the sharp, clean lines and the flat white and dark gray color scheme leave no room for messy, no room for soft, and no room for fun. My office, like my life, is uncompromising when it comes to all work and no play.

I imagine if he was wearing a dark suit, with his hair combed back and his stubble shaved he'd fit. But in jeans with shaggy hair, he doesn't fit at all.

He asked what happened to me, but what happened to him?

I walk past him, holding the daffodils as far away from me as possible. Outside my office, my assistant Cleary is at her desk. She's my third assistant this year, and my sixteenth since I started working. I tend to burn out staff at an unnatural rate. Half have left in tears, a third in a rage, and my last assistant left with the words, *"You are a cyborg and you expect the rest of us to be machines too! I won't do it. I have a life. I pity you!"*

Cleary arrived three hours later. She's lasted two months, which is longer than most. I work seven days a week, average eighteen hours a day, and my assistants have a hard time keeping up.

I hand her the daffodils. "Put these in a vase please."

Her eyes widen behind her round glasses when Reid smiles warmly at her.

It looks like my assistant just fell in love, because a huge flush is staining her cheeks and her hands are fluttering at her chest.

"Keep your smiles to yourself," I hiss at Reid as I stride toward the elevator.

He laughs, and calls, "Have a nice day," to Cleary as he hurries after me.

My office is in the Tower, a few floors below my dad's offices and far enough away that I feel like I'm in a separate building.

I had the entire floor renovated when I started, choosing to eschew all color and instead mimic the metal of the city in gray paint, concrete floors, and steel furniture. It looks an awful lot like my apartment. The only soft piece of furniture in my apartment is the gray couch in my living room, and honestly, it's fairly hard and uncomfortable in that trendy form-over-function kind of way.

Reid keeps a good distance between us as we descend the elevator and then silently walk through the mirrored lobby, my heels clicking over the marble floor. In the mirrors, I can see my flaming red dress tightly wrapping around my thighs and cutting low on my chest.

My expression is still flat, but for once, my cheeks are pink with color.

Reid nods at the doorman and then gestures for me to proceed him.

The humid, soupy heat hits like a wet wall as soon as I leave the air conditioning of the lobby. In the three seconds it takes Reid to follow me outside, my dress is already clinging to me, and I'm coated in a sheen of sweat.

We're in Midtown, near the park, and the heat bouncing off the metal of the traffic, the steam rising from the sidewalk grates, and the exhaust hanging in the humid air only adds to the oppressive heat.

"Wherever we're going for lunch, make it cool," I tell Reid, then I glance at my phone. "And make it fast. I have work to do."

He steps close to allow a mom with a double stroller, and a dog walker to edge past us on the sidewalk. As he does, I look up at him. Even in my heels, he's still inches taller than I am. When a group of boisterous tourists pass, jostling him, he keeps himself between them and me.

After they've passed he looks at his watch and says, "I can do cool, but I can't do fast."

I frown. "That's not what we agreed. I said lunch, I didn't—"

"Andrea. You said you'd give me a lunch, and after that lunch, if you want, you never have to see me again. At least give me *time*."

Okay.

That's fair.

"Besides," he says, looking down at me with searching eyes, "when's the last time you had a leisurely lunch? Just for fun?"

Well.

Eight years.

It's been eight years.

But I don't need to tell him that.

I stare at him, at the sweat already beading on his brow. The sun beats down on us, directly overhead, and the rays reflect off the Tower and the bank across the street, hitting us with more heat. It's miserable. A horn blares, and I think I'll agree to just about anything if it means I can sit down in a cool restaurant and sip a cold drink.

"Fine. Yes. I'll give you time. As much as you like if we can find someplace cool."

Reid gives me a magnificent smile and it reminds me again of mischief and fun and carefree wild days.

"Poutine or chowder?" he asks.

"What?"

"You know, poutine is French fries covered in cheese curds and gravy, it's comfort food heaven. I'm craving it. But I could also go for chowder. Fish, vegetables, spices. It would be fresh. Delicious. Healthier than the poutine, obviously." He holds out his two hands and makes a gesture as if he's weighing the two options. "Which one?"

Chowder would probably be faster, I can eat a bowl of soup in no time. The poutine sounds messy and too filling. I'd struggle to stay awake this afternoon if I ate something so heavy in this heat.

"Chowder."

"Final answer?" He raises an eyebrow.

"Yes," I frown at him.

He grins. "Bermuda it is."

"What?" He's already walking down the sidewalk, so I hurry after him.

"If you wanted poutine we'd go to Montreal, it's cool

there. But I'm glad you chose chowder, I really want to take a swim. The water will be perfect."

He pulls open the backdoor of a sleek black Maybach, the same style as the car he sent me home in all those years ago. There's a driver in the front seat, waiting to pull into traffic.

"Are you out of your mind? You said lunch...not an international trip." I cross my arms and step back on the sidewalk, away from the open car door.

"It's a two-hour flight to Bermuda. We'll be there by this afternoon, just in time for a late lunch. I'll have you back before bedtime. I promise."

The car door is open wide in silent invitation.

I shake my head. No. This is too much. It's too fast and it's too much.

First the daffodils and now flying off to Bermuda for a lunch?

I take a step back.

Reid's eyes turn grave as he considers my retreat. "Andrea, you're allowed to live. You were given this life, you're allowed to live it. Stop punishing yourself."

I lift my chin. "I'm not punishing myself."

He holds out his hand. "Then come with me."

I could turn around, walk back into the Tower, take the elevator back up to my cold, sterile office, and spend the next twelve hours working, and then the next twelve or fifty years doing the same thing.

Or I could take Reid's hand and make a different choice.

I once made a different choice and left this life for Jace. It broke me into a thousand pieces and when I put myself back together I was without joy.

"I'm not going to fall in love with you," I say quietly. "If that's what this is about."

He gives me a somber look. "That's not what this is about."

"And I won't marry you."

He nods. "Are you hungry?"

My stomach growls then, echoing the rumble of the buses and the taxis passing on the street.

"Yes. Fine. Let's have lunch. I want snacks on the plane."

His eyes lighten to turquoise green and his smile stretches, both triumphant and relieved.

I take his hand.

36

ANDREA

AS I BREATHE IN THE RICH SEA SALT BREEZE AND LISTEN TO the foamy surf lap at the shore, I can't help but think that Reid may be on to something.

I expected him to take me to one of the resort restaurants where celebrity chefs reign and five stars are awarded. That's pretentious enough to fit the Reid I once knew.

Instead, we're at a secluded cove on the north shore of the island, sitting in the fine pink sand, with cardboard take-out containers spread on the ground between us.

The sand feels like powdered sugar and is the rosy pink of the inside of a conch shell. It sticks to my legs and tickles my toes. I'm in a navy blue bikini, a cotton cover-up, and a wide-brimmed straw hat. I grabbed the bikini when I hurried to my apartment for my passport. Reid bought the straw hat for me at a stand outside the little take-away restaurant on the road to the beach.

The sun is high in the sky, stroking my shoulders and back with prickling heat. It's only three o'clock. Reid was right, when you have a driver, a helicopter to get you to the airport quickly, a private jet, and a liaison to walk you through customs, it only takes a few hours to get to the beach.

I thought he'd want to chat on the jet, but instead, as soon as we sat down in the wide leather seats, he closed his eyes and fell asleep.

I spent the two-hour trip typing notes on my phone and snacking on cheese, crackers, and wine.

I'm not especially hungry anymore, but the fish chowder is loaded with bacon and spices, black seal rum and sherry peppers and the savory smell floating on the steam is too much to resist.

"So, you have me here. Now what?" I ask Reid as I pull a cardboard container of chowder toward me and grab a plastic spoon.

He stops, his spoon halfway to his mouth, and lifts an eyebrow. "Now we eat."

He says this like it's the only answer. The obvious answer.

I shake my head. "Did you forget we grew up together? I know that you never do anything without an ulterior motive."

He swallows his bite of chowder and puts his spoon back in his dish.

"Maybe I've changed," he says.

I want to argue, but I can't. I'm the prime example of people changing. I went from joyful to joyless in one night and I never changed back again.

I make a noncommittal noise and then taste the chowder. It's smooth and creamy and my eyes widen as the flavor of bacon, fresh caught fish, and rum mingle to create perfection.

If I had to capture this setting—the towering gray rock slabs jutting out of the calm turquoise sea, the salt spray, the breeze petting my pinkening skin—I would capture it with the flavor of this chowder.

I give a small, delighted moan and then say, "That's so good."

Reid flashes me a grin.

I look away from the amusement in his expression and back down to my bowl of chowder, spooning out a pepper.

Reid's in a blue swimsuit, a baseball hat, and nothing else.

He stripped his T-shirt off as soon as his feet touched the sand.

His shoulders are bunched with muscles, his abdomen is flat, and his skin is golden, as if he regularly hops on his jet and spends afternoons on sun-drenched beaches.

I wonder if he still fences. That would explain the corded muscles on his back and the toned sleekness of his chest. Then again, how would he have time? If he's as successful as my dad claims, if he's "worked like a dog" to prove himself, then he wouldn't have the time.

Except...

The way he's eating his chowder with relish, the casual way he's lounging in the sand, the relaxed line of his mouth—he doesn't look like a man who works one-hundred-and-twenty-hour weeks.

I take a sip from my bottle of water and look out at the

shallow turquoise sea. Suddenly there's a pinching in my chest, an uncomfortable weight, and I recognize it immediately. It's the feeling I get when something reminds me of Jace.

I realize what it is.

The beach. The sand. Even though this quiet horseshoe-shaped cove in Bermuda is miles and years away from the beach at Coney Island, my heart doesn't know that.

"Where did you go just now?" Reid asks.

I shake my head and turn to him. "What?"

"You were fine and then you weren't."

He's perceptive, I keep forgetting that.

"Why did you bring me here?" I ask instead of answering.

He holds out a piece of cake, wrapped in plastic. "Have some rum cake."

If the rum cake is as good as the chowder, I'm a goner. I frown at him and he drops it back into the paper bag. "Or not. That's fine too."

"Remember when I caught you beating up..." I clear my throat and skip his name. "In the Ramble? I have a hard time reconciling that version of you with this version. You were an ass then and I can't imagine you aren't an ass now. I didn't much like you then and..."

I shrug, letting "*And I still don't like you*" hang in the sea-salt air.

Reid regards me with a solemn expression. When he leans forward, the breeze tugs at his sandy blonde hair and sends the scent of sunscreen my way.

"I should've said this yesterday," he says slowly, "but I was nervous."

I lift my eyebrows. Reid nervous? That's not an

emotion I ever thought he felt, or at least, that he'd admit to feeling.

A seabird lets out a long, piercing wail and soars with wide wings on the wind overhead. Its shadow flickers over Reid, there then gone.

There's a ring on his middle finger, it's silver, smooth, unembellished. He twists it round and round.

I frown, he's nervous again. "Said what?"

He clenches his hand and then looks away from me, out toward the white waves cresting far out, breaking on the coral reef.

When he looks back, his eyes are open and searching.

"You're right. I was an ass. The things I did when I was younger..." He clenches his jaw and shakes his head. "I hated myself for a long time. Every time I thought about what I did I felt buried under a mountain of shame. It seemed impossible to get out from under it. But I couldn't do anything about it. What I'd done was in the past. Done. Over. I did it. I hurt people."

He's quiet for a moment, his eyes distant, remembering some part of his past. I wait as the sound of the waves drifts between us.

Then he says, "I couldn't go back in time and change the past. No matter how badly I wished I could. And I realized I was letting the garbage of the past rule my present. I was punishing myself with a mountain of guilt and shame. I won't bore you with all the details, I'll just tell you the conclusion. I realized I didn't want to live the rest of my life hating myself. I forgave myself, and if you've never done that, I have to tell you, it's easy to forgive someone else and nearly impossible to forgive yourself. But there it is. I stopped hating myself, I stopped being an ass. I didn't want to spend the rest of my life stuck under self-hatred."

Reid gives me an earnest look, "You don't have to condone the me of the past, but I thought you might judge me for who I am today, and not yesterday?" He gives a rueful smile, as if he knows it's a lot to ask.

It's interesting, I never thought I'd hear Reid talk like this. The only people I know who talk like this are...

"Are you in a cult?"

He laughs. "No."

"Rehab?"

"No."

"Born again? Near-death experience?"

"No and no."

"Hypnosis? Years of therapy?"

His laugh is like the water tumbling over the sand. "No. Jeez, Andrea, can't I just be an introspective person who came to terms with my demons?"

I stare at him, at his lopsided smile, so at odds with the earnest expression in his eyes.

"Hmm," I say, not ready to give him an answer. "I guess I don't understand why you're here. Why you brought me here." I gesture at the cove and the sunlight flashing off the water. "The only logical reason is because you want something."

I tilt my head, remembering him telling me years ago that everyone expected us to marry someday.

I shake my head. "I'm not ever going to fall in love or get married. You came to terms with yourself? Well so did I." I look down and drag my finger over the warm sand. "I know you said that isn't what this is about, but in case I need to repeat myself, I don't have anything to give you."

Finally, I look back up. Reid's staring at me with an

expression that I can only describe as a man leaving his home and knowing he's never going to see it again. Not ever. There's a hollow sadness there.

"What?" I ask, pulling my wrap closer, shielding my heart with a thin piece of cotton.

"I always envied Jace."

I flinch when Reid says his name, but I don't think he notices. He's looking over my shoulder, frowning.

"He had a good family. His brothers. His parents when they were around. His music. He always knew where he was and where he was going. He was confident. He had this way of standing that made you want to be him. It drove me crazy with envy."

I search Reid's face, surprised that a boy who grew up with everything was jealous of another that grew up with nothing. Except, hadn't I been the same way? I saw that Jace had love, a whole life full of love, and that was the only thing I'd ever really wanted that money couldn't buy.

Maybe Reid had felt the exact same way.

"I don't envy him now," Reid says. "I thought he was smart. I thought he had it all. I was wrong though. He let you go."

I shake my head.

Reid studies my face and whatever he sees there has him nodding. "I listened to their songs last night after I saw you. It was educational."

I give him a flat look. It should be a warning to stop, but Reid continues.

"The titles alone—'The Wrong Girl,' 'You Said it First,' 'Forever Doesn't Mean Always,' 'I Didn't Love You Like You Loved Me—'"

"Stop."

"I'm sorry," he says, and I can't tell if he's saying sorry for mentioning the titles of the songs, or sorry because my heartbreak is written in the lyrics of dozens of songs loved by millions of people.

"They're just songs." I shrug, the lie as dry as sand in my mouth.

Reid nods, studying my expression. "Exactly. And you don't let the garbage of the past rule your present either. Right?"

He's holding out his hand again. I stare at it, not sure what he wants me to do.

Besides, he's wrong. I do let the past rule my present. I have for the last eight years.

It's not garbage though, it's...I've loved him for eight years. I've loved him so long.

"Andrea." Reid's hand hangs in the air between us, his fingers long and fine-boned, the tendons in his forearm belying his strength.

"What?" I whisper, my throat raw.

"Let's go for a swim."

"A swim," I say flatly.

He nods. "We have two hours until the driver comes to take us back to the airport. We've eaten lunch, we've spilled our hearts, now it's time for a swim."

"You are a strange person."

His mouth kicks up into that lopsided smile. "I don't know. You are one of the richest women in New York, yet you hole up in your tower, work yourself to exhaustion, and never have any fun. You could fly anywhere in the world on a whim—take a dip in the Blue Lagoon in Iceland and toast the northern lights, take a bubble bath in the world's most expensive champagne, build your own ice palace in the Arctic—

you could do anything, but instead you chain yourself to your desk, glare at the poor sods who dare to speak to you, and never, ever smile. I'm not sure I'm the strange one."

Fair point.

But...

"Who takes a bubble bath in champagne?"

He lifts his eyebrows. "I don't know. I always thought it sounded fun."

"Or sticky."

Reid tilts his head. "You take umbrage to the champagne but not the ice palace?"

"It just sounds uncomfortable."

He grins. "All you have to do is rinse off after."

He stands then, stretching out his long legs and rolling his shoulders. I crane my neck up, peering at him and the sun spraying golden sunshine over his smooth skin.

"Coming?"

Am I?

I don't know.

I don't know that I can.

I've tried to put everything behind me, but it's hard. It's so hard that it's been impossible.

I don't buy it that Reid only wants to see me smile. There's no reason for him to want that. There's no reason for him to care. Even if he hasn't told me his ulterior motive, I know there is one. People aren't kind unless they want something. I learned that lesson again and again.

Even Jace. He was kind because he wanted my love. And then he didn't.

But I don't think that Reid has the power to hurt me

like Jace did. You can't hurt someone if they don't care
about you. And I don't care about Reid.

So, I say, "Alright. Let's swim."

I pull my cover-up over my head and toss it into the
sand.

"Good choice," Reid says, then he bends down and
scoops me up.

I gasp, then grab his neck so I don't tumble down to
the sand. His hands are hot and they prickle when they
rub over my sun-warmed skin, gripping me under the
knees and around my back.

The sensation is like needles pricking my skin, hot
and uncomfortable.

"Let me go," I say.

He's made it to the water, his feet splashing noisily in
the surf.

"Reid. Let me go."

He grins at me, his teeth flashing white against his
tanned skin. That's when I realize my mistake.

"I mean don't. Don't let me go."

He laughs and then he keeps ahold of me as he dives
into the water, sending us both deep, deep under the
cool, turquoise, sun-studded sea.

Hours later, when the jet lands in New York, I drift
awake from the sun-induced fatigue. Reid's pulling my
bag out for me. His hair is messy from air-drying after the
swim and his nose is pink. He looks even more tired than
I feel. I guess the sun really took it out of him.

I stretch and then clear my throat, looking around
uncomfortably. The crew is still at the front of the jet.

"So. Is this it then? We had lunch. We won't see each other again?"

Reid stills and I sense something in him, almost a fearful desperation. It's there then gone, as quick as a wave coming ashore and receding.

"Unless," he says.

"Unless what?" I wait, the salt still coating my skin making me shift uncomfortably as he weighs my expression.

"Unless you'd be willing to come out tomorrow for dinner?"

I lift an eyebrow. Outside the jet window the bright lights of the airport and New York beyond shine white and yellow in the dark.

"In New York?" I ask, just to clarify.

He swallows, then nods. "In New York. With my parents."

There's something funny about Reid's expression, but I can't put my finger on it. His parents aren't my favorite people. His father was always bullish and ill-tempered, and his mom's personality is so pale she's almost translucent.

"What's the catch?" I ask.

He shakes his head. "No catch. It's just dinner with my parents, from eight until late."

"Anyone else?"

"No."

I have a lot of work to do. Taking off most of the day put me way behind schedule. Tomorrow morning my dad will ask about the assessor's office and the legal department. But tomorrow is Sunday...a day that *some* people rest.

There's something in the way Reid is waiting for my

answer, like he's holding his breath and saying please with his eyes, that has me remembering what he said yesterday, *I need you. Please.*

"Yes," I say then.

His shoulders sag, and I hear it, a quiet breath, exhaled.

Then he smiles. "You won't regret it."

I shake my head, "I already do."

At that, he laughs.

37

ANDREA

THE FIRE-TINGED SCENT OF THE WORLD'S MOST EXPENSIVE steak fills the restaurant, permeating the air with sizzling meat, smoky char, and luxury.

There's something primal about steak grilled over open flame, but there's something *exotically* primal about a five-hundred-dollar steak grilled over open flame. Which I suppose is why Clive Shilling, Reid's father, chose to make the Miyazaki Wagyu with caviar the signature dish at his luxury hotel's restaurant.

I've never been to Brasserie—the Shillings are a competitor of the Leighton-Hugheses after all—but I've heard Clive is a die-hard red meat enthusiast and eats here at least twice a week.

Reid asked me to meet him in the entry of the restaurant at eight. I'm ten minutes early. Brasserie is on the top floor of the hotel, with a view of the southern end of Central Park.

The restaurant is dimly lit, the darkness adding to the nineteen thirties art deco atmosphere. The ceiling is high, with brass chandeliers. Mirrors line the walls, separated by dark wood paneling inlaid with brass triangular designs. The tables are heavy dark wood with purple velvet chairs.

The entire place has an aura of indolent luxury. Even the way the cutlery scraping over the plates echoes off the mirrors and people's conversations bounce off the walls has a superciliousness that's surprising.

I wore a silver dress. It's tight, hits at my knees, and its lines are severe. I chose taller heels so that I wouldn't feel so much at a disadvantage next to Reid and his father.

I don't know what to expect tonight so I thought it would be better to come dressed for battle. My hair is pulled into a tight crown braid and my makeup is dark, with bright red lipstick the only slash of color.

Yesterday was nice—okay, better than nice—but that doesn't mean I trust Reid. I especially don't trust his father.

"You're early."

I turn as Reid strides to me, a surprised smile on his face.

He's in a suit tonight and he looks more like the golden boy with the dark heart that I remember.

He comes forward and I think he's about to lean in and give the greeting so common in our circle, a kiss on both cheeks, that I take a step back and instead thrust out my hand.

He isn't expecting that, so I jab him in the stomach. He stops, looks down, and then smiles.

"Sorry." He takes my hand. "Hello."

I grip his hand and shake firmly. "Hi."

I let go quickly. I made it awkward.

Reid's watching me with an odd expression, but he recovers quickly, taking a step back.

He looks up at the brass fixtures on the ceiling and the painting of a naked brass woman holding a candle.

"I'd forgotten how gaudy this place is."

I nod. "It's dripping supercilious indolence."

He likes that, I can tell. His eyes light up with mirth. "I believe my father was trying to match the splendor of the lobby of the Tower."

"Poor him. He didn't come close."

Reid lets out a low chuckle, then holds his arm out for me to take. Good breeding and years of etiquette lessons have me automatically placing my arm in his.

His suit is soft, light wool, and when I touch his arm I can feel the outline of the muscles I saw yesterday on the beach.

"No one can match a Leighton-Hughes," he agrees. "You're the Carnegie to our Mellon."

"Are you a melon? If I knock you on the head will I know if you're good or bad?"

He leans close and I feel the heat radiating off him. "I suppose you could try."

We're standing like that, arms entwined, our faces close and intimate, when Reid's father walks up.

"Ah," he says, "I didn't know whether or not to believe the illustrious Ms. Leighton-Hughes would actually condescend to dining with my son."

It's those words, that short sentence that tells me everything I need to know.

No.

That's not quite right.

It's Reid's reaction to his father's words that tells me everything I need to know.

Ten seconds ago, Reid was relaxed, his eyes were smiling, his arm was loose under my hand. Then his father caught him unaware, in an open, intimate moment, and instead of turning and smiling, Reid flinched.

It was subtle.

I might not have noticed it if I wasn't staring into his eyes, with my arm in his, standing only inches away. But I felt it and I saw it.

His arm tightened, the muscles under my hand corded. His jaw clenched, his eyes hardened, and he *flinched*.

Then, just as quickly, a half a second later, Reid wiped that tension away as if it had never been. I doubt he would've reacted at all if he hadn't been distracted by our conversation, that's how quickly he was able to hide his response, but all the same, I saw it.

Then we turn as one, my arm still in Reid's.

I'm watching Reid from the corner of my eye and so when we face his father—Clive—I see it again.

His father has grown even more snake-like over the years, his eyes are still yellowish-green but they've become flint hard, his head is bullet-shaped and has narrowed over time so that he looks just like a striking cobra.

Reid doesn't look at his father's face though, he looks at the cane in his hand.

And when he does, his arm tightens again and his face, it loses a little bit of the color that he gained from yesterday's swim at the beach.

"I am honored to dine with your son," I say as coolly as possible, tilting my head in that condescending way that I mastered years ago.

My heart is beating in double-time, punching at my chest. Next to me Reid is quiet. Still. Like a rabbit caught in a snare. I want to elbow him, pinch him, get him to snap out of whatever dark place he's gone.

His father smirks, the kind of cruel smile all the worst bullies give, and runs his veiny hand over his ebony cane and the circular brass handle at the top.

Reid's mom stands a few feet behind and to the left of his father. She's aged since I last saw her, while my mom has become more vibrant and more regally beautiful with age, Carol has faded with age, her white yellow hair is nearly translucent, her blue eyes are pale and watery, and her sepia dress makes her appear wraithlike. I wonder now if she's made herself almost invisible to avoid her husband's snakelike attention.

"I doubt that," his father says, and then as he pushes past us he says, "but you'll learn. You'll learn."

Carol follows her husband, drifting through the restaurant toward a secluded table at the back. I imagine it's Clive's table, where he has a standing reservation and no one else is allowed to sit there. My family has a similar arrangement at a few restaurants around the city.

Reid comes to then, like he's waking up from a particularly bad dream.

"Okay?" I ask quietly.

He nods, and I feel him consciously loosening his posture and letting out a slow breath.

"I haven't seen them in four years, not since I left for Paris," he admits. "I apologize."

He gives me a rueful smile. And like I said, I wouldn't

have thought anything of this if I hadn't been touching him, standing close enough to feel his tension. I'd just have thought he was overwhelmed at seeing his parents again.

I'm still not certain why Reid invited me, but I'm used to navigating shark-filled waters.

"Well, are we going to eat or not?" I ask.

He gives me a relieved smile. "Thank you."

38

ANDREA

CLIVE SHILLING HAS MASTERED THE ART OF GIVING compliments that are actually insults.

As we eat the famed Wagyu, slicing into the tender steak and letting the blood run, I'd say that Clive's tongue is sharper than the steak knives and his words more cutting.

Not that he's said anything wrong, exactly.

It's the way it's said.

"Reid catapulted our market share in France, but New York is a different story."

"I admire your father, he has two sons to make him proud."

"Reid understands business, but he doesn't understand family loyalty like you."

We're at the round table in the back corner of the restaurant. A long white tablecloth, candlelight, a bottle of wine from a French chateau's best season—twenty years ago—all of it should make a lovely, easy evening.

Ha.

Even the waiter, busboy and sommelier tiptoe around Clive.

Carol hasn't said a word.

Reid's seated in the high-backed purple velvet chair next to me, we're scooted so close that I can feel the tense line of his thigh.

"My sources tell me your progress on the Carraway is stalled," Clive says, narrowing his eyes on me.

I raise my eyebrows and slice my knife through my butter-soft steak. "Really? Then your sources are incompetent. It was a mere inconvenience, already taken care of." I put the steak in my mouth and chew with relish. It is *delicious*. If nothing else, Clive knows how to hire superb chefs.

Clive frowns, his flat mouth drifting toward his chin. He can't intimidate me or bully me. I'm my father's daughter and he knows this. I guess Reid does too, because there's a small smile playing at the corners of his mouth.

He's cutting his steak, his head is down. I doubt his father can see his smile.

"Well. Bravo." Clive tosses his cloth napkin onto the table. His steak is gone, there's just blood left running over his plate into the shining black spheres of caviar. "You have spine, you have class, you're a league above my son and we both know it. I didn't believe it when he told me you were his date." He shakes his head. "I don't particularly believe the attachment now."

His date?

Reid told his parents I was his date?

Okay, yes, maybe I am, in a manner of speaking, but we aren't *dating*.

Clive watches me through slitted eyes and I recognize that he's waiting for a reaction. A blush, a smile, a laugh, a stammered defense. But he should know, I don't do any of those things.

Reid's gone still, he's waiting for my response, I can feel all of his attention on me, even though he hasn't looked my way.

Maybe he expects me to deny being his date, or maybe he expects me to agree with his father, that he's a worthless and useless son.

Or maybe, because Reid knows me, has known me since I was young and naïve, he expects something else entirely. After all, he was a bully once too.

So instead of answering right away, I reach over and place my hand over Reid's.

I let the warmth of my fingers seep into him.

His hand is bunched on the tablecloth, his fingers in a tightly curled fist. When I lay my hand over his, his hand loosens, his shoulders relax and he lets out a nearly imperceptible breath.

"Believe it," I say in a cold voice. "I haven't met a man as loyal, as interesting, or as intelligent in years."

I know Reid wants to turn and stare at me with incredulous disbelief. I want to stare at myself that way too.

Instead, we both stare unflinchingly as Clive snorts, then shakes his head.

"You're welcome to him," he says.

At that Reid stands, pushes back his chair then pulls mine out too. I stand.

"Mother." Reid walks around the table and kisses her on the cheek.

"Goodbye, dear," she says.

"Father."

Clive nods and leans back in his chair. "Tell your dad hello," he says to me.

"Goodnight," I say.

Then I put my hand on Reid's arm again and walk straight-backed from the dark, fire-scented, rumbling restaurant.

When we make it out to the still-warm evening air at the edge of the park, I tug my arm free of Reid's and take a step back.

He takes a deep breath and tilts his head up to the indigo dark sky.

The traffic at the edge of the park is thick and the headlights of the taxis slice through the night. The roar of engines and hissing buses fills the space between us and the humid air is thick with diesel fumes and the grilled hotdog scent pumping from a nearby food stand.

I give Reid a minute to shake off whatever memories pulled him under tonight. I know enough about that not to rush him. Years ago, there were full months where I felt like my body was in a room, but *I wasn't*.

The pain of losing what I'd had was so much that my mind just flipped a switch and turned all emotion off. I went numb as self-preservation.

That lasted...a long time.

Well, let's be honest, it's lasted up till now.

Reid, for some reason, is trying to start the fire inside me again, so that the ice around me cracks and maybe melts.

A few dozen people have walked past while we've

stood outside the door of his father's hotel. The doorman has politely ignored us.

I only live a few blocks away and if there's anything that might help, it's a hot drink.

Reid finally opens his eyes and looks over at me. He looks tired, really tired. There are shadows under his eyes and his face is drawn, almost as if he's in pain. But still, he gives me a smile and his eyes light with amusement.

"I'm the most loyal, the most interesting, the most..." He shakes his head. "What was that last bit?"

I lift an eyebrow, glad that he's smiling, "I don't recall."

"I think you said...most good looking."

"That definitely wasn't it," I say, looking over his stubble-lined jaw and sandy hair brushing his collar.

He smiles but there's still tension lining his shoulders.

"What was that all about?" I ask, nodding up at the restaurant, back to where his parents are likely having dessert and coffee.

"They approve of you," he says, as if that explains it all.

I step forward and take his arm, pulling him down the sidewalk toward my apartment.

"And why does that matter?" I ask, stepping around a woman walking her Pomeranian.

Reid looks away, out toward a pair of white horses pulling a carriage along the grassy line of the park.

"Can it wait until tomorrow?"

I bite my bottom lip. I don't want to wait until tomorrow, I want to know now, but I can tell by the way he's holding his shoulders and the tired lines around his mouth that tonight took a lot out of him.

I don't know what's going on, but I haven't been

working with my dad for years without learning the art of patience.

"I suppose," I say.

Reid squeezes my hand, the one resting on his arm. "Thank you."

"You can come up to my place, I live around the corner. I'll make you tea," I tell him.

You'd think that I just told him that the earth was in actuality flat with the way he looks at me.

"What?" I frown and then pull him around the corner, onto my tree-lined side street.

"I wasn't expecting the invitation, that's all."

"For tea. Nothing else."

"I know," he says.

So we go up to my apartment. I put a kettle on and tell him to make himself at home.

It's funny, bringing Reid to my apartment. No one has ever been inside my home except for my cleaner. Not my family, not my assistant (former or present), not any colleagues, not...anyone. Now that he's here, I look around and see it as he must.

It's cold.

The floor is gray concrete. The walls are gray. There isn't any art. It's just flat, empty walls. The blinds are drawn and the space is dark.

The couch is gray. The low coffee table is, shocker, gray. There's a bookshelf along the wall, but instead of books, there are piles of documents from the office, manila folders, and unopened mail.

It looks sort of like a prison cell. A lonely, drab prison cell.

When I walk out of the kitchen carrying a tray with

two steaming cups of Earl Grey tea, I find Reid standing in the living room, staring at the couch.

I pull to a stop and the teacups clank in the saucers. Reid turns at the sound.

There's a frown on his face, a line between his eyebrows, but when he sees me, he starts forward. "Let me help you."

He takes the tray and sets it carefully on the coffee table, pushing aside a few back issues of *The Wall Street Journal*.

I clear my throat, embarrassed. "Thank you."

He nods and then hands me a white and gray lined teacup, politely ignoring the fact that there isn't anywhere for us to sit.

There aren't any chairs. There's only the couch. The uncomfortable, rock-hard couch. Where I sleep.

My white sheets are tucked into the cushions, my gray blanket is rumpled, and my pillow is there with a slight impression in the middle.

"Sorry. I...sleep out here."

Reid nods, taking a sip of his black tea. He filled it liberally with a spoonful of honey. I guess he likes it sweet.

He doesn't say anything, and he's not judging me, but I feel exposed and prickly uncomfortable all the same. Why didn't I think of this when I invited him in?

My apartment shows exactly who I am, how empty I am.

Reid said I should stop punishing myself, and I'd said I wasn't, but this apartment tells a different story.

"This is good. Thank you," he says.

And the kindness in his voice makes the backs of my eyes burn and my throat tighten.

Then for a few minutes we stand silently in my barren, gray living room and stare at my couch while sipping steaming hot tea, full of bergamot and lavender. It's so quiet I can hear the rumble of traffic, and a lone siren, many stories below. For the first time I wish I had a sound system or a stereo or speakers or *something*. But home is for working and sleeping, and music is a minefield, so I never bothered.

So after minutes of quiet, when Reid has nearly finished his tea, he turns to me and asks, "Why do you sleep on the couch?"

He's curious, not judging.

I didn't sweeten my tea and the bitter flavor curls over my tongue.

"Because I don't have a bed," I say, choosing the simplest explanation.

He frowns at this, a lock of hair falling over his forehead. "Why don't you have a bed?"

I look into his blue-green eyes, try to find the sardonic jerk that he once was, the one who would revel in others' misery, but I don't see him there. I only see a man who has his own demons.

I wonder if this is going to end up like my friendships from long ago. The ones where I shared myself with school-friends and then they wreaked havoc on my dad's business and my life.

Get close, get burned.

Besides, what can I say? Yes, Reid, I used to have a bed. It sat in my bedroom, a king-size bed with white sheets and a fluffy white comforter. And every time I laid in it, it felt like a eulogy.

I'd remember the way I lay in his arms, the way I kissed his lips and fell into his eyes, the way he held me close and promised me forever. Every time I lay down it hurt and I didn't sleep.

So I had the bed taken away. How's that, is that what you want to know?

Reid's patiently waiting for my answer, watching me quietly, so I finally lift a shoulder and say, "Beds are..."

I don't finish my sentence.

He reads my hesitation as easily as a book, thumbed open to the proper page. "Andrea, you can trust me. Anything you tell me, I'll take it to my grave."

I look at him skeptically. "No one can promise that."

Slowly he reaches his hand to his chest and crosses his heart, watching me solemnly the whole time. "There. It's done. To the grave."

I shake my head, but then, whatever he's imagining is probably worse than the reality. It's better to skate on the surface and tell a partial truth.

So I say, "I can't sleep in beds. Not anymore."

Reid searches my expression, "Did he...did he hurt—"

"No," I say quickly.

By his expression he doesn't quite believe me. But Jace never hurt me, not like he's asking.

"No," I say again. "Nothing happened. At least nothing that hasn't happened to a million people before me. I wanted him and he didn't want me. That's all. Nothing to be upset about."

Reid looks at the couch, the visual evidence that it is something to be upset about, even so many years later.

"I'm sorry," he says.

"There's nothing to be sorry about."

Which is a lie.

He knows it too.

"Will you come to my place for dinner tomorrow?" he asks suddenly. "I want to cook for you."

I look around the living room, so empty our voices echo off the concrete floor and the bare walls. He probably wants to go to his place because mine is a barren modern cell.

"Does cooking for me involve ordering food from a nearby restaurant and putting it on a plate?" I ask.

He smiles. "Maybe."

Ha.

"And then?" I ask.

"And then after we eat, I'll tell you my ulterior motive."

There it is.

"I knew you had one," I say, and I don't want to admit that I'm disappointed he does. "I thought you said you just wanted to see me smile."

He makes a small hum of assent. "That's still true."

"But there's more to the story?"

"There's always more to the story. You know that."

Yes.

I do.

39

ANDREA

REID'S HOME SURPRISES ME.

It's a quaint brownstone near Riverside Park, tucked in a homey row of townhomes on a sunny side street.

Leafy green gingko trees line the street, and the sun spirals through the green, making lacy stars on the sidewalk. His home, like the rest, has window flower baskets overflowing with July's firecracker red blooms.

It's the kind of quiet street that moms and nannies push strollers down, where little kids hold hands on their way to school, and where grandpas take their cocker spaniel out for a walk and contemplate the peace of a neighborhood side street in the Upper West Side.

If I had to imagine Reid's home, this would be the last place I'd envision.

"Sorry, it's a bit of mess," Reid calls from the kitchen.

Yes. He's actually cooking. I thought he'd order food

and pop it onto a plate, but when he said he wanted to cook for me, he actually meant it.

I'm perched on the window seat in the living room, looking out over the street bathed in the summer evening sun.

"It's fine," I say. "It's not messy at all."

And it's not. *Comfortable* might be the better word.

The brownstone is from the eighteen hundreds, and you can see its age in the whiskey-toned wood floors, the deep window seat, and the thick wood crown molding. There's even a built-in bookshelf that looks original to the house.

Unlike my bookshelf, Reid's is actually full of books. Hundreds of them, on every topic, in every genre, including children's books, which makes me think his decorator bought a load of books and filled the shelves for the ambience.

You can smell the age of the house too. It has that subtle beeswax and lemon scent that comes from hundreds of years of polishing wood and cleaning floors. It's a bright cozy smell, that's overlaid by the rosemary and butter drifting from the kitchen.

The difference between my sterile, cold, unscented apartment and Reid's home is almost too much to contemplate.

There's a navy couch with fat, comfortable-looking cushions, pillows, and a yellow cashmere throw. Then there's a loveseat, just as comfy. A low, round wood table, with more books and an empty to-go coffee cup on a coaster. In the corner of the room, there's a potted plant with yellow and green variegated leaves shaped like hearts.

It's quite possibly the quaintest, coziest home I've ever been in.

"How long have you lived here?" I call to Reid.

He steps out of the kitchen and wipes his hands on a dishtowel. "Sorry?"

I stand. "I was just wondering how long you've lived here. It looks..." It looks like a home, actually. "Comfortable."

He follows my gaze and takes in the couches, the books, the sun streaming over the window seat. "Thanks. Yeah. About three weeks."

"Three weeks?" I say, my voice rising in surprise.

How is that even possible?

I've been in my apartment for years and it still barely looks like anyone lives there.

He smiles at my surprise. "Sure. When I realized I was coming back, I expedited the process. Found a place, found a decorator, got it all set, made it a home."

Wow.

"Why are you looking at me like that?" he asks, throwing the dishtowel over his shoulder.

"I guess this isn't the sort of place I pictured you living in. I always imagined you in some modern-art penthouse with lots of mirrors. On the walls, on the ceilings, all over. Mirrors everywhere."

He raises in eyebrow. "Well...I mean, that is what my last place looked like. Because if you're this good looking, why waste time staring at anything else?"

"Exactly," I agree. "But there's not a mirror in here. Not even a shiny metal surface. It's so weird."

His eyes are full of laughter. "So you like it?"

I nod, taking in his casual stance, his navy T-shirt and faded jeans, his bare feet and his tousled hair.

"It's nice," I say.

He nods back at the kitchen. "The food's ready. Do you want to eat at the table or out here?"

"Here," I say, looking toward the coffee table and the overstuffed couch.

I spent nearly fifteen hours, from four in the morning until now, working and liaising with the assessor's office and the title company to sort the mess that is the Carraway project.

The entire thing reminds me of when you put a thin gold necklace away and then in the morning there are knots all through the metal. You have to unravel it *very* carefully or you'll destroy the necklace. So, I'm moving carefully. It's fine, it'll work out, but in the meantime, I'm working myself to the bone.

And when this project is done my dad will hand me an even bigger project to manage.

Somehow, for the first time, instead of making me glad, that thought makes me weary.

So I sit down on the comfy cushions, pulling the table close.

Reid sets plates, silverware, and glasses on the coffee table, then brings out a ceramic dish with steam curling from the top.

He lays it on a hot pad and then he slides onto the couch next to me. The cushion dips and I edge closer to him.

"What is it?" I ask, peering at the dish full of bubbling cheese.

"Mac 'n' cheese," he says with a prideful flourish.

Then he takes the spoon and scoops a gooey spoonful of macaroni onto my plate. It smells like heaven and my mouth starts to water right away.

"This isn't mac 'n' cheese," I say.

Reid scoops some for himself, and the cheese stretches between his spoon and the plate as he dishes it out. "Well. What *is* mac 'n' cheese but macaroni and creamy cheese?" he says philosophically.

I take a forkful, blow on the steaming noodles, and then bite, and ohhhh. Okay. That's good. There's brie, roasted fig, rosemary and cream. I used to not like fig, but tastes change.

"We can call it mac 'n' cheese," I say, "We can call it anything you want as long as I can keep eating it."

He grins at me, then takes another bite. "Good. For a second I thought the mac 'n' cheese would descend into a full-blown identity crisis."

I almost smile, and that would be the first in a long time, but instead I pop another forkful of sweet, savory, cheesy deliciousness into my mouth.

"You can have me over again," I tell Reid. "As long as you make me this."

A smile drifts along the edges of his mouth, waiting to come out. He looks at me from the corner of his eyes and then reaches for another bite.

"We'll see," he says.

And then I remember that after we eat, he's going to tell me the point of all this. Why he barged into my life, why he's here, his ulterior motive.

I don't blow on my macaroni and when I bite into it, the heat burns my tongue. I wince and then swallow.

Get close, get burned.

"Reid?"

I drop my fork to my plate and turn toward him. I put my hands on my knees and quickly build up a wall around myself.

"Hmmm?" he asks, savoring his meal. But then he must hear something in my voice because he stops and turns my way.

When he does, our knees nearly touch and the couch feels crowded and over-warm.

He sets down his fork. "What?"

"I need to know," I say. "Tell me. We've known each other a long time. I won't be surprised by whatever you have to say. Just tell me."

He's flown me to a secluded beach in the Caribbean, taken me to dinner with his parents, he's cooked for me and brought me to his home, and all this is leading up to...something.

Reid's watching me, and there's a slight tension around his eyes, and that hint of some private fear again, some desperate hope.

The look in his eyes wraps around my chest and squeezes.

"Reid."

"Alright," he says, his voice gravelly and solemn. "I need you."

I lean forward. "You already told me that."

Lots of people need me or want something from me. In my life, relationships are business transactions, nothing more.

Reid closes his eyes and runs his fingers through his hair, then when he opens his eyes, there's determination in the blue-green depths.

"Andrea."

"Reid."

"Marry me."

40

ANDREA

THE YELLOW SUNLIGHT FROM THE WINDOW SPLAYS OVER US, as transparent as my shock. Marry him?

Marry him?

After three "dates"? Has he lost his mind? I told him I wouldn't love him, I told him I wouldn't marry him. He promised that love wasn't what this was about.

"No—"

"I'm sorry—"

Reid and I speak at the same time.

"No," I say again.

"I didn't mean to—"

Then there's a loud, piercing cry and Reid cuts off. He stiffens and looks toward the wooden stairs that run along the side of the house.

"What is that?" I ask.

Although, I know what it is. It's obvious.

Reid stands and I do too.

The cry is a high, unhappy wail.

"That?" Reid looks toward the stairs, and it's clear he wants to run upstairs. "That's my daughter."

Then he does.

"Sorry," he says. "I have to see if—"

He doesn't finish, he just hurries from the living room, up the creaky wooden stairs to the second floor.

I don't stay in the living room, I follow him up the old wooden stairs, down the daffodil-yellow hall and into a dimly lit bedroom.

The walls are a lighter shade of yellow, the shades are drawn, and a stuffed bear playing ocean wave sounds sits on a side table next to a crib.

I hesitate at the doorway, but Reid strides in, like he's done this a hundred times before, and bends down over the crib and scoops out a tiny baby in a mint green onesie.

"Hey," he murmurs, holding the baby close, "I'm here. I'm here now. Shhh. Shhh."

I don't think Reid knows I followed him up. His arm is curled around the baby and he's bent his face close to whisper soothing sounds. It's a private, unguarded moment and I don't think I'm supposed to be here for it.

As Reid rocks his daughter, holding her against his heart, I slowly back out of the room. The baby shampoo, lavender smell fades and so do the baby's cries.

I walk to the end of the hall and sit on the top stair, resting my elbows on my knees.

Reid is a father.

A father.

I mean, sure, these things happen. Once upon a time, I thought I might have kids too. But the only person I ever

wanted to have a family with was Jace, and when he was
gone, a future with kids was gone too.

The cries from the nursery are fading, and instead of
a high wail, they're a tired, sleepy cry.

I can hear the low rumblings of Reid singing a
lullaby.

Now the children's books on the bookshelf downstairs
make sense. So does the comfortable brownstone on the
quiet, family-friendly street. Reid moved here three
weeks ago to give his daughter a home, and apparently,
a *mom*.

That's not me though.

Reid could've asked me days ago and I would've
told him.

The answer is no.

I look up when I hear the floorboards creaking. Reid's
there, walking out of the nursery, a wet spot on his
shoulder from his daughter's tears.

When he sees me sitting on the stairs, he stops.

"So."

"So," I say. Then I stand and smooth out my dress. "I
can't marry you," I tell him. "I can't be a mom."

By the way his shoulders slump, I know this isn't what
he was hoping to hear. But there's a stubborn tilt to his
jaw that I recognize from when we were kids.

He nods his head back toward the nursery. "I know it's
a deal no one would take. A husband that you don't
particularly like. A month-old baby that isn't yours. I get
that. I knew when I moved back to New York that I had a
one-in-a-million chance of you saying yes."

"Then why ask? Why move back?"

"Come meet her," he says.

I don't especially want to meet her. I want to go home

and bury myself in mountains of work for the next few years. But his earnest expression draws me back toward the nursery. When I step through the doorway the baby smell hits me again and the teddy bear sound machine plays a classic lullaby.

"It's okay. She's asleep," Reid says quietly.

I step into the nursery, over the soft carpet to the crib. The room has all the baby things—a humidifier spraying cool mist, a baby swing, a play mat with bright colors, a rocking chair.

In the crib, Reid's daughter sleeps, her mouth slightly open, her tiny brow wrinkled. Her hands are curled into fists and she makes little sleep sounds. She has wisps of sandy blonde hair—the same color as Reid's when he was little—perfectly arched eyebrows, and the roundest cheeks I've ever seen.

I grip the cold wooden edge of the crib and lean down to watch the rise and fall of her chest.

"She's so little," I whisper. It's hard to imagine that any human is ever this small. Or this vulnerable. She's completely dependent on Reid for *everything*.

I look back at him. He's watching his daughter with a sad smile on his face.

"What's her name?" I ask.

"Claudia Marie," he says.

"Where's her mother?"

Reid shakes his head. "She overdosed. Three days after Claudia was born."

"But..."

If Claudia is only a month old, then Reid—

"I didn't know she was pregnant. I didn't really know her. We had a one-night stand. We used protection..." He shrugs. "She showed up at my home in Paris, on her way to the hospital to have the baby, demanding I come along. I was the dad—the blood tests proved it—but it's obvious just looking at her. Romy, that was her name, apparently she was an addict. She didn't use during pregnancy, but as soon as she was released from the hospital she...I don't think she meant to overdose, just...it happened. I was a dad, with an infant, and..."

"You thought it was a good idea to come back to New York and ask me to marry you? What? So we can live together and play happy family for the next few decades?"

"No," Reid says.

"No?"

He shakes his head. "No. I don't have decades, Andrea. I have months."

What?

I'm not sure I heard him right. But the way he's looking at me now, with a grave, somber expression, I think I must have.

And as I stare into his eyes, I remember what he said on the rooftop, *"Don't think too long, I don't have a lot of time."* And what he promised last night, *"Anything you tell me, I'll take it to my grave."* And when he swore, this wasn't about falling in love.

I don't want to say it out loud, but there's no getting around it. "You're dying."

He nods, then looks down at Claudia and brushes his finger over her curled hand.

"Romy...didn't have family?"

"No," he says. "And you..." He looks back at me then, his eyes full of fire. "You saw my parents."

"Yes."

His jaw clenches and I see the same dark pain in his

eyes when he says, "I would die a thousand times again and again to keep them from raising my daughter. I'll do anything. I'll get down on my knees and beg. I'll crawl on my hands and knees over broken glass. I'll give you anything you ask. I will do anything."

In her sleep, Claudia has wrapped her hand around his finger, and she's holding him tight.

I think, if she weren't holding onto him, Reid would get down on his knees and beg me to help him.

"Why?" I ask. "Was it so bad?"

"My father has a cane," Reid says.

I nod. I remember it. Ebony, brass handled, cruel.

"There are a million ways you can hurt someone without leaving a mark," he says. "I told you I hated myself for a long time. Every time he hurt me, I hurt someone else. It was a compulsion. I can't...he's a monster. I can't let him raise her. And when I'm gone, he'll want her. He'll do anything to have her. If I designate a guardian in my will, he'll use all his power, all his influence, and he'll fight my will, he'll win. I don't have time for this battle. I don't have the strength. There's no way he'll let his grandchild be raised by anyone else but him. And I can't..." Reid clenches his free hand then and looks down at the ground as if he has faced his worst nightmare and there's only one way out. "I can't let him do that. But I won't be here. I won't be here to protect her. As soon as she was born, she let out the smallest cry and looked at me with these muddy blue eyes, like she was saying, *oh hello, there you are.* I fell in love. I love her. She's the only good thing I have ever done in my life. I've been a fool. I've been a wreck. She's it. She is the only good thing. And I don't want her to be hurt like I was. I don't want him to destroy her too."

I take a step toward Reid, brush my hand over his.

"Why are you giving up then? You could fight. Maybe you aren't really dying."

As soon as I say it, I realize how naïve I sound.

But still Reid smiles at me, "No. I am. I found out the day before Claudia was born." His mouth twists in an ironic smile. "Life has wonderful timing. When I was at Yale I had cancer. They said if it ever came back my chances of survival would drop drastically. I didn't take the warning seriously. I kept living the same way. All work. All arrogant asshole. Then this. Inoperable terminal cancer. One hundred percent mortality. It's spread so fast, metastasized so far that I have six months tops. A year maybe, if I go through chemo and radiation." He looks at his daughter then and says, "I chose to spend six months living rather than a year dying."

He pulls his finger free of his daughter's then and she makes a small sleepy noise of protest. "Do you want me on my knees?" he asks.

I shake my head. "No."

"Then what?"

"I still don't understand. What would marrying you do."

He smiles at me and the tinkling lullaby from the stuffed bear fills the momentary silence. I recognize it now, it's Chopin's *Berceuse*. My own nanny, Grace, used to play it for me when I couldn't sleep.

The shadows of the room play over Reid's face, shrouding his features.

"Do you remember what you said to me all those years ago? When you told me to leave Jace alone?"

I stare at the smile playing on his lips.

I remember the night. I remember my anger. I remember our dance. But I don't remember what I said.

I shake my head. "I told you to leave him alone."

Reid's eyes crinkle, "You told me if I didn't leave him alone, you would break me."

I nod. I remember now. I would have as well.

Reid reaches out, touches my hand. "I came looking for that woman. She's the only woman I know powerful enough and strong enough to keep my daughter safe. If you were her mother, then my father, my parents, they'd never stand against you. You would break them. If you protect her, I won't be so afraid to go anymore."

I shake my head. "I can't love her though." I reach up and touch my chest. "I don't have that in me anymore. I..."

At the look on Reid's face I pause, then I tell him the truth, "My heart broke and there's all these pieces on the floor and I've never been able to gather them up again. I don't know how to love your daughter. I grew up with a mom who couldn't love me. I know how much that hurts, I don't—"

"Please," Reid says. "You know my parents won't stand against you."

"I know," I agree. The Shillings won't dare to stand against a Leighton-Hughes. It's as true today as it was eight years ago. I would break them.

"We can get married, the adoption can go through in three months."

"And then?"

I look down at Claudia sleeping in the crib, her eyelashes fluttering with her dreams.

"And then I'm gone. And you can have a full-time nanny care for Claudia. God knows that's how we were raised. I'm not asking you to love her. I'm not asking you to love me. I'm just asking, no, I'm begging you for your help."

"That's all? We get married. I adopt her. You die." I flinch at the last, but Reid doesn't. He just stands there, watching me with grave eyes. "And then I raise her."

"Yes," he says, "And I leave you my estate. All my assets, this home, I have a trust fund already prepared for Claudia. Everything is ready. You just have to say yes."

It's dark now, the music spins around us and for the first time in years I'm not numb. No, my chest is aching again.

He's not asking for love, he's asking me to keep his daughter safe. To raise her as my own.

"What do you want me to tell your daughter, when she asks me about you?"

Reid reaches out, sets his fingers against mine, "I want you to tell her that I loved."

His eyes are dark and I can't decipher the emotion there, but it feels as if there's a hand curling around my heart, squeezing it tight.

"Anything else?" I ask, staring into his eyes.

He nods. "Tell her I lived. I really, truly lived."

My lips are dry, my throat aches at the words. Reid asked me why I'm not living. Truly living. I wonder, if I say yes, will I truly live these next few months with him?

"I'll think about it," I tell him. "I'll tell you my answer tomorrow."

Like he said before, he doesn't have a lot of time.

He draws his hand back, steps away. "Thank you."

I go home then and spend a sleepless night on my couch deciding whether or not to marry a dying man I won't ever love.

41

ANDREA

THE COLD, THIN METAL—CHEAP TIN—HAS DULLED WITH age. The blue-gray plastic gem and plastic diamonds wink at me, reflecting the harsh light of my living room. I hold the ring that Jace gave me in the palm of my hand.

The ring is feather light and the tin is hard and cold on my skin.

I've kept the ring buried out of sight in the fire-proof safe built into the back of my closet. It stays hidden there with the photograph of my mom and me, tickets from Jace's show at the bowling alley, the receipt for the guitar I bought, and the recipe book I bought while on tour—Jace scrawled with a hotel pen the lyrics for a song he's never sung, next to the grilled ham and cheese panini recipe.

Let's dance on the bed, all night long.
We did.

Let's get married at Christmas.

We didn't.

"What should I do?" I ask the empty room.

Obviously the room doesn't answer.

I curl my fingers gently around the ring and let the warmth of my hand sink into the metal and the cold plastic gem.

My apartment is quiet. It's four in the morning, the sleepy, melancholy time, when the sky is dark, the birds are silent, and most of the city is still lost in dreams.

There's a cup of tea on my coffee table, half-finished and now cold. I sigh and try to sink further into the unyielding cushions of my couch. The metal of the ring pokes at my hand.

Last night, Reid sent me his medical records. His diagnosis, the second opinion, the third opinion, the even more forcefully delivered and pessimistic fourth opinion. They were all a variation on a theme, like one of those classical piano pieces where you play the same melody in four different ways.

All of them suggested treatment to extend his life by a few months. All of them suggested pain management and hospice for the end. All of them sang a tune with the exact same ending.

So.

He wanted me to know that he wasn't trying to trick me. That this wasn't anything but what he claimed.

Reid's father is a monster, his mom, I have to assume, knows this, and Reid is terrified they'll gain custody of his daughter after his death.

I stare at the far wall, where the blinds are drawn tight, and no morning light can ever seep through.

I wonder if I can do what Reid's asking. Yes, I know

that if I marry him and adopt Claudia that I can protect her. But I think, even if he isn't saying it, he hopes that I'll love her.

Children need love.

People need love.

I open my hand and let the ring tumble free.

42

ANDREA

"IF I SAY YES," I BEGIN HESITANTLY, BUT AS SOON AS I SAY this Reid grasps me in a hug, picks me up, and spins me around.

"Thank you, Andrea. Thank you."

He's spinning me, as fast as a top, and I hang onto his shoulders, growing dizzy at the bright pink cherry blossoms and green grass of the park swirling past.

My dress flies around me like a kite, and the cherry blossoms falling from the trees and blowing on the breeze flit around us like pink butterflies. My stomach flips like I'm on a rollercoaster, as the warm air rushes over me.

At that thought I pinch Reid's arm. "Put me down. Reid."

He slows then, grinning down at my serious expression, as he carefully lowers me to the ground.

"It's a yes," he says happily. And even though he looks exhausted—like he got even less sleep than I did—he's full of expectant energy. "Thank you."

I shake my head and walk down the wide dirt trail, passing the long row of blossoming cherry trees. "If I say yes," I begin again, and Reid restrains his smile, "what exactly would happen next?"

He puts his hands in his pockets and relaxes his shoulders. He's the perfect picture of ease.

Tall, lean, striding with the languid grace of a lifelong fencing champion. He's in dark jeans, a casual collared shirt, and his sandy hair is a mess.

If you didn't know him, you'd think he was a man in his late twenties without a care in the world. The only thing that might let you know otherwise is the deep purple lines under his eyes, the hollows in his cheeks, and the slight tightness around his mouth that I think might be the only sign that he's in pain.

I saw that in his records last night. He's tired. All the time. Dizzy. Headaches. Weight loss. And pain. He's in pain.

Reid smiles down at me. "We would apply for a marriage license. Get married this weekend."

He watches my expression carefully to see how I take that news. "That's fast."

"Ye-es." He lifts an eyebrow, but I can tell, he's hiding how nervous he is. Behind his back, his left hand is shaking.

"What else?" I ask.

"We'd be married with our families there, so everyone can see—"

"How in love we are?" I ask, taking a breath of the sweet blossom-scented air.

Reid's mouth twists. "Not what I was going to say. But sure."

"Would we dance at our wedding?" I ask, thinking about how Reid always managed to maneuver me into dancing with him.

Down the path, past the cherry blossom trees standing like bridesmaids dressed in fuchsia, a man sits on a bench and plays his cello.

It's not a waltz, it's not really a dancing song at all, it's a rendition of a popular song drawn out in the low tenor hum of the cello. He has his case open in front of him to collect change as people walk past.

Reid must see the shadow cross over my face, or feel the dampening in my mood, because he holds out his hand and says, "We could dance now."

"In the park? In the grass? Here? Now?"

I look around at the joggers running past, at the dog walkers, at the group of tourists, at the couple lying in the grass under the shade of a cherry tree.

Reid looks too, then shrugs.

"Why not?"

Why not? Because people might think it's strange. Or people may stare. Or because I never do anything spontaneous anymore. I never...live.

"Why not," I agree.

I step out of my heels, let the lush grass cushion my feet, and then place my hand in Reid's. He smiles and pulls me close. I brush against the soft fabric of his shirt, feel the warmth of his hands, and take in the lingering smell of his shaving soap.

Then he spins me, twirling us around the floating cherry blossoms, whirling us through the maze of trees, and as we dance, I feel the tangled, knotted chain around my heart unraveling.

We spin past the cellist, and when he sees us dancing, he bridges into a love song.

When he does, Reid laughs, his eyes alight with the sardonic humor I always associated with him.

I hold him tighter, one hand in his, the other clutching the muscles of his back, as we float over the grass, twirling like cherry blossoms falling through the bright blue sky.

"God, this is fun," Reid says, grinning down at me. "You always were the best dancer."

"I'm actually a terrible dancer," I say, thinking about Jace's concerts.

Reid shakes his head. "Not with me you aren't."

He dips me then and my stomach flips over itself, and when he pulls me back up I'm pressed against the warmth of his chest. He slows then and we dance together, and I can feel the beating of his heart matching the rhythm of my hips.

"What happens if I say yes?" I ask.

His hand presses into the curve of my spine. "You'll move in with me and Claudia. The nanny, Mary, lives in full time. For the next few months, we'll...look, my daughter isn't going to remember me. I know this. But if you're there with us, someday, when she's older, you can tell her about me. And maybe, if I do it right, you'll tell her good things. How we danced in the park, and had a picnic on the beach, and how we put her to sleep at night when she needed us. For the next few months...we live."

I nod. The breeze floats over us, and the falling cherry blossoms coat the grass in a carpet of pink. The love song is finished. The music has stopped.

Reid looks down at me, and the sun stings my eyes as I look back.

Slowly, we stop dancing, but I keep ahold of him and he holds onto me.

"Well?" he asks, and even though his expression is even, I can feel his heart pick up speed.

"If I say yes," I begin again, "I won't ever be able to tell anyone why we really married?"

If I did, if I told my dad, or my brothers, or anyone, it might get out, and then I wouldn't be able to protect his daughter. Not like he's asking me too.

"Right. You'd take it to your grave."

I nod. And then I give my promise.

"Yes," I tell him, "I'll marry you."

He smiles at me then and it's the happiest but also the saddest smile I've seen in my entire life.

43

ANDREA

BREAKFAST THE NEXT MORNING IS DISMAL AND DAMP. LOW, grumbly clouds hang over the buildings and shower a gray cold rain over the city.

Even high up in the Tower, the sun isn't any more visible. The mist clings to the windows and the wet patter-patter of rain plinks against the glass.

My dad is buried in the business section of the morning paper.

Rob Jr is nursing a cup of coffee. His eyes are bloodshot and he looks like he had a rough night out. Sometimes, Rob Jr's business dinners go late into the night and he always, always orders copious amounts of drink to toast burgeoning deals. Unlike Elliot who becomes stupid after two drinks, Rob Jr can swallow a barrel of bourbon and you'd never know it. Not until the next morning when he's as caustic as acid and nasty tempered.

Elliot can tell as well as I that Rob Jr is hungover, so he's reading on his phone, while nibbling on a piece of sourdough toast slathered in butter.

My mom is distractedly stirring her hot turmeric chai —a nod to the rain—her spoon clinking against the edge of the glass.

All business talk is done, we'll be going to our separate offices soon, so I clear my throat.

"I have an announcement."

My mom stops stirring, my dad rustles his paper as he lowers it, and Elliot looks up from his phone. Rob Jr keeps nursing his black coffee.

All eyes are on me, even the mist outside the window seems to be moving closer to hear what I have to say.

"I'm getting married on Saturday. To Reid Shilling."

Silence.

Complete. Stunned. Silence.

My dad drops the paper, and it flutters to the floor, unnoticed.

Even my mom who, I think, has wanted me to marry Reid for years is staring at me as if I've been replaced by a person who *looks* like Andrea but can't possibly be her.

Because the Andrea they know wouldn't do something like this.

Except...

Rob Jr's caustic laugh fills the room, echoing sharply off the glass, steel and marble floors.

I give him a flat look.

He shakes his head and wipes at his bloodshot eyes. "I knew it. I knew you weren't as perfect as you've pretended to be. You ran off once. You're doing it again. My word, you're so predictable." He turns to Dad. "And you think she's a reliable choice for running your—"

"Are you in love?" My mom interrupts.

She's still looking at me like she can't quite believe I'm the same person that was sitting in this exact chair yesterday, and the day before.

At that question, even Elliot gives me a searching look.

Under the table, I clench my hand into a fist. She told me, all those years ago, that the next time I fell in love I should use my head and not my heart. I wonder if I'm using my head, or if I'm letting my heart carry me away again.

I don't love Reid. But I think maybe I'm using my heart more than my head in this decision.

"The wedding will be at ten, at Wagner Cove in Central Park. You're all invited."

My dad has finally shaken out of his momentary shock. I can see his mind working behind the quick movements of his eyes and a new energy buzzing around him.

"Does he have you over a barrel?" he asks point-blank.

I'm not surprised this is where his mind went. He's someone who frequently leaves his competitors in helpless positions where they have no choice but to comply.

"No," I say firmly. "I want to marry him. He asked. I said yes."

Rob Jr snorts.

Elliot shrugs.

My dad rubs his hand over his chin, his eyes dancing with possibilities.

"You'll run the Shillings' companies one day, you and Reid. If we join ventures..." He trails off, rearranging the future, moving companies and lives like pieces on a chess board.

He approves.

He's humming with that same energy he has every time he discovers a new business game to play. And my marriage to the Shilling heir? That's a fabulous game for my dad.

Well. That's settled.

My mom stands, scraping her chair over the marble floor. We all turn to her, she's in a pink pantsuit and pearls, probably in rebellion against the dreary weather.

"Well. What are you sitting here for? You need a *dress*."

44

ANDREA

"I CAN'T TELL YOU HOW SORE I AM," I SAY TO REID, stretching my arms over my head.

He just rocked Claudia and sang her a bedtime lullaby. She fell asleep in his arms, having finished a full bottle. Now, if she wakes in the night, Mary will come down. Which is good, because Reid's eyes are smudged with dark shadows and he looks worn thin.

But still, he smiles at me as he falls back into the comfortable cushions of the living room couch. "I'll bite. Why are you sore?"

I sit down next to him and lean back into the cushions. "Because I tried on one hundred and eighteen dresses today. I spent hours lifting, bending, twisting, zipping, squeezing, parading—"

"That sounds—"

"Painful."

He laughs.

"My muscles are quivery masses of pain. But"—I lift a finger—"I'm going to be the best-dressed bride that has ever lived."

My mom took my wedding dress as seriously as NASA took the space race. She called in her team—dress designer, veil designer, glove designer, stylists, shoe consultant, make-up artists, jewelers—and set to dressing me with single-minded determination.

If I'm going to be married, then I'm going to be married looking like a billion dollars.

And that is that.

Reid shifts and when that jostles me, I let out a moan at the twinge in my shoulders.

"That's it," Reid says as he stands.

"What?"

"You. In the bath." He points down the hall.

I lift my eyebrows. I brought my suitcase with me when I arrived after dinner.

When I finished my dress fitting marathon with my mom, I was too tired to go to the office, so instead I went back to my place. Then, seeing the cold, lonely living room and the narrow, uncomfortable couch, I pulled out a large suitcase, filled it with clothes, shoes, work files, my laptop, and the contents of my safe, and then I called a driver to take me to Reid's.

When he opened the door, holding Claudia in his arms, and saw me standing on his stoop with my suitcase, he just smiled and opened his front door wide.

But just because I moved in doesn't mean I'm going to strip down and take a bath with him.

I cross my arms and frown at the pinch. "Reid. I'm not going to take a bath with you."

He raises both his eyebrows. "With me?"

Oh.

He pushes his hand through his messy hair and gives me a funny look.

"Come on," he says.

I push off the couch, my cheeks heating as I follow him down a long hall, the wood floors glistening, and the light yellow walls lined with paintings of the parks around New York.

He opens the door to the master bedroom. I've not been in here before. There's a large bed, with a fluffy down comforter, a buttery yellow blanket, and a dark mahogany wood frame. It's the nicest, prettiest bed I've ever seen.

Back at the Tower, all our beds were as luxurious as something Louis XIV would've slept on, and we had burgundy and gold silk sheets and gold brocade wallpaper.

Here though, the walls are a soothing cream, the wood floors are covered with thick rugs, and the tall windows have soft yellow drapes. It's so comforting and peaceful that I stop for a moment and just look.

Reid's still walking though. He opens the door to the en suite bathroom and tilts his head. "In here."

I follow him, finding a bathroom with white tile floors, cornflower blue walls, and a massive porcelain clawfoot tub.

But the tub isn't what has me shaking my head.

"You were serious," I say.

He flashes a grin my way. "Why say something if you don't mean it?"

"Oh my word."

"You'll like it," he promises.

There's a funny feeling at the edge of my mouth, almost like my lip is twitching. It's as if I'm waking up, trying to smile.

Reid notices it too. "I promise, I'm going to make you smile or I'm going to die trying."

"You are so..." Infuriating, gallows-humored, unexpected?

"Amazing?" he asks.

"Hmm."

He turns on the faucets then, and almost right away steam rises from the water that's filling the tub.

"How will this work?" I gesture at the bath, it's at least six feet long and three feet deep.

"Well, you see, when you take a bath, you usually get undressed, climb in, and let the water run over you."

"Alright, funny guy. If we're doing this, I'm keeping my bra and panties on."

He grins. "There you go again, thinking I want to join you."

Whatever.

I pull my dress over my head, not noticing the twinge in my muscles because of the hot flush covering my cheeks. I drop my dress on the white tiles and peek at Reid, but he's not even looking at me. Granted, my bathing suit revealed more skin than this, but somehow this feels different.

Maybe it's the clouds of steam rising from the tub, the gurgle of the water, the humidity soaking the air, or maybe it's the small, intimate space.

Reid has always been large, even when he was little, he was always big for his age. And it wasn't just his stature, his personality always took up space too. This narrow bathroom, with the cold white tiles under my feet and the hot steam-filled air, is too small.

Oh well.

I grip the cool edge of the bathtub and climb over the lip, dipping my toes into the bubbling water. It's hot in that way where your muscles immediately relax like chocolate melting in your mouth.

I climb in and sit at the far end of the bath, my legs folded to the side, the water pooling around me.

Finally, Reid turns.

When he sees me in the tub, his blue-green eyes fill with laughter.

"Come on then," I say, splashing water at him, "I'm not doing this by myself."

The water sprays over his T-shirt and he grins at me. "You won't regret it."

"You say that a lot."

"I mean it a lot."

Then Reid lifts the champagne bottle and a loud pop echoes off the tiles as he uncorks it. He pours the champagne into the bath. It streams through the air like a golden rainbow, fizzing as it hits the water. Then he uncorks another. And another. And another.

And with each bottle of champagne that he pours into the bath, his smile gets wider and wider.

I lean back against the porcelain and thank all that's holy that I wore a black bra and underwear today. The water's nearly up to my belly button and if I'd worn white, there wouldn't be anything left to the imagination.

Finally, Reid strips off his T-shirt, steps out of his jeans—thank goodness he's in navy briefs, and not commando—and climbs into the champagne bath.

He sits at the other end, and the faucet runs over his

bunched shoulder muscles and the tanned lines of his chest.

He has a dozen more bottles of champagne ready to go, and now that he's in the bath, he pours the fizzing, bubbling champagne over his head, dousing his hair. When the bottle's empty he shakes his head, the droplets fling from the ends of his hair, arching through the air, and then he wipes his hand over his face.

He's drenched in champagne. His skin is wet and sparkling and his eyes are alive with laughter at the ridiculousness of taking a bath in champagne.

The air is blooming with a sweetness, like ripe peaches and summer rose petals crushed in your hand.

Reid grabs another green glass bottle from the tiles next to the bath and uncorks it. The champagne flows over his fingers.

He shifts toward me and then before I can tell him to stop, he empties the bottle over me. The sticky sweet champagne runs like a waterfall. I sputter and shove at him and he laughs.

"You're a wretch," I say, wiping my face and pushing my wet hair back.

"I know," he says, pulling up another bottle.

I lick my lips. The champagne tastes like citrus, and cream, and golden slices of toast.

The cork pops and Reid tosses it into the bath. It floats between us, like a little boat.

Instead of pouring the champagne into the water, Reid tips the bottle and takes a long swallow. "That's good."

He smiles and grabs another bottle, opens it and hands it to me.

"Drink up. Be merry."

He leans back on the porcelain, takes another drink from his bottle and closes his eyes, luxuriating in the champagne.

But I'm not drinking. Instead, I slowly inch across the bath, and then I tilt my bottle and pour it over Reid's head.

He jerks upright, his eyes open in shock and then he coughs, sputters and shakes off like a wet dog as I empty the entire bottle over him.

"Andrea! I didn't know you had it in you." He's narrowing his eyes on me, contemplating the remaining bottles by the tub.

"I don't regret it," I say. "I really, really don't regret it."

He grins and then grabs another bottle.

I do too.

Then we're shaking the bottles, spraying champagne at each other, soaking each other with bubbling drink. And when the bottles are all empty, we're splashing each other, and Reid's laughing and me...I catch myself in the mirror.

My cheeks are pink, my eyes are bright, and I'm smiling.

45

ANDREA

I'M SHOWERED, SCRUBBED CLEAN OF CHAMPAGNE, AND SNUG in my pink cotton nightgown.

When I turn my head I still catch a hint of citrus and peaches in my hair, but that just makes a bubbly feeling, similar to laughter, lodge in my chest.

The living room is lit by a single lamp next to the couch, my feet are tucked under my legs and I'm warm under the soft cashmere blanket. There's a strange feeling niggling at me, one I can't quite put my finger on, but I think it's happiness.

No, that's not quite it.

Once, when I was sixteen, I went up to the roof of the Tower. I leaned against the brass railing, felt the cold spring breeze, and watched the sun paint the city in reds and oranges and pinks. It was the most beautiful sunset I'd ever seen. It was like the sun was spilling watercolor over the buildings and turning the grays and browns into fiery golden hues. When the sunlight hit me, and lit my skin too, I felt transformed.

There was happiness there, deep awe and wonder, but circling the edge of it there was also grief because I knew that in a few minutes, maybe even seconds, the sunset would be gone, and it wouldn't ever return. Not like that. There wouldn't ever be a sunset like that again.

So that's the feeling.

And I don't know whether to delight in the sun's rays or close my eyes.

I look at the hall as Reid steps into the living room, the floorboards creaking under him. He's in shorts and a T-shirt, his feet are bare and his hair is still wet.

When he sees me sitting on the couch, obviously waiting for him, he smiles.

"So."

"So," I agree.

He steps into the light of the lamp. Outside, the noise of a siren rolls past, breaking the quiet of the night.

"I was wondering, was it everything you dreamed of?" I ask.

He sits down on the couch next to me and stretches his legs out in front of him. He shakes his head and I can smell champagne on him too.

"You know," he says with an apologetic smile, "I have to be honest, I never thought about taking a champagne bath until the other day."

"Really? But you claimed you always wanted to."

He nods. "I just went with it because it was so ridiculous I thought it might make you smile."

I give him a stunned look. "You poured fifty bottles of champagne into a bathtub to make me smile?"

"It worked, didn't it?"

Huh.

I guess it did.

"And you want me to smile because…"

He looks at me like it's as obvious as why the sun rises every morning and sets every night.

"Because I like you. Because I've always liked you. Because plenty of people are alive but not living. But you shouldn't be one of them."

He means it, I know he does. Even when we were kids he liked me. "It's funny, you liked me as a kid, but I never particularly liked you."

"That's because I was a shit."

I can't disagree. "Do you remember your eighth birthday? How you wouldn't let any of the other kids have any cake? You sat there eating it in front of all of us and—"

"You dropped my presents in the pool to teach me a lesson."

He's laughing and I want to join him.

"Or remember how you hid from your nanny that day at the Met? What were we, four?"

"Five," he says, grinning at me.

"Grace and I were looking too, all the docents, security, your nanny—"

"Bernice—"

"Was frantic. And we finally found you after two hours of searching, eating a giant lollipop behind a sarcophagus."

"That was a good lollipop."

I lean toward him, my wet hair falls over my shoulder, and I smile. My lips turn up and more than that, I smile inside.

Reid sees my smile, sits straight and reaches into his pocket. When he pulls out a small box he says, "I got this today. If you don't want to wear it, that's fine, I..."

He opens the box and there's a ring nestled on a white satin pillow.

My heart thuds in my chest, slow and painful. The ring is slender, white gold, with a perfectly round creamy white pearl and chips of aquamarine studding the band.

"I know it's not a diamond. That didn't seem right. But I thought...your birthstone is pearl. And mine is..."

He stops when I reach out and take the ring from the case. "You were born in March," I say, "so it's aquamarine."

It reminds me of the cove we swam at, all pearly sand and turquoise water.

"If it's too much—"

"It's not too much."

I take the ring and slide it onto my ring finger. I've not worn anything there since I took off Jace's engagement ring. It fits perfectly, and I imagine he must've asked my mom for my ring size.

The gold is warm and heavy on my finger.

I never imagined this moment. There's nothing that could've ever prepared me for it.

Reid's watching me carefully. His expression is the one I've come to recognize as the look he wears when he's nervous.

"Thank you," I say, then I lean forward and wrap my arms around his shoulders. I stay there until I feel him relax, his shoulders loosening and his breath steadying.

He doesn't lift his arms to hug me back, he just stays still, sitting in the lamp light, my arms around him, my head resting on that hollow place between his shoulder and his neck.

A few minutes later he heads to bed and I make up the couch, pulling a sheet over the cushions and plumping the pillows.

I fall asleep rubbing my thumb over the warm gold of the ring.

An hour, two, maybe three later, I wake to find Reid shaking me.

"Andrea. Andrea."

I jerk upright and look desperately around the room, sweat drips from my brow and down my back. My nightgown twists around my legs. The living room is dark and oppressive. My heart gallops around my chest, pounding so loudly I think Reid must hear it, and there's a metallic dryness in my mouth.

"You were crying. You were having a nightmare. I came and—"

"Okay." I nod, licking my lips, my eyes darting around the room.

I remember now. I was at the playground, under that bench, and everything was dark and I was crying and crying, but I wasn't calling for my mom, I was calling for...I don't know. I don't know who I was calling for, only that they weren't there and I needed them.

"Are you alright?" Reid asks, searching my face.

I want to say yes. I want to pretend, just like I have for the past eight years, that I'm perfectly fine. But it's the middle of the night, and the room is dark, just like my nightmares, and when Reid leaves, I'll be all alone.

I scoot further into the couch, making room.

"Will you stay?" I ask, "Just for a little bit."

He considers me, watching my face as the light from a

passing car flickers over the room. Then slowly he climbs onto the wide, comfortable couch and wraps his warm arms around me.

He holds me and then whispers into the dark, "I'll stay as long as I can."

I fall asleep to his promise and this time I don't dream.

46

ANDREA

"DO YOU KNOW, I THINK I NEEDED THIS," I TELL REID, tilting my face up to the afternoon sunshine.

We're lying on a checkered blanket in Central Park, the grass tickles my toes, and dandelion fluff floats past on the breeze. To our left, the pond tends green, the sleepy turtles laze in the sun, and Belvedere Castle rises from the sheer rocks thrusting out of the water.

"The pyramids wore you out, did they?" Reid asks as he picks a long piece of grass and twists it between his fingers.

"Hmm. Maybe."

Yesterday, we flew down to Tulum, because, as Reid put it, he'd always wanted to see the pyramids and Egypt was too far for a day trip.

This past week—all the days leading up to our wedding on Saturday—has been *full*.

Not like you would think either.

I haven't been planning wedding festivities—my mom gladly took over that task.

I haven't been working—for which my office staff are *incredibly* grateful.

No. I've been living.

Tomorrow we'll be married. Reid hasn't wasted any time. The night after he slept on the couch with me, I woke up with my mind made up. I told him that I was going to take the next six months off work. I was going to spend every day with him and Claudia—living.

By the look he gave me you'd think I'd given him the world.

So we toured the sun-scorched ruins of Tulum.

We meandered the gray cobblestone streets of Montreal and gobbled down poutine.

We took a sail in New York Harbor to see the Statue of Liberty set aflame by the setting sun.

And now, we're lying in Central Park, napping in the midday sun under the fairy-tale castle.

The air smells of crisp green leaves and freshly mowed grass. A group of kids on summer break kick a soccer ball across the grass nearby. There's a family having a picnic, classical music playing from their stereo. A passel of tourists pass, arguing over which way to Strawberry Fields.

We spent the last hour trying to make Claudia smile. We made faces, tickled her, and pointed out the cheeky squirrels hopping from limb to limb. Reid says she hasn't smiled yet, that babies don't until six or eight weeks, but since he made me smile, he's confident he can make his daughter smile too.

But when Claudia got tired and restless, Mary

volunteered to come down and take her home for a nap so that we could stay a little longer in the park.

I like Mary, she's from Guyana and she's been a nanny for twenty-five years. She's helped raise four other—now grown—kids, and her no-nonsense, calm, patient manner is as comforting as the soft yellow walls of Reid's house.

Nothing fazes her, not middle-of-the-night wakings, not crying for hours, not hopping on a plane with us to bring Claudia on an international trip, none of it. She's like a grandma who, having raised all her own kids, and helped raise others too, is so confident that nothing can ruffle her.

"Should we head back soon?" I ask, stretching my arms over my head. "Rest up for the big day tomorrow?"

Reid covers a yawn and shakes his head. Although hearing all we've done, you'd think that his energy is boundless, it's not. He sleeps a lot. On the plane. During the day. And at night he sleeps like the dead.

He smiles when he sees me watching him and then reaches up and pulls a strand of grass from my hair.

He tosses the grass aside, a smile in his eyes. Then I reach out and brush his hair off his forehead, tousling it so the bit of dandelion fluff that settled there flies free.

We watch it catch the breeze and float away.

"Do you know," Reid says, sitting up, "that some people think you can wish on a dandelion seed? That it'll float your wish right up to heaven."

He's following the seed, a look of concentration on his face, watching it until it's out of sight.

He rolls his shoulders then, his T-shirt stretching across his chest.

"What did you just wish for?" I ask.

He shakes his head, a line forming between his eyebrows. "You don't want to know my wish."

I skim my hand over the spiky grass and frown at him. "Why not? What happened to taking secrets to the grave?"

He leans close and the scent of his soap and the grassy afternoon surrounds me. "This wish, I take with me."

My mouth goes dry at the intense look in his eyes. Across the field, the kids playing soccer start to shout and laugh.

Finally, Reid shifts back and says, "Did you know, I never trusted anyone in my entire life. Not like I trust you."

I understand.

"Life's terribly lonely when you don't have anyone to trust, isn't it?"

He nods.

Then he takes my hand, threading his fingers through mine. His hand is so much larger that I feel wrapped in him, like it's not just his hand holding me, but all of him.

Behind him, the gray stone of Belvedere Castle sparkles in the sun, and beyond that the dark green trees of the Ramble stand against the blue sky.

"Do you mind if we walk by the castle?" I ask.

He shakes his head. "And then...coffee. I need coffee. And...sushi. Do you want sushi for your pre-wedding night?"

We gather up the blanket and stroll across the wide, emerald-toned lawn, taking our time, debating over whether sushi or foie gras is the better pre-wedding dinner. Or should you carb-load with plates of spaghetti like you're preparing for the New York Marathon?

"I think you're on to something," Reid says, drawing me toward the stone terrace at the base of the castle. "Tonight we'll have buckets of fresh spaghetti. We'll have so much pasta we could bathe in it."

"No." I shake my head, a bubble of laughter rising. "I will not bathe in pasta."

"Come on, Andrea. Live a little. Imagine, a bathtub full of spaghetti. You won't regret it."

I laugh then. Because I can imagine it. Reid and me in his white tiled kitchen, swimming in a plastic kiddie pool full of spaghetti. The noodles running through our toes and glopping on our heads.

"I won't do it," I tell him.

His eyes get that glint and I laugh again.

It's a high, ringing, joyful laugh. It sounds like summer, and speeding on a bike down a street with your arms thrown wide, and spinning in the park, dancing to a cellist, and shooting bubbling champagne in the bath. It sounds like joy. I haven't laughed like this in years.

Reid is grinning at me, the happiest expression on his face.

Then I see a figure in the distance.

He catches my eye as he strides from the shadows of the Ramble. He's far away, too far to see his face. Yet I'd know that stride anywhere.

It's confident, long-legged, as if he knows exactly where he's been and where he's going.

When he hears me laughing, he turns in my direction. I know if he were close I'd be able to see the gray-blue of his eyes, the softness of his mouth, and the gentle strength in his hands.

Jace.

He's here.

He's here in New York.

A fist tightens around my heart.

And my laugh, the joy, all the hilarity of the previous moment cuts off as if it had never been. Like a bird shot from the sky, it plummets to the earth. Done. Gone.

I stop walking, and I see that he has too.

"What?" Reid asks, pulling up next to me. "Are you alright?"

I can't say anything.

I can't breathe.

My heart isn't beating anymore, the fist around it is so tight that the world is going dark. I take a step back.

Breathe, I tell myself.

And then I do. I drag in a burning, painful breath. I can feel my heart beating again, it's thrumming wildly in my chest, not knowing whether it wants to run to him or away from him.

Reid's touches my arm. "Andrea?"

Then, he follows my gaze across the terrace, past the wooden gazebo, toward the trees and the shadows and then he sees Jace too.

Reid stiffens, but his concern is for me. He steps close, studying my expression.

"What do you want to do?" he asks quietly. "Do you want me to stay? To go?"

He's asking because Jace is striding our way, moving confidently through the crowd, his eyes on me.

After eight years, Jace and I are finally going to meet again.

Right here, right in the same spot where it all began the first time.

"Go," I tell Reid, my voice coming out as dry as a husk.

He nods, squeezes my hand, and then he's walking

away, striding across the stones, leaving me alone to face the man that broke my heart.

And then Jace is there. He slows and then stops in front of me, only a few short feet away.

And he's Jace, but he's not Jace.

He's at least two inches taller than the last time I saw him. I guess that final growth spurt he had at eighteen wasn't quite finished. He's about six three now, and with him standing so close I have to tilt my chin to look into his eyes.

When I see the scar on his face, the thin line running from his temple to his chin, my stomach twists and I want to reach out and touch him, to make sure he's really okay.

I saw the scar years ago, on a photo in a magazine, but it's different now. In the magazine it was a picture on a page, in real-life...he was hurt, he was *hurt*. And I don't know how. I don't know anything about the past eight years.

Suddenly I hate the years that separated us, making it so that I don't know when he grew those final inches, or how he got the scar traveling down his cheek, or when his face became more angular and his eyes more gray and less blue.

I don't know why he started wearing this black leather jacket, so worn that the elbows are creased and faded, and I don't know what lyrics he has written in the small notebook tucked into the front pocket of his jeans.

I don't know anything.

I stand there silently taking him in, running my eyes over him as if I can catalogue everything that's the same —his long eyelashes, his bottom lip, his thick black hair —and everything that's changed—too much to say.

He's doing the same as me. He looks as if he's

drinking me in. Like he's been dying of thirst and he's finally found cool, clear water.

It's funny, we used to look at each other like this after we made love. We'd lie in bed just drinking each other in.

It's that thought that has me blinking, taking a small step back, even though I want to stay close, because I can smell him again, that ocean-tinged, guitar-cedar scent that always drew me in.

When I step back, Jace's eyes clear.

"I thought it was you," he says, and when he speaks, the rich tenor of his voice weaves over me like a song. "I heard your laugh."

He searches my expression, like he's looking for something, some signal or clue. But I don't know what he wants or what he's searching for.

"Hi Andi," he says, with the sun shining over him.

I suck in a breath. No one has called me Andi since him. The name punches me in the gut.

"Hello Jace."

We stand there silently for a moment, a family weaves around us, a tour guide draws a crowd toward Belvedere Castle, touting its history.

I wonder what Jace is doing here. He and his brothers promised never to come back to New York, not until they'd made it big.

Which they have.

So.

"You're in New York," I say stupidly.

He nods, "We played a concert in Times Square, for the morning show."

"Ah."

He's watching me now, and there's a sort of helpless yearning on his face that I don't know how to respond to.

He's the one who cheated. He's the one who broke up with me. He's the one who said he never wanted to see me again. What does he have to yearn about?

"How...how have you been?" he finally asks, his hands twisting anxiously at his sides, as if he wants to reach out and hold me and is barely able to stop himself.

I swallow the peach-sized lump in my throat. "Good. I've been...good. And you?"

I ask this politely, but inside I'm shouting, *Why did you do it, why did you promise forever and then take it away, why did you write the end of our love for the world to hear, why?*

He nods and there's a pained expression on his face. "I'm good."

"That's good," I say, and then I nearly laugh hysterically because if we say *good* one more time...

It's awful. It's so painfully awkward. We used to talk for hours, about nothing, and anything, we could talk and talk, it was so easy between us. And now, we can barely string two sentences together.

"How's your family?" he asks, looking across the park, toward the Tower.

"Good," I say, "They're all good."

Oh god.

Good.

"And yours?" I ask.

"They're good too." He nods slowly, his eyes shadowed even though the afternoon sun is shining fully down over him. "Everyone's good."

Okay.

I have to go. I can't do this.

He looks so similar to the Jace I knew. The one I never stopped loving.

But he's not the same. He's not the man I could share everything with, the man whose arms I lay in and bared my soul to. He isn't him. And even the Jace I did know was capable of coldness and cruelty, I just never realized it until the end.

I lift my hand in a wave, "It was good to see you again, I—"

"Andi," he says, his voice low, urgent.

I cut off, wait for whatever it is he's going to say.

"How are you really?"

I stare at him.

He's looking at me as if he can see inside me, as if he can see all the pain of the last eight years. How dare he?

How am I really?

Really, really?

A ball of anger lodges in my chest. He doesn't get to ask that. He has no right to ask that.

I shake my head. "I'm good. And I'm glad you're still making music," I tell him. "I know it's what you wanted. I'm glad the world gets to hear your songs."

He nods then and smiles at me, and I feel it then, the draw. That magnetic force that tugged me toward him the first time I saw him and hasn't ever let me go. The need to take two steps forward and fold myself into him is nearly overwhelming.

Except, he hurt me. He broke me. And it's only now, with Reid, that I can see that someday I might be able to put myself back together.

As if Jace can hear my thoughts he asks, "Was that... was that Reid who was with you?"

I nod. "Yes. It was Reid."

This time it looks like Jace is the one who has been punched in the gut.

Then his eyes flicker to my hand and my left ring finger. The one that used to have his ring on it. When he sees the pearl and aquamarine ring his eyes flash up to mine.

"Are you—"

"We're getting married tomorrow."

His face loses color. His breath comes short and quick. "Andi."

I shake my head.

I know what he wants to say, I can see it in his eyes.

Why Reid?

Why him?

Why would you marry him?

Don't you remember what he's like? Who he is?

But then, I guess after all these years we can still read each other's thoughts, because he says, "You don't love him."

I think about Reid, holding me in his arms, promising to stay with me for as long as he can.

"It's not always about love," I say.

Jace shakes his head, his expression stunned. "It is always about love. Andi, you don't promise to spend your life with someone if it isn't about love."

But love fails, doesn't it? We're the proof of that.

Jace steps closer, lifts his hands as if he wants to pull me to him, then stops. "What happened, Andi?"

Funny. That's the same thing I wanted to ask him.

A red-tailed hawk screeches overhead, soaring back toward its skyscraper roost. Its shadow passes over the gray stones, and then it flies beyond the spires of Belvedere Castle.

The stone and the leafy summer smell surround me,

and I can't help but remember another time we stood here outside this castle, needing each other.

It's a sad truth in life that even when your mind knows that someone isn't good for you, your heart can't understand. I still want him. I still love him, and by the expression on his face, he knows.

I give him a smile as bright as the sun, the backs of my eyes burning, and say, "It was good seeing you, Jace. Good luck in life."

Then I hurry past him, blindly pushing into the dark of the Ramble. He doesn't follow me.

47

JACE

I'VE TRAVELED THROUGH SOME BAD DAYS IN LIFE.

The day my parents died. Their funeral. The months after.

The day Andi left.

The day I woke up in the hospital and realized she was gone.

The day when Dallas was sentenced to prison again —put away for assault of the men that attacked Andi— even though he always swore he'd never go back, and then when he was thrown in the hole—a place he hated —after that first day in.

The days of surgeries, metal pins, metal screws, metal rods, and persistent agony.

The day we were dropped by the producer because Dallas was in prison, and I was in too much pain to tour, to sing, to record, to do anything but stay numbed out on prescriptions.

The day River's fiancée Serena miscarried when she was five-months pregnant.

The day Pauly collapsed from taking too many beta blockers trying to control the fear of climbing up on the stage.

The days I couldn't find my voice, not even in my dreams.

Even the day we started touring again, when I limped onto the stage, my leg burning, my throat aching, and I found that I *could* sing, no matter how much it hurt, if I imagined Andi, somewhere out there, still hearing my song.

I've traveled through some bad days.

But none of them compare to this one.

I stare at the bottle of cheap vodka—straight-up, nasty, throat burning liquor. I picked it up at the first liquor store I passed on my way back to The Plaza.

If the clerk recognized me he didn't say anything. Maybe we'll see it in the news tomorrow, *Jace Morgan's Downward Spiral.* You never know, I've had worse written about me, for things less true.

I strip off my leather coat, tossing it over the back of the chair, the saddle-soap smell strong.

I'm in the penthouse suite at The Plaza, finally back in New York. But instead of a two-bedroom, cockroach-infested, graffitied building in the South Bronx, I'm staying in a two-story penthouse, with gold fixtures, chandeliers, velvet furniture, and a view of Central Park.

It's that view that tempted me to walk across the park and wander the Ramble. I was thinking about Andi and then suddenly there she was, like heaven had sent her to me again.

I crack open the vodka, the cap snapping as I twist the bottle.

I'm not a drinker.

I don't drink, I don't do drugs, I don't smoke. I'm a musician and all those things would get in the way of that.

But today?

Today is an exception.

I hear the suite door open, gliding almost silently over the polished wood floor. It's down the hall, around the corner from the main room, but I can hear footsteps and know my brothers are back from their victory tour.

Dean, in particular, wanted to see the old neighborhood and reminisce about how far we've come. River, always up for anything, went with him.

Dallas and Pauly stayed in, ordering food from all over the city, binging on every meal they've dreamed about for the past eight years. I ran into Pauly outside the elevator, he had a stack of pizza boxes so high they nearly reached his nose.

I look up from my contemplation of the vodka when Dean strides into the room, River behind him, and even Dallas and Pauly.

"It's my afternoon off," I say when Dean stares pointedly at the big, plastic jug of vodka.

Dean's thirty-two now, and he looks almost exactly like my dad, especially when he's playing music. It's startling sometimes the resemblance, but Dad wasn't much older than Dean when he died. I think the day he passes his thirty-eighth birthday is going to hit hard.

"I told you he didn't look good," Pauly says, shooting a

glance between me and the vodka.

"You all need to mind your own business," I say.

At that River laughs.

Yeah. We've been living in each other's business our entire lives.

"What happened, Jacey?" River asks, grabbing a mustard-yellow velvet chair and yanking it across the rug to the glass table.

I scowl at him. He hasn't called me Jacey since I was in kindergarten.

Everyone takes that as an invitation to make themselves comfortable. We all have our own suites. The morning show paid all-expenses, our agent handled the travel and accommodations, but even so, he knows to keep our rooms close.

We're famous in the industry for being one of the tightest knit bands out there. We play together, we work together, we laugh together, and we mourn together. Our loyalty to each other and our dedication to the music is one of the reasons we're still here.

There's a silver tray with glass tumblers on the side table. I grab them and splash a thumb of vodka in each of the glasses. Since everyone's here, I may as well share.

"I'm not drinking that," River says, leaning back in the velvet chair. "Serena would kill me. She said I'm not allowed to drink this trip."

Serena lives at their place in LA, with my two-year-old nephew Augustus and their golden retriever Frank. River flies there every other weekend, and when he isn't in LA he doesn't eat, drink, or sleep without Serena's permission. Her word is his gospel.

It fits though. He spent years jumping from girl to girl, then when he found Serena she didn't want him. It took four years of trying for him to convince her he was worth taking a chance on. River's the only one of us lucky enough to have someone.

Since Andi, I've just concentrated on the music. Besides, you can't be in a relationship if you're still in love with someone else.

"Anyone else?" I shove the tumblers across the burnished glass table.

The harsh, chemical scent of the vodka—like floor cleaner and rubbing alcohol—smothers the scent of the rose bouquet on the side table.

The suite really doesn't deserve such a cheap liquor tainting the atmosphere. The ceilings are soaring high, the chandeliers are dripping with crystals, the walls are a sedate dove gray, the furniture is spindly gold and plush velvet, and the windows are tall and arched with one of the best views in the city. In fact, this suite is exactly the kind of place that Andi grew up in, and the place she claimed she wanted to go back to.

I wonder if she and Reid will live in a place like this after they're married.

The thought burns like acid in my throat.

"Okay, what?" Dean says, his voice as deep as his bass guitar. "What happened. I haven't seen you look this bad since—"

He cuts off.

Yeah.

The days after Andi left were bad.

"I ran into Andi in the park," I say.

That has a different effect than I thought it would.

Dean's mouth drops open, and he sort of falls back down onto the blue velvet couch across from me, like his legs can't support him.

River picks up a tumbler and shoots the vodka down in one gulp. Then he coughs, his eyes watering. "That shit is nasty."

Pauly lets out a loud, shocked breath and shakes his head.

The only person who does something predictable is Dallas. He crosses his tattooed arms over his chest and says, "Damn."

I let out a bitter laugh, even though I've never been bitter, not really.

Empty yes.

Hopeless yes.

But never bitter.

"She's getting married tomorrow," I say, my voice breaking on the word *married*. "To a man she doesn't love. That's what she said." I clench my hand. "Damn it."

Dean has recovered, he's watching me with a sort of tormented expression. You'd think he wouldn't feel that bad, he didn't approve of me and Andi after all.

River grabs another tumbler and shoots down the liquor. This time he coughs less.

"What's wrong with you?" I ask him.

Thanks to Serena, he's a health nut who does liver cleanses. Alcohol isn't in his diet.

"I'm empathy drinking," he says.

"Are you going to be okay?" Pauly asks.

I poke at the thing inside me, the howling thing that doesn't understand how the only woman I'll ever love can be marrying another man.

"No," I say. "I don't think so."

Dean hits his palm against his leg and the sound echoes off the walls and the high ceiling. "You knew this was coming. You'll get over it. You did the last time."

I stare at him, open up the shutter I keep over my feelings and let him see inside that place where I've been missing her for eight years.

"I *never* got over it. You don't *get over* that kind of love. You keep living. You keep going. But you don't *get over* it."

Dean flinches and looks away from me, not able to meet my eyes.

I can taste the acrid vodka lingering in the air and it burns my throat.

I knew, theoretically, that someday Andi would get married. That she wouldn't be mine. But the theory and the reality were two different things. It was the idea of pain versus the reality of pain.

In the past few years, I've almost come back to New York a thousand times to find her. But then I remembered that she left and said she never wanted to see me again. I respected that. Just because you love someone doesn't mean they'll love you back. I respected her enough to do what she asked.

I said out loud once, when I was penned in my hospital bed after another surgery, *"I don't know why this happened,"* and Dallas—he was just done with his year-long sentence—said, *"If you knew God's plans then he wouldn't be God, would he?"*

Which is probably the most profound thing Dallas has ever said.

"Jace?" Dean says.

I look up at him, at the rest of them.

"Are you crying?" Dean stares at me, a shattered look on his face.

I shake my head. "No."

But they're all staring at me with a sort of stunned discomfort that tells me I am.

"You should tell her," Pauly says in a quiet tremor. "Don't let her get married without telling her. It's not right. You should tell her. You love her like your dad loved your mom. For life. Right?"

I can't speak, so instead I give one sharp nod.

Pauly speaking up reminds me of when we started touring again, when we walked into that first club.

We had a new booking agent finding us gigs, a drummer just out of prison, a lead singer—me—who could barely walk and who might not be able to sing, a horn player with severe anxiety, and a bass player who was willing to do whatever it took to make it to the top. Then we walked into that club and realized that the aluminum barn in the middle of the field, surrounded by the big, grassy parking lot was a club full of people who hated who we were and what we represented.

Dean told us we could go. Dallas wanted to leave. River was ready to pack up the van.

But Pauly, hands shaking, eyes scared—he was certain they were going to kill us later out behind that big barn in the vacant lot—he said, "Your dad always told us music doesn't have a color. He said music can connect anyone. Your dad said music can heal the world. This is our chance to prove him right. This is our chance to make him proud."

When Pauly, the smallest, most scared, most timid of us all said that, we couldn't do anything but stay and play.

We played like the whole world depended on the outcome of that night. And maybe it did. Because at the end of the show, there wasn't any hate in that room. Everyone was coming up to us, shaking hands, hugging, clapping us on the back, and the bartender called his cousin, the man that introduced us to our current record label. So if Pauly hadn't spoken up, and we'd left, we wouldn't be where we are today.

So since Pauly's speaking up again, we're all listening.

"Dean," River says, his voice is somber and his eyes are serious, which isn't at all like River.

People say we used to look like twins, but that was before the accident when I got a scar down the side of my face, a crooked nose from the break, and my eyes lost that spark of joy. Now, River is like a mirror of what used to be, back when I was more carefree and had a lifetime with Andi to look forward to. Instead of twins, people now say that even though we're brothers, we look as different as the saint and the sinner.

That's what they call me, the man with the voice of an angel and the face of a sinner. It's funny, because that's what my mom once said too.

"What?" Dean snaps, his voice raw. He's refusing to look at River.

"Tell him."

Dean shakes his head.

"Tell him," River demands. "Tell him or I will."

"River. No." Dean clenches his fist and leans forward, finally looking at River, trying to stare him down.

"Tell me what?" I ask, looking between my brothers.

Dallas and Pauly don't know what's going on either. Pauly's frowning and Dallas has his eyes narrowed on Dean.

"Nothing," Dean says.

River stares at Dean, his face flushing. "It's not nothing. I'm tired of keeping it from him. Look at him. Look. It wasn't right eight years ago. It's not right today. I justified it. She was a crutch. She was a liability. I can't justify it anymore."

"What," I say, my voice hard, my stomach dropping.

River's talking about Andi.

Dean shakes his head. Then River leans forward and reaches out to touch Dean's hand.

The chair, even though it's upholstered, is hard and uncomfortable beneath me, and my leg throbs in that insistent, angry way I've grown accustomed to.

Dean jerks his hand away and River gives him a beseeching look.

"Dean. Mom and Dad would be ashamed of us. You know they would. Dad wanted us to play for the world, but he didn't want us to hurt each other. I know you thought it was for the best, but how do you know what's best? How do you know?"

Dean looks down at his hands and when he does, a trickle of fear spreads through my chest, running through my veins.

"Tell me what?" I say again, my jaw aching from clenching it.

The light shining through the windows casts the opulent suite in an unnatural light, painting the mustard-yellow velvet garish and the gold tawdry. The rose and alcohol odor clogs my throat and I grab my glass and hold the cold crystal tumbler in my hand, breathing in the fumes.

Finally Dean looks up at me and I see guilt and shame and maybe fear.

"What did you do?" I ask.

And then Dean looks at River and River nods.

And suddenly I feel it, this is one of those moments, where your whole life changes in an instant.

And then Dean takes a breath, looks me straight in the eyes, and says, "I lied."

48

JACE

"WHAT DO YOU MEAN YOU LIED?" I ASK.

There's a loud pulsing noise in my ears, an insistent bass drum beat that I realize is the throbbing of my heart.

No one else can hear it. Pauly and Dallas stand next to the blue velvet couch, the pink marble fireplace and giant gold-framed mirror behind them, they're staring at Dean, not me. River's gripping the mustard-yellow velvet, his fingers leaving marks in the fabric, his expression determined.

And Dean, he doesn't hear the pounding in my ears. He rubs his hand over his face and looks at me like he can't bring himself to say whatever it is that River thinks needs to be said.

I catch my face in the massive gold-framed mirror. I see now why River thinks I need to know. My face has lost its color, my eyes are dead, the scar that runs the length of my face is deathly white, and there really are tears running down my cheeks.

Hell.

I used to imagine lyrics to write for Andi, every time something happened, good or bad, I'd write down a lyric for her. I'd imagine telling her, this is what happened, here's the lyric for today. What's yours?

But this moment? There isn't a lyric on earth that can describe it.

There aren't words, there's just the painful, insistent booming of my heart realizing that something happened that shouldn't have happened.

"What did you lie about?" I ask again. I'm clenching the crystal tumbler so hard, that I think it's about to shatter. I push it onto the table, sloshing the vodka over my hand.

"I thought..." Dean clears his throat, looks at River then flattens his mouth into a hard line. "I thought I was doing the right thing. I still think I did. It was the right choice."

River shakes his head. "The band isn't everything. Music isn't everything."

"It is," Dean says insistently, then he looks around at all of us and lets out a sigh. "Look. Before you crucify me, remember where we are today. Back in New York, at The Plaza, playing in Times Square. We're on top of the world. We got here because of the choices we made."

"What the hell?" Dallas says.

I look at my brothers, at Pauly and Dallas, all of us a thousand miles away from who and what we might've been. It's why we left. We all know what could've been. We left to break out of the prison of our futures.

"What does this have to do with Andi?" I ask, and it's painful, like skin tearing over gravel when I speak.

"You remember the night that Andi left?" River asks.

I don't have to answer, of course I remember the night she left. It's the dividing line that separated my before and my after.

Down below, twenty stories beneath us, an ambulance siren screams past, rising and then fading.

"Remember I had sex with a woman in your room," River says.

I nod. River had plenty of sex with plenty of women before Serena. I wasn't happy that he'd used my room, but it wasn't important considering the rest of the events of that day.

"I remember."

"Yeah," River says.

Dean grips his thighs and then lets out a low curse. "Andi saw River and the woman, but the lights were out and Andi thought it was you."

"What?" I shake my head. Try to take in what Dean is saying. "She wouldn't have thought that. She would've asked. She wouldn't—"

"She would if I told her it was you. If I told her that you'd been sleeping with other women for months."

I stare at Dean, the pounding so loud in my ears that I can barely hear him. He's my brother. He's my friend. He raised me after Mom and Dad died. He cares about me. He—

"What did you just say?" I ask, my lips numb, my mind denying what I just heard.

No, no, no, no, no.

"I told her it was you. That you were a cheater." He's talking in this monotone, like what he's telling me didn't break my life, break my heart, and the expression on his face tells me that he thinks he was justified.

"She was attacked by those scum. She saw River having sex and you told her it was me. She left. And then—"

"She called when you were in surgery," Dean says, and he begins to look uncomfortable, shifting on the velvet and gold trimmed chair. "I deleted her voicemails. She wanted you to tell her it wasn't true. Then she texted and I wrote back and—"

"And what?" I speak through gritted teeth.

River glances worriedly between me and Dean, but I can't care how worried he is. River can be the peacemaker some other time.

"And what Dean?"

He closes his eyes, then opens them, a plea for understanding. "I pretended to be you. I told her you did sleep with other women. I said you didn't want to see her again. Then I deleted the messages and showed you only hers."

There's a howling inside me, a desperate howling clawing at my bones.

"You lied."

Dean's face is stone. It reminds me of the face he wore at Mom and Dad's funeral. He didn't show grief, he didn't show regret, he didn't shed a single tear. I thought it was because he wanted to protect us. Now I wonder, was he protecting us, or was he always only protecting himself?

"I lied," he agrees, then shaking his head he says, "Jace. It was necessary. You were a kid. You didn't know what love was. She was a crutch and she was holding us back."

At that, the howling inside me unleashes. I lunge out

of my chair, my leg screaming in pain at the sudden movement. I thrust the glass table, turning it over, and charge at Dean.

"Shit," he says, scrambling back.

The glass table shatters as it hits the ground, spraying shards across the oriental carpet and crunching under my feet as I race at my brother. The vodka spills, soaking the air with its acrid alcohol scent.

"Jace, no!" River shouts.

Too late.

I punch Dean, striking him in the jaw. His head snaps back and his stupidly opulent chair flips, throwing him on his back.

He slides across the polished wood and I jump on him, throwing another punch. He throws out his hands to cover his face and tries to shove me off.

"Jace!" River shouts again.

And then Dallas is there, and River too, both of them tearing me off Dean.

I fight them, my chest heaving, my lungs burning.

"Calm down," Dallas says in his deep, demanding way.

I try to shake off his hands, but even though I'm six three and built, Dallas is still as immovable as a mountain.

"Jace," River says, shaking my arm.

I shrug him off and stare at him, unable to believe that my brothers, my own brothers, would've done this.

"You knew..." I say to River, my voice aching. "You knew how much she meant to me. Dean, I can understand," I shoot him a look of loathing, "He cares more about music than people. But you? You know what this did to me."

And her.

My heart booms in my chest.

She was hurt. She was scared. And then she thought everything I promised her was a lie. So she went back to the life she thought she'd escaped. And now she's marrying a man she doesn't love.

"Let me go," I say, shrugging my arms. "Damn it, let me go."

"You're done fighting Dean?" River asks.

I shake my head, not looking at Dean on the wood floor, his lip bleeding, his eye swelling. "I don't care about Dean. I have to find Andi."

River and Dallas step back then, letting me free.

"I'm sorry," Dean says, wiping his lip.

I shake my head. I don't have time for sorrys.

Andi is getting married tomorrow. That means I only have hours to find her and take us back to where we used to be.

She has to know what happened. She has to know I still love her.

I grab my coat, my wallet, and then sprint toward the suite's door.

After me, I hear Pauly shout, "Good luck, Jace."

I don't need luck. I need a miracle.

49

JACE

THE TOWER IS AS GLEAMING, GOLDEN, AND IN-YOUR-FACE as ever. It truly is a monument to the ego of one man and the empire he's built.

The first time I came here as a seventeen-year-old I was more concerned with looking at her than at the ludicrous amount of marble and mirrors. Now, I'm more concerned with looking *for* her.

"She's not here," her brother Rob Jr says.

He hasn't aged well. They say you get the face you deserve by the time you're sixty. Rob Jr got the face he deserved at thirty—all the cruelty, disdain, and malice show in his thin lips, the veins on his nose, and the deep lines on his forehead.

I never knew him, but I heard about him while at Darby, and Andi told me enough for me to know that he isn't a friend.

He came down to the lobby after the doorman called up to let "the family" know that I was asking to see Andi.

"Where is she?" I ask, keeping my voice even.

At that, Rob Jr looks me up and down, from the scar on my face, to my black leather jacket, all the way down to my leather boots. There are a dozen reflections of the two of us in the mirrors lining the lobby. I see his smile in every one of them before he begins to laugh.

When he does, the sound bounces off the marble and the mirrors.

"Jace Morgan," he says, baring his teeth in a smile that reminds me of a barracuda.

"Yes."

He puffs out his chest, sizing me up. "The musician. This is perfect."

I look around the lobby, measuring the distance between the glass doors and the elevator. I wonder if Andi is upstairs.

The lobby smells like a museum, all cold marble and glass. It feels cold too. Cold and empty. I hate to think of Andi back here, thinking I didn't want her.

"Do you know where she is?" I ask, my patience straining.

Rob Jr nods and although I don't trust the delight on his face, he says, "She lives on the Upper West Side now. I'll give you the address. I hope you convince her to give up Shilling."

I narrow my eyes. "Why?"

There's no reason for him to care.

He shrugs, "Because I like it when she makes bad decisions."

After that, there's nothing much to say.

50

JACE

THE BROWNSTONE IS AS FAR FROM THE IN-YOUR-FACE luxury of the Tower as you can possibly get.

It's an understated three-story home on a quiet side street near Riverside Park. There are flower boxes full of red flowers, and large shining windows built to let in lots of afternoon light. If the Tower is a showpiece, then this is a home.

The sun shines through the green leaves of the gingko tree behind me and down the street a little girl laughs as she runs in front of her mom, pushing a stroller down the sidewalk.

I stand out on this street. It's for people who have two kids, a dog, and like doing the crossword on lazy Sunday mornings in their cluttered living room. It's for people who have a home. The only home I've ever had is Andi.

Maybe that's why my hand shakes as I ring the doorbell, the buzzing sound jangling through me.

Sweat trails down my neck as the sun shines down on me. Even so, I'm cold.

On the other side of the door, I hear footsteps. I hold my breath.

Andi.

Andi.

Please.

The door opens.

It's Reid.

We stare at each other, neither of us speaking for a good twenty seconds.

He's different than I remember. At Darby he wore arrogance like a suit, and he had a way of looking at you that let you know he was on top and you were far, far, far lower down. His Paul Newman looks, that blond-brown hair, the ice-blue eyes, and carved face always added to the Reid Shilling persona. Now. Not so much.

He's in old jeans and a t-shirt. He's even barefoot and his hair is longer and messy, like he just woke up from an afternoon nap.

His cheeks are more gaunt than they once were. He has shadows under his eyes. He's thinner. It's all different.

And although he's not looking at me like I'm beneath him, there's a bit of that arrogance there still, because the right side of his mouth lifts and he drawls, "I thought you might stop by."

On the street behind us a car backfires, the noise is loud, like a gunshot, and I flinch. When I look back at Reid he's studying me, his eyes grave and closed off.

"Hello Reid," I say.

Reid steps onto the stone stoop and quietly closes the thick wooden front door.

"Jace."

I stare at the navy blue lacquer of the front door, shiny and glistening in the sun.

"Rob Jr told me Andi lives here. Is she in?" I watch Reid carefully, and when his expression shifts, like a cloud drifting over his face, I lean forward. "I need to speak with her."

Reid considers me. "I imagine you want to tell her not to marry me tomorrow."

I don't say anything. A gust of wind blows past, dragging the warm summer smell of hot concrete and the Hudson on the breeze. It's been years since I smelled this city smell of baking pavement, sizzling window air conditioners, exhaust, and river. It brings back so many memories. Most of all, it brings back the last summer I was here.

"You know she doesn't love you," I say.

Reid's face stays expressionless, not a flicker of surprise or denial. So he knows. And he's still going to marry her.

"Is she here?" I ask.

Reid shakes his head. "No."

I close my eyes, draw a long breath. "You're going to marry her, even though she doesn't love you?"

When I open my eyes, Reid's mouth has lines around it, as if he's in pain.

"It's not really any of your business what I do."

He's right.

Except.

"I know you don't care about me, but I think you care

about Andi. If you do, don't marry her. She'll regret it. She will regret it."

At that, something flickers in his eyes, like the sun flickering through the leaves behind us, but then it's gone and he shakes his head. "Maybe. I don't know."

I don't understand him. He has everything. Wealth. Prestige. Family name. A future paved in gold. He has it made and he always has. Why does he want Andi too?

"At least let me know where she is, so I can speak with her."

Reid doesn't answer me. Instead he takes his phone from his pocket, hits a number and puts the phone to his ear.

"Jace is here," he says.

I stand straight, my muscles tensing. Andi's on the other end.

"No. He didn't say," Reid says, eyeing me. "He says if you marry me, you'll regret it."

Whatever Andi says back to that makes Reid smile. When he does he turns his face to the side, so I can't see his expression anymore.

"No...uh huh...no...I'm fine."

It's torture not knowing what she's saying and knowing that she's on the other end of the phone deciding whether or not she wants to see me.

"Tell her," I interrupt. "Tell her..." What can I say that Reid will pass on? "That I have a lyric I want her to hear."

Reid shrugs. "He says he has a lyric."

He nods, the sun glinting off his hair. "Okay. Sure. See you tomorrow."

My throat tightens at that, and the warm humid air suddenly feels oppressive.

Reid slips the phone back into his pocket, eyeing me as he does.

"She says she'll see you."

Golden relief, like sunshine breaking through the clouds, courses through me.

Reid holds up his hand in the wait gesture. "I've wanted to tell you for some time...I'm sorry for how I treated you when we were younger. More sorry than you can know. And maybe someday you'll forgive me."

I brush it off. After all, how he treated me pushed Andi and me together. "You're forgiven. It was years ago."

Reid looks at me as if I misunderstood. "I meant forgive me for marrying her."

"You're not going to marry her if I can help it."

He nods. "I know."

He shrugs then and a family walks past, laughing, talking, and dragging their Saint Bernard behind them.

As they pass, Reid gives me Andi's address, then as I'm turning to go he grabs my forearm to stop me.

I halt, my feet on two different steps.

Reid stares at me for a moment, his eyes weighing me, then says, "You still love her, don't you?"

I consider not saying anything. I consider shrugging his hand off and running to find Andi, but something in his eyes has me pausing to say, "I never stopped."

"Will you still love her in six months?"

I frown at him, pull my arm away. "That's not even a question."

Reid nods, "And if she gets married. Will you still love her then?"

I shake my head. "She's not getting married to you."

"Will you?" he demands.

"Yes," I say, frustration boiling out of me. "Yes. I will. I will always love her. I can promise that. Maybe you should reconsider tomorrow, knowing that."

He smiles then, his eyes warming. "Remember you said that. Try not to break her heart tonight. She only just started living again."

I shake my head.

I told Andi eight years ago that I'd never hurt her. I promised it. She was hurt, we both were, but now I'm trying to fix it.

So I hurry down the street, to Andi.

51

JACE

ANDI THROWS HER DOOR OPEN WIDE AND STANDS IN THE doorway, her chin tilted haughtily, her eyes challenging.

I have to fight the urge to step forward and either take her in my arms or fall to my knees and beg her to hear me out.

"Reid said you have a lyric?" she asks, her voice that cold hauteur that she used to do so well. I would laugh when she used it, then roll her under me and kiss her until we were desperate for more.

She changed her outfit since I saw her in the park. She's in a burgundy silk dress with a gold belt and towering gold heels, the kind of outfit I think her family would approve of. Her honey-amber hair is pulled tightly into an intricate twist and she has deep red lipstick on.

If this moment was the first time I'd ever seen her, I

would've fallen down on my knees and worshipped her. Seeing her is equal measure heaven and hell. The pain is equal to the pleasure, like I'm sliding down a razor blade, edging between both.

But all the pain could go away in a moment if I could just hold her.

I wonder how much of herself she had to hide away when she came back?

Because even though she's sleek, poised, and framed by the darkest, grayest apartment I've ever seen, I can see the Andi I love peeking out from behind her flat, painfully polite expression.

She thinks I broke my promise.

She thinks I never loved her.

"Can I come in?" I ask, my mouth dry and my heart pounding.

Andi considers my question, the harsh industrial modern light in the hall buzzing overhead.

The building is one of the luxury places that caters to people who want to pay millions for a monochromatic black and gray box with a view of the city beneath them. The dark hall has a cold, depressed feel that extends into Andi's apartment. The concrete floors. The gray walls. The single gray couch and coffee table. There isn't any color. There isn't anything in there that shows me what Andi's life has been like.

Unless this is what it's been like.

Finally Andi tilts her head and steps back, her heels echoing on the concrete.

I follow her inside and close the door behind me. The silence of the apartment closes around us, like a gray, smothering blanket. We're so high up there isn't any noise from the city, and even though there are windows, all the curtains are drawn, shrouding the room in dim gray light.

I stop at the entry and Andi turns back to me. When she does, the smell of strawberries drifts toward me and I nearly fall to my knees.

"If you're here to convince me not to marry Reid..." She shakes her head, and the diamonds in her ears flash in the light.

"I've missed you, Andi," I say raggedly. "I've missed you every second of every day since the moment you left."

She lifts her hand to her chest and shakes her head, her eyes wide. "Jace...you can't..." She swallows and turns aside for a moment then looks back to me. "You show up, eight years late, and tell me you've missed me? No."

"Do you remember the day you left?"

She flinches, it's almost imperceptible, but I can see the still-sharp memory of pain.

"After you went for a drink I waited for you to come back, and when you didn't I went looking for you. I found Dallas in the hallway, in the middle of handing out a beating that sent him to prison—"

"What? Dallas—"

"Served sixteen months."

Something passes across her expression and she clenches her hands. "I thought he didn't care."

"He cared. He was gutted when you left."

"Dallas?" She holds her hand high over her head. "Big guy. Tattooed. Doesn't trust anyone."

I smile at her, a warmth starting to fill the cold space between us. "That's him."

But then she frowns. "But I saw you. You weren't with Dallas, you were—"

I hold up my hand. "I was. When he told me what happened I sprinted back to find you. But you weren't there. Instead, I found River coming out of our room with a hookup from the party. Then Dean told me you'd left."

"River?"

I step forward, ache to take her hand. "You know I wouldn't."

It's so cold in here, so gray, but I can see it in her eyes, the fear and the hope warring. "I don't though. Dean said you did. And you wrote me. You said—"

"I didn't say anything. I went after you. I took Pauly's motorcycle to catch you. I got in an accident. I was in surgery for sixteen hours, in a medically induced coma for twenty-four. Whatever was said to you, it wasn't me."

Andi's hand shakes as she lifts it toward my face. "You..."

I nod. "I nearly died. This scar on my face is the least of it. It took me months to walk again. More surgeries than I want to remember. But what hurt the most was that you were gone."

She does touch me then, her fingers gently stroke the side of my face, trailing over my skin like she's trying to soothe an injury nearly a decade old. And maybe it works, because her touch is like the flutter of warm lips over a cold heart, blowing breath and life back into a shattered soul.

I reach up and rest my hand on hers, linking her fingers with mine, and when I do, I let out a broken breath. Just holding her hand sends a wave of *right* through me that's so strong I could weep.

"You didn't send those texts," she says, the pulse in her wrist fluttering under my fingers.

"No. I didn't know about them until Dean told me today. The only text I saw was the one you sent telling me you never wanted to see me again. The one where you asked me to write you a lyric."

She makes a small noise in her throat and she steps closer to me, the heat of her, the strawberry scent of her pulling me close.

"You didn't get my voicemails?"

"No," I say, stepping closer so that only a whisper of yes separates us.

"Why?" she asks, tilting her head up.

"Dean thought you were a crutch. I couldn't sing without you there. He decided he knew best."

I block out the shame and grief in Dean's eyes, I don't want him here right now, during this.

She places her other hand on my heart, feeling the rhythm there. "I didn't know you were hurt," she whispers, "I wish I could've been with you."

I reach up and run my fingers over her face, over her eyebrows, her soft eyelashes, over the curve of her cheekbones, the dimple that always drove me crazy, and finally, I rub my thumb over her bottom lip. "I didn't know *you* were hurt. I'm sorry I wasn't there."

"You never cheated," she says, a touch of wonder in her voice.

"No. Never," I say. "I would never."

"You never said you didn't mean always."

"God no," I say. "Andi, when I said I'd always love you, I meant it."

At that she presses her cheek to my chest, wraps her

arms around my back and rests her head to my heart. It's beating so hard, trying to break free to reach her, that I think she must be able to hear it. Her fingers grasp my shirt, hanging on to me like she never wants to let go.

I close my eyes and send out a prayer.

Please.

Please, God, Please.

"What's the lyric you wanted to tell me?" she asks suddenly, her voice muffled in my shirt.

I smile down at her head tucked against me. I haven't felt this right since the last time she was in my arms.

"I'm sorry," I say, "I'm sorry I didn't come sooner. I thought that's what you wanted. I spent the last eight years loving you and here you were—"

"Loving you back," she says.

I let out a breath that I've been holding for years.

"I sang to you. Every song was for you. I'd be singing under the night sky in LA and I'd picture you listening to me under the same moon in New York."

"Your songs were love songs?" she says, her shoulders tensing.

"Didn't you listen to the lyrics?"

She shakes her head no. "It hurt too much."

I close my eyes. Drop my head to hers, cupping her cheeks in my hands.

"Andi, I've been singing you a love song since the day I met you. Why would you think I'd stop?"

She looks up at me with regret-filled eyes, "I suppose the same reason you thought I'd stop loving you."

"Let's not make that mistake again," I say, my voice a plea.

Eight years.

"Alright. Promise," she says.

And I nearly sag with relief.

Then I realize, it isn't finished. She loves me. I love her. But she's marrying Reid tomorrow.

Reid.

"Don't marry him," I say desperately, my stomach knotting. "Andi, don't marry him."

She stiffens and I pull back, searching her expression. The hollow silence of the concrete gray apartment swallows me as I wait for her answer. Then she smiles up at me, her deep red lips forming a shaky smile.

"Would it be alright if we stayed up all night talking?" she asks, her eyes wide and pleading. "Like we used to? I want you to tell me everything about the past eight years. Everything. We'll have grilled cheese and strawberries. I don't have a bed, but we could sleep on the floor."

My knees nearly buckle.

Thank God.

She isn't going to marry him. I'll stay. I'll hold her. It's going to be okay.

"Tell you everything?" I ask, smiling down at her, my chest expanding. I stroke my fingers over her cheek, drowning in the way it feels to be near her again.

"I want you to fill all the empty spots, fill all the dark spots with light. Tell me everything so I never have to wonder again."

She leads me to the couch, takes my hand and pulls me across the gray, dark room, which now somehow seems lighter, less empty. We sit, I tuck her against my side. She rests her head against my chest and her hand curls on my arm.

Even the pain in my leg, which is a constant companion, has lessened its clutch on me.

I put my arms around her and it feels like she never left them.

I fit her and she fits me.

"Okay, I'm ready," she says, her warmth pressed into me, "Tell me what happened in the space between when I was gone and when I was there."

52

JACE

THE SCENT OF CRISPLY GOLDEN GRILLED CHEESE AND strawberries surrounds us.

We're on the floor, Andi sits between my legs and leans against my chest. A pile of blankets cushions the concrete floor.

It's three a.m. and we've been talking for hours. Around one a.m. Andi decided she'd always wanted to build a fort, so we spread a sheet from the couch to the coffee table and made a nest of blankets to lie in.

The lights are off, but even in the middle of the night, the city is never fully dark. The light seeps into the apartment and Andi holds a flashlight, like the small light can illuminate all the dark places.

Andi plucks another strawberry from the bowl and bites into the tart sweetness of the glistening fruit. Every time she wraps her mouth around the strawberry I think about kissing her. But I don't. Not yet. Not while she's still engaged to Reid.

Instead I hold her. Feel the warmth of her sinking against me.

"So even though you've gone platinum twice, played at Red Rocks, won a Grammy, you're still..." She tilts her chin back to look at me. "You."

"A more tired me...but yes."

We smile at each other in the light of the flashlight. I brush back the tendrils of her hair that have fallen free of her twist, their silky warmth sifting through my fingers.

I told her everything that I've done for the past years. The excruciating year I spent recovering when the pain made it so I could barely play. The phase where I could only write sad songs. Our first record deal. Our first time in a recording studio. Traveling to different countries. The creative burnout after touring too long. How Dallas became even more silent after his last release from prison. How Pauly collapsed on stage and how sometimes he has panic attacks during concerts—and how he makes it through. River and Serena. How much I love my nephew. How Dean is so driven he doesn't see anything else but making Dad's dream come true. How we've made it, the world is singing our songs, but—

"I don't know if it was worth it, if it meant missing you."

"Don't say that," Andi whispers, taking my hand. "Don't say that. I saw it myself, your songs help people. I think...no I know...your songs have saved people's lives. So, maybe we don't know what was supposed to happen or what's supposed to be."

I tuck her close and rest my head under my chin. "You're right. We're here now."

"We're here now," she agrees.

There's an empty bottle of red wine next to us, the glasses on the floor nearby. There's a low hum thrumming through me, like the resonance of a plucked chord. It's a content, happy feeling. The only worry is that she has to tell Reid it's done.

To untie the knot of worry inside me, I say, "The same goes for you. Even though you manage multi-million-dollar development projects and live in this boring, concrete, gray apartment, you're still..." I study her wide brown eyes and her small smile. "You."

She told me everything from her last eight years too. How her coming back was contingent on her being the perfect Leighton-Hughes. Columbia. Business under her dad. How she worked eighteen-hour days to drive out the emptiness. Work with contractors, construction crews, permits, assessors, loans, legal, more. How she couldn't listen to music, because every time she heard my voice it broke her heart all over again. How for the last eight years she felt as if she was just going through the motions, her body there, but not her heart.

Andi buries her face against my chest and lets out a long yawn.

"Tired?" I ask, my voice scratchy from the hours of talking.

"No," she says, but she yawns again.

I lie back then on the blankets, taking her with me, resting her in my arms. I stare up at the white sheet, the light of the flashlight spreading over it, like a tent under the stars.

"Will you tell Reid tomorrow?" I ask, then I realize it's nearly four, and say, "Today, I mean."

She makes a noise and curls into me.

"He'll be at Wagner Cove. It's fine," she says tiredly.

"He knows you don't love him," I say. I take a deep breath, breathing in the strawberry smell and the warmth. "Why did you say yes?"

"It's complicated."

"Do you need my help?" I ask, my muscles tensing at the thought of her being hurt. "Complicated how?"

She doesn't answer. Maybe she's not ready to share this part of herself yet. That's okay, we have years. I'm not going anywhere.

"I have a lyric," she says suddenly.

I smile against her hair, my cheek pressed against her head. "I'm ready."

Her hand splays over my chest, her fingers pressing kisses into me. *"Remember, I love you."*

I wrap my arms around her, holding her tight.

She's warm, she's soft, she's in my arms, and it's not a dream, it's real. With that thought, and a smile on my face, I fall asleep.

When I wake up to a siren screaming past on the streets below, the apartment is light, the flashlight is dead, and Andi is gone.

53

JACE

I FLY ACROSS THE GRASS, SPRINTING THROUGH CENTRAL Park, desperate to stop the only woman I'll ever love from marrying another man.

I weave through the crisscrossing paths, past green benches that stand empty like mourners, over hills and jutting gray rocks.

There's the Alice in Wonderland statue where Andi fell when she was small.

A playground with kids shouting and sliding.

There. Gone.

My lungs burn as I round the path climbing toward Bethesda Terrace, the angel of the waters rises high, her hand outstretched, her wings flared.

Tourists crowd around her, the bronze angel of healing in her fountain, holding a lily in her hand.

There's a raucous wedding party taking photographs,

a bride in white, a groom in black, my heart thunders—but it's not Andi.

My feet pound across the red brick, past the arched stone, past the lake and the rowboats with couples bobbing in the sparkling green waters.

The sun is already high over the leafy green trees, the dirt and grass smell strong with the evaporated dew, the bright blue sky mocking.

It's the perfect day for a wedding.

He'll be at Wagner Cove in the morning, she said.

I charge down the path lined with tall shade trees and leap over the wire mesh fencing separating the grass from the path.

When I land, my leg screams in pain, the old injury flaring, and I grab my thigh, dig my fingers into the pain and keep running.

I jump over another fence. I don't have time to take the prescribed path.

I dodge a bicyclist and keep running as they shout after me. Then I'm on the small stone and dirt path tumbling down to the lake and the cove.

The woods are thick with green, the boulders rise out of the ground and trees dig their roots into the stone.

The path winds down, down, and my chest heaves as I drag in the summer air.

Sweat runs down my back, and every step down the stone path is like a hot poker stabbing bone.

But I see her.

I see her now.

I round the path. Down below, cascading down the forest toward the lake, there's a rustic wooden gazebo, hewn from roughly cut logs, perched like a fairy tale on the edge of the shimmering lake.

And standing underneath the sloped wooden roof, surrounded by a carpet of red rose petals, is Andi.

She's in white.

Of course she's in white.

She's getting married.

But the white nearly strikes me down. She looks like an angel, radiant and beautiful.

I almost can't reconcile the Andi lying in my arms last night with the Andi standing in the gazebo.

Her dress is the most brilliant white I've ever seen. It floats around her like a cloud and must have a thousand diamonds sewn into the fabric because it gleams like the noonday sun.

The top of the dress is tight, strapless, showing the thin line of her shoulders and the smoothness of her skin. The bottom, though, flows out, like a cloud blowing in the breeze, sparkling as the sun lights over her.

Her veil is pulled back, settling over her hair, a diamond and pearl tiara rests on her head. And on her neck, there's the thickest diamond and ruby choker I've ever seen.

She looks like a billion dollars.

She looks like a bride.

The sight punches me, robs me of breath, but I fly down the stone path, desperate to stop her.

She hasn't noticed me yet.

No one has.

Andi's holding his hands, staring up at him with a solemn, grave expression, her face pale and serious.

A gust of wind hits me then, bringing the voice of the officiant...do you take...to have and to hold...

Andi tilts her chin, that defiant, stubborn, take-on-the-world look I've dreamed about for years.

It means she's going to say *I do*. She's looking at him, holding his hands, and she's going to say yes.

I reach out my hand, as if I can stop it all with a gesture, and say raggedly, my lungs burning, "Andi, don't."

At that, Andi turns to me, but the only part of her that shows surprise is the flaring in her eyes. I can see it, the surprise, but also the overwhelming love.

I take another step forward, my leg burning, my chest aching. I reach out my hand, palm up.

She can take it, she can take my hand and we can walk away, leave all this behind together.

"Don't do this. Come with me."

I let my hand hang there and all she has to do is take it.

My heart thuds a heavy, desperate beat as she looks into my eyes, a bright, shining love there.

Around us, her family is shifting, her brother laughing, her dad murmuring angrily, the groom's family confused and stunned.

And him, he's still holding her hands, a somber expression on his face.

But I don't see them, I don't hear them, I only see Andi.

None of them matter.

None of them.

"Andi," I say, the taste of her riding on my lips, the memory of her kisses, the memory of her laugh, the memory of her touch.

When I say her name she gives me a brilliant smile, one like the sun coming out from behind the clouds on a rainy day.

It's a joyful smile, the one that first made me fall in

love with her all those years ago. The one she's only ever given to me.

The one that says, *I love you.*

And when she smiles that smile, I know exactly, without a doubt, what she's about to say.

Slowly, she turns back to Reid, looks up into his eyes, and says in a loud, clear voice, "I do."

Thunder cracks in my mind, a sharp, rumbling sound. I stumble back, drop my hand.

The ceremony continues, the blood-red flowers pooled around a diamond studded bride and her groom.

I take a step back, and another, and another, and another, until somehow...somehow I've left Andi behind.

54

JACE

"WHAT HAPPENED?" RIVER ASKS, PUSHING THE DOOR TO MY suite's terrace open.

I turn away from contemplating my guitar and say in a numb voice, "She married him."

My throat burns and the taste of cheap vodka scalds my tongue. The wind pushes at me, and the sight of Central Park twenty stories below sends a raging howl through my veins.

River stops, and behind him, Dean, Dallas and Pauly hesitate to come out onto the terrace.

I grip my leg, digging my hand into the twisting pain, and turn away from my brother.

"I'm sorry," River says.

I ignore him.

The private terrace has comfortable furniture set amongst lush potted plants. It's an oasis above a concrete city. The floor of the terrace looks like sandstone. Solid. Fireproof.

I stare at the guitar Andi gave me all those years ago. I've played it every day since she gave it to me. I've written songs on it, I've played it during my shows. I realize now that I prayed on this guitar, I wrote and played songs of love and hope on it.

It was like my dad's Martin, a falsity, a lie. A guitar can't connect you to someone that's dead. And a guitar can't connect you to someone that's gone.

There isn't a song in the world that can bring someone back from the dead and there isn't a single lyric that can fix what's broken.

"Jace," Dean says, stepping across the terrace, his voice low.

"No," I tell him, my voice harsh and pained like a wounded animal.

He stops.

Looks at me helplessly, his eye swollen, his lip busted.

That's right, Dean, you can't help me.

I take the jug of cheap vodka, the one I bought yesterday when I thought I'd seen the worst, and I empty the liquor onto my guitar.

The liquid spirals through the air, arching as I dump it over every bit of wood, every string, every surface, until the entire guitar is covered in alcohol.

The acrid scent of it rises on the wind and fills my mouth with its bitter flavor.

"What are you doing?" River asks, stepping close. "Jace?"

"What I should've done a long time ago."

Dallas steps forward then, lays a heavy comforting hand on my shoulder, and pulls a flask from his pocket.

If I could smile I would.

Leave it to Dallas to be the first to understand.

I toss aside the plastic vodka jug, unscrew the flask, and then dump the gin onto the body of my guitar.

Nobody's saying anything. They're just watching me dump liquor onto the guitar that has taken us around the world. Shows in Paris, in LA, in Cape Town, in Belarus. From touring clubs, colleges, and festivals, to playing Red Rocks and Times Square. This guitar has been with us for the whole ride. And it's time to say goodbye.

I pull a small pack of matches from my pocket, picked up at the bar across the street.

"Jace, no," Dean says.

But it's too late.

I strike the match, the flame sparks and lights, bursting into existence. The sulfur smell mixes with the alcohol scent, and the match burns blue and orange, flickering in the breeze.

"Holy shit," River says, finally catching on.

Then I toss the match through the air, the flame spins, rotating as it falls, falls, and then the match hits the liquor-soaked guitar.

The flames whoosh with a hungry hissing roar, covering the guitar in licking, writhing fire.

"Shit," River jumps back.

Dean runs back toward the suite, probably to grab the bottles of water they leave all over the place for us to drink.

I don't care.

Instead I stare at the flames smothering the guitar. It groans as the heat warps and burns the wood, making a keening, dying sound. It's the final song it will ever play.

I stare into the deep blue flame, breathe in the cedar-scented thick black smoke rolling off the fire, and say goodbye.

The guitar moans, the fire crackles and snaps in fits and starts, and all those years of telling myself that when I sang, Andi was listening, burns on this funeral pyre.

River, Pauly, Dallas, they all stand behind me and watch the fire burn, sending angry black clouds up past the spires of the skyscrapers nearby, out over the green of Central Park.

Below the rumble of a siren booms over the streets and horns sound, honking angrily.

My eyes burn from the smoke, my throat tightens, my lungs ache, out past the trees of the park, through the buildings, the Tower rises, golden and mocking.

She's gone.

She's gone, just like the smoke dissipating on the breeze.

Dean runs through the doors, his feet pounding across the stone. He's carrying a silver bucket with water sloshing over the sides.

"You're too late," I tell him.

He stops, his face pinched and pained.

The fire has burned down. It was quick to start, lighting up bright and wild, and it burned up all the alcohol and all the wood, as fast as first love, and now... there's only the charred remains of my broken guitar and its ashes.

"I'm done," I say to Dean, to them all. "We're done."

55

ANDREA

I CLENCH MY HANDS AND CRUMPLE MY WEDDING DRESS—
the yards of white silk, tulle, and hundreds of diamond
studs inlaid in the fabric—and stare across the suite at
Reid.

So.

We're married.

The suite at the St. Regis is a wedding night gift from
my parents.

It's the only suite in the city that suits the Leighton-
Hughes flair. The walls are covered in hand-dyed deep
red silk, the ceilings are layered in gold, the chandeliers
drip with fat crystals, the handmade furniture is richly
made and has enough gold gilt to satisfy.

Every available surface is covered in tall crystal vases
of long-stemmed red roses. There are hundreds of them

and their scent fills the air with the fragrant hopes of wedded bliss and romance.

My fingers are beginning to lose circulation from how tightly I'm gripping my dress.

This suite is an opulent seduction scene, beyond the couches and the table with champagne on ice and a tray of chocolate-covered strawberries, is the bed. It's a sprawling four poster with a down comforter as white as my dress, set dramatically against the red silk walls.

Reid notices where I'm looking and shakes his head. He strides to the table in the center of the room, his dress shoes silent on the thick carpet, and pulls the champagne from the gold ice bucket.

His fingers are swift and efficient as he unwraps the gold foil and pops the cork.

I take a step forward, my diamond-studded heels sinking into the plush carpet.

The champagne fizzes over the edge of the bottle and splashes on his fingers—and onto his wedding ring, a simple gold band.

There's a soft understanding light in his eyes, and I step closer, taking in the tangy sweet scent of the champagne.

"You know, it's not too late for an annulment," Reid says, giving me a somber smile. "I think a divorce would take longer than just waiting for me to die. But an annulment..." He shrugs.

I swipe a champagne flute off the dark wood, gold-trimmed table and grip the cold crystal glass.

"I'm not getting an annulment. Or a divorce," I say, swallowing down the pulse frantically beating in my throat. "I married you."

He smiles then, a wry twisting of his lips, and pours the fizzing golden champagne into my glass.

Reid is in a formal black tuxedo, with jet buttons, a snow-white shirt, and gold cufflinks studded with rubies—a present from my dad. There's a red rose pinned to his chest.

Years ago, he wore a suit just like this. It was to my sixteenth birthday party, held in the ballroom of the Tower. We had a full orchestra, a pastry chef flown in from Paris, a six-tier chocolate fountain, and all my dad's competitors were invited so they remembered who was on top. Reid and I danced. He wore a red rose then too.

He pours himself a glass of champagne and then takes a long swallow, draining the entire glass in one gulp.

The right side of his mouth lifts then and he says, "Thank you. I know I told you yesterday that if you wanted to go with him, I wouldn't blame you, but...there's this selfish part of me that's desperately glad you didn't."

The backs of my eyes burn and the tightness of the diamond choker around my throat feels like a hand gripping me, preventing any tears from coming.

"You're not selfish," I whisper, shaking my head. "I'm the selfish one."

Reid frowns, drops his glass to the table and steps forward. He rubs his thumb over my cheek, taking away the wetness there.

"Don't cry," he says, taking my hand in his.

The room is muffled with the silk on the walls, the thick carpets, the giant bed, so that every word is quiet and intimate.

And this is Reid. My friend. The one who promised to never share my secrets with anyone.

"I love him," I say, my voice breaking.

"I know," he whispers.

"He stayed with me last night, we talked all night, and he held me and...I was so selfish, I couldn't tell him I was still going to marry you in the morning. He never stopped loving me, all these years I was wrong. It was a mistake and he was in an accident and it took him years to recover and he's..." My throat tightens and Reid squeezes my hand. "He loves me. And I just wanted one night with him. I didn't think I'd ever get that again. I didn't want that last night to be spent fighting, so I let him think I wasn't going to marry you. And I gathered it all up inside, I gathered up how he looked and how he talked and how it felt. Because I knew, after I left, he'd never want to see me again. And this time, I know how not seeing him ever again feels. I'm the selfish one, Reid. I was so selfish I let him believe I was going to stay with him."

It hurts.

It feels like the guttering of a flame.

"Andrea." Reid runs his fingers over my cheeks, brushing aside my tears. "You can still go after him."

"No," I say, picturing the broken expression on Jace's face when he realized I was going to marry Reid. "Do you know why I married you?"

Reid brushes his hand through his hair and gives me a questioning look. "No, actually. I thought I could make you happy enough that you wouldn't mind being tied to me for six months. Then I thought I'd appeal to that core of decency inside you that always has to protect those weaker than you. But now..." He shrugs. "I don't have an ego left, no pride, I know I'm a terrible bet. I'm not a catch, I'm the opposite, I'm a millstone around your neck. I'm the villain here, thwarting true love—"

"Stop," I say. I set my glass down on the table and step toward him.

I brace my hands on his shoulders, strong and muscled beneath his tuxedo.

"You're my friend," I tell him. "You reached me when no one else could. You cared when no one else did. You see me. Maybe not the same way that Jace does. But you see me. And I see you. No one has ever much liked you, Reid Shilling, God knows, but I do. I like you. I care. You and me." I step into him, my wedding dress rustling as I move between his legs. "We might not have a lifetime of love, or a whirlwind romance, but...we have this." I place my hand on his heart and look up into his eyes. "We have six months, maybe twelve, and I'm going to be your friend for all of them. I'm going to care about you, and I'm going to love your daughter. Okay?"

He stares down at me, and his hands shake as he places them on my hips, as if we're dancing without moving at all.

"Okay," he says, then, he nods. "Okay."

The scent of the roses overwhelms me as we sway, and beneath us, petals crush beneath our feet, sending up a floral medley.

"What now?" I ask.

We have an entire day and night in front of us, yawning like an abyss full of red roses and an aching heart. Mary is watching Claudia today and tonight so Reid and I can have a "wedding night." The white-glove butler service will provide anything we need, and we can have a gourmet dinner and a full breakfast, all served in the suite's bright red and gold dining room. But other than that...what's there to do?

Reid smiles down at me, his fingers gently circling my hips in a soothing rhythm.

"Did you know there are more therapists in Manhattan per square mile than there are cockroaches?" he asks, his eyes full of laughter.

"Really?"

He shrugs. "It's a fact. They come in all types. Cognitive behavioral therapists, dialectical behavior therapists, psychodynamic therapists, hypnotherapists, sex therapists, divorce therapists, marriage therapists, clinical therapists...the list goes on. They even have therapists that specialize in talking people through dying. It's really helpful actually. And my therapist said that the best way to move through grief is to concentrate on the *right now*. Not the past, not the future, just this moment right here. That small space between the past and the future. Like the moment between the inhale and the exhale."

"This moment right now?" I ask, realizing for the first time that Reid has gold flecks around the blue-green of his irises that look just like sunlight shining through champagne.

"This moment right now," he agrees. "Nothing else."

"Alright."

Across the room, sunlight streams through the sheer curtains, gilding the roses in gold. The air conditioning turns on, rustling the delicate lace of my veil.

"And do you know what that means?" Reid asks, still watching me somberly.

"What?"

"That we are finally, finally—"

"Finally?"

"—going to dance in our underwear."

I laugh. It bubbles up and Reid grins down at me, his eyes crinkling.

"What are you talking about? I'm not dancing in my underwear."

He nods, "Yes you are. You are going to get out of that truly, incredibly ostentatious yet beautiful diamond-studded dress, and I'm going to get out of this tuxedo, and we are going to put some Elvis on the surround sound, and we are going to dance."

I laugh, the cold rose-scented air blowing over me and I shake my head. "Elvis. Really?"

He nods. "Yes. You won't regret it. I promise."

Then he steps to the side table beside the sofa, picks up the remote, and turns on the surround sound. When he turns back to me, there's a light in his eyes, and the sound of piano and guitar floats across the room.

I shake my head. "You're serious."

He reaches down to his sleeves, pulls off his cufflinks, drops them to the table. "I'm serious."

Overhead, the song begins, *Wise men say...*

He pulls off his tuxedo jacket, drops it to the floor.

"Come on, Andrea," he says, his fingers loosening his black bow tie, then moving down the jet buttons of his white shit.

I watch, stunned, as he pulls his shirt off.

"Fools rush in," I say, laughing as he tugs his undershirt off and tosses it on the couch.

"They sure do." He grins at me, the golden tan on his bare chest shining in the sunlight.

Then he points to my veil and tiara. "Take it off."

I look into his eyes, sink into their blue-green depths, and decide to join him in the space between the inhale and the exhale. Just there, with him.

I reach up and loosen the pins holding the tiara, tug it free. My hair spills across my shoulders, loosened from its confines.

He grabs the tiara—a quarter-million dollars' worth of diamonds—and tosses it onto the sofa. Then I unclasp the choker around my neck and lay the necklace on the table. The diamonds wink in the light, and suddenly, I can breathe again.

Reid slips out of his black shoes, kicking them aside. They thud against the sofa, landing quietly on the carpet.

I step out of my shoes, more heel than leather, more diamond than not, and then lift my train and walk toward Reid, swaying to the rhythm of song.

"You have to unbutton it," I say, turning my back to him.

I can smell him now that he's taken off his tuxedo jacket and shirt. The sweat, the fresh air of the park clinging to his skin, the shaving soap he uses.

I dip my head as he gently brushes my hair over my shoulder, his fingers grazing the intimate space between my shoulder and neck. Goosebumps rise at his touch and I drag in another breath filled with the scent of roses and him.

Then he's slowly unbuttoning the long row of pearl buttons and as he does, my ribs expand, my lungs fill with air, and dizziness rushes over me because I can finally take a full breath again.

When he reaches the last button, at the base of my spine, he pushes the waterfall of my dress over my hips, his hands brushing my thighs.

The cold air runs over my bare skin, tingling against the heat of my flush. When I step out of the folds of my dress and turn to Reid, I tilt my chin in the air and say, "Is this indecent enough for you?"

He grins, his eyes lit with laughter.

My mom hired a lingerie designer from Paris to create a rush-order ensemble. My strapless bra is silk and handmade lace, my panties thin strips of lace and silk, and both are as white as the pure driven snow. My garters are deep, crimson red ribbons pinned over my thighs, like an erotic pin-up girl from the forties, and my thigh-highs are sheer satin, virginal white.

Reid laughs. "You look like my teenage wet-dreams."

I put my hands on my hips, "Did I make you horny as a seventeen-year-old?"

He laughs. "I was seventeen. Concrete sidewalks made me horny."

I grin at him, then point at his pants. "Take them off."

"Yes ma'am."

He flicks the button on his pants, drags the zipper down and steps out of the black tuxedo pants. His legs are long and lean. His stomach is flat and smooth, muscled and tan.

I hold out my palm.

"Take my hand," I whisper, joining in with the music swirling around us.

He does. And then we're dancing, spinning around gold furniture, velvet divans, tripping over shoes, jumping over the mountain of my dress, stumbling over his jacket, and laughing at the absurdity of spinning around the jewel-box room in our underwear to a song meant for falling in love.

Then the song shifts, and it's no longer about love, it's about shaking and moving. It's the kind of 1950s song that makes you swing, and jump, and dance, and we both know it. The piano is banging out the tune, the stereo is loud, and Reid's eyes are bright.

He gives me a challenging grin. "Regret it?"

"Never." And then I shake my hips and move my hands, and Reid grabs me, lifts me and spins me in the air.

I laugh and shriek as he chases me around the suite. Until we find ourselves in the red-silk bedroom by the massive four-poster bed.

The music swings around as I edge toward the bed, the backs of my knees hitting the satiny feather-filled duvet.

Reid grins at me. "Are you thinking what I'm thinking?"

"I've always wanted to do this," I say, gripping the thick plush comforter.

"Yes." He lifts me easily, tosses me on the bed. I laugh and he's jumping onto the bed after me.

Then we're scrambling up, jumping up and down, bouncing like two five-year-olds, and I'm laughing so hard I'm crying. The bed groans and creaks and the headboard hits the wall with the rhythm of our bouncing.

"Having fun?" Reid laughs, his hair flying up and down in time with his leaps. He's jumping so high he's nearly hitting the ceiling.

"Shut up and dance," I tell him.

We grab hands and spin and jump. We're dancing on the bed. The thick pillow mattress sinks under me, and the thumping is as loud as the music, and my heart is bumping wildly around my chest.

This moment.

I stare into Reid's laughing eyes, grip his warm, solid hands, and dance in my underwear on the bed.

After that we don fluffy robes and watch classic cartoons, eat loads of chocolate-covered strawberries while lying in bed, and order everything on the room service menu. That night, I don't sleep on the couch, I fall asleep in bed next to Reid, the TV on, my hand in his.

56

ANDREA

THE NEXT DAY, WE'RE BACK AT REID'S—AND NOW MY— home, sitting cross-legged on the floor of the living room, trying to make Claudia smile.

Reid crosses his eyes and sticks out his tongue, which makes me laugh, but only makes five-week old Claudia stare at him as if he's some strange species she's never seen before.

The oriental carpet is soft under us and even if there's a heavy ache in my chest, like the weight of the Tower pinning me down, I breathe through it and concentrate on this moment right here.

"There," Reid says triumphantly, grinning at me. "Did you see that? She smiled! I did it."

Mary tsks. She's perched on the couch, her reading glasses low on her nose, perusing a book on baby sign language, "That's gas, Mr. Shilling."

The deflated look on his face has me hiding a smile.

"You think that's funny?" Reid whispers to me.

I bite my bottom lip and shake my head no.

He scoffs and goes back to making funny faces at his daughter, tickling her stomach, and trying in vain to make her smile.

"Maybe you should try dancing with her," I say cheekily.

Then I pick her up, cradling her head in my hand. I hear she was a small baby when she was born, and she's only nine pounds now. Even though she's light as a feather, and wearing the cutest purple gingham ruffle dress, she feels solid and warm in my arms. Her muddy eyes are moving toward the blue of Reid's, but less green and more aquamarine.

I breathe in her baby smell, the baby shampoo and the newness of her, and stand, holding her close. She looks into my eyes, her gaze questioning, suckling her fist. I smile down at her, then I spin her around the room, dancing through the afternoon light streaming in from the windows, past the bookshelf, around the plush couch.

"I'd be careful," Reid says, watching with an amused grin.

"I am careful," I say, holding her close.

"That's not exactly what he means," Mary says.

Then Claudia makes a little mewling cry, her eyes form a wide O, and she spits the contents of her last bottle all over my chest. It's wet, warm, and it smells like curdled milk.

"Oh. Okay. Not smiling," I say, wrinkling my nose at the spit-up running down my shirt. "I guess she didn't inherit your love of dancing."

Reid laughs, and stands. "I'll take her. You go get changed."

He pulls her gently from my arms, a warm smile on his face, and settles back on the couch, letting her rest in the crook of his arm.

Mary had the day off, since she stayed with Claudia all yesterday and last night, but she wanted to stay to make sure Reid and I have adequate time to spend together as newlyweds. It's sweet.

She's digging through a basket now, finding a towel to scrub Claudia clean.

I hurry off to change, not wanting to miss a single second of the days we have left.

When I come back, wearing a red cowl dress, there's a change in the atmosphere of the living room.

First, Claudia and Mary are gone. So the laughter and sweetness that come with Claudia being near have left the room.

Second, Reid's standing now, his fists clenched behind his back, his jaw tight, and his eyes shifting around the sunlit room worriedly.

He's trying to hide his nervousness, but I can see it clearly. It's obvious to me now, in the same way I can tell the difference between the Reid he shows the world and the one that he only shows me.

The room I've come to love is no longer a cozy haven. The light yellow paint, the soft couches, the cheery bookshelf, they're all dark and forbidding now. Even the gentle beeswax and lemon smell is gone, replaced by harsh, astringent cologne.

I stop at the edge of the oriental carpet and stay on the solid footing of the wood floor.

Clive and Carol Shilling have come for a visit, and

with them the temperature of the room has plummeted about thirty degrees.

No one is sitting. I assume Reid didn't offer. They're all still standing at the edge of the living room, near the front door, as if they only just came inside, and Reid is blocking their entry.

"Hello," I say, drawing their attention to me.

Reid shoots me a look I can't decipher.

"We came to see the happy newlyweds," Clive says, shouldering forward. "And our granddaughter."

"She's taking a nap," Reid says, his voice even and hard.

He must've sent Mary upstairs with Claudia as soon as his parents rang the bell.

I doubt Reid realizes that he's blocking his parents' entry, physically barring them with his width, but his father recognizes it.

They haven't met Claudia yet. From what Reid tells me they haven't shown any interest. He claims they won't, not until he's gone.

Yet here they are.

I look at Reid's hand, clutched behind his back, and see his fingers shake.

His father smiles and strokes the brass top of that hateful cane.

"Thank you for your congratulations, but we're busy enjoying our honeymoon," I say, stepping closer to Reid, putting my hand through his arm.

When I do, I feel the tension in his muscles, and then I feel it slowly melt away.

Behind Clive, Carol's gaze darts nervously between her bullish husband and her son. I asked Reid about her, and he said that when he was young, he went to her, told her what was happening, and she told him to stop spreading lies about his father. When he persisted she slapped him and told him to mind his mouth. He never mentioned anything to her again.

I squeeze Reid's arm and Clive narrows his eyes on my hand.

"Well, you married him," he says, his lip curling. "Got yourself an illegitimate in the process. He moved fast. But I never doubted my son's silver tongue, I only doubted his intelligence. If I had known he could catch a Leighton-Hughes, I would've pushed him harder."

I can't take it.

I can't take the feeling of Reid's arm tensing beneath mine, the haunted look in his eyes, the way he blocks the living room, and the stairway leading up to his daughter.

This man is *hateful*.

I can't watch for a second more the transformation of Reid going from laughing friend to solemn, tense, shamed son.

"There's something I've always wanted to do," I say, turning to Reid.

His brow wrinkles and he shakes his head, "What?"

"You wanted champagne, I want this."

Then I let go of Reid's arm and stride toward Clive. I take in the sneering lip, the snake-like eyes, the short shaved gray hair, and the ropy lines of his arms, a body built for malice. He hides it in public well enough, although I always sensed the snake in him, but here, with his son, it's plain to see.

I open my palm. "Let me see your cane."

"Pardon me?" he asks, his voice scathing.

His cane, this piece of wood, Clive doesn't use it for

walking, Reid said he doesn't need it, he never has, he uses it for intimidation, for abuse.

"I want to see it," I say, keeping my hand open.

Behind me, I hear Reid shifting, the whisper of his clothing as he steps closer to me. Protectively.

There's a tension in the air, as if Reid's father realizes that a new chess piece is on the board, and she's a queen.

I watch the calculation in his eyes, drilling through all our moves and countermoves, and I see the moment he realizes that my family will always win.

My father didn't achieve his crown through flowers and hugs, no, he did it with cunning and ruthlessness. I put that in my gaze, show that if I choose, everything Clive is will disappear. My dad wouldn't deny me, he'd enjoy it.

Clive jerks the cane up and drops it in my hand. The wood is black, thin, lacquered and shining. There's a heavy brass globe at the top, weighing it down. I grasp the cold wood in my hand and heft its weight, considering it carefully.

Then I look up at Clive, stare into his mean, hateful eyes and say in a hard, cold voice, "You do not get to come into my home and speak to my husband that way. You may have raised him, but you are not his father. You will leave this home and you will not come back. You do not speak to my husband. You do not speak to my daughter. You do not speak to me. If you try, I will destroy you. I will break you."

Then I raise my leg and bring the cane down over my thigh.

It hits the flesh there, hard, it bends, but it doesn't break. And dang it—it hurts. It hurts like a mother.

Clive leans forward, his bullet-shaped head angled toward me in disbelief.

Carol gasps.

That was a nice speech, but that part where I was supposed to break the cane to make a point, well that fell a little flat.

But then Reid steps up beside me, casually pulls the cane from my hand, lifts it in the air and snaps it in half. The crack of the cane breaking is loud in the silence.

Then Reid says, his voice even and steady, "I think what Andrea meant was, if you come again, *we* will break you."

My heart pounds wildly in my chest, my mouth is dry with the metallic taste of adrenaline and all I want to do is limp to the couch and sit down.

But Reid's face. My word. He's staring at his father with a promise of retribution in his eyes. And his father... he takes a step back.

Reid throws the cane to the floor and it clatters across the wood.

When he looks at me there's a bit of awe there, and gratitude, and that Reid that I know is back, the one that smiles and does all the things that he's always wanted to do.

"You'll leave my family alone," I tell Clive. "Do we understand each other?"

Reid has a wide, tooth-baring smile directed at his father.

Clive's eyes dart between the two of us. Then instead of realizing that he is the originator of everything that's happening, he says, "You deserve each other. I hope you rot."

Then he spits on the ground.

"Get out," I say.

And they do. Clive takes his wife's arm, thrusts open the door and careens down the stairs, slamming the door behind them.

For a moment both Reid and I are silent, letting the vibrating door still. The lingering scent of Clive's astringent cologne fades. The heavy, dark atmosphere they brought lifts. The only evidence that they were here at all is the splinters of the ebony cane on the floor and the throbbing bruise forming on my leg.

Finally, Reid lets out a loud sigh and his shoulders sag as if he's just been relieved of the weight of the world.

He turns to me, his eyes wide and incredulous.

"I will break you?" he asks, laughter tinging his voice. "I will destroy you?"

He picks me up then, lifts me from under my legs just like he did on the beach. My stomach flips and then settles. I reach my hands around his neck and breathe in his warm scent.

"You said we're your family. You said I'm your husband. You said she's your daughter." He's repeating it all, as if he can't believe it.

"It's all true, isn't it?" I ask, frowning at him. His neck is warm, the stubble on his neck and jaw scratches my hand.

He holds me close and gazes down at me as if he wants to spend the next fifty years holding me in his arms. My heart skips a beat and I flush, tingling warmth spreading through me.

"My leg hurts." I wince at the throbbing pain.

"I'll say." His eyes light up with humor. "Poor you. Let me find some ice."

He strides into the kitchen, me in his arms, and when

we're there, in the bright, white quartz and white cabinet space, he slides me onto the counter. The stone is cold beneath my thighs.

Reid opens the freezer and sticks his head in, then pulls out a pack of peas.

"Here." He presses it to the purpling bruise on my leg.

I sigh at how good the cold feels on the bruise.

"I could kiss it and make it better," he offers, laughter in his eyes. Then he presses his hand to his mouth, and gently runs his fingers over my thigh, rubbing the kiss into my skin.

I let out a shaky breath, feeling the cold counter beneath my legs and the cold iced peas on top.

"I've always wanted to do that," he says, leaning against the counter next to me.

"Kiss me better?"

He laughs. "No. Break that damn cane. Stand up to my father. You are a miracle, do you know that? You're the answer to every prayer I've ever made."

I smile at him, looking at me with calm, happy eyes.

"You're going to love her," he says simply. "You're going to keep her safe."

I reach forward and put my hand to his jaw, feeling the rough stubble under my hand.

My mom couldn't love me—I wasn't hers and she couldn't make herself care—but that doesn't mean I'm the same. Reid's right, I'm going to love her.

"I'm going to love her as best I can," I promise.

He smiles at me, a lightness in him that I've never seen before. We stay there for I don't know how long, quiet in the lengthening afternoon shadows, the peas slowly warming from the heat of my leg, melting ice dripping onto the floor, in a steady drip, drip, drip.

Eventually, Mary brings Claudia down to the kitchen to start a bottle, and Reid says we should have dim sum delivered for dinner, because he's always wanted to eat dim sum by candlelight while sitting on the floor, and as everyone moves busily around the kitchen, heating bottles, trying to make Claudia smile, and calling for delivery, there's a niggling question at the back of my mind—is it possible to love in more than one way?

57

ANDREA

IF IT'S POSSIBLE TO LOVE IN MORE THAN ONE WAY, THEN IT'S
also possible to break your heart in more than one
way too.

As the days pass I concentrate only on the moment,
the one right in front of us.

We take Claudia to the house in the Hamptons and
dip her feet in the salty water and watch her surprise at
the splashing waves.

We fly to Napa and take off our shoes to walk barefoot
through the grapevines, breathing in the lush, green and
sweet grape smells.

We spend the day in New Orleans wandering the
French Quarter, sipping espressos and burning our
fingers on the freshly made, steaming hot beignets.

Reid brings us to the Natural History Museum so he
can hold Claudia beneath the great behemoth dinosaur

fossils and show her the vastness of the universe in the planetarium.

We swoop over the Grand Canyon in a helicopter, and because I really thought we were going to crash into the towering red canyon walls, I clutch Reid's hand the entire time.

Each day is endless. Each day is gone.

Reid hides it—I know he does—but he's losing time. The clock ticking shows in the deepening hollows in his cheeks, the shadows under his eyes, his ever-diminishing appetite, the cabinet full of pills, the fatigue, the naps, the sleep, the lines of pain around his mouth.

The night after Napa, I slipped into bed next to him, fear eating at me like a moth gnawing silk in a dark closet, and when he made a noise of pain, I said, "Maybe you could try, maybe it's not too late, what if we—"

"Don't say it," he said, his voice muffled in the darkness. "Don't ask me, if you do, I would do it for you, but I don't want to. Please don't say it."

So I didn't. Instead I curled into his side, rested my hand over his heart, and laid there listening to his breathing slow into the rhythm of sleep.

He'd told me he'd rather spend six months living than a year dying, and even if I want him for a year, it wouldn't be the year that he would want.

So now we're in the Arctic Circle, at the only snow hotel open year round because Reid wants to see me in an ice palace with the northern lights lighting the midnight sky.

The chill of the snow, an odd sensation in August, bites at my nose and when I breathe out, big puffs of white form in front of me.

"Are you cold?" Reid asks. He's in a sweater and a

down jacket, and his hair sticks out from the bottom of his wool hat. Even so, his nose is pink and his cheeks are red.

"Yes," I say, and then I rub my mittened hands over my arms.

"Come here." Reid smiles and tugs my hand, pulling me against him.

He tucks my back into his front, then he wraps his arms around me, rubs his hands over me and holds me against his warmth.

I lean back into him and let him warm me. A contentment spreads through me, soothing like the peppermint hot chocolate we drank on our arrival at the snow hotel, it warmed me all the way to my toes.

We've been married for a month now. I never knew this before, but Reid is affectionate, he likes to rest his hand on mine, or sleep with his arms around me, or take my hand in his while we're walking. Every time he does, I look at him, to see what he's thinking, but he just gives me a lopsided smile and a wink.

I rest against him, enjoy the feel of his arms around me, and take in the ice suite. The air has the clean, fresh snow scent mixed with evergreen and ice.

The walls of the suite are built from thick, rectangular snow blocks, each about twenty inches wide and eight inches high, sloping up to a rounded ceiling.

Light shines into the room through the ice sheet windows, which show a blurred, wavy blue and green outdoors, trees and sky distorted by the ice. There's a faux brick fireplace carved from snow, with a snow fire burning. The floor is soft, powdery snow that crunches under our feet. And the furniture—that's the best part— it's all carved from ice.

There's a massive claw-footed ice table with thronelike chairs. There's an ice couch and coffee table with a vase full of delicate ice roses. And then, there's the bed. It's a sleigh bed, with an elegantly rounded headboard and footboard, with curlicues and scrollwork carved into the ice, it looks just like an antique wooden bed once slept on by royalty. Except it's completely carved from ice. Luckily there's a mattress and a white down comforter, and on top of that, there's thick, luxurious gray fur blankets.

The snow crunches under my feet as I tilt my head to glance at Reid.

"Well, is it everything you imagined? An ice castle fit for a haughty ice princess?" I ask him, breathing in the soft wool scent of his sweater.

"Mmm." His arms tighten around me. "I love it when you play haughty ice princess."

When he came back to New York, he said he was looking to see if I was still that haughty ice princess in the Tower, and I'd asked if he was still the same arrogant prick.

I laugh. "You know, I think you actually do."

"Of course I do. It's the same reason you love it when I'm arrogant."

"You aren't arrogant," I argue.

"Of course I am. I'm arrogant enough to think my daughter is the smartest, most beautiful baby in the world, and also to think that you actually like my brand of fun. That's arrogance."

I turn in his arms and set my hands on his chest, pressing into the down jacket. "It's not arrogance if it's all true."

He grins down at me, looking like a tired ruffian come to raid the ice palace.

"Should we go hunt down the northern lights?" he asks, setting his hands on my hips. "Or do you want to stay here and stare into my eyes? Remember, the woman at check-in told me my eyes are the exact shade of the aurora borealis." He widens his eyes, showing off the blue-green color, and wags his eyebrows.

I scoff. The woman at check-in was flirting with him, awed by his good looks and how cute he looked holding his two-month-old daughter.

"I changed my mind, you are arrogant."

He laughs.

And then we head to the rustic wood cottage nearby to find Mary and Claudia nestled on a soft couch next to an open fireplace.

Reid and I hike up the wooded hill, full of early autumn flowers and crisp cool tree smells. I carry a backpack with a blanket and a metal canteen full of hot cocoa. Reid carries Claudia.

Down below, there's an ice-blue, toe-numbing lake, surrounded by rolling, pine-studded hills, and gray lichen-covered outcroppings. The snowy ice structures and cottages cluster near the pebbled shore.

Claudia snuggles in a fluffy quilted one-piece, resting against Reid's chest, as he points out a gull soaring over the lake, a white and blue fishing boat knocking against the rocky shore, and the deepening indigo of the sky. Her eyelids droop at the quiet lull of his gravel-deep voice and the rhythm of us climbing higher and higher.

It's only half a mile, but it takes a good thirty minutes to make it to the top of the slope. Reid's breathing is labored and he stops frequently to lean against a tree trunk or lichen-dusted boulder, resting. Neither of us says anything about what that means.

The sky has shifted from indigo to startling black. At the top of the hill there's a wooden bench carved from thick cedar logs.

I sit down on the bench, scooting all the way to the high back, and then pull the soft fur blanket and the hot cocoa from the backpack. Reid sits next to me, his thigh pressing against mine, his body heat traveling through the cold air to reach me.

I drape the blanket over us, and Reid holds Claudia in the crook of his arm.

I pour the hot cocoa into the small carved wooden mug the kitchen provided and breathe in the warm chocolate steam rising up. It's full of cream and melted dark chocolate and a dash of crushed peppermint. I take a sip, letting it warm me, then hold it out to Reid.

He takes a sip, his eyes laughing at me over the rim of the mug, and then hands it back to me.

I hold the warm mug in my hands, resting in the silken softness of the fur blanket tucked around us. It's late autumn, cold, but not quite cold enough for the night insects to have stopped singing. The sound draws over us, a high, violin-like hum.

"Well. Now what?" I ask, looking out over the valley and the endless expanse of blackness spread out before us.

"Now we wait," Reid says.

Then he looks down at Claudia and makes a funny face, wrinkling his nose and sticking his tongue to the side—still trying to get her to smile.

It's been his daily mission for the past weeks, she's

eight and a half weeks now, and Reid is certain it will happen any moment.

Reid bends close, presses his nose to hers and rubs it back and forth. Claudia swings her arm up and grasps at Reid's nose, he makes a startled oof, and then—

"She's...she's smiling," he says, his voice filled with awe.

He doesn't move, he just lets her keep whacking his nose, as she looks up at him with her lips curved into a happy smile.

He smiles back, joy lighting his face, and then he laughs, "You smiled for me," he says. "I knew you would. I knew it."

Then he lifts her up and bounces her in the air, she lets out a startled giggle and Reid's eyes light up as he glances quickly at me.

His expression seems to say, *this is the best day of my life, how could I be so lucky?*

I wish I could capture this moment and hold onto it forever. I promise myself I won't ever forget it, so when Claudia is eight years old and asking for stories about her dad, I'll be able to tell her about this very moment. Every detail.

The wind rustling through the pine leaves, the smell of hot cocoa, the soft warm fur, Reid's joyful laugh, her baby smile, and—

"Look," I say, breathing out in wonder.

Reid follows my gaze and there, dancing above the lake, twisting between the hills, ethereal and wondrous, are the wispy, misty green northern lights.

The crescent moon shines over the lights, and they move, shifting through the black sky, like illuminated strands of silk flowing in water.

Reid turns Claudia to the stars and the moon and the aurora borealis, and it must be the best light show a baby has ever seen.

As the brilliant green streams across the sky, my chest expands, and I reach over to Reid and take his hand, weaving my fingers with his.

"She was right," I tell him. "It is the color of your eyes."

He smiles softly at me, and while I rest my head on his shoulder and watch the northern lights, Reid watches Claudia, now asleep in his arms.

And me, he watches me.

58

JACE

SAYING YOU'RE DONE AND ACTUALLY BEING DONE ARE TWO
different things.

There are contracts, obligations, recording sessions,
promos, venues, tours booked, tickets bought, talk shows
scheduled, interviews, awards ceremonies, the list goes on. If
you've spent your life driving full speed down a certain path,
you can't just walk away, no matter how much you want to.

I suppose it's like the Titanic, it's not as if they didn't
try to turn the boat. It was just too big and the speed it
was going was too fast.

That's me.

Jace Morgan, lead singer, Grammy-winning artist,
man desired by millions, followed by paparazzi,
photographed by strangers in the street.

Too big.

The Morgan Brothers are too big and we rocketed to the top fast.

If we were still small, limping from one small club to the next, faceless and nameless, it wouldn't be hard to walk away.

But it's not possible to just walk away when people depend on you—people in the industry, your producers, your fans, your brothers, your friends—in fact, it's damn near impossible.

They say when bands break up it's like the bitterest, most explosive divorce you can imagine—bands are relationships too, after all, and often musicians are closer to their bandmates than their spouses.

For the first time in our history, the rumors about a potential band break-up are true. Tensions are so high that we're speaking in monosyllables. Dean has become more controlling, River more placating, Dallas more distrustful, and Pauly more anxious. Everyone's worst trait has been amplified, the speakers turned up.

If you asked River—who has always understood everyone and never judged anyone—he'd say my worst trait is not letting go.

I won't let go of what Dean did.

I won't let go of what River did.

I can't seem to get past it. Every time I play with my brothers—which is the only time we see each other now —I can only see them in the hospital lying to me, and then I can only see Andi, smiling at me before marrying another man.

River says, *you have to let it go.*

But I've never been able to do that. I never let go of my dream to sing for the world. I never let go of my love for my mom and dad. I never let go of my loyalty to my brothers. I never let go of my promise to Andi.

How am I supposed to let go?

It's only been a month. Am I supposed to let it go in a month?

We flew to Malibu yesterday, down on a chartered jet, to spend two weeks in the recording studio doing live sessions. We have a new album lined up, it's orchestral, so crammed in the studio space we have the full complement of strings, brass, and woodwinds, along with the band. That's more than twenty musicians in a small space.

Our producer Gary Martin, Dean, and I worked through the instrumentation after I wrote the lyrics and the basic guitar and piano parts. We chose the tonal styles and the theme. Hired the musicians and engineers.

Now we're here. Ready to record.

The white walls are ugly, the floors are drab wood, there's more music stands, instruments, microphones, wires and electronics than you could fit on a semi-truck.

The engineers are set up in the control room on the other side of the soundproof divider, with our producer Gary guiding the process.

We already laid the scratch track, and typically we come in and record parts separately, but we decided—months ago, when we were still talking—that this time around we'd record an instrumental album in the studio, live.

We wanted the energy and the "live" feel that you can only get when everyone is feeding off each other.

Unfortunately, there isn't much energy in here today, unless you count the anxiety rolling off Pauly, the dark looks coming from Dean, and the false cheer of River.

The musicians brought on, luckily, can't sense the undercurrents or are wisely choosing to ignore them.

Typically, we record a scratch track for reference and then record parts separately with the mixing engineers fixing tempo and notes. After that, Dean and I always consult with the engineers working the EQs, compressors, and reverb. And then we decide on the stereo and tonal balance to fit our vision.

It's worked for all our past albums. But this album. They wanted it to have all the energy and harmony of The Morgan Brothers.

I clench my jaw at that.

I'm in the isolation booth, my headset on, one mic for singing, one for my guitar, my heart as tight as a fist because this song...this song. I don't know what I was thinking when I wrote this song. It was before I saw Andi again, obviously. Before the wedding. Before all of this.

But still.

The cellos and violins begin, a mellow chord rising and falling, like waves crashing over a yellow sand beach. Then Dean and River come in, Dallas beneath them, and it's already my cue.

Sing.

Except there's a tightness in my throat, a clenching I haven't felt for years, and why the hell did I write another love song?

The rule I've always kept—the one passed down from my dad—be honest in your music. Always.

You can't hide what's inside from the audience and you can't hide it from yourself. If you're singing a song about love, you have to feel that love, otherwise the song falls flat and leaves everyone feeling dead.

But I wonder what happens if when you're singing a love song *you* only feel empty inside?

"Jace," Gary comes over the headset, and outside the music falters and stops. "You missed your cue."

"Sorry. Yeah."

Dean shoots me a look, his dark eyes unreadable. If this happened in the past he would've been on me, *what's going on, you alright?* But now, he only looks at me darkly, then turns away.

The booth is hot, the air stagnant and full of the new lacquer smell of my brand new Fender—not a Martin, I didn't want a reminder of ashes.

The song begins again.

Violin...cello...bass and piano coming in and then—

"Sorry. I need five," I say, pulling off the headset and pushing out of the booth into the cooler air of the studio.

I stride quickly through the maze of musicians, past stunned faces and scraping chairs, and push out the studio door. Jog down the hall and shove out into the Malibu sun.

I squint into the sunshine, my chest tight, my lungs burning and take in great lungfuls of hot ocean air. The breeze whips around me, and down below, over the tall cliff's edge, the deep blue water crashes in frothing currents and hidden undertows.

Slowly the tight band around my chest loosens and I walk to the edge of the cliff, sit with my legs hanging over the side, and dig my hands into the August-dry grass. I tilt my face to the sky and let the scorching sun beat down on my face.

The door bangs shut, but I don't turn to see who's come out. They'll be here soon.

"Hey."

It's River.

"What?"

"Do you want to scrap the song?" he asks, keeping his voice light and nonjudgmental.

Of course he knows what this is about.

I imagine all of them know what this is about.

I think about the lyrics, *Every time I look in your eyes I'm transported. The waves crash over me, your love,*" and my throat tightens again.

"No," I say. "I'll be in. Just give me a few."

"Alright," he says, then he claps me on the back and makes to go, but hesitates.

"What?" I ask, wanting to be left alone to listen to the waves hit the shore and feel the sun scour away the ache in my chest.

"Serena told me to tell you that if Andi married someone else then she's not the one. She thinks you need to let it go and look for someone else," he says it in a rush, and it's the longest speech he's given since that day at The Plaza.

I stare out over the white crashing ocean and think about the conversation I had with Reid. He asked me if I still loved Andi. If I'd still love her if she married him. I'd said yes, confident that she *wouldn't* marry him.

River leaves then, the door blowing shut behind him, and I'm left alone with the waves and the wind.

From behind me, I can hear the normal noises of musicians practicing during a break, the doors open, long notes held, tuning, a few chords played, a partial melody plucked out.

There's footsteps again, and I expect River's back to tell me it's time to come in, but instead, Pauly settles on the grass beside me and dangles his legs over the edge.

He doesn't say anything for a good minute. The wind whistles over the rocky cliff and the waves make a ferocious roar. His shoulders turn in at the stiff breeze and he gives me a sidelong look.

"Did you come to tell me to let it go?" I ask, looking over at him.

"Nah," he says, staring nervously out over the open air beneath our feet.

I don't know how someone who plays the horn so fearlessly and drives his motorcycle like a maniac can be so afraid of everything else. Except I do, I was there when he was a kid too.

"Alright."

My chest is loose again, the tight fist around my heart relaxing its grip.

"I remembered something," Pauly says finally, looking out toward the hazy blue horizon.

The grass and stone itches as it scratches against my palms. "What's that?"

"When I was eight," he says, looking over to make sure I'm listening. I nod. When he was eight he was tiny, more like a five-year-old than an eight-year-old, and even now he's only Andi's height. "I was sitting in the hall outside my place."

"Yeah," I say.

He'd sit out there a lot. He didn't want to go home but he didn't want to be on the street. There was a rubber mat in front of his door that he'd crouch on, underneath a fluorescent lightbulb, down the hall from the fumes of the trash chute.

"Your mom and dad, they came by, I don't know why, but they did. Your dad knocked on my door and he told my parents I was coming down to hear you play. Then your mom took my hand and your dad bent down and said to me, "Son, if you want to heal hurts, then you do it with music." I didn't get it. I was eight. But I've been trying to heal hurts for thirteen years now..."

Thirteen years. That's how long it's been since my mom and dad died.

"Has it worked?" I ask.

"I don't know, but I keep trying." His brow draws down and he looks like that scared dog shying from a friendly hand when he says, "Don't give up, Jace."

Then he stands and walks with his head down back to the studio.

I stretch back, breathe in the salt and the seaweed and feel the wind wicking away the sweat on my brow. The grass bends under the wind, flicking my fingers.

I have twenty-six musicians waiting on me. My brothers, Dallas, Pauly. A roomful of engineers. And all the people who have written to tell us how they danced to our songs on their first date, at their wedding, played them for their baby just born, or how our songs saved their life. All those people are waiting.

So I stand, stride back toward the studio, and accept what I accepted eight years ago, that every love song I sing, I'm singing for her.

She might not know it, she might not hear it, but it's for her.

59

ANDREA

I GRASP THE GLOSSY BIRTH CERTIFICATE, RUNNING MY HANDS over the paper, my name printed in block letters. It's so new that I can still smell the ink and the paper is crisp and unwrinkled.

It's official.

I'm a mom.

The three-month wait was long and torturous, and nightly I prayed this day would come quickly, but I also prayed that it would never come, because that would mean Reid would be leaving us.

But that was the entire point, wasn't it?

Reid and I weren't about a grand love, or an all-consuming romance, it was about Claudia.

He's done everything he said he would. We've lived—really lived—and we've stored up so many memories, thousands of photos, a million little stories that the feel of him will never leave me.

When I asked him what he wanted me to tell Claudia when she asked about him, he told me to tell her that he'd loved and he'd lived.

I wish I wasn't the one that had to tell her, I wish he could tell her himself.

Reid pulls me into his side, tucks his arms around me as I hold the brand new birth certificate.

"I'm a mom," I say, smiling at him.

We're cushioned on the couch in the living room, a soft breeze blows through the open window, bringing the scent of autumn leaves and crisp October air. Outside a taxi honks as it passes a car double-parked and I look over to Claudia to make sure the noise didn't wake her.

But no, she's still asleep in her swing, a lullaby tinkling across the room.

"You're a *good* mom," Reid says, running his hand over my arm.

I'm trying to be. It's easy, I think, with Mary, who taught me how to swaddle, bottle, change diapers, and rock to sleep. The only thing she didn't have to teach me was how to love, that came on its own.

Claudia is mine as much as Reid is mine. They're both lodged permanently in my heart.

"How does it feel?" I ask, sliding the birth certificate back in its envelope.

He makes a noise, shifts me against him, and I try not to worry about how much weight he's lost, how I can count his ribs, and see the sharp lines of his collarbone through his shirt. I try not to think about how last week he was too tired to get out of bed three of the seven days.

When he's up, he's still charming, laughing, and I think he's doing it for himself—living—but more than anything, I'm coming to believe that he's doing it for me.

"I've never been happier," he says. "The great Andrea Leighton-Hughes Shilling, mom."

Then he turns serious eyes on me, takes a strand of my hair and tucks it behind my ear.

"I don't want you to leave me," I say suddenly, wanting to hold him to me and demand that he never go.

His hand stills and then he pulls back and gives me a solemn look. "Andrea."

"Reid," I say, swallowing.

Across the room Claudia makes a sleep sound and the soft swish of her swing rocking back and forth and the quiet lullaby fills the space.

Reid looks into my eyes, searching my expression. Behind him the autumn light shines through the window, spilling over the three pumpkins on the window seat, two big and one small, and over the caramel apple-scented candles I demanded we buy at the farmers market in Union Square.

He's in a sweater and comfortable jeans, his hair messy and his stubble golden in the light. His eyes are tired, the hollows under them deep, but there's a wry light there.

"I have a serious question," he says, taking my hand.

"Yes?"

My mouth goes dry.

"Would you like cake to celebrate? Chocolate, with mousse, and caramel and...ice cream, mountains of ice cream." He yawns. "I feel like cake, don't you? We could have it delivered."

I nod. There's a French patisserie down the block that has the exact cake he's describing. "That sounds perfect."

"I thought so."

So we eat chocolate caramel cake and mountains and mountains of ice cream.

60

ANDREA

DECEMBER IS HERE AND WITH IT THE LAST OF THE LEAVES have fallen from the gingko tree out front, the flowers in the pots have died, and I've strung white twinkling lights on every bare, lonely surface.

It's late and the night is the clear sparkling dark that you only find in the cold winter months.

Outside the gusty wind rolls through the streets, rattling the Christmas lights against the window, throwing shadows and light across the living room.

I'm tucked against Reid on the couch, his arm wrapped around my shoulder holding me close. I rest my head on his chest, and the steady thump of his heartbeat thrums against my cheek.

Two mugs of hot chocolate filled to the brim with marshmallows sit on the coffee table and let off the sweet scent of creamy Belgian chocolate. My mug is almost empty, Reid's is still almost full.

I was worried, really worried that he wouldn't make it to December. The past few weeks were bad. But then a few days ago he had a sudden burst of energy and I think, maybe, just maybe we'll have a Christmas together.

But just in case we don't—although I won't admit it out loud—I told him that since it's now December I wanted to give him a present.

Yesterday we had a balsam fir delivered, it's full with green-blue needles and a fresh, woodsy pine tree smell.

We stood it in front of the wide bow window and wrapped it in white lights. Then while Reid watched from the couch with Claudia crawling across the rug trying to grab the strands of twinkling lights, I put an angel on top.

Now we're wrapped in the warmth of the living room, the blustery cold outside, the lights casting a soft glow, our angel watching over us.

There's a stack of presents on the coffee table. I wrapped mine in thick gold paper, with a velvet burgundy bow.

There's a small pile next to it. Reid brought them out, an envelope, a white package with a blue satin bow, and a small box wrapped in sparkling silver paper.

"I'll go first," Reid says, and I shift upright, moving out of the comfortable warmth of his arms. He smiles at me, the gentle lights brushing his hair gold and hiding the fatigue lines around his eyes and mouth.

"If you don't like it, don't tell me," he jokes.

"On my honor," I say, crossing my heart.

I sit with my legs tucked under me and my hands folded in my lap, suddenly nervous.

I've never received a Christmas present like this before. Growing up, my dad had personal shoppers choose, wrap, and deliver gifts, and once we were teenagers we flew somewhere warm and were given a lump deposit into our bank account on Christmas Eve.

This is the first time in my life that anyone has actually picked out a present for me themselves.

Reid reaches over to the table, the sleeve of his cashmere sweater softly brushing against my arm. He shaved today, his jaw is smooth, and the soapy scent that I associate with him lingers.

He takes the envelope and the white box and holds them loosely, "So, these two are actually for you to deliver," he says.

He hands me the envelope first. It's cream-colored vellum, thick and smooth. I take it in my hand when he holds it out to me.

"I want you to give this to Jace the next time you see him."

I look quickly at him, and the letter in my hand is suddenly as heavy as the world.

I shake my head, "You're so sure I'll see him again?"

A slow smile spreads across his face, lighting up his eyes. "I don't know what will happen tomorrow, but I do know that you'll see him again."

I'm not so sure. I saw the look on Jace's face as he was walking away.

But Reid's watching me like this is important, so I say, "Do you mind me asking what it says?"

He shrugs. "It's just some unfinished business."

Ah, that makes sense. Reid has mentioned how much he regrets the way he treated Jace when they were kids, so I think this is an apology.

"I'll give it to him," I promise.

Reid lets out a breath that I think he must've been holding and says, "By the way, when he meets Claudia, can you tell him to only say good things about me? Like how handsome I was, how charming, how intelligent—"

I scoff and tuck the envelope onto the couch next to me. "How arrogant."

He grins, then takes the little package with the blue bow. "This one is for Claudia," he says.

I shake my head. "You can give it to her on—"

He holds up his hand, stopping my protest.

"I want you to keep it for her. It's recordings. She likes it when I read to her, so I recorded a book for every birthday. It's all kids' books, so maybe when she's older, she won't like it as much. But I found that I like *Goodnight Moon* again, and *The Runaway Bunny*, so maybe she will too. I don't know. I don't have advice, or lists for living, and I can't sing, but I can read. And she can hear my voice and listen to the words when she's tired, or lonely, or sick, and maybe, even though I'm not here, hearing *I Love You This Much* will remind her she's loved."

I think of Reid, lying in bed, Claudia snuggled on his chest as he reads her a book, his quiet voice rumbling, his head tucked near hers.

I take the package, brushing my hand across the satin bow, and nod. "I'll give it to her. Every birthday. I promise."

"Thank you," he says, squeezing my hand.

Then he takes the silver wrapped package and shifts it nervously in his hands.

"Is this one for me?" I ask.

"If you don't like it—"

"I won't tell."

He smiles and nods. Outside, another gust of wind howls down the street, rattling the lights on the window. They tap and tink against the pane and flicker over the room.

I hold out my hands and he sets the present gently in my palms. Slowly I unwrap the silver paper. I tear a small corner of the paper, it curls up, and I look at Reid smiling.

He nods and there's a soft gleam in his eyes, the reflection of the Christmas lights in their blue-green depths.

I slowly tear the curled edge, the paper crinkling as I take off another small strip of paper. The anticipation thrums through me, it feels delicious and full. Reid leans closer, his eyes on me as I keep peeling the paper strip by strip.

This is my first real present, and it's from Reid, so I'm going to enjoy it.

Finally, the edge of a white leather box pokes free.

I look back to Reid. He nods again.

Then I can't take it anymore. I yank at the paper and tear it free.

I hold a six-inch-long, four-inch-wide, two-inch-high white leather box in my hand.

"What is it?" I ask, rubbing my hands over the smooth leather.

"Open it," Reid says, laughter in his voice.

So I do.

Inside the box is a necklace.

The chain is delicate links of gold woven together, and at the base, there's a pendant the size of a penny, but in the shape of a flame. It's gold with rubies and diamonds sprinkled across it like embers burning bright.

"I know you have lots of jewelry," Reid says, "But I had

this made because I...I didn't want the fire in your heart to go out again. When I'm gone, don't let it go out." He reaches out, touches the flame. "I thought, if you wore this, you'd remember to keep it burning, no matter how cold it gets."

I stare at the flickering lights winking off the rubies, dancing like a flame, and my heart aches. He's right. When he came back to New York the flame in my heart had died. He brought it back though, holding the ember in his hand and breathing it back to life.

But what happens when he goes?

I brush my hand over the tiny chips of fire. The metal is cold.

"I'll always wear it," I tell him. "I won't forget."

He smiles and there's relief in his eyes as he takes the necklace, brushes my hair aside and clasps it around my neck.

My heart thunders as his hands skim over my neck and collarbone. He's only inches away, his smell, his heat surrounding me.

"Now yours," I say, pulling the gold wrapped present from the table and dropping it on his lap.

His eyes crinkle as he picks it up and shakes it, holding it to his ear. There isn't anything to hear though. It's as big as an encyclopedia and solid.

Then, unlike me, he doesn't have any patience. He tears off the burgundy bow, tosses it on the floor, and rips open the wrapping paper, shredding it with abandon.

I suppose that's the difference between us. I revel in the anticipation and he delights in the doing.

I grin at him, at his smile and the paper flying about him. He holds up the thick leather album and then looks at me, his eyebrows raised.

"Open it," I say, repeating his words.

So he does.

It's a handmade memory book. And it isn't just the past few months, it's all the pictures I had of us as kids too.

We're four years old, there at the Met for art class, bright red paint on our smocks. We're eight, at his infamous birthday party when I tossed his presents in the pool. We're at my sixteenth birthday, dancing under the ballroom chandelier. We're seventeen, at a gala, I'm scowling at him, and he's giving me that sardonic smile, holding out his hand. We're at the beach dipping Claudia's toes in the water. We're in the park, pink cherry blossoms raining around us. We're eating a mountain of ice cream, and he's smearing chocolate on my nose.

It goes on, pages and pages, he turns each one carefully, running his fingers over the images.

And I didn't realize it when I made this album, but I realize it now—I thought I was just putting together a photo album, but I wasn't, I was telling our story.

And—

"Andrea?" His voice is low, he's watching me somberly.

"Yes, Reid?"

"Did you go and fall in love with me?"

I give him a helpless look.

That's what this album is. It's a love story.

I nod, my throat tight, my lips wobbling. "Yes."

He gives me a wry smile. "Why'd you go and do that?"

"I'm sorry. I couldn't help it," I whisper.

He nods. Then he sets the album on the coffee table, and reaches out and takes my hands.

He's warm, his hands are strong and comforting. He

rubs his thumb gently over the pulse in my wrist, and the only sound is the wind, the lights against the window, and his soft exhale as he runs his fingers over my skin.

I look into his eyes and I see what I should've recognized before, what I should've known.

"You love me too," I say.

He gives me a rueful, apologetic smile.

"How long?" I ask brokenly.

He thinks for a moment, his eyes crinkling. "When we were four. You came with your nanny to our weekend French class. You were in a red velvet dress, with a big bow, and your red-gold hair was braided in a crown on your head and I said, 'Bonjour, Andrea,' and you said, 'Au revoir, Reid,' and...that was it for me."

"Reid—"

He nods and I feel as if I'm breaking apart, fragmenting like the hundreds of lights on the Christmas tree.

"Why didn't you ever say anything?"

He shakes his head. "There's a wide chasm between loving someone and *knowing* you love someone."

I take my hand from his, brush my fingers down the smoothness of his jaw, running them over his cheekbones and finally his mouth. He lets out a pained exhale.

How long have I loved him?

How long without realizing it?

"It took me a long time too," I say, tracing my hand over his bottom lip.

"I realized it when I came back to New York," he says, "but then, it looked like I was nearly a decade too late. Late to arrive, early to leave," he says, smiling wryly against my fingers.

"Don't say that," I whisper, "I want you to stay."

I press my fingers into his lip and he nods. "As long as I can."

Then he reaches up and grasps my hand in his. "I never needed you to love me back. It was enough knowing I loved you. Making you smile and laugh again. But now...Andrea."

"Yes?" I say, my pulse fluttering beneath his fingers.

"There's something I've always wanted to do."

The air between us turns warm, soft, like candlelight and gold, and then Reid reaches up, and cups my face in his hands.

"Yes," I whisper.

"I love you," he says.

Then he spans the space between us and brushes his warm mouth over mine. I reach out, lay my hand on his heart, hold on to him as the room spins, like we've been lifted in the sky and are dancing, spinning in the blue-green of the northern lights, in the gold of the stars, and the gentle light of the moon.

He traces his tongue over my bottom lip, tasting the memory of chocolate and sugar still lingering there.

He savors my mouth, luxuriates in it, and if I ever wondered what kissing Reid would be like, I should've known.

He kisses like he lives.

Fully. Openly. Delightedly.

He drags his fingers through my hair, tugs me closer, and then he pulls on my bottom lip, sucks it, and I feel the echo of it sparkling through my veins, pumping all the way to my heart.

I open to him. He makes a happy, appreciative, rumbling noise that I feel down to my toes.

I bite at his bottom lip, taste him, the heat of him, the

flavor of him. I run my hands over his chest, feel the fast beating of his heart, calling to mine. I send my hand under his cashmere sweater, tug it up, and run my hands over the smooth warmth of his skin.

Reid runs his hands down my neck, over my pulse, across the sensitive space between my throat and collarbone.

All the while, we're kissing.

Tasting.

Living.

Loving.

He sends his tongue into my mouth, exploring me, claiming me, and at the thrust and withdrawal of his tongue, a spark lights and grows, and grows, like a diamond shining in the dark.

All those times we danced, they were a prelude to this. Making love with our kiss.

The slow dances when we were kids, the waltzes under glittering ballroom lights, the spinning dance by the cherry trees, the joyful dance on our wedding night, they were all building to this.

His mouth.

His hands.

My heart.

His love.

We're not the love story I'd ever imagined, but we're one all the same.

I hold on to him as I sink into his mouth, lose my breath to him, give him all the love that I didn't know I still had to give.

"Andrea," he whispers against my mouth, and it sounds like a prayer.

"I love you," I say, and he takes it, presses kisses over

me, sends his hands over me as if he's memorizing me, capturing this moment for eternity.

And I wonder, can you capture eternity in a kiss?

He pulls back then, draws his warm, wet lips from my mouth. He stays an inch away, looking into my eyes, his are full of love, achingly blue-green. My mouth is bruised and tingling and I can feel the warm puffs of his breath caressing my lips.

When we kissed, it felt like falling backwards, arms wide, trusting that at the bottom Reid would be there to catch me.

And he was.

"Do you regret it?" he whispers, his fingers stroking my jaw and cheeks.

"I've never regretted a moment with you."

He smiles then and the gold flecks in his eyes light up like Christmastime.

"You?" I ask.

He brushes his thumb over my lip. "You're everything I ever dreamed of and never deserved."

I lean forward then, crawl over the couch cushions, to wrap myself around him, and hold him in a tight, tight hug.

He stays still for a moment, then he tucks me into him and wraps his arms around me.

We lie there, twined together, watching the Christmas lights sparkle, listening to the wind and the beating of our hearts.

"Love you," I murmur tiredly.

He strokes a hand through my hair, gently brushing it, letting his fingers trail over my skin. Pressing kisses across me with his hands.

I close my eyes, settle into him, and slowly drift off.

I come awake when Claudia starts to cry.

I sit up, shake my head, and come fully awake.

Reid stretches, yawns, he looks tired again, and I have a memory, that while I was dozing he was stroking my hair, holding me close. While I was drifting off, he was collecting memories.

"I'll get her," I say, yawning. "You should sleep."

Reid shakes his head and stands. "I want to. It's okay. You can go to bed."

Mary's visiting family, so it's just the two of us. I'd offer again, but Reid leans forward and presses a kiss to my forehead.

I smile sleepily up at him.

"Thank you," he says, "for your gift."

I lift a hand to my mouth and he smiles at me, a happy smile, one I'll never get tired of seeing. Then he's striding across the living room to go change a diaper, make a bottle, cuddle his daughter back to sleep.

I go to the bedroom, change into pajamas, climb into the large, comfortable bed and fall asleep happy.

I wake up to darkness and silence. The wind has stopped, the lights no longer tap against the living room window, and the city is quiet. I reach over for Reid, but his side of the bed is cold, as if he never came to bed.

The clock on the nightstand says it's two in the morning.

He probably fell asleep in the rocking chair, he's done that a few times, and I always go up, shake him awake and draw him back down the stairs to bed.

I throw the covers back and hurry across the cold wood floor, the boards creaking beneath my feet.

I'm warm, my mouth still tingles, and I'm thinking

about cuddling into Reid's side back in bed when I step into the nursery.

It takes me a moment to realize something's wrong.

Reid isn't in the rocking chair. He isn't standing by the crib. He isn't sitting cross-legged on the floor, reading a book to his daughter.

No.

He isn't doing any of those things.

The room is quiet except for the hum of the humidifier puffing out lavender-scented cool steam. The stars and moon nightlight casts a yellow glow over the nursery.

Claudia is asleep in her crib, her hand reaching through the slats, her fingers open and splayed out toward her dad.

As if she fell asleep reaching for him.

And Reid.

He's there.

But he's on the floor. He's face down, his arm reaching out toward the crib. And he's not moving. He's not moving at all.

My heart thunders and I shake my head, refusing to see. No. No. No. No. No.

He's fine.

He's fine.

I drop to my knees, they crack against the wood and I scramble across the floor to him.

"Reid?"

I shake him.

"Reid."

I shake him harder, push him over. "Reid!" I shout.

Claudia wakes up then, and when she sees me she starts to cry.

"Reid!" I shout.

I press my head to his chest, listen for his heartbeat.

It's not there.

There's no sound.

Claudia's crying, reaching for me. For her dad.

I claw at his chest, push down on his heart, try to pump it back, to make it work.

I try to make his heart beat again, pumping my fist against him, breathing into his mouth.

"Reid," I cry.

He came back to New York, he found me, and my heart was broken, and to fix it he gave me his own. And now, I can't make his start again.

Claudia's cries are so loud now they're piercing my ears. Reid's not moving. Not breathing. His heart isn't beating. And his skin, it's lost the warmth of life.

But I can't—

I sprint down the stairs, grab my phone, and call the ambulance.

He's not gone.

He isn't gone.

Not yet.

He promised to stay as long as he could.

He promised.

And I only just realized that I loved him.

The ambulance comes. Their red and white lights brighter, harsher than the Christmas bulbs. They take Reid away. But not before telling me—he's gone.

My love is gone.

Andrea

The funeral was something I never want to live through again.

My bones ache, my body is heavy, and my heart is guttering.

But I keep my necklace on, and every time I feel like my light is going out, I reach up and touch the flame burning there.

My family came, my brothers grim-faced, my dad shrewdly considering my blank expression, my mom casting worried glances my way. Reid's family came too, but they left as quietly as they arrived.

It's after now, the winter blue of the sky is fading to twilight, the clouds moving slowly by, the air cold with the smallest crystal snowflakes falling but not sticking. Not staying.

I hold Claudia in my arms, her solid six-month weight

heavy in my arms, and rock her in the fading light shining through the living room window.

We're alone.

It's just her and me now.

The Christmas tree is lit up, the angel looking down over us. The bookshelf is full, the couch is still comfortable, the yellow walls still soothing, the house still smells of beeswax, and now fir tree.

But he's gone.

I kneel down to the Christmas tree and pick up the white package with the blue satin ribbon. Slowly, I unwrap it, and Claudia watches me, grasping for the bits of paper.

She's in a white ruffled dress, her golden hair wispy, her eyes bluer than Reid's blue-green. She frowns up at me, her lower lip wobbling, her hands clenched in tight fists. She's getting ready for a good cry after a long day.

I gather her up, pull her to the couch, and settle her in the crook of my arm, just like Reid used to do.

Then I turn on the first recording, the one marked, *Claudia, six months*, and push play.

I wait, my breath held, my eyes burning, my chest aching as Reid's quiet voice fills the living room.

"*This is How Much I Love You*," he says, his voice a soft rumble that reaches across the emptiness and grasps my heart, "*Read by your dad.*"

I rock Claudia to Reid's words, and his voice, the rhythm of his love, soothes her to sleep.

I sit with her for a long time and watch the sky fade from blue to black.

62

Jace

Six months in we're nearly done with our tour.

We dropped the album and have been touring hard since. I'd like to say things have gotten better since recording, but they've only gotten worse.

Tonight is the final concert, after that it's on record that we're taking a "break for creative recharge." Everyone expects we'll take six months, maybe a year off and then come back together, ready to roll again.

Gary suggested we do like The Beatles and take a joint meditation retreat. I didn't remind him that they broke up shortly after that retreat. When it's over, it's over.

We're all in my suite at The Four Seasons in New York.

The Plaza wouldn't have us back after the flaming guitar incident.

I didn't want to come back to New York, but it's the

final stop on our tour. We're sold out at Madison Square Garden.

As soon as we stepped off the charter jet, I had a feeling, gentle and insistent like a breeze blowing through an open window, that Andi's here, waiting for me.

But she's not. I have to remind myself of that. She's not.

Even so, every woman with honey-amber hair, every musical laugh, has me looking and then looking again, certain she's there.

My skin is tingling, my chest is tight, and I'm certain that she's just around the corner and I'll see her soon. Any minute.

She's here, in this city, and so am I.

And it's the last time I'll be singing for her.

I lean back on the white couch and look at my brothers Dean and River, sitting across from me. At Pauly on the couch next to me, and at Dallas standing by the tall toffee-colored marble fireplace.

We're all in black. Jeans, T-shirts, leather, we stand out against the tasteful white fabrics, the white marble, the silver floors encrusted with dark wood, the walls wrapped in silk and embossed leather.

I'll try not to burn anything this time around.

"I called you over," I say, my voice steady and quiet, "because this is the last show I'm going to play. Tonight, we're done with our tour, we're done with our shows. This is it for me."

Dean shakes his head. The Empire State Building and the Chrysler Building rise up behind him, perfectly positioned in the floor-to-ceiling windows.

We haven't had a proper conversation in months, this is it, right here and right now.

Dean's shoulders are bowed, and he looks tired, worn out, and somehow, even though we're in a four-thousand-square-foot suite, on top of the world, he reminds me of how he looked when he came home to our run-down apartment from his job hauling concrete. Like his dreams were slowly being crushed to dust beneath the weight of that heavy load and he'd lost his joy.

"Don't," he says, his voice deep with emotion, "Take a break. Take all the time you need. But don't give this up because of a mistake. Jace." He looks up at me, his eyes weary. "It was a mistake. Don't let a mistake stop the music."

She was the music.

He doesn't get that. He never has.

"You can keep playing," I say, "I'm only one person. There's four more of you."

Dallas shakes his head, crossing his arms over his chest.

"She married someone else," River says, swearing angrily. "It sucks. It's terrible. But it's done. I'm sorry I ever lied to you, but let it go. Let it go."

"It's not that you lied to me, it's that you kept lying for eight years. What was any of this? Was it real? Is this what family is? You lie to each other, use each other, all for what, fame, money, to get out of a life you don't want?"

Dean stands, walks across the room to the sunlit windows, Manhattan sprawled below. He gently hits his fist against the glass, and the quiet thud echoes through the room.

He turns to me then, his face lined and his eyes

pleading. "You know that's not what this has been about. It never has. You *know* that."

Then he strides from the room.

River shakes his head, then shoves off the couch, following Dean from the suite. Dallas doesn't say anything, he just follows them out.

Soon, it's only Pauly and me sitting on the sofa, staring at the sun glinting off the shining silver top of the Chrysler Building.

The air blows cold and dry from the air conditioner, humming steadily and blowing the scent of oranges, pears, and mango from the fruit basket discreetly tucked on a side table.

"Are you going to try to change my mind?" I ask tiredly.

"No," Pauly says, shifting on the couch, looking nervously at the door. His shoulders hunch and he tucks into himself, like he does when he's anxious about something.

"What?" I ask.

"You should forgive Dean."

He says Dean, because he knows, I've already forgiven River. We all know it's Dean who makes the decisions.

"Why?"

Pauly looks down at his hands, at his short, bitten nails, and the callouses, and when he sees that they're shaking, he buries his fists in his lap.

"You're really leaving the band. This is it? No more music?" His voice shakes.

"I'm sorry."

He gives me a long, considering look, as if he's deciding whether or not he should run or stay. The flight or fight of the timid mouse under the eagle's talons.

Except, I'm not an eagle, I'm his friend.

"I'm telling you this," he says, then he whispers to himself something I can't hear, and then he says more loudly, "I'm telling you this because I think you deserve to know what Dean is really like."

"I know what he's really like," I say. He's my brother, I've known him for twenty-six years.

"No," Pauly says, shaking his head. "You don't."

That's the most forceful I've ever heard him. He stares at me, then says, "When I was fifteen my dad gave me the beating of my life."

"I remember," I say.

He nods, digs his fingers into his thighs. "I found a gun in my dad's closet. It was stolen."

The feel of a low, cold, numbing acid starts to run over my skin, working a chill over me. I sit still, absolutely still, because if I do, maybe what I'm suddenly thinking won't be true.

"I took the gun and I told myself if he ever hit me again, I'd shoot him. But he did, and I didn't. It was..." He shakes his head. "So I decided I was done. I took the gun, went down to the bodega. I was going to go out in a big way. I wanted to steal something big, pull out the gun, end it—"

"Pauly, no." My lips are numb, my skin is burning.

"The guy behind the counter was yelling, I was waving the gun, waiting for the cops to come, then your dad stepped out to stop me. He said, "Son, what are you doing?" and I was so startled, so jumpy, and hair-trigger, that I started shooting, just shooting everywhere. And your mom, she jumped in front of your dad, and they knew, they knew it was me, and—"

His mouth twists, his eyes flare wide, and an animal noise wrenches out of him.

I sit there. As cold as ice, burning hot.

I can't move. Because this isn't real. There's no way that the person who gunned down my parents is the same kid I grew up with, the one who I've always thought of as my family.

"Dean knew it was me as soon as he saw the security footage," Pauly says. "I was holed up at my place, considering that gun, thinking of finishing it all. And he busted down the door, came in, hauled me up, and said, "I didn't want my parents to die, but I sure as hell don't want my friend to die either. Get up. Get up, Pauly. You're going to play. You're going to play and you're going to make my mom and dad proud. Clean yourself up. Stand up." He shook me so hard I thought I was going to die and sometimes I wish I had. But Dean said he knew I didn't mean it and I was going to heal the world and heal all the mistakes I'd made by making music."

I'm shaking my head.

Shaking because it's not true.

It's not true.

"He forgave me," Pauly says. "He saved my life. He always does what he thinks is best. Sometimes he's wrong, sometimes he's right. But don't walk away. Don't give up. Jace. If we don't fall, if we aren't human, then there's no need for grace. You have to forgive."

Slowly, I clench my fist, one finger at a time.

I'm able to move again, so I do. I stand. Take a breath.

Pauly looks up at me, eyes wide and white.

"You killed my parents."

"Don't stop playing music," he says.

"Dean knew you killed my parents."

He shakes his head.

"Jace, your dad said music can heal anything."

I point a finger at Pauly and he flinches. "Get out. You are dead to me. You are not my family. You are not my friend. You killed my parents and took their place. You are dead to me."

I stand there, my lungs burning, my throat clenching, as Pauly stumbles from the room.

63

JACE

THE ROAR OF THOUSANDS CRASHES OVER ME, THE SWELL OF shouts vibrates across the stage and shakes me to the core.

I step into the lights, smoke rises, the drums pound in a steady beat, and my guitar hangs like a noose around me. My throat is tight and clenching, and still they scream.

Cheer.

Shout.

And all I feel is emptiness devouring rage.

Dallas pounds out the beat, Dean and River join, knocking out the rhythm.

I should be concentrating on the song, the lyrics, the notes, but all I can hear is my words, *you're dead to me, you're dead to me.*

It's Pauly's cue now, the trumpet for the opening. I turn to him, and he's there, looking at me.

Then the lights flash, blue, purple, smoke, and instead of lifting his trumpet, Pauly collapses.

It takes a second to understand.

But then the crowd noise dims, Dallas stops first, the drums cutting out. Then I'm running across the stage, my guitar beating against my thigh. I throw it off, drop down to the hard black stage.

"Pauly," I say, grabbing his shoulder.

This has happened before. He takes too many pills to keep down the anxiety. He's always taking too many.

His eyes are closed, his head to the side, River's shouting for the EMTs. The Garden is deathly quiet. Then Dean is there, Dallas, River skidding to the ground next to us.

I thrust my hand against Pauly's neck. His pulse flickers like a dying light, there, gone, there, gone.

"Pauly." I shake him, fear, cold and hard clutching me. "Pauly. Listen to me. I didn't mean it. I didn't mean it."

He doesn't open his eyes. I don't know if he hears me.

I beg him, thinking of if I'd been in Dean's place I wouldn't have wanted him hurt either, how I've never wanted him hurt. And my parents, they loved Pauly, they wouldn't want him hurt. Like my dad says, music heals, it's healed Pauly, it's healed Dean, River, Dallas when he came home from prison, it healed me, kept me afloat all these years.

"Pauly. I'm sorry. You were right, if we didn't do wrong, we wouldn't need grace. You were right."

His pulse stops then, doesn't flicker back.

"I didn't mean it," I say. "You're my brother. You've always been my brother."

Then the EMTs are shoving through, checking his pulse, shouting for a defibrillator, then rolling him away, tied down to a stretcher.

I stay, kneeling on the stage, smoke rising around me, until Dean takes my hand, lifts me, and he says, "We play the show."

I nod, my chest empty, aching, tearing apart.

Dad would tell us to play.

Mom would tell us to play.

Pauly would beg us to play.

"We play," I say.

One more show. One more song.

When we get to the hospital, hours later, the doctor tells us that Pauly is gone.

And then Dean does something I've never seen him do.

He weeps.

And I grab him, pull him to me, and let thirteen years of tears fall, while we stand in the harsh, fluorescent light of the emergency room lobby, our song playing on the speakers above.

64

ANDREA

WINTER PASSES, A BLUR OF WHITE AND GRAY, ENDLESS DAYS
that melt like dirty snow trickling down gutters. An entire
season washed away.

Spring comes and goes, the drip drip of icicles
melting, birds returning to empty nests, bulbs pushing
free of the cold dirt seeking gray skies.

Summer arrives, the sun insistent, the sky blue, I
draw the curtains and leave them closed.

It's June, the week of my birthday, when my mom
finds me.

She sweeps into the house, let in by Mary, her white
dress flowing around her, her hair shining, her make-up
bright. She stops when she finds me on the couch, takes
in my unbrushed hair, my wrinkled shirt and sweatpants,
and purses her lips at the hollows under my eyes.

Her perfume, the same lily-scented floral water she's

always worn, surrounds me. I look at her, my eyes bleary, and I feel like I'm peering up at her from the dark, huddled underneath that bench in the park. It hurts to look at her.

"Get up," she says.

"Why?"

It hurts to ask even that.

Claudia is on the rug, by my feet, playing with a set of wooden blocks that Mary brought home yesterday. She toddles over to my mom and holds out a block to her.

My mom leans down, takes the block with a smile and says, "Thank you, Claudia."

"Ma ma ma ma," Claudia says, as she tromps back to me, and grasps my leg.

"Hi baby," I say, and she gives me a cheeky smile, and for a second she looks just like her dad.

My mom strides over to the curtains and yanks them open, and for a moment, I'm disoriented, blinking into the bright sunlight.

"You're getting dressed and we're going to the park," my mom says, dust motes flying around her in the streams of sunlight.

The park is a foreign concept. I've not been since—I can't remember. Mary takes Claudia out. They go to playdates, toddler story time, the library, the park. I don't go out. I stay here, in the living room, on the couch.

"Why?" I ask again, wondering why she's here, why she cares, why.

I dig my hands into the soft cushions of the couch and grip the fabric to remind myself that I'm still here.

"We're going to find a swing at a playground and push Claudia. You'll feel the sun on your face. You'll smell the summer breeze. Perhaps we'll buy Claudia a popsicle from a stand, although...hmm. Never mind, not that last bit."

She stands then, her arms folded in front of her, her face placid, waiting for me to stand up, get dressed...act like a Leighton-Hughes?

But since she said the word *playground*, all I can see is my mom, holding my hand, crossing a busy street, the cars loud, the wind cold, taking me to an abandoned playground, and—

"Why did you do it?" I ask her, looking at Claudia happily knocking two blocks together. Even if I'm having a hard time keeping my head above water, I can't imagine ever wanting to abandon anyone so small, so precious. I'm here for her. I'm doing the best I can.

My mom stills. She holds herself in that way she has, where the light shines over her, and she's so flawless and smooth, it's like she's from a different plane. One not reachable by the rest of us.

"What do you mean?"

Claudia's happy gurgle fills the living room, the tink tink of blocks knocking together, and then, from outside, a motorcycle rumbling past.

My mom's lily-floral scent pulls me upright and I lean forward and say what neither of us, what none of us has said before. "Why did you leave me? I know you didn't want me. I know I'm not yours. But why did you leave me?"

My mom's face pales and her hand comes up to her throat. "You remember that?"

Claudia stands, grasping the couch for support, and hands me a block, delighted at the game of giving block presents.

"Thank you," I say, kissing her on her forehead,

taking in her almost-baby-scent. She gives me her beautiful baby smile, her cheeks pink and round, her eyes wide.

When I look back to my mom she's watching Claudia and me with a faraway look that I've never seen on her before.

"You were beautiful like her as a baby," she says, her voice quiet. "The most beautiful baby I'd ever seen. I loved you right away."

I shake my head, that's not the way it was.

But she gives me a direct, firm look and nods. "I loved you so much it scared me."

"Mom—"

She holds up her hand when I shake my head, the gold bracelet on her arm catching the light from the window.

"You were my light. I took you everywhere. We did everything. Then I had a bad year." Her face twists. "Bad is putting it lightly. I was done with life. I thought I'd have one last good day. I'd take you to the playground, then...I left you there and went to the bridge nearby to end it. I could see you still, at the playground far below. I stood there for hours. Until...I saw someone coming to take you and I couldn't...I ran down the stairs, gathered you up, took you home. After that, I got help, but you never looked at me the same again, and I...I never thought I deserved you or your love. I kept myself locked away from you, but Andrea, you've always been my light."

I reach up, grip the flame pendant, let the sharp edges dig into my hand, and remember what Reid said. Don't let that fire go out.

I'm trying.

I am.

"Please, Andrea," my mom says, her hand out to me. "Get up."

I taste salt in my mouth and realize it's tears tracking down my face.

"Ma ma ma," Claudia says, then, "Da-da, Da-da."

I run a hand over her smooth cheek, brush back her silky-smooth flyaway hair. Outside the sky is cerulean blue, the gingko tree is full of sea-green heart-shaped leaves, and a family walks by, their laughter loud and bright.

There's an ember in my chest, and as I look at my daughter, at my mom holding out her hand, that ember starts to grow, to flame.

I stand, take a step, then another, and another, and then I walk into my mom's open arms and rest against her.

"It will be okay," she says, stroking my back. "It will be okay."

Then, I get dressed, brush my hair, wash my face, and walk with my mom and Claudia into the blinding summer light.

65

JACE

WE GATHER IN THE KITCHEN OF RIVER'S CALIFORNIA ranch.

Serena has chili cooking on the stove, the tomato and pepper spices make the air sting and taste like smoke and fire. My nephew Augustus and his dog Frank play under the long, wooden plank table, weaving between our legs, scrambling over our toes.

River's home is a large, sprawling, hodgepodge of his music memorabilia and instruments, Serena's rehabbed furniture projects, and Augustus's toy cars, dump trucks, and action figures thrown in unlikely places—like the dog bowl.

It's a happy, sun-lit home, full of bright orange and yellow walls, plush furniture, and music and laughter.

Dean, Dallas, and River sit at the table, our wooden

chairs pulled close, the question hanging between us, unanswered.

I grip my glass of ice water, the condensation running over my hand, warring with the heat coming off the gas stove and from the summer sun shining through the window.

"Well, what'll it be?" Dean asks, his voice a low rumble, "The six-month hiatus is over. Do we end it for good or do we keep making music?"

We're putting it to a vote.

There's an empty chair at the table, where Pauly would've sat. We all know what his vote would've been.

Serena taps her wooden spoon against the chili pot and then quietly pulls Augustus and Frank from under the table, leaving us in the kitchen alone.

River watches them go, a contented smile on his face. Being married, being a dad suits him. It fits him as much as being a musician ever did.

I glance at Dean and he shares a look with me, one of understanding. After Pauly died we sat down and talked, and what we said had been more than a decade overdue. I'll never agree with the decisions he made, but I understand why he thought he had to make them.

I realized you can forgive without condoning.

Dallas leans back in his chair, his face hard, his neck and the left side of his face covered in more tattoos than ever, a tribute to his friend and brother.

The question is laid out in front of us—what road will we take?

Do we step away, part ways, choose a different path?

Or do we continue the promise we made years ago, to make the world sing.

Heal the world with music.

And maybe in the process, heal ourselves.

"Let's vote," Dallas says.

I think of Andi then. She's always there, in the background, like a song playing softly. I wonder how she is. I wonder if she's happy. I won't look for her. I won't try to discover how she's doing. I'll let her go.

That's what River said, I need to let her go.

I send her all my love, I send her my wishes for happiness, and this time around, if she hears me singing, I hope she feels only joy.

I raise my hand, the sunlight streaming over me, and say, "I vote for the music. We keep playing. We keep making music. We stay together."

At that, Dallas raises his hand, River too, and finally, Dean.

We'll keep going. Keep singing.

And if there's ever a night I'm lonely, or a day where I'm missing her, I'll sing.

I'll sing a love song.

PART III

FIVE YEARS LATER

66

ANDI

"MOM, HURRY, I WANT TO GO TO THE PARK!" CLAUDIA shouts from the living room, the thumping sound of her jumping up and down excitedly echoing all the way to the bedroom.

I smile and finish putting my hair in a bun, a quick glance in the mirror shows I'm presentable—a flowy white blouse, tight jeans, boots, my flame necklace and the chunky yellow and blue bead bracelet Claudia made for me at family art day at the Met last spring.

"Coming," I call to her, putting on deep red lipstick, a bright flash of color that Claudia says makes me look as beautiful as a princess.

Which of course means that I'll wear this lipstick every day.

Claudia turned six last month, and her zeal for living each day with boundless enthusiasm and limitless energy makes me think the first six months of her life had a lasting effect on her personality.

Or maybe she just inherited it from Reid.

She loves playing in Central Park, rolling in the mud with her friends just as much as she loves her shopping trips with her Grandma Leighton-Hughes, hunting for pearl-encrusted, gold-dusted dresses. She plans outings to the ice cream shop with as much passion as excursions to Paris to visit the Shilling real estate and development branches there.

She's fearless too, she's the first to jump off tall rocks in the park or to dive into crashing ocean waves, but she also loves the quiet times, where we snuggle on the couch and read a book, cozied under a blanket together.

She's my joy. I'm thankful for her every day.

I stride into the living room, the old wood floor creaking, my footsteps soft.

Claudia's at the bookshelf, bouncing on her toes, running her fingers over the spines, waiting impatiently. The bookshelf is more crowded than ever, it's stuffed with all her latest book finds. The overflow, piles of books on unusual insects—her latest love—is spread across the coffee table.

The room is cluttered, full of framed pictures of Reid and Claudia as a baby, all of us together in the ice castle, Reid and me dancing, and then more pictures, of me and Claudia, my mom and Claudia, and even my brothers and dad.

On the window seat there are pillows and a throw so we can cuddle and watch all the dogs, and families, and people walk past.

This house isn't ever what I imagined I'd live in. It's

not a Leighton-Hughes-style house. It's not even a Shilling-style house. But it's a *home*.

It fits us.

After Reid died, and the will was read, I learned again how much he'd loved me.

He gave me his heart, he trusted me with his daughter, and he left me this home and all his assets. There was a trust for Claudia, she'll inherit the shares, this home eventually, everything he could give her, but he also...he wrote me and said, *"Don't waste time doing something you don't love. Live, Andrea."*

So after my mom took me back into the sun, I picked myself up and instead of going back to work at the Tower, I started my own real estate firm, a small boutique brokerage that specializes in family homes in the city. Sure, I still work with my dad on occasion, and I consult at the Shillings' branch in Paris, which Reid's estate owns, but other than that—I'm doing what I love.

"You ready to go?" I ask Claudia, holding out my hand.

"Yes, Kiki is already there! Let's go!"

As we skip down the sidewalk, Claudia pulling me along, past sniffing dogs, scaffolding and crowded bus stops, Claudia breathlessly tells me about how she and Kiki—her best friend—don't like a boy in their class.

"He's horrible. He always takes the red crayon, which is the one I want. And when I told him so, he called me a spoiled princess. It doesn't matter though. He's a Caulfield, and I don't like Caulfields."

"Hmm. Well..." I hide a smile and look down at her serious expression. "Maybe save a little room for the possibility that someday you might change your mind?"

She considers this for a second, but brushes it aside,

and then she's off. We're at the edge of the park, and she's running past the boulders, over the green grass, her blonde braids bouncing and her legs flashing as she cartwheels across the lawn.

I wave as she grabs Kiki's hand and they pull out a bright red kite to fly.

The breeze is light, the sun is soft, the summer scents perfume the air with tree blossoms and sweet green grass, the clouds float overhead puffing past, and I'm happy.

As we stroll to the lawn in front of Belvedere Castle, past the deep green shade of the Ramble, I'm happy.

I'm really, truly, almost perfectly happy.

67

JACE

WHEN I SQUINT ACROSS THE SUNLIT PARK, THE DAY BRIGHT
and golden and hot, I have only two things on my mind—
tonight's concert in the park, and the lyrics for a new
song.

Around me, the sounds of the park buzz—kids
shouting, laughter, dogs barking, a pickup game of soccer,
birds singing in the shade of the trees—and I settle into
the noises of the park in the center of the city.

My guitar thuds against my back as I walk. I came to
play in the shade of a tree, sitting in the grass below
Belvedere Castle. I'm in sunglasses, a hat, a T-shirt and
jeans, but even so, I think I might be too conspicuous.
Even in New York, where people leave you alone, I'm
getting second and third glances.

A squirrel chatters at me and I consider turning
around. I was drawn here by the tree-filled view from my

balcony, and my desire to see the park, quiet and peaceful, before the bright lights and roaring crowds of the concert tonight.

It's a big deal for us. At least Dean thinks so.

We started playing in this park, an open guitar case, coins thrown inside by passing strangers, and now, we're playing on a stage in the same park for thousands.

I've made it to the lawn, the grass soft beneath my feet, the lake glittering, the turtles still sunning themselves on flat rocks, and Belvedere Castle rising above. It smells the same, wet rock, lake grass, and fresh air full of hope. The Ramble is there too, as shaded and wild as ever.

I stare at it a moment, my chest thrumming painfully, like a string plucked, a song played but never finished.

The breeze runs across my skin and I take a deep breath and tilt my head toward the sky, ready to turn back.

"Excuse me, mister?" A little girl with braided blonde hair and the biggest blue eyes I've ever seen tugs on my shirt.

I look around, trying to find her parents but don't see anyone watching her.

"Yes?" I say, crouching down so we're eye level. She has freckles over her nose, long gangly legs, and a mischievous smile that reminds me of River when we were kids.

She hops up and down and points at the wide trunk of the oak tree behind me. "Can you get my kite for me? Please?"

I look back then, and sure enough, there's a red kite tangled in the leaves of the lowest branch.

"Sure I can," I reassure her.

While she watches, bouncing from foot to foot, I reach up and grab the ribboned tail of the kite, and gently tug it down.

"It's a little rumpled," I tell her, smoothing out the red fabric, as she watches the repair with solemn eyes.

When it's smoothed out I hand it to her. "As good as new."

She gives me a wide, dimpled smile.

"Thank you," she says, and runs a few steps, then stops and turns back, her blue eyes narrowed.

"Excuse me, mister?"

"Yes?" I say with a smile, squinting through the leaf-laced sunshine streaming down.

She frowns and the wind tugs at her braids and tries to lift the kite from her hands, but she holds it tight.

"I know who you are," she says, tilting her chin high in a familiar way that makes my chest tighten, like the strings of the kite are tugging on it.

"Oh yeah?" I lift an eyebrow.

Lots of people know who I am, but usually not little kids with freckles and lisps from missing front teeth.

"You're Jace Morgan," she says, pointing at my guitar case.

She doesn't sound impressed.

I nod slowly, and laughter and the sounds of kids playing drifts across the lawn.

"I am."

She frowns, digging the toe of her shoe into the dirt.

Then she looks back up and says defiantly, "My mom doesn't like you."

I hide a smile and say as solemnly as I can, "I'm very sorry to hear that."

She nods and says in a rush, her chin tilted high, "I

know she doesn't like you, because whenever your songs come on, she cries. She doesn't know I see her, but I do."

Then she adds, "So even though you got Kiki's kite down, I don't like you either."

"I see." I don't tell the girl that sometimes when a person cries to our songs, it doesn't mean that they don't like them, it means they like them a lot. Instead, I smile and say, "Is your mom here with you?"

Her eyes light up and she points across the grass, toward the lake and Belvedere Castle. I follow the direction of her finger, looking for the mom of this girl, the woman who doesn't like me.

And when I find her, the world tilts, shakes me around, and I stumble.

I shake my head and reach out and grasp the rough bark of the oak tree for support, my heart booming noisily in my chest. I drag in a sharp breath of cut grass and green leaf-scented air, and remind myself to breathe.

But who can breathe when she's here?

She's the same. She's exactly the same, but infinitely different.

She looks different, her face is softer, her figure fuller, the way she stands is different—as if she's taking everything in around her, pulling it to her and treasuring every sight, every sound as something precious.

She's in jeans, casual clothes a world away from diamonds and gowns, and her lips are a bright, alluring red. She's talking with another woman, and a little girl, then she tilts her head back and laughs at something they say.

The breeze carries her laugh to me and it sounds like the notes of a song, crescendoing up a harmonious scale and then down.

The sound of her happiness, the whisper in my heart, the voice that says, *she's the one*, that's the same. Everything is different, all of it, except the way she makes me feel. That's exactly the same.

The bark of the tree scratches my hand and I drag in another breath, trying to steady the world.

Andi.

Andi cries when she hears my songs.

I turn back to her daughter then, struggling to tear my gaze from Andi. The girl is frowning at me.

"I know," she says. "She doesn't look like me cause I'm 'dopted."

I nod. "I see. What about your dad? Does he like my music?"

I can barely breathe, I'll just ask this one question and then I'll go, happy to have seen Andi, her daughter, to know that she's happy with Reid.

She kicks at the dirt again, toeing the root of the tree. "I don't know if he does. My dad died when I was a baby."

There's a loud rushing noise in my ears, louder than the roar of the loudest crowd, and I crouch down.

"Your dad died?"

Reid died?

She frowns at me. "It's okay. I have my mom." Then she looks back toward the other girl and says, "I'm going to go play now. Bye."

She waves the bright red kite as she runs back across the lawn, shouting that she got the kite, and then, Andi laughingly looks across the grass at her daughter, waving at her.

I move then, walk out of the shade of the tree, into the golden sun.

And then, she sees me.

68

JACE

IF SOMEONE TOLD ME THAT I'D BE HERE, FOURTEEN YEARS after I first saw Andi, and that I'd accomplished all my dreams but I didn't have her, I wouldn't have believed them. I would've told them that I'd rather Andi than all my dreams.

But all the same, here we are.

Andi steps away from her friend, and her daughter and the other little girl run across the lawn, trailing their kite behind them. It twists in the air and rises.

The breeze tugs at me, pulls sun-warmed grass and light over me, and then Andi's walking to me, her eyes on mine.

We meet at the edge of the water, the tall grass rustling in the wind, and a turtle slips into the water when we come too close, leaving behind ripples flowing outward.

Andi stops, tilts her chin high, and her eyes fill with a warmth, but also with wariness and hesitancy. It makes me want to step forward and hold her, she never, ever was wary before, and she shouldn't be now.

Maybe she's afraid I hate her for marrying Reid, or that I'm bitter over what happened, but you don't have room for hate or bitterness when there's this much love.

She twists her hands in front of her and the wind tugs her scent to me, and she still smells like strawberries and long days lying in the sun.

"Hi," she says simply.

I pull off my sunglasses and drink in the gift of seeing her one more time.

"Hello."

She smiles at me then, the wind tugging tendrils of her hair free and she takes another step forward, although I don't think she realizes she has.

"I met your daughter," I say, smiling at her running past pulling the kite, with it twisting in the wind, diving and swooping.

"Claudia." Andi really smiles then, a wide, flashing, happy smile. "She's pretty great, isn't she?"

I nod, but it reminds me. "I'm sorry."

Andi lifts an eyebrow. "About what?"

"She said Reid died when she was a baby. I'm sorry."

He and I were never close, but I never wished him harm, and I'm sorry that Andi had to go through that and that his daughter is without him. I know firsthand how it feels losing your dad.

"Thank you," she says, and for a moment a sadness shifts over her gaze, like clouds across the sun, there, then gone, and I realize what I didn't before—she loved him.

But then she blinks and says, "I just remembered. He

left a letter for you. He said I should give it to you the next time I saw you."

"How long has he been gone?" I ask.

"Five years. Six this December."

So long.

"How old is Claudia?"

Andi gazes steadily at me, knowing exactly what I'm asking. "She's six. She was Reid's first, and then she was ours, and now she's mine."

A bird swoops low, skimming over the water, its feet grazing the surface of the lake. "Is that why?"

I think about the night before her wedding, how I was certain that we'd be together for the rest of our lives, but also how she never said that she wouldn't marry him.

She glances to the side, up the gray stone walls of Belvedere Castle rising out of the water, and then back to me.

"There are a thousand reasons, but yes, I didn't want Claudia to ever be waiting in the dark, scared, and needing love. I didn't want another little girl hiding under a bench all alone."

I nod, wanting to take her hand.

She has that tilt to her chin, the same look she had when I first met her, after she'd chased off three teenage boys twice her size, that defiant, willful need to care for others. To love.

Then Claudia runs up and grabs Andi's hand, and barely casting me a glance, she asks, "Can I go to Kiki's for a sleepover? Her mom said it's okay. Can I? Can I please?"

Andi's eyes flash to mine quickly, then back to her daughter's pleading expression.

"Yes," she says. "But no junk food."

And then Claudia's off, and Kiki and her mom are making plans with Andi and Claudia, and then in a whirlwind they're gone, leaving Andi and me alone, standing in the cool shade of the castle.

"Will you come with me?" she asks, "For the letter?"

I nod and we walk back across the park, down a shaded side street, past honking taxis, rumbling buses, and families out for a Saturday afternoon stroll.

Andi doesn't speak, instead she casts me indecipherable glances, and when I glance down at her, she quickly looks away.

I don't know what she's thinking. All I know is how I feel, the way that rightness is there again, like a chord struck in perfect harmony, and how she unconsciously leans toward me, like she wants to stand as close as possible, our hands nearly touching, but not.

We wait at an intersection, a hot dog vendor pumping out savory smells, and buses rolling past, and I ask into the silence, wanting to hear her voice, "How's your family?"

She gives me a startled glance, and then a rueful smile lights on her lips. "Don't make me say good."

I lift my eyebrows. "I won't."

"They're the same. My dad is onto even greater conquests. My brothers are still wrestling like Jacob and Esau for the most-favored son. And my mom...well, she's a good grandma."

I smile at the softness in her voice and say, "I'm glad."

The back of her hand brushes against mine and she doesn't pull away.

"I was sorry to hear about Pauly," she says. "I called with my condolences. Did you get them?"

I shake my head. "No. We had thousands of letters

and calls. Yours must've been lost in the mix. But thank you."

She nods and then the light has changed and we're moving with the crowd across the crosswalk, walking down a shaded side street, and then coming to a familiar brownstone.

I pause at the stoop in the cool shade of a tall gingko tree, a bird singing in its branches, my guitar solid against my back, and ask, "Andi?"

"Hmm?" She holds her keys in her hands, ready to open the tall wooden front door.

I look at the sun glossing off her hair, at the soft tilt of her eyes, and ask, "Do you ever feel that you've ended up exactly where you were meant to be? Even if you didn't know the road was leading this way when you took it?"

Her face softens and she nods. "Yes. All the time."

Then we're inside her home, a comfortable, wood-floored, yellow-walled space with bright open windows, and books on every surface. It's worlds away from the Tower, but it fits her.

She leaves me in the living room to find the letter, and I stand there, looking at the framed photos of her and Reid, and if I hadn't seen it in her eyes at the park, then I'd see it now.

She loved him.

And I'm glad she did, because I've only ever wanted her happiness.

I turn when I hear her footsteps and when she steps into the living room her cheeks are pink and she's holding an ivory envelope in her hand.

"I'm not sure what it says." She holds the letter in her hands, almost like she doesn't want to let this piece of him go.

"I don't have to read it if you don't want me to."

"No, it's not that." She shakes her head and steps forward, giving me a smile that shows the dimple in her chin. "It's only..." She shrugs.

"You loved him," I say.

She looks at me then. Really looks at me.

"I did," she finally says.

"I understand," I say, and when she holds out the envelope I take it from her slowly, holding the smooth, heavy-weighted paper in my hands.

Her fingers brush against mine as she pulls away and I can smell her again, that teasing fresh smell that makes me want to fall at her feet and love her. It's softer here, mixed with lemon and furniture polish.

She's watching me with careful, solemn eyes, waiting for me to open the letter.

So I fit my finger under the seal and slowly tear the envelope open. There's only a single folded sheet of thick ivory paper inside. I pull it out, it makes a rustling noise as it slides free of its envelope, then I uncrease the letter.

I can feel Andi's gaze on me like a touch, heavy and yearning.

The floor creaks as she shifts, and I read the letter Reid left for me.

A thick, tight band closes around my heart and the back of my eyes burn as I stare at the words. My throat starts to ache as I clench the letter in my hand.

"What does it say?" Andi asks, her voice barely above a whisper.

I shake my head. "Nothing. It's just Reid, thinking he knows best."

I look at her then, and she smiles at me, sharing a memory. "He usually did."

I nod and look back to the letter. It's in a bold, slanted scrawl. There are only seven words.

You promised. Make good on it.

-Reid

He remembered what I said the day before he married Andi. That I'd always love her. That I'd love her even if she married him. That I'd love her no matter what.

He must've been worried for her, for what would happen after he was gone. He never needed to worry on my account.

The sun shines low in the window, pooling its warm rays across the living room where Andi's lived for the past six years, a life without me. I fold the letter and put it back in the envelope, the scent of aged paper floating up to me.

I look back to Andi. She shifts on her feet again, uncertain what comes next.

Outside, the afternoon light fades. "I have to go get ready for our show," I say, nodding toward the park. "But...will you come?"

"To your concert?" she asks.

I nod. "I'd like it if you came." I reach into my pocket, pull out a card. "If you call this number, they can get you a stage pass."

She takes the card, holds it between her fingers, and says, "You're sure you want me there?"

I stop myself from reaching out, and instead say, "Always."

But hours later, when I ask, she hasn't called, and when the crowd starts to cheer, and the stage is set, and we're ready to go, she isn't there.

69

ANDI

I SIT ON THE WINDOW SEAT, MY ARMS AROUND MY LEGS, MY chin resting on my knees.

I watched Jace walk away, a slight, nearly unnoticeable limp to his stride. My heart nearly broke watching him leave, and I had to tell myself, it's not for good this time.

It doesn't have to be for good.

He's here.

He's here.

When Reid gave me the letter for him, I didn't think I'd ever see Jace again, but Reid was certain. *I don't know what will happen tomorrow, but I do know you'll see him again.*

I reach up and clasp the flame necklace and let out a shuddering breath.

He's here.

The last of the sun's rays shine through the window, stroking across my face, reminding me of how Jace used to brush his fingers down my cheek, his smile full of love.

The house is quiet without Claudia here, even the street outside is silent. It's a comforting, restful quiet, at odds with the tumultuous hope singing through my veins.

Jace asked if I ever thought that maybe where we've ended up, is always where we were meant to be.

If I hadn't met him, I wouldn't have known his love. If I hadn't left, I wouldn't have found Reid. I wouldn't have Claudia. I wouldn't have my mom. I wouldn't have now.

I'm so grateful for now.

Jace is here.

Seeing him, it was like that piece of me that's been missing, it's here again, and I feel whole.

But...what about Claudia? What about the past? What if. What if.

"What should I do?" I ask—I'm asking the sun on the yellow walls, the photos of my life, the books on the table, the warm beeswax scent, Reid.

I don't expect an answer.

The room stays silent.

But then, I think there is an answer because I hear a whisper in my heart.

Live, it says, *live and love.*

70

JACE

I SQUINT INTO THE SPOTLIGHT, THE MUSIC REVERBING, lighting up the dark.

We're on the Great Lawn, the stage set high, a massive screen behind us, playing effects, speakers rolling our music across the park.

Thousands of people fill the lawn, glowsticks held high, like starlight flickering bright.

Sweat rolls down my back, sticking in the humid air. Back when we played on corners, in the subway, in this very park, we'd play music to make a connection.

Every song you play has a feeling, an emotion, and if you do it right, it'll grab people, bring that good feeling back, and remind us that we're all human.

Once we gathered crowds of ten, twenty, now we have crowds of thousands upon thousands.

The connection is still there, it's just bigger.

The way Dean started tonight—it reminded me of what my dad used to tell us when we were first learning to play. He'd lecture us, *keep it in the pocket.*

"When you're in the pocket, whoa, you got 'em," he'd say, his eyes lit from playing Louis. And when we learned to hit that sweet spot, one hair beat behind the groove, the whole thing warmed up, and the music was ours.

We're in the pocket and the whole crowd, the whole park is singing our songs.

The words roll over me like thunder, shaking the stage, vibrating through me. Before we came out, Dean said, "*Let's do this, let's play so loud Mom and Dad hear us in heaven."*

We're back in New York.

It's the first stop on our world tour. Tokyo's next.

We're on top of the world.

And as my fingers fly over the notes of our last song, I search the stage, the crowd, for Andi.

I always wanted her here, I pictured the ghost of her here for years, and whenever I played I wished she could hear me. Now with thousands of people singing along, can she hear it now? Can she hear my love?

The final notes hover in the air and then crash into silence.

It's time to go, I take one last look over Central Park, at the trees, the people, the skyscrapers lit high in the sky, feel the rumble of the crowds roar, breathe in the nighttime city breeze, and lift a hand to the sky, pointing to heaven.

"Thank you New York!"

My brothers hold their hands up, a thank you, a goodbye, and then I turn to go, and when I do, I catch the flash of amber-honey hair, big wide eyes, a cherry red mouth.

I stop, feel the weight and warmth of my guitar and look into her eyes.

Andi's at the front of the crowd, mashed shoulder to shoulder with a tall, bearded man, and a woman in a fluorescent pink dress, more people—she's crowded in, without an inch of breathing room, barely able to move. Everyone is jostling, hollering, shouting, and there's Andi, just holding still, her smile wide, her eyes proud, the quietest, calmest refuge in a sea of noise.

When our eyes connect her smile grows, and there's the gap in her front teeth, and that dimple on her chin, and when she lifts her hand to me, I realize, she's been here, she's been with me the whole time.

"Actually," I say, my voice rising over the crowd, "we have one more song."

I smile at Andi, at the oversized gray Morgan Brothers T-shirt she's wearing over tight jeans, her hair in a messy ponytail, her cheeks flushed, and then say, "I wrote the lyrics today, so bear with me, because we've never played it before."

The response is instantaneous, there's a roar, an energy, and Andi hides a smile, because this is what we do.

Tell me a lyric.

I turn to my brothers. River is up for it, he's grinning at me, because he's always up for anything. Dean's looking at me, then looking at the crowd, and I know he's seen Andi too, because he gives me an understanding look, one that says he'll do whatever he can. Dallas waits patiently, ready to start the beat.

"One o' eight," I say, talking quietly, turning to my

brothers, setting the beat. I strum out a few chords, the melody. "It goes like this, and this, and *this*, got it?"

It's one note away from jazz, one chord away from classical, and because we've played thousands of songs together, from the minute we could hold an instrument, and the progressions, the chords, they come easily, they get it.

I walk to the side of the stage, pick up my dad's Martin, it's always here, although rarely played. But it fits this song, and Andi's the reason it's still here. I roll my fingers over the strings, warm to the mellow resonance.

Then I turn back to the crowd and find the woman I've been looking toward for nearly my whole life.

She's waiting for me, pressed against the stage, the stage lights glowing over her, the breeze catching her hair, and I swear I can taste strawberries and feel the warmth of her hand in mine.

We'll be friends. You'll tell me your secrets, I'll tell you mine.

I catch her eyes, and it's like holding starlight, bright and lovely.

Then for the first time in nearly fourteen years, I look into her eyes and sing her a love song.

"*Love, I'm yours. The road's been long, the years have been hard, but I'd do it again, just to see you one more time. The road's been long, but it's always been leading home.*"

Behind me, Dean strums the bass, River plays the chords, and Dallas comes in with a steady beat, but I barely hear them, because all I can see is Andi, holding me in her gaze.

When the last chord plays, when all the lyrics are sung, and all my secrets are told, I step to the edge of the stage. And because I don't want to lose her in the crowd, or in the night, or to some chance of fate, I reach down, take her hand, and pull her onto the stage.

Then to the cheering, thundering applause, and the surprise of thousands—but not to my brothers or Dallas —I take Andi's hand in mine and lead her backstage and on to the waiting line of black SUVs, ready to take us safely away.

71

I slip my shoes off and dig my toes into the soft wool rug at the entry of Jace's penthouse apartment, and try unsuccessfully to calm the heavy thudding of my heart.

He's here.

I'm here.

Jace pulls off his jacket, the smell of leather and ocean breeze and *him* drift over me.

The yellow light is soft and warm and the penthouse is open, white-walled, wood-floored and expansive. It's tasteful, not showy or flashy, but Jace never was either of those things.

There's dark leather furniture, armchairs, tables with books, and a large open kitchen with a bowl full of apples and oranges on the counter. There's a mug on the kitchen table, next to a notebook with an open pen, and even from here, I can see Jace's familiar scrawl on the lines of the page.

I realize suddenly, seeing the red ribbon and the gold-tinted pages, that the notebook is the one I bought him for Christmas all those years ago. My heart clenches. *The road's been long, but it's always been leading home.*

"I bought this place a few years back," he says, studying my reaction, "for whenever we played here. I don't know why, it just felt right."

I nod, take in the wide, homey space with all the lights of Midtown glowing bright, the cool hum of the air conditioning blowing over us, and the dim sounds of traffic far below.

His place is on 57th Street, near the edge of the park, a discreet, stainless steel and glass apartment building tucked near the center of it all. Not far away, you can see the golden light of the Tower shining over the city.

He hangs his coat on the rack near the door and then turns to me, a question in his eyes.

"Andi?"

I step closer, my heart pushing me to move near, to hold him.

Live.

Love.

"Yes, Jace?"

He smiles down at me, his gray-blue eyes as wide open as the sea.

"I've missed you. I've missed you so much."

At that, the last fear tied around my heart unwinds and I step forward and wrap my arms around him, press my face against his chest, bury my hands into his side, and listen to the steady beat of his heart.

"I've missed you too," I whisper, breathing him in,

reacquainting myself with the feel of his heart against mine.

We always fit, it was always easy between us, and whenever we touched it felt as if all our cells were aligning and pointing in the same direction. It's the same, my body softens, my muscles relax, the strain I've been holding onto for years melts away, and I can breathe again.

He settles his hands on the hollow at the base of my spine and when he touches me, it's as if he's plucked me like a guitar string and my body is vibrating, warming to him.

I want him to touch me again, stroke me everywhere so that all of me remembers how to sing again.

"I was scared," I tell him, gripping his shirt, feeling the hard line of his back, the strength of him. "I thought I'd lost you. I thought you wouldn't ever be able to forgive me."

He reaches up, strokes my hair, running it through his fingers like he's missed the feel of it. "No. You never lost me. Never."

He rests his fingers on my cheek, takes me in, then says, "I won't regret what happened. It brought us to now, and right now...it could be something wonderful. Don't you think?"

I look up at him, thinking about having no regrets, none.

Jace is playing for the world. I've known love. So much love. I have my family, my daughter, and this moment, right here.

I love him so much.

Before I didn't know that there were different ways to love. With Reid, his love was like a morning mist, so light and softly cool, that I didn't notice it until the sun had nearly burnt the short hours of its time away.

With Jace, his love has always been like a wave, crashing over me and lifting me up. The wave receded, but it was never gone, his love is my ocean.

And if I let him love me again, it won't be replacing any love, it will only be adding to it.

"Yes," I say, my voice thick, my skin humming. "No regrets."

I step out of Jace's arms, and he reluctantly lets me go. I reach into my pocket and find the sharp edges and warm plastic waiting there.

I close my fingers around it and the metal prongs dig into my palm.

"I wanted to ask you something," I say hesitantly.

Jace watches me patiently, a warm look in his eyes.

I keep my hand closed, feel the bit of plastic that kept me afloat for years, and then slowly, I open my hand.

The light catches the plastic diamonds, the blue-gray plastic gemstone, the dull tin that faded with age.

Jace sucks in a sharp breath, his eyes devastated. "You kept it. Andi, you kept it."

"I was wondering," I say, my voice shaking, "if you still felt the same. If you still want that lifetime?"

He closes his eyes then, a prayer on his lips, and when he opens them there's a fire there, and a need so strong that it nearly bows my legs. I understand it though, because I feel the echo of it in my own heart.

"I love you," he says brokenly, "I've always loved you and I always will. No matter how long the road to get here, no matter the twists and turns, I'm yours."

I step forward, offer him the ring, and he takes it,

holds it in his hands like it's the most precious thing he's ever seen.

"I have a lyric," I say, smiling at him.

His blue-gray eyes are warm, the love shining from him so bright. "What is it?"

"I love you too. I always have and I always will."

He smiles then and when he reaches down and picks me up, cradling me in his arms, he says, "That's the best lyric I've ever heard."

I smile at him, reach up to cup his face, and ask, "Will you love me?"

"Always."

Then he carries me through the living room, his arms thick and muscled, his chest warm. He opens the door of his bedroom, and in the center of the room, framed by the lights of the city, is a wide white bed.

A bed for loving.

He gently lays me down, the comforter pooling around me in soft waves, the dark and the light flickering over us. He stares at me in his bed, as if he never thought he'd see this sight again.

"I just want to look at you for a moment," he says.

I smile up at him, then slowly draw off my cotton T-shirt—the one I bought to let him know I was his. It scratches my skin as I drag it off, and then I throw it to the wood floor.

Jace's eyes gleam in the dark. His long body is tense, as if I'm a feast and he's a starving man, barely able to restrain himself.

I unbutton my jeans, drag them down my legs, kick them to the ground.

The feather comforter is cold against my skin, but

even so, the fire in Jace's eyes warms me, and a hot flush spreads over me.

I'm not wearing a bra, just a red lace thong. The cold air from the air conditioning makes my nipples pucker and Jace's eyes hood when he sees them. He lets out a small, pained noise.

Finally, I reach up, pull my hair free. It cascades around my shoulders, letting out the strawberry shampoo scent.

He smiles at that and if music carries memories, then so does scent, because I can see in his eyes that he's remembering our first day together, the strawberry shake, lying in the park, and how everything felt right, absolutely right. How at that moment we both knew, we were meant for each other.

Below, on the street, a bus lets out a long honk, and another car honks, blaring its horn, but the sound is muffled, and here, in this bedroom, we're in our own world.

Jace steps forward, one step, then another, his footsteps soft on the wood floor. I lie before him and luxuriate in the feel of his gaze stroking me.

"Once we make love," he says, a question in his voice.

I nod. "When we make love."

He smiles at that, and says, "Tell me this isn't just for tonight. Tell me there's a tomorrow. Andi, I want a tomorrow with you."

My heart expands, and it feels so big, so wide. I lift my hand, reach out to him, and bridge the space between us. "I want tomorrow too."

I want always.

I want forever.

Then he's there, gently moving over me, the bed tilting beneath me, lifting my hips. His jeans, his cotton shirt drag over my skin, and I raise my arms to his shoulders, and love the feel of him over me, looking down at me like I'm his.

I'm rocking against him, feeling the wave of his love, finding that rhythm.

His fingers drag over me, playing music with his hands, drawing sounds from my lips. And when he does, he catches them, presses his lips to mine and drinks them in.

The taste of him, it's the same, pleasure and love, soft lips, murmured words.

Then I'm dragging his shirt over his head, revealing the smooth line of his chest, his thick shoulders, the dip of his muscled abdomen, taut with need. I tug at his jeans and he lets out a soft plea. I pull them down, throw them aside, free him.

I kiss him then, wrap my hand over his heat, and he jerks and buries his mouth against my neck, whispering his love.

In the flickering shadows, there's the long line of scars down his leg, white and painful, and I press my hands over them, soothing the past.

Then he clasps my wrists with one hand, raises my hands over my head, and slowly pulls my thong down my legs.

I look at him through hooded eyes, drunk on the feel of him, the heat of him, the sweat on his brow, the musical sound of his voice.

"Thank you," he says, pressing down over me, skin to skin, heart to heart, his lips kissing mine.

"For what?" I ask, rocking to him, feeling the heat of him, right *there*.

"For your love."

He unclasps my wrists then and I take his hand, thread my fingers in his, and hold on as he crashes over me, into me, carries me away.

I love you, my heart whispers. I love you, my kisses say. I love you, my body sings.

"I love you," I say.

And then he's inside me, a part of me, building me higher and higher, until I'm clenching around him, pulsing, cresting, and I hear him, calling my name, filling me, loving me, and I ride the wave of his love until my entire body is lit from within and I feel whole—I feel so loved.

He rocks me then, his hips moving lazily over mine, his lips trailing over me, his hand clutching mine, the warm press of his skin on mine, the whisper of his stubble against the hollow of my throat, we rock together, slowly coming to shore, slow, gentle waves, spent after a storm.

"I'm so grateful," I tell him, cocooned in his warmth.

"For what?" he asks, his voice a soft rumble, his lips pressing into my neck.

"For you. For life. For everything."

"Yes," he says, and that one word sounds a lot like *I love you too*.

Then without letting me go, he pulls me to the side, wraps his body around mine, and we spend the night, not sleeping, but talking, making love, making plans, loving.

72

ANDI

THE WARMTH WAKES ME, I'M COCOONED IN IT, THE SOFT, peaceful warmth. I shift and smile when I realize the warmth is Jace's arms, and I'm still curled against him, his arms around me.

The morning light trickles across the room, slowly sending its early glow over the bed.

The sheets are crumpled, my face is buried against Jace's chest, the ocean and wind scent of him strong. I press a kiss against his heart.

He makes a low noise in his throat, reaches up and strokes a finger down my cheek, playing with the hair at my neck.

We didn't sleep much last night. We talked and talked and loved some more.

I told him my secrets and he told me his. Five years of catching up through words and kisses and loving.

"Come with me," he says suddenly, his voice rough from sleep.

I push my hand against his chest and lift my head, my hair spilling over him. I smile at the sleep lines on his face. I reach out and brush my hands over them.

"What?"

He stretches his hands out and pulls me closer, "When we leave tomorrow for Tokyo. Come with me. You and Claudia. I don't want this to end. We have today now. But I want tomorrow. And the next tomorrow. Come to Tokyo, then Seoul, then London, then Paris. Come. Please."

I regard the solemn look in his eyes, the hope and the love there. My heart flutters in my chest, expanding, growing.

If we go with him...

His eyes are ocean gray, a promise there.

I'd join him on tour again. This time a world tour.

Claudia would love it.

It's summer break. She's wanted to see Tokyo Tower and ride the London Eye again.

I could shift work around, manage most things remotely, and...

"I love you," I say, dropping my mouth to his. "Yes. We'll come. Yes."

The strain in his muscles relaxes and he drags his mouth over mine, whispering words of love, then he flips me over, pins me beneath him.

"You're my heart," he says.

And right when I think we're about to start loving again, a seven o'clock wake-up, there's a loud pounding at the door, and then the sound of a key turning and feet banging, and then—

"Wake up! We brought bagels. Jace, you aren't going to believe—"

It's River.

And I can hear Dean's voice, and Dallas's deep rumble.

I flip to the side, underneath Jace's arms, scramble off the bed and dive for my jeans and t-shirt.

"Go away!" Jace shouts, smiling at me as I hop on one leg, trying to shove my foot through my jeans.

"We've got coffee," River shouts. "Where are your mugs? Where's the cream?"

"Whyyyy," I whisper, crawling across the floor, hiding behind the bed to grab my t-shirt and thrust it over my head.

"I'll get rid of them," Jace says, climbing out of the bed, the long line of him gleaming in the early sun.

He grabs his jeans, also from the floor, puts them on, and then smiles at me one last time before he walks barefoot and shirtless out to the living room.

As I hurriedly put my hair in a ponytail, I hear Jace say, "You guys need to go away. What did I tell you about the spare key? It's for emergencies only."

"This is an emergency," River says. "You have cream. At least I think you have cream."

I hear the opening and closing of a refrigerator door.

"What River means," Dean says, "is that Serena put him on a dairy-free cleanse and he's afraid to have cream anywhere else but here."

I peek around the bedroom door. River's sitting at the kitchen table, pouring a massive amount of cream into a mug, a look of ecstasy on his face. Dean's pulling tin-foil wrapped bagels out of a paper bag, the crinkling of the foil loud. Dallas has his arms crossed, a frown on his face. And Jace, he's shaking his head, pointing at the door.

But they're not leaving.

So I straighten my t-shirt, pat my messy ponytail, tilt my chin high, and stride barefoot out to the living room.

River sees me first, and he's so stunned that instead of pouring the cream in his cup, he pours it all over the table.

"Watch it," Dean says, swiping the cream and tossing him a handful of napkins from the bagel bag.

The scent of toasted cinnamon and raisin hits me then, mixed with a dark, roasted coffee flavor.

"But..." River pulls himself back together and gives me his wide, happy River smile. "Hi Andi."

"Hi River."

Both Dean and Dallas jerk their heads toward me as I step into the kitchen. The tiles are cold against my feet. I walk to Jace and slip my arms around his waist.

He smiles and pulls me into his warmth.

Dean clears his throat and looks between Jace and me, the napkins and bagels forgotten. And even though the last time I saw Dean he lied to me, and even though he caused so much pain, I can't bring myself to feel any resentment.

"Hi Dean," I say. "Good to see you."

At that, his shoulders relax and he nods. "It's good to see you too."

I see it then, the difference in him. He isn't so hard anymore. His stance is more relaxed, his face is softer, and there's an understanding in his eyes, one you only get after you've lived a bit.

Jace squeezes me to him and brushes a kiss over my hair.

River's smile grows wider, delighted. "So I guess you like Jace, huh?"

I nod. "I guess I do."

He laughs and then Dean shoves him and tells him to clean up his mess.

"You want a bagel, Andi?" he asks.

"Do you have strawberry cream cheese?" I ask, raising my eyebrows.

"I have some in the fridge," Jace says.

"I don't trust people that like cream cheese," Dallas says, and I turn to him, take in his tattoos, his height, his dark eyes.

"Hi Dallas," I say. "Thank you. For what you did for me. Thank you."

He didn't betray me. He helped me and he paid the price.

He nods then, takes in Jace's arm around me, all of us here in the kitchen together, the warm breakfast scent surrounding us, and then he says, "I used to not trust people who like cream cheese. But I've changed my mind. This once."

I smile then, and after that, we're all unwrapping hot bagels, the steam curling around us, burning our fingers on the hot sugar and cinnamon.

We drink coffee, and laugh, and joke, and when there's only crumbs on the table, and splatters of cream missed in the hasty cleaning, Dallas asks, "So is Andi back now?"

They're all quiet, watching me with expectation.

Jace reaches over and takes my hand, holding me, waiting for my answer.

"I'm not back," I say, shaking my head, "because I never left."

At that Jace stands, tugs me close and says, "And now, you all really need to leave."

They do.

And Jace loves me.

And he loves me some more.

And some more.

73

ANDI

TOKYO, WITH ITS FRAGRANT PINK CHERRY BLOSSOMS, Imperial Palace, Skytree, and the elegant red and white striped Tokyo Tower.

Seoul with Gyeongbokgung Palace, Gwangjang Traditional Market, all the rich food smells and the modern luxury of the shopping district.

London with its gray skies and rain, sharing umbrellas, double decker buses, cobblestone roads and dizzying rides on the London Eye.

Paris with the reverence of stained-glass windows, towering cathedrals, and the romance of the Eiffel Tower, and kissing next to the lazily flowing Seine.

All of it, together.

Me, Claudia, Jace.

We stay in hotels with two or three bedroom suites, we tour the cities, we take in the sights and the smells, or we stay in and cuddle on the couch. And every concert, Claudia and I come, and watch from the side of the stage, letting the music flow over us, dancing together.

When Claudia found out that Jace had known her dad as a kid, she asked him, *"What was he like?"*

And Jace crouched down, looked her in the eyes, and told her, *"He looked a lot like you, and he was smart and funny, and he could do anything he put his mind to, and he was lucky, because he had your mom and he had you. He lived and he loved."*

At that, I think that every doubt I might have had fell away.

So back in New York, after touring for a month, with summer break nearly over, while Jace and I lie in the grass of Central Park and watch Claudia cartwheel across the lawn, I ask him.

"Last time, when you said you wanted always and forever, you asked me to marry you."

"Yes," he says in a low, happy voice, taking my hand, pulling me to his side.

The breeze blows across the park, sending the fresh-cut grass smell over us and bringing the sounds of kids playing happily nearby. In the distance, past the lake, stands Belvedere Castle and the dark green of the Ramble.

Where it all began.

I sink into Jace, feel the lush grass, smell the green smells, and watch my daughter play in the sun.

"This time," I say looking up at him, "I thought...do you remember how you asked? You said, will you be my wife?"

He nods, stroking his hand over mine, "And you said, as long as you'll be my husband."

"I want that," I say. "I want that with you. I want always."

He smiles at me then, and it's as bright as the sun in the sky, as he says, "You've had my always since the day we met."

Then I'm kneeling and he's kneeling and we're holding hands, and this time, when I'm saying yes, and he's saying yes, I know that we're exactly where we're meant to be.

74

Jace

One Month Later

When you have a lazy weekend, a clear blue sky, a soft ocean breeze, and leaves still green before the autumn, there's only one thing to do.

The sound of laughter bounces around the backyard, as Claudia gleefully chases River's sons Augustus and, his youngest, Angel around the yard. Frank, the old dog, gallops behind them, as much a puppy as ever.

I smile after them, then wrap my arm around Andi's side, pulling her close.

She leans into me, and I hold her tight—the sun streaming over us, the day bright—and send up a thanks for this moment.

She looks up at me, her hair in a ponytail, no makeup

on, barefoot in the lush grass, and blushes—probably because of what we just got up to in the bedroom five minutes before everyone arrived.

"I'm not cooking all these burgers," River calls, waving a spatula at the grill, the smell of charred meat and smoke rising, "unless someone gets me a drink."

Serena strides across the lawn, swats him on the back of the head, and hands him an iced lemonade. He grins and kisses her, patting her pregnant belly affectionately.

Dean walks by, a platter of corn in his hands ready to be grilled. He shakes his head and says to Andi, "Are you sure you're glad you joined this family?"

She laughs and puts her finger to her lips, considering. "I don't know. What dessert did you bring?"

"Strawberries," Dallas says, thudding a glass bowl overflowing with bright red berries onto the picnic table.

"Yes then," she says, smiling at Dallas. "I'm very glad."

He nods, like he at least never doubted it.

I take Andi's hand, brush a finger over her wedding ring, now gold, with a sapphire and diamonds, and kiss her palm, then her wrist, kissing her pulse.

"What's your lyric?" she asks, reaching up and brushing her hands, as light as the breeze, across my face.

"Happy ever after is right now," I say, kissing each of her fingers one by one.

She curls her hand, presses her fingers into my lips.

"Yes it is," she agrees, and I know, by the look in her eyes, that later today we are going to be making a different kind of music together.

"Food is ready," River shouts, and then Claudia is there, tugging on my sleeve.

I let Andi go and kneel down, smiling at her red cheeks and bright blue gaze.

"Jace?" she says solemnly.

"Yes?"

She frowns, a little line appearing between her eyebrows. "Are you my dad now?"

My heart stops, then slowly starts up again. The backs of my eyes burn and I hear Andi let out a slow breath.

I look at Claudia, at her wide blue eyes, at the smudge of dirt on her nose from rolling in the grass, at her wispy blonde hair—the same exact shade as Reid's—and at the serious question in her straightforward gaze.

"What do you think?" I ask solemnly, my voice quiet. "Do you want me to be your dad?"

She tilts her head, considering, then says, "I already have a dad."

I nod, my throat tight. "You do. He's a good dad."

She looks at me, gives me a small smile. "But I think it's okay if I have two."

"Yes," I say brokenly. "That just means you have double the love."

"That's what I thought," she says, then she lifts her arms, and I pick her up, lift her to my shoulders, and then Andi grabs my hand and we're striding to the picnic table, where everyone is laughing and eating and enjoying the sun and one of the last days of summer.

Then I let Claudia down and she's running to sit next to her cousins, and Andi reaches up, wraps her arms around me, and gives me that smile, the one I know means that I have all her love.

Always.

Always and forever.

EPILOGUE

JACE

FIVE YEARS LATER

I FLY ACROSS THE DARKENED CITY, SPRINTING OVER THE sidewalk to reach Andi in time.

It's after midnight, our show let out late, and even though I was on the stage for hours, I was with her, in my heart, the whole time.

Bright headlights cut across the intersection, a taxi rushing by, honking his horn. I dodge it and race across the crosswalk, my leg burning. It doesn't matter. I have to reach her.

A cloud of steam rises from the sidewalk grate, throwing up that subway tunnel scent, fully New York. My feet pound against the pavement, I leap onto the sidewalk, my lungs burning.

Almost there.

The bright lights ahead beckon me.

I shove through the front doors, squinting into the bright fluorescent hospital lights. The antiseptic smells, the clean sterile walls, the signs pointing to check-in, laboratory, surgery.

I don't have time for the elevator.

I run through the nearly deserted lobby, push through the doors to the stairwell and take the stairs two at a time. I grip my leg, pushing back the ache.

My heart trips double time, booming in my ears, one-twenty if I had to guess.

And then I'm to the floor, running down the hospital hall.

And finally, finally I'm there.

I slow at the door, steady my breathing, step into the white-walled hospital room.

Andi's on the bed, her amber-honey hair curled around her, a sheen of sweat on her brow, her cheeks pink and her butter-brown eyes tired.

"Am I in time?" I ask, stepping close, grasping her outstretched hand.

"Yes," she whispers.

And then I hold her, stay with her as our baby girl is born.

SHE'S SLEEPING, WRAPPED TIGHTLY IN HER RECEIVING blanket, warm in my arms.

Louisa Morgan.

It's quiet now. Andi's eyes are drifting closed. She's tired after a long night.

Outside the room, I can hear our family hurrying down the hall. Eleven-year-old Claudia with her four-year-old twin brothers, Sebastian and Jon, and her almost three-year-old sister, Olivia, and of course, her grandma and Mary.

Later today, River and his family will fly in, and Dean and Dallas will come by.

I run a finger over Louisa's soft pink cheek. "You've got a busy day ahead of you," I tell her, "Meeting all the people that love you."

Andi looks over at me then, her eyes opening wide. "Giving her advice?"

I shake my head. "No. Just telling her she's loved."

Then the room is crowded, full of everyone wanting to see Andi and Louisa and there's oohs and ahhhs and laughing and crying and Claudia looks skeptically at her new sister and says, "Do you think five kids is enough?"

Andi laughs, pulling Claudia onto the bed with her. "I don't know. It's a crazy thing, we haven't run out of love to give yet."

"Grandpa says you're trying to build another family band," she frowns.

I laugh, and that wakes up Louisa. She stares at me, confused and bleary eyed, and then, she decides, I think, that she's going to be a singer, because she lets out the most powerful cry I've ever heard.

Then Sebastian and Jon and Olivia climb onto the bed too, and Claudia makes room, and Andi tries to wrap her arms around all of them, and above the noise, and the laughter, Andi looks at me, and I see it in her eyes.

Tell me a lyric.

For right now.

But I can't, because this time, the happiness is too big,

my love is too wide, there aren't any words to describe the feeling of how much love I'm holding inside.

ANDI

"AND THAT IS HOW I FELL IN LOVE," I say, yawning as I finish the bedtime story.

"It isn't really," Jon says, his eyes tired, his blanket grasped in his hands. "It's just a fairy tale."

I look over at Jace and he gives me a wink, rocking a sleeping Louisa in his arms. Olivia's nearly asleep, her eyes drooping, leaning against her dad.

Claudia lies on the floor, her head in my lap, her hand in mine.

"It *is* really," I say, "There was a princess in a tower, a dragon, a chivalrous knight, a golden harp, and true love's kiss."

"Is it true, Dad?" Sebastian asks, turning to Jace for confirmation.

Jace nods then, a smile in his eyes. "It's true. It's all true."

And so the kids are tucked into their beds, secure in the knowledge that there's a love like this out there, a love so big, a song so beautiful, that it heals the world.

THE END

ACKNOWLEDGMENTS

A huge thank you to Art for answering a million questions about the nitty gritty of life as a professional musician. Hours and hours of interviews ranging from the minutiae of band dynamics, hotel rooms on tour, what it's like playing in small venues versus arenas—your knowledge was invaluable.

Your philosophy on music and your decades of experience making music for the world were inspirational. Thank you.

Your lifelong desire to bring happiness to others through the music you play is a gift to the world!

JOIN SARAH READY'S NEWSLETTER

When you join Sarah Ready's Newsletter you get access to sneak peaks, insider updates, exclusive bonus scenes and more.

Join today at:

www.sarahready.com/newsletter

ABOUT THE AUTHOR

Author Sarah Ready writes contemporary romance and romantic comedy. Her books have been described as "euphoric", "heartwarming" and "laugh out loud".

Her works include *Josh and Gemma Make a Baby*, *Josh and Gemma the Second Time Around*, *French Holiday*, *The Space Between*, and romcoms in the Soul Mates in Romeo series.

Her debut novel *The Fall in Love Checklist* was hailed as "the unicorn read of 2020".

She lives in the Caribbean with her family and water-loving pup. Find more books and interesting tidbits at: www.sarahready.com

ALSO BY SARAH READY

Stand Alone Romances:

The Fall in Love Checklist

Hero Ever After

Once Upon an Island

French Holiday

The Space Between

Josh and Gemma:

Josh and Gemma Make a Baby

Josh and Gemma the Second Time Around

Soul Mates in Romeo Romance Series:

Chasing Romeo

Love Not at First Sight

Romance by the Book

Love, Artifacts, and You

Married by Sunday

My Better Life

Scrooging Christmas

Stand Alone Novella:

Love Letters

Find these books and more by Sarah Ready at:

www.sarahready.com/romance-books

CPSIA information can be obtained
at www.ICGtesting.com
Printed in the USA
BVHW031920060723
666855BV00013B/84